Bad Sports

By

Stuart Guinn

TO BEN —

BEST WISHES!

ISBN 0-7414-2571-8

Published by:

INFI∞ITY
PUBLISHING.COM

1094 New DeHaven Street, Suite 100
West Conshohocken, PA 19428-2713
Info@buybooksontheweb.com
www.buybooksontheweb.com
Toll-free (877) BUY BOOK
Local Phone (610) 941-9999
Fax (610) 941-9959

Printed in the United States of America

Printed on Recycled Paper

Published May 2005

Dedication

This book is dedicated to my beautiful parents, who taught me always to look into the heart to find the truth, who supported my travels and seemingly ill-considered career diversions as I chased the dream of writing, and who waited patiently all these years to see that dream fulfilled.

Acknowledgments

Thanks to my agent, M.T. Caen, who remained steadfastly enthusiastic about the story, the characters and the prospects for publication through seemingly endless rewrites and delays; and whose eleventh-hour suggestion to ratchet up the mayhem gave me a chance to have fun with the story all over again.

A million thanks to Kenya Bradford, whose Ninth Ward New Orleans charm, boundless optimism, and inspired contributions added the creative spark to this project at precisely the right moment – # 2 will always be # 1 in my book. Thanks as well to Nacquinta Johnson, who, along with Kenya, welcomed me on my first fact-finding mission to New Orleans as if I was a long-lost relative; after only two days, I had two "old friends" that shall remain so forever.

Special thanks to Bruce Thompson, who allowed me the invaluable opportunity to read the manuscript aloud. Special thanks also to Leslie Burton and Markita Cooper who offered specific and sometimes-harsh criticisms to improve the book.

Fond Thanks to Ronald Allen, Dwayne Jones, Catherine Glaze, Jon Sylvester, Eric James, Nicole Schilder, Leonis Word, Omar Abdul-Hakim, Bomani King, Anne Roberts, Ibula "Jacques" Katakanga, Nevil Neil, Terrence Black, Haleem Williams, Joyce Smith, Joel Crow, Peter Fenno, Jerome Walker, Lonna Willis, Beth Terry, Roger Nadeau, Michelle Brown, Adriana Bate, Ernell King, and others who served multiple roles as proof-readers, advisors, cheerleaders, and all-around good sports as I worked obsessively on this project.

Thanks to James Hines, who is without question the finest bartender on the planet, and to Dayon Wiltshire and the rest of the staff and management of Scott's Seafood, which served as my secret hideaway for countless hours or plotting, writing and rewriting. Thanks also to Robert Harris of Dockside Boat and Bed for his impromptu tour and lesson on the ins & outs of pleasure boating for this hopeless land-lubber.

Thanks as well to Tramal Polk, Mike Polk, Prentisis Polk, Allen Alexander, and Johnell Carr who took me into the world of the Bourbon Street tap-dancers and the creative spirit of New Orleans. Thanks to Sean Gaines, who went above and beyond his professional duties during my second visit to New Orleans in a perfect example of the "lagniappes" that always make The Big Easy such a pleasure to visit.

Finally, thanks to all the others in that city who reach out every day with the best of Southern hospitality…New Orleans is truly the only city I know where one can indeed depend on the kindness of strangers.

Prologue

The real party had just begun. Cruising down Highway One with the top down on his custom-built Rolls Royce convertible, "Jackhammer" Hamilton, the six-foot seven-inch power forward for the Golden State Warriors, had four adoring young ladies along for the ride. Jackhammer and his entourage had just emerged from a late night of dining, dancing and partying at several of San Francisco's most exclusive venues – clubs frequented by the innermost circles of The City's political, sports, and entertainment establishments.

Born Jack Hamilton, he had become known to his fans and the press as "Jackhammer" both for his hard-driving style of play and for the obvious alliteration of his name. After the sudden banishment of Latrell Sprewell six seasons earlier for attacking and choking the Warriors' coach, Jackhammer had quickly stepped into the vacuum – laying claim to the role of team superstar. Leading his teammates this year in nearly every significant statistic, he had played a key role in boosting the team's morale and injecting a glimpse of real talent into an otherwise disappointing season.

But he had also stepped quite comfortably into his predecessor's role as team "bad boy" and media pariah, as his on-court temper and off-court playboy foibles garnered more attention in the local press than either his considerable talents or his budget-busting contract. Many among San Francisco's old-money elite were put off by Jackhammer's brash manner and troubled lifestyle, but he had earned his entry into these bastions of privilege through indisputable talent and the raw purchasing power of his NBA salary.

After making the party circuit, Jackhammer and his companions embarked upon the twenty-mile drive south along one of the most beautiful stretches of highway on Earth, destined for his lavish estate in Moss Beach, a tiny coastal hamlet at the foot of the Santa Cruz mountains. The views were always spectacular, as the highway twisted with the contours of steep sea cliffs, high above the crashing surf and secluded beaches of the Pacific. This scene was repeated nearly every night of the off-season, and frequently during regulation as well. Only the female companions changed from one night to the next.

Tonight's catch included Debbie, sharing the front seat with Jackhammer; LaTanya, who was seated directly behind the basketball star; and Julie and Roberta, occupying the center and right rear passenger seats, respectively. It was an unusually warm July night, completely free of the chilling fog that so often gripped the California coastline during the summer months, and all of Jackhammer's passengers were scantily clad. Debbie and LaTanya were wearing halter tops and shorts, revealing as much silky skin as possible – Debbie's a designer denim outfit and LaTanya's fashioned of black Italian leather. Julie and Roberta, on the other hand, each donned tight satin evening dresses that left no detail of their figures to the imagination.

LaTanya retreated in her seat, pouting jealously and washing away her cares with a bottle of Remy Martin Louis XIII cognac. Julie and Roberta seemed more content with their roles, eagerly fulfilling the star's explicit instructions for them. He had turned his rear-view mirror to watch them, and had described his fantasy of watching them sniff lines of cocaine from the exposed portions of each other's breasts, licking the skin before applying the white powder so it would not be lost to the wind. Their back seat performance, illuminated by the full moon and enlivened by soft moans of real passion, had exceeded his expectations and most certainly ranked as the best such display he'd seen this week.

Debbie, however, had won the nightly competition and had earned the favored position in the front seat, with full access to the player's ear, aura and physique. She wriggled her way strategically under Jackhammer's right arm, allowing him to maintain control of the gearshift without disrupting her mission. Placing her hand seductively on Jackhammer's thigh, she gushed, "I just love tall men. Tell me again how tall you are?"

"Baby, I'm the biggest man you'll ever be with!" Jackhammer bragged. "I'm six-feet seven-inches of pure athletic ability, but my women all tell me that I'm even tall lyin' down!"

2

"I've dreamed of this night since the very first time I saw you," Debbie continued, skillfully inching her fingers to his inner thigh. "So many times I've seen you from across the room, but you always had other women hanging on all sides. I can't believe I'm here with you tonight, going to your mansion."

"I call it my playground, baby! I've got six bedrooms, with king-size round beds and sunken marble Jacuzzis in each one. I've got an Olympic-size pool, and I've even got my own studio hook-up, so we can film every freaky thing we do tonight and watch it again in the morning."

Looking in the rear-view mirror, Jackhammer could see that Julie and Roberta were straying somewhat from his stage directions, taking turns sprinkling the white powder liberally from their necks down to their cleavages, then licking it off. He liked what he saw, shaking his head and biting his lip as he imagined how they would soon be doing the same to him. Glancing to the other side, he saw that LaTanya was in her pout mode again, curled up tightly in the corner and nursing her bottle. *As soon as I finish with Debbie, I'll spank that little pouting LaTanya*, he thought to himself, smiling with anticipation of the antics to come.

Debbie allowed her fingertips to glide up Jackhammer's inseam, but she knew better than to proceed further while he was driving. Resting her head against his shoulder, she continued to expound her star-struck admiration. "This playground of yours sounds like a palace. It must have cost a fortune."

"Sixteen million for the house and a dozen acres of the most expensive real estate on the planet. I have a completely unobstructed view of the ocean from my master bedroom, and nearly a quarter mile of private beach. Throw in a quarter million for this car and a half million dollar wardrobe custom-fitted for me by some of the world's best-know designers – money ain't a thang for me, baby! I'm making eight million a year, and I'm just halfway into a ten-year contract. The NBA thinks they can tame me with a twenty-five thousand dollar fine – fuck that! Those freaky chicks in the back seat will have sprinkled and licked that much away by the time we pull into my crib!"

"They'll never tame you, baby!" Debbie exclaimed.

"Damn right!" Jackhammer raged. "The NBA can suck my dick! I get paid to play the game, and that's what I do. So I pull a few fouls, so I'm a little rougher than some of these punks – damn, some of these pretty boys coming up now act like they don't want to scuff their precious little promo shoes. They're so caught up making commercials for soft drinks and fast foods, they forgot what this sport is about. If they can't handle getting jacked by the Jackhammer they need to take their sissy asses outta the game!"

LaTanya, who had far surpassed the threshold of sobriety, leaned forward to caress the star from behind. As she nibbled his left ear, he could smell the sticky-sweet scent of cognac on her hot breath. "I can take the Jackhammer, baby! Give me all you've got!"

"Damn, girl, sit back! Your breath stinks!" He reached over his shoulder and pushed LaTanya backward, his massive hand covering her entire face. "How much of that cognac have you had?"

"Don't push me!" LaTanya screamed. "Don't ever put your hands on me! No man puts his hand on me like that!"

"Aw shit, here we go!" Jackhammer muttered, shaking his head and rolling his eyes. "Homegirl got drunk, and now she's got attitude! Why don't you just sit back and chill?"

"Fuck you! You know I'm better than that airhead bitch you got riding with you up front, with her fake-ass bleached blond hair, or these freaks doing each other back here. What you need them for? I'm all the woman you need."

"Shut up, bitch!" retorted Debbie. "What makes you think you can handle a man like Jackhammer? You can't even handle your liquor, you drunk-ass whore!"

LaTanya lunged forward, swinging the nearly empty cognac bottle wildly. "Who you calling a whore? Bitch!"

The argument erupted into a full-scale brawl inside the car, with LaTanya swinging her cognac bottle fiercely, and Debbie leaning back over the seat, flailing her arms to block the bottle while trying to land a few punches of her own. In almost surreal juxtaposition, Julie and Roberta, so preoccupied in their own personal performance, were completely oblivious to the battle raging literally right over their heads.

Unable to land a good blow swinging the bottle, LaTanya recoiled in her seat then threw the bottle as hard as she could toward Debbie. Missing Debbie's head by inches, the bottle sailed past and crashed into the inside of the windshield, chipping the glass.

"Damn! Look what you did!" Jackhammer shouted, almost reflexively turning in his seat and smacking LaTanya across the face with a backhand.

LaTanya exploded with fury, boxing the star athlete's ears from behind with both hands. "I told you no man puts his hands on me!"

The car swerved wildly across the lanes as Jackhammer tried to drive with one hand while using the other to defend himself from the woman scorned. Debbie joined in the fight, trying to assist the beleaguered driver, and even Julie and Roberta seemed finally aware of the commotion that had interjected itself into their private party. Suddenly, as the car shimmied around a sharp hairpin curve, they were confronted by an oncoming tractor-trailer straddling both lanes of the highway. The truck was flashing its headlights and blowing its air horn repeatedly.

"Oh, fuck!" Jackhammer cried. The urgency in his voice, coupled with the approaching air horn, cut through the melee like a referee's whistle, and all heads turned to look forward at the source of the distraction. The flashing lights were bearing down on them, the truck showing no inclination to slow down or retreat into its own lane.

"Oh, fuck!" Jackhammer repeated, as he tried desperately to steer his speeding automobile out of the truck's path – but there was no shoulder, no guardrail, no room to maneuver. The right front tire left the pavement, traveling quickly up and over the low dirt embankment that served as the only barrier between the roadway and the sheer cliffs, causing the entire vehicle to tilt oddly to the left. For what seemed like an eternity, the car rolled along the edge of the precipice with one tire dangling out in open space, the undercarriage scraping the rocks and soil of the ridge, and the rear tires screeching as the brakes locked. Then the front bumper snagged a notch in the uneven surface of the ledge, and the car flipped end over end, tumbling down the nearly vertical slope toward the crashing surf one hundred feet below.

There were no screams. Those inside the athlete's Rolls-Royce convertible were in a state of complete shock as they fell to their deaths. A horrific noise pierced the night air as metal slammed against stone and glass shattered explosively, the sounds blending in a strange, discordant way with the roar of crashing surf. Then, silence, as gasoline trickled out of the ruptured tank, spilling onto the rocky beach and gradually seeping toward the white-hot wreckage of the car's hand-crafted engine. Thunder once again erupted from the beach as the car exploded in a massive fireball.

On the roadway above, the truck had disappeared silently into the night. But a charcoal gray sedan pulled slowly to the edge of the roadway at the site of the crash. If Jack "Jackhammer" Hamilton's rear-view mirror had not been positioned to observe the action in his own back seat, he might have noticed the gray sedan following him all the way from San Francisco. The second car's occupants had not been concerned with that possibility – they had done their homework and were confident that the bad boy of basketball would be preoccupied with his female companions.

The passenger of the sedan got out of the car and peered cautiously over the edge of the cliff. Seeing the flaming wreckage below, he turned and gave a thumbs-up sign to the driver. The driver spoke a few words into a cell phone then signaled the passenger to get back into the car. Spinning in a tight semi-circle, the sedan moved into the opposite lane and sped back toward The City.

1

"Sean! Get your butt in here, NOW!" bellowed Lillian Kramer, in a voice that was at once husky and shrill – much to the displeasure of those who worked with her. Lillian was Sports Editor for the San Francisco Star-Reporter, and had established a reputation as one of the most uncompromising managers in the business. Her tough demeanor was understandable – it had taken a large dose of grit along with exceptional talent, finely-honed instincts, and dogged perseverance to become one of the first women heading the sports division for a major metropolitan news organization. Nonetheless, the running joke among the staff at the newspaper was that her name was the reason lilies had come to represent death and funerals.

Sean McInness, the object of her immediate attention, was quite a different story. Almost completely lacking the drive and ambition that had so characterized Lillian's life, Sean displayed the tell-tale attributes of one who had reached his early forties without ever really trying to succeed: ten or twenty extra pounds on his six foot frame, graying blonde hair receding rapidly from his wrinkled forehead, and a job with no prospects for promotion. He had chosen a career in sports writing because he had thought it would be as close as he could come to making a living as a couch potato and armchair quarterback.

While Lillian was unceasingly appalled at his lack of motivation or work ethic, she had been mortified in the spring of ninety-seven when Sean had become one of the most vocal and visible opponents of the city bond issue to build a new stadium for the 49ers. Sean had been caught on camera discussing his outspoken opposition to the plan on one of the local television stations, and Lillian Kramer had gone ballistic. The greatest sin, in her view, was not that he opposed the stadium, but that he had granted an interview to a competing news organization. Television, no less! That was fraternizing with the enemy. Throughout the years that had passed since that fateful media event, Lillian had focused considerable energy on a quest – no, a vendetta – to give Sean the most unappealing assignments to cross her desk. One such gem had just come over the wires.

"Sean, they've identified a car that went off Highway One last night as Jackhammer Hamilton's Rolls. The bodies are just being recovered, but it looks like Jackhammer finally pushed the limits too far. I want you to get down there and get something together for the afternoon edition. That gives you two hours, so move!"

"Oh, great!" Sean muttered, just loudly enough for Lillian to hear. "How I do enjoy hanging out in morgues. All those *lilies* give me the creeps! Then again, how tough can it be to interview a dead person? 'Can I quote you on that, Mr. Corpse?'"

"Cut the funny crap," Lillian retorted. "Just get down there and do your job, and keep it simple. Remember, you're on deadline!"

Without further contention, Sean grabbed a windbreaker from the back of his chair, scooped his keys and notepad off the edge of his desk, and rode the elevator to the lower level garage where he parked his red Mazda Miata. Actually, he thought to himself as he flashed his staff pass and pulled out of the garage, this assignment met all of his criteria for a great story: half a day driving up and down the California coastline with the top down on his little Miata convertible; a brief "Q&A" with some local cops, without the self-promoting bluster and imperious third-party pronouncements that so often cluttered interviews with sports icons; and a simple story with a clear beginning, middle, and end – not subject to a dozen rewrites, a score of verification calls or a hundred angry letters to the editor. This was going to be a day for making deadline and heading home early to relax by the pool with a pitcher of gin and tonic.

Turning onto I-280 just south of the downtown San Francisco financial district, he was able to catch quick glimpses of the glistening SBC Park, home of the San Francisco Giants baseball team, as well as the proposed site for the on-again-off-again Stadium Mall planned for the 49ers football team. Together, these two stadium projects represented nearly a billion dollars of public and private financing. *There's so much money to be made in professional sports*, he thought. *How is it that I'm only pulling forty G's as a sportswriter for the San Francisco Star-Reporter?* He knew the answer, as he had known every time he pondered The

Big Questions of Life: motivation, drive, determination – others had them; he didn't. In the end, he was not unsatisfied with his life. He had a nice little apartment in one of the world's most beautiful urban areas, he had a fun car and a fun job, and he didn't have to deal with the life-shattering stresses that had broken so many sports heroes just as they reached the pinnacle of their careers. Like Jackhammer Hamilton, whose envied success, fame, and fortune had just gone up in flames.

As I-280 merged into southbound Highway One, Sean could see the Pacific Ocean, its gray-blue waters spotted with giant freighters whose man-made enormity appeared as mere specks on the vast expanse of the sea. Just beyond the town of Pacifica to the south, the Santa Cruz Mountains rose abruptly from the water's edge, with precipitous cliffs along the seashore giving way to rolling hills and dense foliage further inland. These coastal mountains acted as natural buffers for the San Francisco Bay Area, protecting the inland communities from the harsh, erosive forces of wind and water that rolled ashore after six thousand miles of unchecked acceleration across the Pacific. They were also key contributors to California's awe-inspiring natural beauty.

No matter how many times Sean made the drive from San Francisco to Half Moon Bay, it was always exhilarating. The road had been carved into the sides of mountains where no sane engineer would imagine constructing anything for human use or habitation. Solid rock lined one side of the highway, while the other side abutted sheer drops of a hundred feet or more to the beaches and rocky outcroppings below. There were literally hundreds of tiny, isolated beaches along this drive, occupying every inlet and cove. Many were operated as state parks while still more were private enclaves. On a warm summer day such as this one, thousands of The City's residents would migrate to their favorite beaches for an afternoon of surfing, hang gliding, volleyball, or sun-bathing.

Sean was so deeply lost in his California daydream that he nearly forgot the purpose of his drive. He was jolted back to that awareness when he sped around a hairpin curve to find the road crowded with highway patrol cruisers, ambulances, fire trucks, and other emergency vehicles. He slammed on his brakes as he saw that the southbound lane was completely closed, red flares burning to mark the forbidden territory and a highway patrol officer directing traffic, alternately allowing northbound then southbound traffic to pass through the one remaining lane. Sean pulled his Miata over to the side of the roadway, stopping just a few feet behind the row of official vehicles. Stepping from the car, he flashed his press badge at the patrolman who was directing traffic and the officer motioned him into the restricted area.

As Sean made his way past the parade of parked vehicles, he peered over the edge of the cliff. A pair of inflatable boats were tethered near the still-smoldering wreckage, with a Coast Guard helicopter hovering just a few yards off shore. Looking ahead, he saw a small group of highway patrol officers and turned to walk toward them. As he approached, he quickly selected the officer who appeared to be in charge, glanced at the officer's badge for a name, then reached out his hand in introduction.

"Hello, Lieutenant Vasquez, I'm Sean McInness with the San Francisco Star-Reporter. What've you got here?"

"Well, the automobile you see down there is registered to Jackhammer Hamilton, and we've got five victims – one male and four female. The bodies have been removed to the San Mateo County Coroner's office for positive identification, but there is little doubt Jackhammer was the driver. It may be a few hours before we get ID's on the three females who died in the car with him."

"Three, or four?" Sean asked, noting the inconsistency.

"Three females died in the car with Jackhammer. A fourth was thrown from the vehicle as it left the roadway. She's been airlifted to Stanford University Medical Center. She was broken up pretty bad – I doubt if she'll make it."

"So were there any witnesses – anybody see the car go over?"

"No. None that we know of. In fact, we're still unsure of the exact time of the accident. Traffic could've passed by up here all night without noticing the wreck below. Our first call actually came from a fishing boat that spotted the flames just before dawn and notified the Coast Guard."

"So, Lieutenant, what *really* happened up here? Any sign of another vehicle involved in the accident?"

"Definitely not. We have only one set of skid marks – it looks like Jackhammer almost managed to regain control – and there's no debris or other physical evidence of a collision or second vehicle. Nope, my guess is this one will go into the stats as a DUI, but the coroner will be able to confirm that for you."

"Thank you, Lieutenant Vasquez," Sean said, as he closed his notepad and reached out to hand the officer his card. "Please call me if anything unusual turns up." He began walking back toward his car, then stopped and turned back to the officer, who had already returned to his own paperwork.

"One other question: this survivor – has she made any sort of statement?"

"No. She was unconscious when our first officers got to 'her, and I'll be very surprised if she wakes up anytime soon."

"Okay. Thanks again."

Sean returned to his car and, after waiting nearly twenty minutes for his turn to pass through the single lane of Highway One, continued south toward Half Moon Bay. He then turned inland toward Redwood City, one of a score of bedroom communities sandwiched on the peninsula between San Francisco and San Jose. He needed to make a stop – a brief stop, he hoped – at the county coroner's office.

Turning off the coastal road, Sean followed state highway Ninety-two on a winding course across the ridges and valleys of the Santa Cruz Mountains, much of the trip stuck behind a slow-moving motor home. Ordinarily, he would have thought nothing of passing the obstructing vehicle, but after viewing the wreckage a few miles back he decided to err towards caution. Upon arriving at the San Mateo County Coroner's Office, he presented his press credentials to the receptionist and asked to speak to the person handling the Jackhammer case. After a few moments, a slight young woman in a white lab coat, whom Sean guessed to be in her early thirties, emerged from the examining rooms. She removed the latex gloves from her hands, and reached out to greet him.

"Hi. I'm Dr. Hahn. I understand you have some questions."

"Yes. I'm Sean McInness from the Star-Reporter, and I'm covering the Jackhammer Hamilton story. What can you tell me?"

"The male deceased has been positively identified as Jack Hamilton, a.k.a. Jackhammer. We have preliminary identifications for all three female victims, based upon ID's found at the scene, but the bodies are too badly burned to identify from photographs. I'm waiting for faxes of their dental records now to confirm those identities before releasing names, but I can tell you none of them appear to be well-known persons."

"And what about cause of death?"

"Exactly what would be expected from this kind of accident – all four suffered massive and multiple traumas, as well as severe burns. If you're looking for anything unexpected or mysterious, you're out of luck."

"Anything else you can tell me?"

"Yes. I'd say the late Jackhammer Hamilton would make a good poster boy for designated drivers. These four were all loaded. Jackhammer had a blood alcohol level of .17, as well as traces of cocaine, cannabis, and amphetamines. There's your story, Mr. McInness."

"That's Sean, but thank you for the information, doctor. Here's my card – would you call me when you get names matched up with the other three?"

"Sure, I can have our receptionist pass that information along to you."

"Thanks again. It was a pleasure meeting you, despite the circumstances." With that, Sean looked at his watch. It was ten-thirty. He just might have time to stop by the Stanford University Medical Center and look in on the surviving victim before deadline for filing the story.

2

Sean arrived at the Stanford University Medical Center a few minutes before eleven and quickly located the recovery ward where the accident survivor had been taken following emergency surgery. Visiting was not permitted but, luckily, there were no hospital staff in the survivor's room. Sean entered and walked quietly to the bedside. The victim was wrapped nearly head-to-toe in bandages, with both of her legs in traction and one arm encased in a plaster cast from shoulder to wrist. Her head was wrapped in bandages as well, and held firmly in place with a traction halo, but Sean could see that she had a strikingly beautiful face, characterized by angular features and a deep ebony complexion. Only one arm seemed to have escaped the carnage of the previous night, her uninjured hand resting on her abdomen. Her eyes were closed, and her shallow breaths were punctuated with faint, guttural moans.

Instinctively, Sean reached out and enveloped her hand in his own. The human contact must have triggered a response deep in her consciousness, because her eyes began to flutter and blink, finally remaining half-open as she stared blankly at him.

"Flashing..." She muttered, her raspy voice scarcely more than a whisper.

Uncertain how to approach the barely conscious woman, Sean tried to initiate a conversation with her. "Hi there. My name is Sean. What's your name?"

"Flashing..."

"What's your name?" Sean persisted.

"Flashing...it was flashing..."

She began to cough convulsively, her attempts at speech proving too taxing for a throat still dry from the dehydrating effects of shock. Sean found a pitcher of water on a nearby table and, after pouring some into a glass, offered her a few sips through a flexible straw.

"Flashing at us…" she tried to continue, her voice trailing off as she wavered on the edge of consciousness.

"What was flashing at you?" Sean finally asked.

"The truck. Flashing lights."

Sean was taken completely by surprise by her answer. *What truck? What in the world is she talking about?* Assuming that she was delirious, he decided to try to turn the conversation back to the question of identity.

"What's your name? Please tell me your name," he insisted.

Her almond-shaped eyes widened and she gripped his hand tightly as she struggled to speak, the words seeping out in a labored staccato. "A truck. Flashing lights. Blowing its horn. Wouldn't stop."

Completely unprepared for this information, Sean could think of nothing to say or ask, other than to repeat her statement back for confirmation. "There was a truck flashing its lights and blowing its horn at you?"

"Yes."

"What kind of truck?"

"Big. A big truck. Wouldn't stop. We had no chance. Are the others dead?"

"No one else has talked to you about the accident?" Sean asked, not wanting to be the one to break the bad news to her.

"No. No one. Are the others dead?"

Sean hesitated for a long moment, then with a resigned sigh he answered softly: "I'm afraid you're the only one who made it. I'm sorry. Can you tell me your name?"

She loosened her grip on his hand, and shifted her eyes to look away from him. After a few moments of silence, she spoke again: "LaTanya. My name is LaTanya Harrison."

"Hello, LaTanya. I'm really very, very sorry for what you've been through, and I don't want to take any more of your time. You need to rest."

Looking back at him, her eyes now fully open and alert, she spoke forcefully, her voice quavering as she tried desperately to find enough breath to speak in complete sentences. "There was a truck flashing its lights and blowing its horn at us. It was in our lane and wouldn't stop. The accident wasn't Jackhammer's fault."

As if that had taken all her energy, she suddenly looked away and seemed to begin fading back into sleep. Sean placed her hand gently back on her abdomen and paused for a moment before turning to leave. The young lady's determination to tell what she had seen had deeply impressed him.

"LaTanya Harrison, you're a brave young woman," he whispered. "I'll be back to check up on you."

As he left the room, he checked his watch. It was eleven forty-five. *Oh, shit! Fifteen minutes to deadline. I've got to put something together.* Realizing that he had left his cell phone in his car, which was parked in a far corner of the hospital parking lot, he rushed down the labyrinthine hallways of the medical center, finally locating a waiting area with pay telephones. After choosing the one that afforded the greatest privacy from nearby ears, he dialed Lillian Kramer's number at the newspaper.

She always answered on the first ring. "Lillian Kramer."

"Lil, this is Sean." Sean knew that she despised the diminutive form of her name, but used it consistently as a small act of defiance. "What good are bosses," he would speculate among his coworkers, "if you can't mess with their minds from time to time?"

"Sean, where in hell are you?" Lillian screeched. "It's a quarter till twelve, and we need your Jackhammer story NOW!"

"That's why I'm calling, Lil. We've got a small problem with this story. If you patch me through to Gus in the copy room I can give him a short piece to run with for this afternoon – Jackhammer has been positively ID'd and had more drugs in his bloodstream than a twenty-four hour pharmacy. But something's not right with it. There's a survivor who claims there was a second vehicle involved."

"A survivor?" she queried, her tone revealing an ambivalent mix of skepticism and excitement. "I saw the clips on the morning news – that car dropped at least a hundred feet. And exploded. How is there a survivor?"

"I guess she was thrown from the car before it went down. She's in pretty bad shape, so I don't know if she's credible – could be hallucinating on medication or delirious from head trauma. But I need to follow up."

"Okay," Lillian concurred. "I'll put you through to Gus. Give him what you've got for the afternoon run. Then get on this second vehicle angle – it might be a chance for us to pull a scoop. Who else knows about this survivor?"

"It's common knowledge at the crash scene that a survivor was airlifted out, but I think I'm the only one she's spoken to, and I don't think they've ID'd her yet. She told me her name was LaTanya Harrison."

"See what you can come up with for the morning run." With that, Lillian transferred Sean's call to the copy desk so he could dictate a short article before deadline. After forwarding the call, Lillian sat quietly pondering the phone. "Why can't he ever do a simple story?" she mused aloud to herself, her voice betraying frustration at the impossibility of supervising a man who cares little for the established rules, coupled with grudging admiration for the combination of luck and instinct that had so often allowed Sean to break new ground where others had seen only routine stories.

After completing his call with the copy room editor, Sean decided to return to the accident scene and question the officers again about the possibility of a second vehicle. Arriving back at the crash site, Sean saw that many of the emergency vehicles had gone, with only two highway patrol cars and one fire truck remaining. Luckily, Lieutenant Vasquez was among those still onsite. Sean approached, and Lieutenant Vasquez nodded toward him. "Back again?"

"Yeah. I've been to the coroner's office, and you were right – Jackhammer had more drugs in him than an Olympic weight-lifting team. Actually, I have a couple more questions for you. You said there was no evidence of a second vehicle?"

"That's right. The investigation has just begun, of course, but the only debris we have found so far is consistent with a single Rolls-Royce automobile. It would be nearly impossible to have a high-speed collision without finding significant debris from both vehicles."

"And what if there was no collision?" Sean prodded. "What if the vehicles never actually made contact, but just had a near-miss?"

"Well, with no collision, you would have no debris. But in a near-miss situation, we would at least expect to see two sets of tire tracks. Even with anti-lock systems, you can't slam on your brakes without leaving some skid marks on the pavement – certainly enough for us to find."

"So the tire tracks you're looking for are from braking?"

"That's right. Sure, there are faint imprints wherever a vehicle has traveled, but thousands of vehicles drive this highway every day – their tracks are all layered one atop the other. Isolating one set of tracks would be like trying to lift one clean fingerprint off the men's room door at a Giant's game – impossible. The only tracks we can catalog are the darker imprints burned into the pavement from a skid."

"So, what if there was no skid?"

"What do you mean?" responded the officer.

"What if one vehicle never applied its brakes?"

"Well, if they never applied their brakes, and never made actual contact, then our only evidence of the second vehicle would be witness testimony. But that would be a highly unusual situation – it's a nearly universal human instinct to slam on the brakes when impact appears imminent."

Sean pondered the officer's answers silently for a few moments, then asked, "Were there any other incidents reported on this stretch of highway last night?"

Lt. Vasquez answered without hesitation. "No. I've been on duty since twenty-three hundred hours last evening, and there have been no other accident responses on Highway One between San Francisco and Santa Cruz."

"Thank you, again, Lieutenant Vasquez. You've been very helpful." With that, Sean walked back to his car. He sat for several minutes before turning the ignition, trying to pull the pieces together. Something just didn't fit. All of the evidence pointed clearly to a drug and alcohol-induced single car accident. Jackhammer was driving under the influence of at least four intoxicants, and there was no physical evidence of any kind at the scene pointing to a second vehicle. It was open and shut – except for LaTanya's claim of a strange truck flashing and honking at them.

There were only two possibilities, Sean reasoned as he continued analyzing the scenario: either there was a second vehicle, or there wasn't. LaTanya had almost certainly been intoxicated as well, and had taken a severe blow to the head, so hallucination or delirium was a very plausible possibility. On the other hand, if there was a truck, why didn't it brake? It wouldn't have braked if it never saw them, but that didn't fit with LaTanya's story – she claimed it was flashing its lights and honking at them, so it definitely appeared to have seen them. A second possibility would be that its brakes had failed. That would explain the flashing and honking, to warn oncoming traffic, but Officer Vasquez had categorically denied any additional incident reports, which would all but rule out a runaway truck scenario.

The hallucination theory seemed most probable, Sean surmised. This was probably a simple DUI, just as the highway patrol and coroner had determined. All the same, he wanted to speak with LaTanya again, hoping that as she continued to regain consciousness, she would remember the accident more lucidly. He started his engine, and began the thirty-minute drive back to the medical center.

He could not have known that LaTanya had already had another visitor. Not long after Sean had left her bedside to return to the crash site, a young man wearing the typical white smock of a hospital intern had entered LaTanya's room. He had lingered for several moments at the foot of her bed, flipping the pages of her medical chart purposefully. Then, walking around to her bedside, he had withdrawn a syringe from his jacket pocket and injected the contents into her intravenous tube. LaTanya never awoke.

When Sean arrived at LaTanya's room, the doctors and nurses of the ward's "crash" team were leaving one by one, some pulling large pieces of equipment behind them. Peering in the door, Sean saw that the sheet had been pulled over LaTanya's face, and a doctor was making a lengthy notation in her chart. Sean grabbed the nearest nurse by the arm.

"What happened?" he demanded.

"I'm afraid Ms. Harrison passed away a few minutes ago, of respiratory arrest. It's not uncommon in cases with severe burns and trauma. I'm very sorry. Was she a friend?"

3

Sean was not the sort of person who carried a briefcase home with him. When the workday was over it was forgotten, and he would head across the bay to his home in Oakland. Relaxing by the pool with his drink of choice, biking around the lake or into the hills, or perhaps taking in a movie at the Grand Lake or Jack London, Sean would turn off his cell phone and be a million miles from the San Francisco Star-Reporter. But on this night, he could not shake the events of the day from his thoughts. *Something wrong...* The thought kept flashing through his consciousness like an amber caution light seen through a thick fog: the source was obscured but the message clear. *Something was definitely wrong with this story.* He sat quietly in the living room of his apartment overlooking Oakland's Lake Merritt, a remote control in his hand, but the television dark and silent.

He had been wrong about a story before, and had even felt a similar gnawing doubt in his stomach after the presses were rolling. For example, he had been among those fooled by Al Davis' shrewdness several years earlier, as the Oakland Raiders' owner had played Oakland against Los Angeles in a battle of economic incentives and political manipulation. Sean had written a column asserting with all his journalistic authority that he did not believe the Raiders would return to Oakland the very same night the team's buses rolled north. Nearly a decade had passed since that colossal blunder and Lillian still had not let him live it down.

But this story had a very different feel to it. *People had died,* and he just couldn't forget what LaTanya had told him from her hospital bed. Something in her eyes had convinced him of her sincerity...and her certainty. She had believed that there was something sinister about the truck approaching them as it had, flashing its lights and honking its horn, but never even tapping its brakes. She had been terrified, as well as bewildered. She had sensed that something had been terribly out of place. That is what he had seen in her eyes. There was no evidence to support her story, and logic dictated that she must have been delirious, but he simply couldn't forget her haunted eyes and the urgency in her voice.

Lifting the receiver of his old "trimline" telephone and thumbing through his tattered Rolodex, he located the number for Jackhammer's personal assistant. Anyone even remotely involved with the world of professional sports knew that a player's PA was always the most authoritative source of information about the player, although often also the most reluctant to divulge that information. A player's coach and team manager would know the player's practice schedule, his prospects in the starting line-up, and his fellow players' views of him as a team player or prima donna. The player's trainer would know the player's physical condition, injuries, and workout regimen, while his agent would know his salary and contract terms, corporate sponsors, and the position he would take in upcoming negotiations. But the personal assistant knew everything.

The PA had nearly unlimited access to the player, his family, and his innermost thoughts, watching out for the player's home and business interests while the player was on the road. The PA would know where to find the player at any time, day or night – he would not only know if the player was cheating on his wife, but would have the other woman's unlisted home number. The PA was the counselor, confidante, friend, and right-hand man every player depended on to make sense of his complicated life and to keep him out of harm's way.

The phone rang six or seven times, then a voice answered with a monotone, "Hello?" It was Tramayne Owens, Jackhammer's Personal Assistant. The flat affect of his single word greeting invoked the twin emotions of shock and sorrow at the loss of his boss, friend, and provider.

"Tramayne, it's Sean McInness. I'm really sorry about Jackhammer. I know it's hit you and his family hard. How are his parents and brothers holding up?"

"They're not doing too well, as you might imagine," Tramayne responded. "This came as a complete surprise. I was always telling Jacky to slow down, cut back. But I guess we all just really believed that he was invincible."

Sean noted the use of the childish nickname, "Jacky." No one else alive could have gotten away with calling the basketball player Jacky. Jackhammer had, in turn, taken to calling Tramayne his "Mayne Man." It was a textbook example of the amazingly close, almost familial role played by most players' personal assistants.

"Have any decisions been made on a memorial service?" Sean asked.

"Yes, actually. The parents are already here, and both brothers should be in town by tomorrow morning. Jacky grew up in Chicago, you know, but he's been identified with the Golden State Warriors for so long that the family wants him laid to rest here in California. They're also talking about setting up some kind of memorial scholarship for promising young athletes, or perhaps a basketball camp for troubled youths – something like that. It's all up in the air, for now. They expect to have a plan ready to make a formal announcement immediately after the service. Oh, the service has been set for Saturday morning."

"Tramayne, off the record, I need to ask you something. Did you have any reason to believe Jackhammer was in trouble? Did he say anything to you or act out of character in the past few days?"

"No," Tramayne answered flatly, "nothing like that at all."

"Did he have any enemies that you knew of? Was anyone threatening him – jilted lovers, ex-business partners, anyone with an ax to grind?"

"No," the beleaguered PA replied. "Why do you ask? You think this wasn't an accident?"

"Well, the coroner and the California Highway Patrol seem to have closed the book on that question already. But there is something a bit odd. You know there was a survivor, don't you?"

"Yes, I heard one young lady was flown out to, what was it, Stanford? But she died a short while later, didn't she?"

"Yes, she did, but I actually got a chance to speak with her before she died. She said there was another vehicle involved – a truck."

21

Tramayne seemed completely taken aback. After a long silence, he inquired, "A truck? Involved in what way? Was there a collision after all?"

"No, the highway patrol is certain about that. In fact, as far as they're concerned, there's not a shred of evidence that this truck or any other vehicle ever existed."

"So, what's the point?" The tone in Tramayne's question reflected neither impatience nor sincere curiosity. Rather, he spoke with the dull tone of one whose mind was too full or preoccupied to absorb a new stream of information.

"I don't know. I don't know where to go with this. It seems to be a dead end, and yet, she seemed so certain. I just have an odd feeling about this. Off the record."

"Well, I'm at a loss," Tramayne replied. "I really don't see what difference this girl's story makes, and I definitely don't know anyone who would have had a reason to hurt Jacky. Everyone he associated with knew what they were dealing with, up front."

"Okay, thanks. Take care of yourself. I'll see you at the service Saturday."

Sean switched off the receiver on his phone and replaced it on the table by his couch. The call to Jackhammer's PA seemed to have accomplished nothing, but Sean knew that sometimes even a lack of information could prove illuminating. He believed that Tramayne had been on the level and really did not know of any threat to Jackhammer's well being. If Sean could find no evidence of any motive for an attack on the player, he would feel more comfortable concluding that LaTanya had simply been delirious – and wrong. Then, he hoped, he would be able to lay to rest the gnawing feeling of unease and put this story behind him. He made up his mind to call everyone associated with Jackhammer over the next few days, and ask each of them the same series of questions he had asked Tramayne.

When he arrived at his office the next morning, the first thing he had to do was to convince Lillian Kramer to give him a little more time to follow-up on the story.

"This sounds like another one of your hair-brained, cockamamie wild goose chases," Lillian had snorted. "But, then, God knows you probably wouldn't get any real reporting done today,

22

anyway. You have two days, but if you don't have something solid we can run with by the end of the week, the Jackhammer story will be closed."

With the formality of official sanction out of the way, Sean sat down with his overstuffed Rolodex and started making calls. Jackhammer's agent, coach, trainer, and current teammates came first. Then former teammates, from both his NBA and college days, followed by business contacts and friends. Sean even called some of the officials who had gotten into shouting matches with Jackhammer on the court. Far from the vicarious glamour that many envisioned in the daily routine of a sports reporter, Sean knew from long experience that most of his time was consumed with the tedium of trying to get past secretaries, waiting for return calls that often never came, and repeating the cycle again and again until finally making his contact.

The unanimous conclusion among Jackhammer's friends and associates was that he had become a victim of his own excesses; an unfortunate cautionary tale for moderation and clean living.

Sean finally satisfied himself that the story of Jackhammer Hamilton had ended cleanly and decisively in the fiery crash off Northern California's coastal highway. There was nothing more to be said or written. The terrifying images the unfortunate LaTanya had recounted had been nothing more than coma-induced nightmares – a final, sad footnote to a tragic event.

After reporting his findings, or rather, lack of findings, to Lillian, he made the appropriately self-effacing comments to deflect her wrath: "You were right, as usual," and "I should have trusted your instincts." Returning to his desk, he picked up his keys, dropped off his notepad, and grabbed his jacket. *T.G.I.F. – it's gin and tonic time!* He thought, a wry smile coming to his face. As tough as Lillian thought she was, he felt smugly certain that he had her wrapped around his little finger. She could bitch, yell, grumble, and criticize all day, but in the end, he always got exactly what he wanted. Most of the time, that meant an easy ride. He turned toward the elevator and waved generically to the room full of reporters, editors, and staffers, most of whom consistently stayed at the office long after he pulled his Miata onto the Bay Bridge.

He was almost to the elevator, when the phone on his desk rang. *Hell with it*, he thought. *I'm done for the day*. Punching the down arrow, he tried to ignore both the phone and the glares of several of his coworkers as he waited for the elevator, but the phone kept ringing. *Damn, when is Lil going to get the voicemail system fixed? It's the twenty-first century, for God's sake!* The elevator seemed determined to outlast him, stopping on each of three underground parking levels, then pausing on the first floor. He was on the fourth floor, and the phone was still ringing. Finally, he realized that the entire newsroom was becoming annoyed with the phone – and with him for not answering it – so he grudgingly turned back and made a quick dash to his desk.

"Hello!" he shouted into the receiver.

"Yo, who's this?" It was a deep but youngish voice, with a very heavy accent that Sean did not immediately recognize.

"This is Sean McInness. Who's this?"

Ignoring the reporter's question, the voice continued. "You the one wrote that story on Jackhammer?"

"Yeah, I wrote it," Sean answered, impatiently. "Who is this?"

"You been askin' too many questions, ya heard me, an' you're in danger. If you wanna know mo', get a room at the Hotel Maison Dupuy in New Orleans tomorrow. The Maison Dupuy, ya heard? Be there!"

Then the line went dead.

(4)

Sean arrived at New Orleans International Airport a few minutes past three the next afternoon, feeling more fatigue than anxiousness. On such short notice, it had been a challenge to get a reasonable flight, and with the time zones working against him on an eastbound route, it had been impossible for him to arrive any earlier. After considerable effort on the part of Lillian Kramer's secretary, Amy, and the newspaper's corporate travel agent, he had been booked on a 6:00 a.m. flight out of San Francisco, with a two-hour layover and connecting flight from Dallas. The early departure time had required Sean to set his alarm for three o'clock in the morning in order to reach the San Francisco airport on time. The short night's sleep and long day of travel had been exhausting, and the damp Louisiana heat assaulted him the instant he stepped off the plane. *My God, this place is a swamp!*

Sean never trusted baggage service on connecting flights, so he had only brought two small carry-ons – a briefcase containing his laptop, cellular phone, and other business essentials, and a small bag packed with three sets of clothes. As he lugged the extra weight down the jetway and into the terminal building, he recalled the whirlwind course his life had taken since receiving the anonymous call the previous day. It had been lucky, he thought, that the call had attracted the attention of so many of his coworkers, because Lillian never would have believed him otherwise. Even with a score of witnesses, she was still skeptical.

"You expect me to sign off on an all-expenses-paid getaway to New Orleans on the basis of some mysterious, anonymous call?" Lillian had asked rhetorically, her jaw agape in wonderment. "I don't suppose this caller also suggested that I pick up the tab on your car payment, a leather coat, or a fine Swiss watch?" Ultimately, she had relented and authorized the travel budget. "You've got two days down there to find out what this contact has...and you pay for your own gin and tonics!"

Following the overhead signs, he turned right and proceeded down the long terminal corridor, then down a short escalator and past the baggage claim area to the ground transportation hub. Bypassing the more economical airport shuttles, Sean opted to hail a cab – it was important that he reach the Maison Dupuy as quickly as possible. He walked to the head of a long line of waiting taxis where a skycap silently signaled for the first cab in line to move forward and accept the fare.

The cab ride into New Orleans proved to be among the most entertaining twenty minutes Sean could remember. The driver was so immersed in local lore and trivia that he found it necessary to speak very fast in order to say all he wanted to say, complementing every anecdotal factoid with wildly animated hand gestures. First came the obligatory remarks on New Orleans' insufferable summer humidity, along with a practical warning on the frequency and suddenness of summer thunderstorms. Then, as they continued along Airline Highway, they passed one of the city's many cemeteries, with row upon row of aboveground mausoleums.

"You know why they bury people above ground in New Orleans?" the driver asked, glancing in his rear-view mirror, then continuing before Sean had a chance to answer. "They tried to bury 'em when they first settled here, but New Orleans sits below sea level, so the ground is permanently saturated with water seeping in from the river and the lake. We can get ten inches of rain here in just a few hours, and the ground becomes so wet that the coffins would pop right up and start floating around the cemetery. Families of the deceased started to complain a bit about that; so they started burying 'em above ground in these mausoleums."

"Each mausoleum is built for one family," the driver continued. "Did you know it's illegal in Louisiana to deny a family member the right to be buried in the family crypt? They have a saying down here, 'if your family wasn't close in life, it will be in death.' Ha! Ha!" The driver seemed to be continuing his monologue as much for his own amusement as his passenger's. "The way it works, there's a large slab, with smaller shelves underneath. When a person dies, they place 'em on the slab for one year. After that, they're cremated, and the urn placed on one of the lower shelves, making room for the next deceased. They got another saying down here, 'whatever your standing in life, everyone gets their turn on top in death.' Ha! Ha!"

As they drew near the central business district, the massive shape of the Louisiana Superdome came into view, rising nearly 300 feet to dominate the New Orleans skyline. Home field of the New Orleans Saints football team and the fledgling New Orleans Cajuns baseball team, and site of dozens of events and concerts annually, the Superdome was at once bold and graceful in design. Sitting just in front of the massive gray dome was the oddly angular, green arena that had served as home of the New Orleans Hornets basketball team since their arrival in 2002.

"There's the Louisiana Superdome," the driver announced unnecessarily as he pointed to the imposing structure. "It's the largest fully enclosed domed structure in the world, with over seventy-six thousand seats. If you get a chance to take the tour while you're here, you should – it's beautiful inside. The seats are all painted different colors. You know why they do that? So when the cameras show the bleachers during a televised game, the audience can't see that the stadium is half-empty. From a distance, the colored seat backs look just like people wearing different colored clothes – sorta camouflage for poor ticket sales. Ha! Ha! But it's a pretty sight, you gotta give 'em credit there."

The cab passed within a block of the Superdome, then continued another half mile along an elevated expressway before exiting at Orleans Avenue, the highway exit signs subtitled "Vieux Carre." Sean asked what that meant.

"It means 'Old Square' in French," the driver replied. "Restaurants and businesses in The Quarter use 'Vieux Carre' in their names or menus to try to sound classy – and to add a buck or two to their prices – but no one local gives it a second thought. To us, 'The Quarter' will always just be 'The Quarter'."

After two quick turns, they abruptly entered the clearly delineated boundaries of "The Quarter," its continental charms evident within the first block. The narrow, cobblestone streets were barely more than a single car-width, and the architecture was dominated by shuttered French doors and balconies with intricately laced wrought-iron railings. The streets were lined with authentic gas lights, and everywhere Sean looked was an explosion of color: the subtle earth tones and soft pastels of the buildings provided a backdrop for brilliantly colored flowers, festive flags, and deep green foliage on nearly every balcony. Even the air was different here – the musty and slightly sour smell of a city whose sewer system was a century out of date invaded Sean's senses as it wafted inside the taxi.

Pulling to a stop, the driver announced, "Hotel Maison Dupuy!" Stepping from the cab, Sean could hear the faint but unmistakable rhythm of jazz in the air.

"Where's the music coming from this time of day?" Sean asked, as he and the driver both walked around the vehicle to retrieve his luggage.

"That's Bourbon Street, two blocks straight ahead. The party's on twenty-four hours a day on Bourbon Street. Great place. You can find anything you want on Bourbon Street – jazz, blues, strip joints – whatever you like. Is this your first visit to New Orleans?"

"Yeah," Sean answered. "I travel quite a bit for my work, but surprisingly I've never made it to New Orleans before now. I'm definitely looking forward to trying some of the local cuisine."

"Nobody cooks the way we do it here in New Orleans!" the driver boasted, as he set Sean's bags on the pavement and slammed the trunk closed. "Crawfish, oysters, gumbo, po' boys – we got it all! One word of advice: the joints on Bourbon Street all jack their prices, and their quality is geared for high-volume tourists that'll probably never come back, anyway. You'll find better food and better prices out St. Charles, up in Mid-City, or out in some of the neighborhoods."

"Thanks for the tip," Sean nodded. "How much do I owe you?"

"That's twenty-eight dollars."

Sean handed him forty, and asked for a receipt.

The driver smiled wryly. "Sure, I can give you a couple!"

Sean thanked the driver again for his informative and amusing guided tour, then turned to enter the hotel. The Hotel Maison Dupuy, at the corner of Toulouse and Burgundy streets, was a magnificent work of understated elegance. The four-story structure, fashioned from a series of seven townhouses alternately constructed of red brick and gray plaster, dated from the early nineteenth century. A wrought-iron balcony ran the full length of the building on both street fronts, wrapping around the corner. The facade was lined with arched windows on the first floor, black-shuttered French doors opening onto the balcony on the second floor, simpler windows fronted with ironwork on the third, and a series of small gables comprising the fourth. As he entered through a large arched doorway, Sean could see an elegant Romanesque fountain centered in a small courtyard lined with banana trees and palms, and a small pool nearly hidden from view by a dense row of shrubbery in a raised planter. A half dozen hotel guests were lounging by the pool, some sheltered by large and gaily colored umbrellas, others soaking in the rays of the afternoon sun. *At least the mystery caller has good taste!*

Turning right, he found the hotel's front desk and stepped to the counter to check in. There were two smartly uniformed hotel employees stationed at the desk. One, a young man in his mid-twenties with reddish hair and a matching goatee, was assisting another guest. The other, a young woman of about the same age, had a light caramel complexion and an ebullient smile. She looked up to greet Sean as he approached.

"Welcome to the Hotel Maison Dupuy. May I help you?"

"I'm Sean McInness from San Francisco. I made a reservation yesterday."

"Yes, Mr. McInness. Your room is ready. If you could just sign the registration, I can have someone help you with your luggage."

"That won't be necessary," Sean demurred. "They're just carry-on bags. By the way, have I received any messages?"

"Just one moment, I can check the monitor for you." After tapping a few keys on her computer console, the young woman looked back at Sean and smiled. "Yes, you had one call, but there was no message. That was about an hour ago."

"If anyone calls for me, please see that they get through. I'm expecting a rather important business call."

"Certainly, Mr. McInness."

Passing the house restaurant, Dominique's, on his way to his room, Sean suddenly realized how hungry he was. He had been awake for almost thirteen hours now, with only juice and coffee for breakfast and a light sandwich snack on the second leg of his

29

flight. Dominique's appeared to be a high-end French restaurant – too stuffy for Sean's tastes and too pricey for his meager expense account – so he decided he would step out for a quick dinner as soon as he received his expected call.

Sean's room was on the third floor, with a north-facing window overlooking the courtyard and pool. Comfortably furnished with a king-sized bed, two adjacent lamp stands, a table, armchairs with ottomans, and floral-patterned bedding that matched the wallpaper trim above the windows, the room was bright and cheerful. At the same time, Sean's journalistic instincts immediately noticed that the two lamp stands were utterly mismatched, adding an element of authentic charm that was so often lacking in the sterile uniformity of even the best chain hotels.

Sean unpacked his toiletries, hung his shirts and slacks in the closet by the front door, then settled into one of the armchairs. He had an excellent view of the entire courtyard, and he could feel his body relaxing slightly – the beauty of the surroundings providing an effective antidote to the tension of the past few days.

Why am I here? The question suddenly imposed itself on his consciousness, and it seemed odd that the thought had not really occurred to him before. It was a valid question, he realized: why had he decided, without a moment's hesitation, to twist Lillian's arm for the funds, then jumped on a plane for a strange town two thousand miles from home, on the questionable merits of a vague and anonymous tip?

He pondered the question for some time, and wanted to believe the noble explanation, that the deaths of Jackhammer, LaTanya, and the others had imbued this story with an importance he rarely encountered as a sportswriter. He had made a profession of playing, observing, and describing games of all sorts, but this story was far more than a game. It was life and death, and it was real. There was some truth to that explanation, but at the same time, Sean recognized that his motivation might well be nothing more than morbid curiosity and self-preservation: he had been told that he was in danger and he simply had to learn the nature and extent of that threat.

The exhaustion of the day's travels was catching up with him and he was drooping in his chair on the threshold of slumber, when the phone rang. He answered on the first ring. "Hello?"

"Yo, is this Sean McInness?" It was unmistakably the same voice he had heard the day before.

"Yeah, this is Sean."

"I see you made it. I was 'bout to give up on you, ya heard me?"

"I got here as fast as I could. So what do you have to tell me?"

"What I have to say has gotta be face to face, ya heard? I'll meet you tomorrow mornin'. You got an ink pen by the phone?"

"Yeah, sure, give me a second," Sean answered, scrambling to get his notepad out of his briefcase. "There, got it. Go ahead."

"Tomorrow mornin' fo' nine, walk up to North Rampart – that's the next block, ya heard – an' you'll see a bus stop in front of a gray buildin' wit' the paint peelin' off, right 'cross from the First District N.O.P.D. Catch the Esplanade bus – it'll take you all the way to City Park. Get off at the park, when the bus turns after crossin' over Bayou St. John, then walk straight up past the museum an' go 'round behind it. After a few mo' steps you'll see 'nother road cuttin' off to the right – take 'bout fifty steps up that road to the stone bridge, an' wait there, ya heard me? There's a train that goes 'round the park fo' the kids – I think it runs 'bout every fifteen minutes. If three trains pass by, you'll know I'm not comin'. One other thing, ya heard: don't try anythin' stupid."

"How will I recognize you?" Sean asked.

"You won't," the deep voice replied. Then once again, the phone went dead.

5

At first, Sean was irritated that the mystery caller had again hung up the phone before he could coax any worthwhile information from him. Then Sean's gin and tonic side took hold and he realized that an evening in New Orleans with no work to be done could be a very good thing, indeed. He jumped in the shower to rinse away the sweat and grime of a long day's travels, then selected a beige and blue polo shirt and a pair of eggshell-white Dockers from his closet.

The hotel's front desk recommended Petunia's, one of The Quarter's ubiquitous Creole/Cajun restaurants, just around the corner from the Maison Dupuy. It was a charmingly small establishment, fashioned from the living room and parlor of a well-preserved Creole mansion. The hardwood tables were brightly accented in shades of green, pink, and mauve, and the walls displayed a dozen artists' renditions of the namesake flower. Surveying the menu, he found the expected offerings of jambalaya, gumbo, and fried oysters, along with a variety of lesser-known local specialties, including soft-shell crab, andouille and boudin sausages, and crab or shrimp remoulade. A server approached the table, clad in casual attire that bore no resemblance to a traditional waiter's uniform. He looked to be in his early twenties – likely working his way through college, Sean surmised – with short blonde hair and a trio of platinum earrings. He was at once cheerful and professional.

"Good ev'nin'! May I bring you somethin' to drink?"

"Sure. Could you bring me a gin and tonic with a couple of olives?" Sean asked. Then, before the waiter could turn to walk away, Sean spoke again.

"You have more dishes on the menu than I could eat in a week. What's your house specialty – what does your kitchen do especially well?"

The waiter's face lit up with a broad smile.

"Anybody can deep fry an oyster," he answered, pronouncing oyster like "erster." "An' everybody's Maw-Maw has a jambalaya recipe that'd put most restaurants to shame. The real test of Creole cookin' is etouffee, an' I can honestly tell you that our crawfish etouffee is the best in The Quarter. I'd recommend our file gumbo to start, followed by the etouffee. Then, for dessert, there's nothin' better than the bread puddin' with whiskey sauce."

"Done! Oh, and please don't forget the olives in my gin and tonic."

The olives were Sean's personal trademark – gin and tonics are traditionally served with a wedge of lime. The substitution of the olives, Sean had explained to bemused friends and befuddled bartenders, qualified this drink for the title "Poor Man's Martini."

The waiter turned and left the table crisply, and returned after only three or four minutes had passed, presenting Sean with a gin and tonic in an oversized crystal tumbler. In the time-honored New Orleans tradition of "lagniappes" the waiter had taken care to give his customer a little something more than had been bargained for – the drink was garnished with four jumbo olives skewered on a long plastic sword. *I'm going to love this town*, Sean beamed.

Peering out the window, he felt a world away from San Francisco. The charm of the French Quarter seemed to radiate from every brick, cobblestone, and shuttered window. As if on cue, Sean heard the unmistakable "clippity-clop" of hoofs, then smiled as an elegant white carriage turned the corner into his view, harnessed to a chocolate-brown mule with a bright bouquet of faux flowers decorating its mane. The driver, wearing a white tuxedo shirt, black bow tie and suspenders, and a tall black top hat, was turned in his seat to face the young couple cuddling in the carriage's jump seat. He was gesturing enthusiastically with both hands, and Sean could only guess that he must be regaling his fares with homespun tales of settlers, pirates, back-alley intrigues, and the enigmatic history of a town that once changed hands among three empires in three years.

As the carriage disappeared from view, Sean turned back to see that his dinner was being served. The gumbo was delicious, and the etouffee was outstanding. The waiter's recommendation had been absolutely on the mark, and Sean made a mental note to tip him accordingly. New Orleans, Sean would quickly learn, is not fond of moderation, and the portions on his plate were enormous. By the time the waiter served the bread pudding, Sean had reached his capacity and was only able to sample a few bites. He ordinarily would have ordered a second or third drink with a large meal, but had decided to pace his alcohol consumption in anticipation of the drinking which would almost certainly accompany his imminent tour of Bourbon Street.

After settling the tab, Sean stepped out the front doors of the restaurant. Despite the late hour, the air was still quite warm, as the deep violet of the twilight sky was rapidly receding into night. Sean could hear the discordant amalgam of music emanating from Bourbon Street and set out to follow the sounds to their source.

He was unprepared for what he found. Bourbon Street on a Saturday night was utterly unlike any place he had seen before. It was the festive frivolity of a street fair, the seamy debauchery of an adult entertainment strip, the unfettered enterprise of a third world village market, the slick commercial banality of a carnival midway, and the sophisticated professionalism of an upscale restaurant and theater district. Bourbon Street.

The street, which was blocked to automotive traffic after sunset, was teaming with masses of humanity in widely varied states of intoxication – locals mingling seamlessly with visitors from every corner of the world. Every tourist visiting New Orleans for the first time felt the same obligation to visit Bourbon Street, but each with decidedly different expectations. Families from the farm belt came with more than a little trepidation, their hearts racing with anticipation at the prospect of witnessing a modern day Sodom or Gomorrah. Students at nearby universities, living away from home for the first time, came to find freedom from the moral constraints under which they had suffered until now. Chic and trendy European tourists came to lose themselves in the world's longest-running party. They came for widely varied reasons, but they all came, and most had the time of their lives.

Bourbon Street ran parallel to the Mississippi River, setting four blocks inland from that artery of commerce. The festive portion of the street stretched ten blocks, from Iberville, near the boundary with the uptown central business district, to Ursalines on the downtown side.

Sean quickly learned that natives of this "Crescent City" had adapted their language of direction to the peculiarities of a town whose narrow streets and broad avenues had been constructed with reference to the random contours of the river snaking through it, and utterly devoid of any correlation to compass directions. The standard grid lines of north, south, east, and west had succumbed to uptown, downtown, riverside, and lakeside. Furthermore, typical of New Orleanians' utter indifference to the norms of the surrounding universe, they applied "uptown" and "downtown" with the precise opposite meanings ascribed to those words in nearly every other English-speaking city on Earth. In New Orleans, "uptown" included the central business district as well as the antebellum mansions of the Garden District, while "downtown" referred to the residential neighborhoods furthest from the hustle and high-rises of the city center.

Approaching on St. Louis Street, Sean emerged onto Bourbon almost precisely at the midway point of its ten-block rampage. The music that had served as his beacon, emanating from the Bourbon Street Blues Company, remained evident as the loudest among a cacophony of sounds permeating his senses. Every restaurant and club along Bourbon had its doors flung open, the varied rhythms of jazz, blues, zydeco and rock bands blending in the warm evening air. Adding to the auditory buffet, doormen at each venue aggressively hawked their wares, shoving menus or placards at randomly selected targets in the passing throng, touting "all you can eat shrimp," "three-for-one happy hour," or "bottomless dancers" with the straight-faced certitude that their chosen patrons could not refuse those temptations.

Sean turned right on Bourbon Street, nominally in the direction of his musical beacon. Drinking is allowed in the streets of the French Quarter, and every bar serves its potables in plastic "go cups." In addition, many of the more popular clubs have "take-out" windows serving New Orleans' classic Hurricanes and other mixed drinks directly to a pedestrian clientele. There were even shops serving Daiquiris in more flavors than a Baskin-Robbins ice cream menu, all "on tap" in giant, churning drums with clear fronts. A frozen drink sounded good on such a warm and muggy evening, so Sean stepped into the nearest Daiquiri dealer and selected a peach-flavored libation.

As he continued his stroll, he noted that a number of the street's visitors had purchased their drinks in tall, slender souvenir glasses, some made of brightly-colored, translucent plastic, others molded to form the shape of a female bust near the top. The glasses were huge, some holding forty or even sixty ounces of frozen decadence. Despite the incredible abundance of alcohol, there seemed to be surprisingly few examples of intoxication's less pleasant side effects: Sean had seen no brawling adolescents, squabbling couples, or gutter-hugging drunks. Nearly everyone on Bourbon Street was smiling, laughing, and chattering.

Having reached what seemed to be the end of the party-zone, delineated by the traffic barricades, Sean turned and walked back toward the other end of the street. The same doormen whose pitches he had respectfully declined only a few moments before now thrust their flyers or signs toward him a second time, their faces showing no hint of recognition.

Passing St. Louis Street, he entered new territory and continued his journey of discovery. At the next corner, a sizable crowd had gathered to watch a group of four shirtless youths in their mid to late teens tap dancing on the sidewalk. Dressed in overly baggy shorts and tennis shoes, the only tools of their trade were cobbler's taps affixed to their soles and cardboard boxes placed to collect tips, but their skilled performance was worthy of any professional dance company. Their audience applauded with delight as the young men locked arms and flawlessly executed their well-rehearsed choreography. Then, in an equally coordinated maneuver, the young men suddenly stopped dancing and fanned out among the tourists – passing their boxes and asking repeatedly, "How 'bout a tip?"

After dropping a dollar into one of the boxes, Sean turned and continued on his way. He noted, for the first time, that the party was three-dimensional. While most of the clubs on Bourbon Street had trendy motifs, they were all contained within vintage town houses dating back a century or more. There were no modern edifices on Bourbon Street. Many of these converted town homes included second and third floor balconies, and the crowds inside often spilled out to watch the revelry on the street below. Patrons on the balconies would taunt, catcall, or otherwise engage the passing crowds, soliciting impromptu amateur strip shows, then tossing down cheap Mardi Gras beads to reward those who complied. No one seemed to mind.

As Sean reached St. Ann Street, he realized he had entered the gay end of Bourbon Street, the corner being home to two of the city's largest and most popular dance clubs. Young men in pairs and small groups crisscrossed the street, clad in whatever attire or lack thereof would best manifest their own physiques – ranging from stunning drag queens in full cotillion regalia, to young hustlers wearing nothing but tight denim cut-offs. The gay clientele passing between these two dance clubs and other nearby havens seemed to intermingle effortlessly with the farm belt families, foreign travelers, rowdy frat boys, and other denizens of this permanent party. On Bourbon Street, no one cared.

Near the end of the strip, Sean noticed a particularly old-looking structure and crossed the street to take a closer look. The sign on the door identified the building as Lafitte's Blacksmith Shop and, upon entering, Sean was taken aback by the darkness. There were no electric lights in Lafitte's Blacksmith Shop, and the dim flicker of candles on hardwood tables, against a backdrop of darkly-hued bricks, was barely enough to cast an eerie glow on the faces of those who had met here for quiet conversations.

Seeing that he had come to the end of Bourbon Street's thoroughfare of delights, he turned on St. Phillip and headed toward the river. While Bourbon Street stood in a class by itself for the shear brazenness of its enticements, St. Phillip and a dozen other streets within the French Quarter buzzed with the harmonious cadences of romantic dining and after-hours entertainment. St. Phillip came to its end at the French Market, a lively open-air conglomeration of fruit stands, souvenir shops, and sidewalk cafes just inside the boundaries of the earthen levee that held the Mississippi within its banks. At the end of this strip, Sean found the Café du Monde.

The Café du Monde must qualify for at least three of the world's "top-ten" lists: for most beautiful location, most abundant free entertainment, and simplest menu: beignets – square French donuts coated in powdered sugar – and coffee in several variations. Seating himself at a small table next to an iron railing that served as the only physical barrier delineating the café's perimeter, he ordered the specialty, "café au lait," coffee with steamed milk and the uniquely New Orleans addition of chickory, along with a plate of beignets. Then he sat back to catch his breath for the first time in several hours.

Consulting a pocket map he had picked up at one of the generic souvenir shops on Bourbon Street, he realized that he had walked nearly twenty blocks. Pulling a notepad from his hip pocket, he decided to jot down a few of his observations from the evening, but he found it impossible to work. The night air had finally reached a comfortable temperature, and a lone musician was making melodic love to his saxophone just past the café's railing. Beyond the jazz artist, the brilliantly lit and imposing presence of the St. Louis Cathedral towered over the open expanse of Jackson Square. Behind him, couples of all ages strolled the Moonwalk – the boardwalk atop the river levee – while steam boats and freighters glided by silently. It was a magical night, as any night must be in so wonderful a place, and he had become so immersed in the pleasures of The Big Easy that he had nearly forgotten the serious purpose of his trip. Glancing at his watch, he saw that it was well past midnight. Reluctantly, he decided it was time to turn in. Tomorrow, there was important work to be done.

6

Just a few hours earlier, but half a continent away from Sean's French Quarter tour, steam billowed from the marble-lined shower of a fashionable Georgetown townhouse not far from the imposing Washington Cathedral and the Vice-President's residence at the U.S. Naval Observatory in northwest Washington D.C. Cassius Banks, point guard for the Washington Wizards, was enjoying the finale to an amorous evening with the latest in his now legendary roster of conquests. The object of his momentary attention was Giselle Hathaway, the stunning and internationally renowned model, who was married to Danny "Hat Trick" Hathaway of the Washington Capitals – one of the greatest hockey players of all time. Cassius had met Giselle at a shoot for a soft-drink commercial a few weeks earlier, and by nightfall of that same day they had had the first in a rapid-fire series of lustful encounters.

This evening, after several hours of passionate lovemaking, Cassius had stepped into the shower. Giselle had followed, stepping behind him and wrapping her arms around his waist, then proceeding to trace the ridge of his spine with a series of soft kisses, from his lower back all the way up to the nape of his neck. *Mmmmmmm..... I love the way she pampers me*, he thought to himself. *Hathaway is a fool to let another man get a piece of this.* Cassius turned around to face her, taking her radiant visage in his hands and kissing her passionately before gently pressing downwards on her shoulders to signal his desire. He had made up his mind before arriving at the townhouse that this would be his last visit with Giselle, and he was determined to enjoy it to the fullest. As she knelt before him to comply with his unspoken request, he marveled at how fully he had mastered the goal he had set for himself nearly six years earlier.

Cassius had always had his way with women, and had been known throughout his high school years as Casanova Cassius. He had skipped college and joined the NBA at the tender age of 18, drafted by the Philadelphia 76ers, whose management saw tremendous star potential in the lanky six-foot-four teenager. His performance that first season had exceeded all expectations, earning him instant fame and the benefit of numerous product endorsement contracts. But despite his fabulous success on the basketball court and in the court of public opinion, Cassius was both puzzled and troubled by the lack of respect he received from his own teammates. On one fateful day, a veteran member of the team had mocked him in front of all his other teammates, asserting that his lady-killer reputation was little more than the empty braggadocio of a schoolboy.

"Casanova Cassius my ass!" the veteran had laughed. "Every girl in high school wants to get with a jock, just so they can wear his letter jacket. That ain't shit! I've been with at least 5000 women since I joined the NBA – I can have ten women in my hotel room any night I want, at home or on the road. Until you show us what you've got off court, as far as I'm concerned you're just a punk-ass schoolboy trying to play a man's game."

You're just a punk-ass schoolboy trying to play a man's game. Cassius remembered how those words had stung him. At that precise moment, he had decided his destiny. He knew exactly what he was going to do. He was going to sleep with the older player's wife. He was going to sleep with *every* older player's wife. It could take a decade to rack up the sheer number of exploits that his provocateur and other players claimed for themselves -- he would be playing a game of catch-up that he could never win, and would always be in second place. But if he could sleep with the wives or girlfriends of those same players, he could one up them on their own home court and instantly prove himself the superior man.

As it turned out, his mission had proven far easier than he ever imagined. Many of the wives had married sports superstars for the glamour and excitement, only to be disappointed and humiliated when their men took them for granted while focusing their energies on outscoring their teammates in the hotel room game. The allure of affectionate attention from another player with charm and charisma often rekindled the women's hopes for the headliner lifestyle they had dreamed of. As an added bonus, the prospect of sharing surreptitious encounters with a member of their husbands' own team proved to be a soothing balm for the wounds inflicted by their husbands' infidelities. It had taken only a fortnight for Cassius to score his comeuppance against the player who had teased him, and within a year it was rumored that he had slept with the wife or girlfriend of every player on the 76ers roster, earning him the new nickname, "The Philly Philanderer."

After Giselle had provided him one last moment of ecstasy, he stepped from the shower and toweled himself dry, then put on his jogging suit in preparation for his midnight run. He enjoyed running the trails of Rock Creek Park, and the location of the Hathaway's townhouse offered the opportunity for a scenic four mile run through the park, past the monuments of the National Mall, and around the cherry-lined Tidal Basin to his luxury condominium at L'Enfant Plaza. He loved living in Washington D.C., both for its visual appeal and for the iconic power of its institutions. But above all, Washington had provided fertile new ground for his bedroom conquests. The Sixers had traded him to the Washington Wizards at the end of his third year, and he had immediately set about the task of introducing himself to all of his new teammates' wives. Soon, local sportscasters were dubbing him "The Washington Womanizer." *I get a new nickname every time I move*, he smiled.

Within a year, Cassius had exhausted the supply of wives among his Wizards teammates, and had decided that it was pointlessly provincial to focus exclusively on his own team. He decided to broaden his horizons, and began seeking out the wives of football players, baseball players, and hockey players, as well as the wives of players on other NBA teams. *I may reach 5000 after all*, he mused, *but mine will all be targeted and seduced, not strangers and groupies*.

Giselle had, without a doubt, been one of the most coveted prizes on his "to-do" list. She was widely regarded to be among the most beautiful women on Earth, scoring countless magazine covers and topping nearly every "who's hot" list since she took the modeling world by storm five years earlier. She stood a tall five-foot-ten, with sultry eyes, pouting lips, and silky straight black hair draped at shoulder length against her slightly olive complexion. Born in southern France, she had moved to New York to find her fortune in the world of fashion. Before long, she had met Danny Hathaway, who was playing for the New York Islanders at that time. Her star was rising rapidly, while his was shining at its most brilliant, and their wedding had been a media extravaganza worthy of a Prince and Princess. Fairy tales never last, and the gild of their storybook romance had long-since faded. Danny was a falling star, on his way down after two disappointing seasons, while she was now making more money in one year than he had made in his eleven-year career. Her publicist had warned her that attempting to divorce her once-popular husband might damage her image, so she remained with him in a marriage of convenience. But her passion had turned to other outlets. Cassius had filled a need for her that she could no longer find with the aging hockey player.

Now, Cassius had reached the limit of his time with her. Cassius never allowed his trysts to last more than a few weeks. No commitments. No messy endings. No lingering questions. Just the tried-and-true hit-and-run before moving on to the next prize. Giselle had emerged from the shower in a white satin robe, barely closed in the front, revealing the glistening wet curves of her cleavage. Cassius leaned forward to kiss her one last time.

"I gotta run, Babe," he announced, trying not to sound scripted as he closed their brief but torrid relationship with the same, oddly passionless words he had used to close a hundred others before: "Until next time..." With that, he turned and opened the door, stepped into the warm, moonlit night, and began to run.

Only a few blocks away, Danny "Hat Trick" Hathaway was drinking the night away at the Brickskeller Dining House and Down Home Saloon. The Brickskeller occupied the English basement of a charming five floor boarding house near the edge of Rock Creek Park, midway between Dupont Circle and the commercial heart of Georgetown. The Brickskeller had a classic pub ambience, with the sunless darkness of its multiple rooms and foyers deepend by the dark hues and light absorbing quality of its brick walls. Most notably, every wall in the establishment was decorated with rows and rows of unique beer bottles and cans, and the proprietor proudly displayed his official Guinness world record certificate for offering the largest variety of beers available anywhere on the planet. Hat Trick, who fancied himself something of an aficionado of imported and microbrew beers, had immediately fallen in love with this establishment when he moved to Georgetown after signing with the Washington Capitals.

Hat Trick had earned his nickname as one of the leading scorers in the NHL, recording more games with three or more points than any other player in league history. He had been universally acknowledged as the greatest player the game had ever known, and had been wildly popular. But all that had changed. His last two seasons had been abysmal, and he had been scoreless for an unprecedented ten games in a row just as this year's season came to a close. In addition, his well-known temper, which in earlier years had entertained fans with an abundance of on-ice violence, had crossed the unwritten line of the sport: he had engaged in two fights with taunting fans, and had body slammed an official after a questionable penalty call. As a result, he was now facing fines and suspension from the NHL, lawsuits from several fans, and plummeting popularity.

But that was not the worst of his problems. Players in every major sport learn to insulate themselves from the fickle tides of public opinion. They focus on their game without concern for the latest popularity polls. But Hat Trick did not know how to insulate himself from the pain inflicted by a wife whom he realized had never reciprocated the genuine love he felt for her, and who was now publicly humiliating him through a barely-concealed affair with one of the most notorious womanizers in professional sports. As a result, Hat Trick now had a third major problem: a sudden plunge into the soulless void of alcoholism.

Hat Trick found himself hunched over a table at the Brickskeller. Drowning in too many beers like a common, broken-down drunk, he was spilling his guts to a sympathetic stranger who had joined him in his private agony and had offered a friendly ear while keeping the player well supplied with beer after beer.

"I'll never under... understand why she would do this with that... that mother fuckin' Phila... Philly... son of a bitch," he stammered to his listener. "She knows... everybody knows... that bastard's just about hit-and-run. It won't last a month and it don't mean a thing. She's destroying our marriage and humil... humil... embarrassing me to the whole world for nothing. Why would she do that?"

"I don't know," the listener responded, pouring another beer for the intoxicated hockey player. "It doesn't make sense, does it?"

"Hell no!" the player exclaimed, before tipping back his mug for another long swallow of liquid relief. "I gave her everything! I treated her like a... like a fuckin' princess! She was my whole world, and I made sure she knew it every day. You know, I never cheated on her once. Not once! Can you believe that? Shit! I gotta piss again!"

Hat Trick excused himself from the table and wobbled toward the back of the bar, steadying himself against the walls with nearly every step. He returned to the table a few minutes later, with his fly unzipped and the dampness of a fresh stain extending halfway down his left pant leg. The stranger who had spent the better part of two hours listening to the inebriated player's laments and who had plied the player with nearly a dozen beers, had just concluded a cell phone call, and announced that it was time to bring the drinking binge to close.

"Listen, Hat Trick," he began, while standing to place his arm around the player's shoulder. "Let me walk you to your car. I'll drive you home."

The player nodded his assent, then draped his arm heavily over the stranger's shoulder and continued to ramble about his heartbreak while the two exited the basement pub, climbed the steps to the sidewalk, and walked around the corner to where Hat Trick had parked his car on Q Street. Recognizing Hat Trick's Jaguar, the stranger took the keys from him, helped him into the passenger seat, then walked around to enter the driver's side and started the engine. The pair pulled away from the curb and disappeared into the night.

Cassius had entered Rock Creek Park at R Street, sprinted down the slope to the jogging trail, and turned south toward The Mall. After a mile or so winding through the thickly forested park, the trail emerged onto the banks of the Potomac River, continuing along the back side of the massive Watergate complex and the elegant Kennedy Center. After passing the performing arts center, Cassius followed the trail as it turned inward, jogging around the southwest corner of the Lincoln Memorial and catching a fantastic view of the Washington Monument and the Capital mirrored side-by-side in the gently undulating waters of the reflecting pool. Proceeding along the water's edge then veering left to follow the arc of West Basin Drive, Cassius jogged toward the edge of the Tidal Basin. As he approached the FDR Memorial complex, the softly lighted dome of the Jefferson Memorial came into full view across the water. Although the view was most famous at the time of the Spring Cherry Blossom Festival, it was unquestionably one of the capital's most beautiful vistas at any time of any day or night.

Cassius was unmoved by the beauty of the monument, however, instead turning his thoughts to the recent revelations regarding Jefferson's affair with his slave, Sally Hemming. *His wife was probably too uptight, with all those ruffled dresses they wore back in the day. Ol' TJ had to get with that slave Sally to get down the way he wanted,* he speculated with a chuckle. *But TJ had it all wrong,* he continued with his smug critique of the former president's escapades. *What's the point of having an affair if you're gonna keep it secret for two hundred years? TJ shoulda put it out there like a real man and let everyone know he was top dog. Sure Clinton took some heat behind that Monica thing, but damn sure every man in America wished they'd been in that Oval Office with that cigar.*

Cassius caught himself laughing out loud with his self-satisfied assessment, matching his sexual prowess favorably against some of history's most famous and most powerful womanizers. He was so deeply distracted that he did not see the hockey stick swinging towards his face until it was only inches from contact.

The impact was devastating, instantly shattering his jaw and splintering nearly all of his teeth into a thousand enamel fragments, as a frothy cloud of blood exploded from his mouth. He hit the ground with a breath-stopping thud, barely remaining conscious as waves of pain crashed through his head like cinder blocks pounding inward in all directions. He lay helplessly as a man wearing a ski mask and a jogging suit in the black, white and gold colors of the Washington Capitals emerged from the shadow of a trailside cherry tree, wielding a hockey stick in a menacing pose.

"That's so you'll never brag again!" the attacker snarled.

Then the attacker swung the stick downward in a dozen swift blows to Cassius' legs, pulverizing both kneecaps and both ankles. The white-hot pain shot through his entire body like lightning bolts surging from his lower legs. He cried out in anguish, but the sound was muffled to little more than a gurgle through his blood filled mouth.

"That's so you'll never play again!"

45

Once again, the attacker raised the hockey stick, and again struck downward in a series of swift blows, this time to the basketball player's crotch. Mercifully, Cassius' body had become overwhelmed with shock, and his mind had disconnected from the sensations of pain as he slipped from consciousness.

"And that's so you'll never mess with another man's wife again!"

With that, the attacker dropped the hockey stick by his victim's side, then turned and began walking through the trees toward the bookstore of the FDR Memorial. A young couple who had been enjoying the romance of a moonlit night nearby had witnessed the entire attack. The young man had had the presence of mind to clasp his hand firmly over the young woman's mouth when she began to scream, and had turned her head away to avert her view of the grisly crime, holding her tightly as she sobbed convulsively. As soon as the attacker disappeared from view, he had taken her by the hand as they turned and ran from the scene, waiting until they reached a safe distance before grabbing the cell phone from his belt and dialing 911.

When the attacker reached the circle drive just past the bookstore, the Jaguar was waiting for him. The friendly listener from the bar emerged from the vehicle and walked around to the passenger side, wrapping the unconscious Hat Trick's arm around his shoulder and pulling him from the car, laying him spread eagle on the nearby pavement. The listener and the attacker worked together quickly, with the listener removing all of Hat Trick's clothes while the attacker stripped out of the blood-splattered black, white and gold jogging suit. Then the listener dressed Hat Trick in the suit, while the attacker changed into a fresh pair of clothes which he had stashed in the trunk of his own car. Finally, the listener placed a new ski mask over Hat Trick's face, taking care not to use the one that had been worn by the attacker, knowing that it could have contained traces of DNA from the attacker's hair or saliva.

After completing the quick-change, the attacker and the listener pulled Hat Trick up from the pavement and, with each wrapping one of his arms around their shoulders, they quickly dragged him the short distance to the scene of the attack. They laid him on the grass a few feet from Cassius, who could be heard struggling for breath in shallow, gurgling gasps. As the coup de grâce, the attacker used his gloved hands to carefully squeeze Hat Trick's fingers around the shaft of the hockey stick in half a dozen places, intentionally smudging and smearing several of the prints to appear that they were made during active and violent use.

Just as they were finishing preparations for the frame up, police sirens could be heard approaching on both 14th Street and Independence Avenue. The friendly listener and the hockey stick attacker looked at each other, smiled, slapped a high-five, walked casually to the attacker's car, and drove slowly away into the night.

7

Sean woke with a start at precisely six-thirty, and scrambled to reach the ringing telephone on his bedside table. In his jet-lagged stupor, he knocked the telephone onto the floor, but managed to retrieve the handset just in time to hear an automated voice saying, "Good morning, room three-eighteen. This is your wake-up call. Remember that breakfast is served until ten-thirty in Dominique's, just off our hotel lobby. Have a pleasant day."

"Damn, what time is it?" Sean wondered aloud. Finding his watch, he continued his morning soliloquy, "Six-thirty-two? It feels like three in the morning! My body is definitely still on California time."

The temptation was strong to lie back for a few more winks of peaceful slumber, but Sean had enough presence of mind to drag himself out of bed. He took a quick shower, selected a pair of Dockers and a Polo shirt for this morning's meeting, and made his way down to Dominique's.

Settling into a booth by the restaurant's window, he ordered a breakfast of eggs, sausages, grits and coffee, then asked the waitress to bring him a copy of the Times-Picayune, New Orleans' leading newspaper. She returned promptly with the paper and coffee, followed a short time later with the food. Sean was in the habit of pulling out the sports section to read first, but when he picked up the paper after gulping down his first cup of coffee, a headline on the front page grabbed his attention: "NBA Star Savagely Beaten in D.C. Park – Hockey Player to be Charged."

Sean read that Cassius Banks of the Washington Wizards was in intensive care at the Washington Hospital Center with injuries that would end his career. Danny Hathaway of the Washington Capitals had been found at the scene, intoxicated and gripping a bloody hockey stick. The article speculated that the assault may have been motivated by a rumored affair between the victim and Giselle Hathaway, super-model wife of the attacker. The U.S. Attorney for Washington, D.C. had scheduled a press conference for mid-morning to detail the charges he planned to file against Danny Hathaway. Giselle Hathaway was reportedly in seclusion, and management for both the Wizards and the Capitals had refused to comment on the developments. The Article closed with the observation that, following only a few days after the tragic accident in California that had claimed the lives of Jackhammer Hamilton and his passengers, the events in the nation's capital would cement this week as one of the darkest in recent sports memory.

Sean shook his head and stroked his chin, his jaw agape in disbelief. *Just when you think you've seen the worst that can happen among professional athletes*, he thought, *a new one steps out of the woodwork and takes it to another level. Now my Jackhammer story is "old news" before I can even wrap up this final lead – Lil is going to kill me!*

After finishing his breakfast and three cups of coffee, he set out on the short walk to his prescribed bus stop. He had been told to start his journey at nine o'clock, but had decided to allow time to familiarize himself with the area around his hotel and with the layout at the bus stop. It had occurred to him the preceding night that this meeting could be a set-up or a trap, and he wanted to be as prepared as possible. Sean walked cautiously around the block, trying to observe as much as possible. He found that the Maison Dupuy straddled the boundary between the commercialized blocks in the heart of the French Quarter and the mostly residential fringes.

The private residences were heavily fortified against New Orleans' notoriously high rates of murder, robbery, and other violent crimes. Ordinary barbed wire seemed inadequate to meet the security needs of average French Quarter residents. Every home had, at minimum, generous rolls of gleaming razor wire lining the tops of their fences. Many went even further, some with custom-forged iron spikes, others with glittering shards of shattered glass imbedded in mortar. Sean had never seen anything like it.

Sean's final destination was North Rampart, a broad, four-lane avenue which, together with Canal Street uptown, Esplanade downtown, and the Mississippi River served as one of the boundaries delineating the French Quarter. The transition was as stark as it was sudden. Emerging from the cobblestone charm of The Quarter, Sean saw that Rampart was lined with commercial parking lots, gas stations, weed-infested vacant spaces, liquor stores, laundromats, and other small storefront operations, along with a sprinkling of bars. It was as if he had stepped out of the scenic bliss of the late eighteenth century into the urban blight of the late twentieth.

Sean spotted the bus stop at the corner of Toulouse and Rampart, but did not go immediately to it. Instead, he walked casually along the block, stopping to "window-shop" at each storefront. After reaching the end of the block, he crossed the street and strolled slowly back toward Toulouse. If he was being followed, he hoped to flush out any unseen pursuer with his circuitous path. At five minutes before nine, Sean finally made his way back across Rampart and stood at the bus stop as he had been instructed.

The Esplanade bus came at two minutes after nine. Sean was doubly relieved that the bus was on schedule and that no one else had boarded the bus behind him. As an added bonus, he found the Regional Transit Authority bus to be one of the most pleasant he had ever ridden – the driver was friendly and courteous, the seats were cushioned and upholstered, and the air conditioning was more than adequate to maintain a temperature just a few degrees above that of an average refrigerator. After following North Rampart for eight or ten blocks, the bus turned left on Esplanade, away from the river and the French Quarter.

While North Rampart had utterly failed as an example of New Orleans historic charms, Esplanade succeeded magnificently. Esplanade was also a divided, four-lane thoroughfare, but its median strip – or "neutral ground" as the locals called it – was cloaked in the shadows of twin rows of majestic shade trees. Stately antebellum homes lined both sides of the boulevard, many of which had probably remained in one family's ownership for several generations. The lawns along Esplanade were immaculately manicured, while flowering ornamental trees added an element of gaiety to the quietude of this old-money neighborhood.

Upon reaching City Park, Sean exited the bus and saw that the tree-shaded double lanes of Esplanade continued through the entrance to the park, while the bus and most traffic turned left on

Carrolton. A quarter-mile or so inside the park, Sean could see the New Orleans Museum of Art centered at the terminus of the tree-lined promenade, the lanes veering apart to curve around opposite sides of the gallery. It was a pleasant walk, and the park was already alive with activity – from joggers and Frisbee-catching dogs, to family caravans setting up camp for a long day of barbecue and touch football.

Passing the museum, Sean found the lanes merging again on the other side, as he had been told, and walked just a few more yards before finding Golf Drive veering off to the right. He walked up the roadway and found the small stone bridge to which the mystery caller had directed him. After taking a brief detour to peek at the streambed underneath the bridge, he was satisfied that no one was lying in wait. Returning to the top of the bridge, he scanned the view. In front of him, the green velvet of one of the city's largest golf courses stretched several hundred yards, framed on both sides by dense stands of live oak trees, Spanish moss hanging from their limbs in picture-postcard perfection. At the far end of the golf course, a huge fountain sprayed its waters thirty or forty feet into the air. Behind him was a small lagoon, populated by a gaggle of geese, ducks, and swans, with the art museum barely visible through the trees beyond.

Despite the beauty and serenity of the scene, Sean felt anything but tranquil. This trip had been such a whirlwind that the potential danger of this clandestine meeting had not fully hit him until now. *What the hell am I doing out here?* He had arranged furtive meetings with sources before – usually to protect the sources' anonymity – but those meetings had typically been about draft choices, contract negotiations or college recruitment scandals. The wrong people would have been angered to learn of those meetings and the sources might have lost their jobs, but this was different. "You're in danger" had been the caller's message, and Sean's instincts were screaming at him that the danger was real.

A pair of joggers approached the bridge -- conversation animating their arms in wild gestures that seemed somehow synchronized to the steady beat of the runners' steps. They passed over the bridge and continued without pausing. Another lone jogger soon followed, wearing headphones and a portable stereo, but he also continued past without stopping. A minute or so later, Sean heard the melodic steam whistle of the park's narrow gauge railroad locomotive for the first time. It came into view near the backside of the art museum, turned left just before the intersection with Golf Drive, and continued along the periphery of the golf course. *That's one*, Sean thought.

He was becoming increasingly paranoid about the imminent meeting. *Why couldn't this caller tell me what he knows on the phone?* A series of cars passed by, each seeming to slow down as it approached the bridge, and Sean gripped the railing reflexively each time, hoping he could jump quickly enough if one of these cars swerved suddenly to run him over. More joggers passed, along with an elderly couple out for a morning stroll and a group of young children carrying fishing poles. Again, Sean heard the sound of the steam whistle. *That's two.*

His thoughts drifted back to the article he had read in the Times-Picayune. He recalled the closing line, "…following only a few days after the tragic accident in California that had claimed the lives of Jackhammer Hamilton and his passengers, the events in the nation's capital would cement this week as one of the darkest in recent sports memory." A sudden chill shot down his spine as he realized the unthinkable possibility. *Oh my God! What if it's not coincidence? What have I gotten myself into?*

Checking his watch nervously, he saw that it was nearly ten o'clock. The sun had climbed well above the tree line and was beating down with the intensity of a thermonuclear beacon. Sean was drenched in sweat, the synergistic effects of heat and anxiety draining him rapidly. *Where is he? Why doesn't he show up?* A car approached from behind, pulling to a stop a few feet from the edge of the bridge. The car's windshield was reflecting the glare of the sun, so Sean could only see a blurry silhouette of the car's lone occupant. As Sean squinted to try to get a better glimpse of the driver, he saw that the man had leaned over the back seat and retrieved a long, cylindrical, metallic object. *Shit! He has a rifle!* The car door swung open, and Sean felt his stomach rising into his throat as the shadowy driver's head came into view.

Glancing away for a split second, Sean took another look at his presumed escape route, and he felt his breath stop as he realized it was too far to jump to the streambed below – the fall would almost certainly break his leg. Finally, the driver emerged into full view, and Sean was nearly overwhelmed with a confused jumble of emotions as he saw that the object in the man's hand was actually the three segments of a rod and reel. The man was there to fish in the lagoon.

Several more cars, joggers, and pedestrians passed, but none stopped. Then, at ten-fifteen, Sean heard the steam whistle again. *That's three. I'm outta here!* He waited on the stone bridge until the train had passed and disappeared from view, just to be in full compliance with his caller's instructions, then he began the walk back out of the park. *Damn! Stood up! I hope this whole trip hasn't been a wild goose chase – I would never hear the last of this from Lil.*

Circling back around the art museum, Sean returned along the tree-lined promenade that merged with Esplanade Avenue beyond the park's borders. The huge family picnic that had just begun when he had passed earlier was now in full revelry. Smoke billowed from two metal grills, carrying with it the twin summertime scents of charcoal and barbecue seasoning. The younger children were running, screaming, and spraying each other with Super Soaker water guns, while the older generation had taken up positions in folding lounge chairs strategically placed to remain shaded throughout the long, hot day. A contingent of teenagers had isolated themselves several yards away from the older family members, leaning against a car and talking as the car stereo blasted a dozen or so decibels above the established threshold of human hearing.

Emerging from the park, Sean crossed Carrolton toward the bus stop for inbound travel, where he saw three young men standing at the bench. One, a rather slender youth who stood at least three inches taller than Sean's six feet, was wearing stereo headphones, bobbing his head and gesticulating rhythmically to the beat of his music. The other two were talking loudly and occasionally laughing. One stood about six-foot-one, the other an inch or so shorter, both with stocky builds. All three were African-American, probably in their early twenties, the tallest with hair in a short Afro, the two nearest him sporting intricately patterned braids. They were all similarly clad: the one with the stereo was wearing black Girbaud jeans, black Reebok sneakers with red trim, a red tee-shirt and a red bandanna, while the other two were dressed in black jeans, white Reeboks, shabby white tee-shirts, and matching white bandannas.

As he approached, the two in white shirts turned to look at him and immediately began speaking in more hushed tones. Instinctively, Sean stopped a few feet from the young men and attempted to maintain a discreet distance. Unfortunately, the location did not lend itself well to such carefully choreographed posturing, because there was nothing but grass and sidewalk near the bus bench – no logical place to stop and stand. Apparently noticing Sean's awkward hesitation, the taller of the two turned and looked directly into his eyes, while continuing to talk loudly with his friend.

"Wuzzup wit' da white boy? You think he's afraid we might fuck him up an' take his platinum card?"

"I dunno," the friend answered. "I don't think he's from 'round here, know what I'm sayin'? Look at dem clothes! Maybe he's lost."

The two friends laughed menacingly, while the third young man seemed completely oblivious, still lost in his music. The two continued their baiting game.

"Hey, Whodi, wuzzup?" the taller one called out. "You lost? You tryin' to get home to June an' the Beaver?"

"Yeah," agreed the shorter young man, laughing. "You sho' 'nough need somebody to show you how to dress! Where'd you get dat whack-ass outfit?"

The two friends cracked up laughing, obviously pleased with the discomfort they were causing their unwilling audience. Sean tried to ignore them, and glanced around in hopes of spotting a police car, convenience store, or any other refuge, but there was none.

"He don't seem too talkative, do he?" the shorter one asked his friend rhetorically. Then, shifting toward Sean, continued the verbal onslaught.

"How come you don't answer when we talk to you, Whodi? That's jus' disrespectful, know what I'm sayin'? You got a problem wit' brothas?"

The taller man continued the harassment where the other had left off, cutting in before Sean had time to respond. "You know

54

where y'at? You in da Sixt' Ward, fool! You don't dis a brotha in his own ward 'less yo' lookin' to get clocked!"

This is just great, Sean thought, trying to maintain his composure despite a growing sense of panic. He was now feeling extreme urgency in his quest to find a way out of the rapidly escalating situation. He tried to stammer a response, but was so completely caught off guard that he found himself at a surprising loss for words. All he could think of was escape. *Come on, bus! Get here!* The two taunters took a tentative step toward him. *Oh, shit!*

"Hey, you deaf, mutha fucka? I'm talkin' to you!" the taller man was now speaking with an openly hostile tone of voice.

"Look," Sean entreated. "I don't want any trouble…"

"It's a l'il late fo' dat," the taller man interrupted, his voice growing louder. "'Cause yo' in a world o' trouble, now, know what I'm sayin'?"

"This is one *stoopid* white boy," the shorter one chimed in. "Standin' out here in da Sixt' Ward dressed like a momma's boy an' actin' like a bitch!"

"You scared of us?" the taller one continued, shrugging his shoulders in an exaggerated gesture. "Wussup wit' dat? You don't even know us. We could jus' be two brothas waitin' on a bus to get to our j-o-b's. We had no beef wit' you, know what I'm sayin'? So how come you can't answer a brotha when he speaks? That's jus' stupid disrespectful!"

The two continued to move slowly but steadily closer, and Sean had nearly resigned himself to the certainty that he was going to be mugged, when he saw the Esplanade bus approaching a few blocks away. The look of relief must have shown on his face, because both of the young men turned to follow his gaze. Seeing the rapidly approaching bus, the two stepped back away from him. At the same moment, the third man turned toward him, and in one smooth motion switched off his stereo and raised the front of his red tee-shirt, revealing an automatic pistol lodged snugly in his waist band.

"Take one step to dat bus an' I'll pop a cap in you right here!" commanded the newest participant in the slow motion assault. Sean ran through a rapid series of calculations in his mind, trying to decide if he could call the muggers' bluff and make a dash for the bus when it pulled to a stop. As if reading his thoughts, the young man with the gun waved to the bus to pass on by, and it rushed past the stop and around the corner without slowing.

As soon as the bus had passed, the man with the gun gave a slight nod of his head, and a car squealed up from an adjacent street. The two who had been baiting him stepped to the car and opened both passenger side doors, then the shorter one slid into the back seat, taking the position behind the driver. The man with the gun gestured toward the back door, saying simply, "get in," as the taller of his original tormentors waited near the door.

Sean hesitated briefly, sensing that if he entered the car he would never emerge alive. He turned slightly and tried to find the courage to run.

"You crazy, mutha fucka?" the man with the gun grasped it tightly, ready to draw and fire on a second's notice. "Get in the fuckin' car! You want this to be a kidnappin' or a murder? Get in the fuckin' car, NOW!"

Realizing there was no escape, Sean ducked into the back seat, the second assailant following and closing the door behind them. The man with the gun got into the front seat and ordered the short, dark-skinned young man at the wheel to step on the gas. Then, turning in his seat to face Sean, he said, "You shoulda known the golf course would be a dead end. Basketball and hockey are where the action's been lately."

8

Sean was too terrified to think rationally, and the odd comment by the young man with the gun in the front seat sent his mind reeling. He had no idea what was happening. He tried to track and memorize their location as the car sped away from City Park, but even that simple tactic for self-preservation proved difficult as the car made a rapid series of seemingly random turns. They turned right from Carrolton onto Esplanade, then after a few blocks, they made a series of four left turns in rapid succession, onto Broad, Gentilly, St. Bernard, and finally onto the access ramp leading to I-610. After what Sean guessed to be a mile, I-610 merged into I-10, then they continued for several minutes before exiting the Interstate toward the Ponchartrain Causeway. No one had spoken to him during the rapid flight out of New Orleans, but when they turned onto Causeway Boulevard, the man with the gun turned around in his seat to face Sean again. Flashing a brief smile, he said, "Everythin'll be chill soon as we get on the causeway. Jus' don't fuck up."

Sean's mind was racing ahead, trying desperately to remain calm, while just as desperately searching for a way out. He believed he recognized the front passenger's voice from the anonymous calls he had received, but it was difficult to be certain. Beyond that, Sean could not imagine what he was doing in this car with four young thugs and a gun. The car slowed as traffic merged ahead of them just before the entrance to the causeway. As they approached the bridge, a highway patrol cruiser pulled even with them in the left lane, and remained alongside for nearly half a mile. Sean tried to think of a way to convey a signal to the law enforcement officer but, again anticipating his thoughts, the young man with the gun looked him in the eyes icily and said, "Stay cool, Whodi, ya heard me?"

Finally, they passed onto the bridge and accelerated to the prevailing speed, gradually outpacing the highway patrol cruiser and blending in with the traffic headed toward the North Shore.

The causeway seemed to go on forever, vanishing where the bright blue sky and muddy-blue water met in the haze of the horizon. The Ponchartrain Causeway, at twenty-four miles, was the longest single-span bridge in the world and it would be quite some time before they reached the other side. The passenger in the front seat turned to face him again.

"You got a press badge, Whodi?" he asked.

"Yeah, I do," Sean replied, surprised by the question. "Do you want to see it?" The young man nodded, and Sean reached slowly into his back pocket, producing his wallet. Opening the wallet so that his identification was visible, he handed it to his inquisitor.

After inspecting the press card carefully, the young man flipped quickly through the remaining contents of the wallet, then closed it and handed it back to Sean before continuing his questioning. "What do you know 'bout Jackhammer Hamilton's death?"

"To be truthful, I'm not sure that I know anything more than what you've seen in the newspapers," Sean answered.

With a half chuckle, the young man pressed on. "Come on, Whodi, you wouldn't have come all this way if you really believed it was jus' an accident."

"Well," Sean conceded. "I do have suspicions."

"What suspicions?"

"I talked to the only survivor at the hospital. Before she died, she told me there had been a truck at the scene, involved in some way. The way she described it, it sounded almost as if the truck had run them off the road intentionally."

The young man in the front seat glanced briefly at the driver, who nodded knowingly back at him. Turning back again, he instructed Sean to continue. Sean described the sense of urgency and certainty he had seen in LaTanya's eyes, and outlined his conversations with Lieutenant Vasquez, Dr. Hahn, and Tramayne Owens. He described the calls he had made to a score of Jackhammer's associates, all without turning up anything that could substantiate LaTanya's frightening recollection. He finished by explaining that he had all but closed the book on the story until he had received their call.

"That was me, yo," said the young man in the front seat, a smile coming across his face. "By the way, you can call me 'Z'."

"Okay, 'Z'," Sean responded, his journalistic instincts re-emerging along with just enough courage to begin recovering from the panic that had gripped him. "I've told you everything I know about this story. Now it's my turn. Why am I here? What's this all about?"

"Okay," Z replied. "Off top, let me introduce the fellas. This is my dawg, 'Cool'," he said, pointing to the driver, a serious-looking young man who appeared to be about five-foot-seven. "Back there on yo' right is Roderick an' on yo' left, his l'il brotha Dewayne," nodding toward each of them in turn. Sean noticed that Z pronounced Dewayne with the emphasis on the first syllable, as if it were D-Wayne.

As they were introduced, each of the brothers nodded politely toward Sean as if meeting a friend of a friend for the first time. It struck Sean as rather bizarre, considering their performance at the bus stop.

"I guess I'm supposed to say it's a pleasure meeting each of you. Now, why did you call me and have me come all the way to New Orleans? And why are you driving me across this damn bridge at gunpoint?"

"I called you 'cause I overheard a conversation an' knew you were onto somethin' real," Z replied. "See, I work at a fitness club in Metarie, where a lotta white businessmen come to walk on the treadmills, play racquetball, or make million dollar deals in the sauna. Metarie is the kinda town where a young brotha like me can get a job carryin' towels fo' the rich white shot-callers, but I'd be askin' to get my ass whupped if I drove down the streets at night, ya heard me? The cops there always be stoppin' an' harassin' brothas. Anyway, I was takin' inventory in a closet off to the side of one of the saunas, when J. Richard Connor walked in. He's the one who got the Cajuns baseball team for New Orleans."

"Yeah, he finally got a team of his own," Sean interjected. "He had been leading the effort to get an NBA team for New Orleans for years, but too many of the people he was involved with got sucked into the riverboat gambling fiasco and the scandals that followed. A lot of big names and deep pockets got caught up in that web – even your ex-Governor Edwards and 49ers owner

Eddie DeBartolo were taken down. What a mess. I still don't know how Connor managed to stay above the fray and avoid prosecution. After another consortium bypassed Connor and brought the Charlotte Hornets to New Orleans, Connor turned his attention to baseball. So, what happened – did Connor speak to you?"

"Nah, Whodi, he didn't even know I was there," Z continued. "He thought he was alone, ya heard, so he pulled out his cell phone an' paged 'The Cardinal,' who controls all the drugs in the white neighborhoods of New Orleans, as well as most of Jefferson, St. Bernard, an' Plaquemines Parishes. Our parishes are what I guess you'd call counties outside The Boot. The Cardinal's territory includes Metarie, Harahan, an' Kenner, out by the airport, Gretna an' Westwego on the West Bank, an' Chalmette out past the CTC."

Sean had caught the reference to the boot shape of Louisiana, and smiled at the apt nickname. "What's the 'CTC'?" he asked.

"Cross The Canal. It means the neighborhood 'cross the St. Claude bridge, on the other side of the Harbor Canal."

"So what about this call?"

"Okay. Well, anyway, he paged The Cardinal – I guess even J.R. Connor doesn't know The Cardinal's home number – an' first thing they talked 'bout was you. It sounded like they'd both heard that you'd been snoopin' 'round tryin' to stir somethin' up behind the Jackhammer accident. Then J.R. said he didn't want anythin' to delay their plans. He said 'Go ahead with the D.C. double-play on schedule, an' I want Mack Vanderhorn an' Tyrone Freeman taken out right away.' That's a direct quote, ya heard me? Then he said if you got in the way, they'd take you out, too, ya heard?"

"The D.C. double-play," Sean repeated. "You don't think he was talking about..."

"Yeah," Z nodded, finishing Sean's thought. "Sounds like he coulda been talkin' 'bout Cassius Banks an' Hat Trick Hathaway. I don't know how, but I think Connor an' the Cardinal were behind that somehow."

Sean sat silently for a few minutes, pondering the wild story he had just been told. His first instinct was to presume that this "Z" character was lying – setting him up somehow – or that he had badly misinterpreted what J.R. Connor had said. But there was an earnestness to Z's recounting of the eavesdropped call that matched the credibility he had ascribed to LaTanya's equally wild tale. After thinking through Z's account of Connor's call to The Cardinal, Sean tried to make sense of what Z had heard.

"I don't get it," He began, thinking aloud. "I don't see the connection. Jackhammer played basketball for the Golden State Warriors and Banks played for the Wizards. Hat Trick is a hockey player for the Capitals, Vanderhorn is a pitcher for the Chicago Cubs, and Freeman is the New England Patriot's star linebacker. I can't see any connection among the five of them. Vanderhorn is the only one with any connection to New Orleans, since he owns a home here. He's also the only one connected to baseball, but his Cubs are in the National League Central Division while Connor's Cajuns are in the NL East – with no division rivalry, that link to Connor looks tenuous at best. None of them has any other apparent connection to the Cajuns organization, so why would Connor go after those five? I just don't get it."

"I don't know, either, yo," Z responded. "But I can tell you one thing f'sho' – if The Cardinal's involved, it's some serious shit. One thing you'd best learn quickly – New Orleans may seem like nothin' but a big party to outsiders, but when it comes to business, everythin's serious. We don't play here in the Boot Camp. This is the toughest town in America, ya heard me, an' you'd better learn fast if yo' gonna stay alive."

"So what about you and your friends," Sean queried, nodding first toward Roderick then towards Dewayne. "Are you playing or for real?"

"Oh, you mean back at the bus stop? Yeah, well, we were settin' you up an' testin' you to make sho' you was 'bout what you said you was 'bout. If this shit is fo' real, an' they set up Jackhammer's accident an' the drama in DC with Cassius Banks an' Hat Trick, then there's sho' 'nough gonna be mo' bodies tagged befo' it's over, ya heard me? An' if The Cardinal finds out I overheard that conversation, I'll be 'gator bait from one end of Plaquemines Parish to the other. When I told Cool I was gonna call you, he thought I was crazy, an' he was prob'ly right. Fo' all we knew, they coulda iced you already an' sent over a decoy to mark us fo' one of The Cardinal's triggermen. We decided to come up wit' a plan to catch you by surprise wit' an unexpected situation. That way, we could stay in control while we had a chance to check you out an' make sho' you were legit. I told Rod an' D to come at you wit' their best ghetto rap, act like they was from 'round that way, an' keep yo' back to the wall."

"And if you'd gotten a bad feeling about me..." Sean's voice trailed off, leaving the obvious question unasked. Z similarly chose not to answer directly.

"We ain't gangstas, yo. Rod got busted sellin' dope a few years back, jus' a couple nickel bags of weed, ya heard, an' D got a record in junior high fo' some petty shit – shopliftin' out at Wal-Mart an' pick-pocketin' some tourists on Bourbon Street – but all four of us are in college now, jus' tryin' to do the right thing. We don't look fo' trouble, ya heard me, but if trouble comes to us, we handle our business. The Nint' Ward is like that."

"The Nint' Ward?" Sean asked, unconsciously mimicking the New Orleans accent, which habitually omitted the final sound of many words and syllables. In New Orleans, "Ninth" loses the final sound to become "Nint'," "corner" sounds something like "coh-nah," and even the city's name is often pronounced "N'awlins." Sean had noticed this trait of the local dialect, along with the maddeningly mangled pronunciations of the city's many French place names, so that "Chartres" was pronounced "charters" and "Burgundy" had the emphasis strongly on the second syllable.

"Yeah, in the Nint' Ward, we have a sayin', 'when it doesn't concern you, mind yo' business, but when it does concern you, *handle* yo' business.' We didn't call you out here to do you wrong, Whodi, but if you'd tried to do us wrong, we would've known how to handle it – there's a lotta water in this lake, ya heard me? That's the Nint' Ward. That's how it is Downtown. Now, if you were Uptown, it'd be a whole diff'rent story. They're crazy Uptown. They'll kill you fo' no reason. I'll tell you what the Uptown thugs are like.

"A few years back, someone came up wit' a new way to pay last respects to some of the brothas dyin' in drive-bys an' pull-ups. All of the victim's friends would get his picture silk-screened onto tee-shirts, wit' the year he was born written underneath as 'sunrise' an' the year he died as 'sunset.' But then some Uptown hardheads started wearin' tee shirts like that *befo'* a hit, ya heard?

62

They would jus' walk 'round town fo' a week or two, wearin' the shirt an' lettin' everyone see what was comin'. If they were hard 'nough, they might even step to the victim face-to-face wearin' the shirt, so he would know he was a dead man. That's Uptown, yo."

"Damn!" Sean exclaimed softly, shaking his head. Unable to think of any other appropriate response, he repeated, "Damn! Now I think I'm beginning to understand the razor wire and medieval spikes on everyone's homes. I'd heard the French Quarter had a crime problem, but nothing like that."

"Oh, The Quarter, that's nothin'," Z laughed. "Houses gettin' broke into an' tourists gettin' jacked fo' their credit cards an' digital cameras. Crime in The Quarter gets all the attention 'cause it involves white people an' white people's money. No offense, but that's jus' how it is. The serious shit happens in the projects an' neighborhoods, jus' like any other city. There's a project called the Iberville jus' a few blocks 'cross Rampart from yo' hotel that everyone calls 'Cop-killer-ville' 'cause so many of the gangstas there got armor-piercin' bullets. The other projects Uptown are the Magnolia, the Melpomene, an' the Calliope, but everyone jus' calls 'em the Mag, the Melp, an' the Callio."

"So, what do we do, now?" Sean asked, almost rhetorically. "I have the testimony of a dead witness that was never recorded or heard by anyone but me. You have a hearsay conversation, pitting the word of a young black college student from a tough neighborhood against the word of one of the richest, most powerful entrepreneurs in the country. We have nothing. All I can do is contact Mack Vanderhorn and Tyrone Freeman to try to find the common link and to warn them to watch their backs."

"You need to watch yo' back, too, Whodi," Z observed, as they reached the north end of the causeway bridge, and looped around to return along the other side. "This ain't a town to play 'round in if you don't know what you're doin'. Here in New Orleans, if you see somethin' goin' down that doesn't involve you, jus' keep walkin'. An' if anyone ever tells you to run, break out fast as you can, an' never look back."

(9)

As the car continued southward, back toward New Orleans, the five of them sat quietly for a few minutes. No one spoke as they all pondered the implications of what they had learned from each other. Breaking the silence, Sean resumed the conversation.

"You said I'd better learn fast if I'm going to survive, and I couldn't agree with you more. You've got to tell me *everything* you know about this story. There is clearly a lot you haven't told me yet. For example, what do you know about this 'Cardinal,' and perhaps more importantly, *how* do you know about him?"

Z looked quickly to Cool, who returned his glance and shook his head silently. Z turned his gaze away, peering out the passenger window at the vast expanse of water rushing by. Stroking his chin with his right hand, he appeared deep in thought and only spoke after several minutes' contemplation.

"Yeah you right – I guess I do need to finish what I started," Z began. "If yo' gonna keep yo' head above water you've gotta know which way the tide is runnin'. Let me break it down fo' you like this – crime in New Orleans is a local thing. We don't have the same organizations other cities have – no Crips, no Bloods, no real Mafia, no loyalties outside the Boot. We have connections, f'sho' – the guns an' drugs gotta come from somewhere, but no one outside New Orleans ever calls the shots. When you see brothas wearin' colors or soldier rags in New Orleans they're representin' their wards, or maybe they jus' like how it looks.

"I told you 'bout parishes, already. Well, parishes are each divided into wards, ya heard, an' each ward represents a diff'rent neighborhood. Wards are everythin' on the street. Yo' ward is yo' country, yo' people, yo' blood. When somebody tells you what ward they're from, you *know* what they're representin'. Most of the violence that happens here is one ward 'gainst 'nother. Projects in the same ward may have beefs, like the Magnolia an' Callio, Uptown, but they never take it to the limit. The same two hardheads who were beatin' the shit outta each other one minute will drop everythin' to back each other up against perpetrators from 'nother ward.

"All the wards in New Orleans are divided into three groups – Uptown, Downtown, an' the West Bank. I already told you Uptown is the roughest, so it's no surprise that a lotta the muscle runnin' the show Uptown is deep into gangsta rap. The shot-caller Uptown is Callio Cal, the biggest rapper to come from the Uptown projects since Master P. He has his own label, an' makes beaucoup cash off his own records an' 'bout a dozen other artists he produces, but heroin is his real business, ya heard me? He jus' uses his record label as a front. He's got some damn good accountants, too – they say the IRS has been tryin' to nail his ass on tax evasion fo' years, the same way they got Capone, but they can't touch him. As fo' the local five-oh, they *won't* touch him. It seems like half the N.O.P.D. is on the payroll, even though they've been tryin' to clean the force out the last coupla years. It's common knowledge in New Orleans that the three most popular cars fo' drug dealin' are Cadillacs, Cutlasses, an' cruisers – police cruisers."

"I remember reading about the FBI sting and scandal that rocked your police force back in the mid-nineties," Sean interjected. "But I thought your last couple of police commissioners had cleaned things up."

"True dat," Z responded. "Gotta give Pennington and Compass their props, they made a lotta changes an' things have most definitely gotten better, but there's still a lotta cops workin' wit' Cal, an' the rest of the force is scared. You mess wit' Cal, they're gonna chop yo' house up – it don't matter if you're carryin' a badge or not."

"What do you mean, 'chop your house up'?" Sean asked.

"That means a drive by on yo' house wit' AK-47's. They call AK's 'choppers', 'cause the bullets come outta an AK spinnin' end-over-end, like power saw blades. You can take down a medium-sized tree wit' a chopper, so you can imagine three or four guys sittin' in a car sprayin' the front of yo' house wit' 'em fo' twenty or thirty seconds. It's like a wreckin' crew, an' nobody inside is gonna survive.

"Like I told you befo', Downtown isn't so crazy. Downtown is run by 'Big T.' He has a legit front too, jus' like Cal, but instead of a record label, his is a chain of hardware stores all over Southern Louisiana. He runs his business a lot diff'rent than Cal, though – he relies mo' on brains an' loyalty than muscle. He plays a sorta 'Robin Hood' role in the Sevent', Eight', an' Nint' Wards – sponsorin' youth sports teams, leanin' on his contacts in city hall to fill a few potholes in front of the projects, an' buyin' stained-glass windows fo' some of the churches so they won't preach against him.

"Don't get me wrong, ya heard me, his hands are jus' as bloody as Cal's. He makes beaucoup money sellin' dope to the same kids he fronts as helpin', an' he'd rip yo' throat out wit' his bare hands if you crossed him. He's six-foot-six an' nearly three hundred pounds, so there ain't too many people that'll step to him. He jus' has a diff'rent style, ya heard – he knows you catch mo' flies wit' honey than wit' vinegar, an' he has the most loyal soldiers anywhere. You'll never hear anyone in the CTC talk bad 'bout Big T – least not in public.

"Last, an' definitely least, is the West Bank. All you need to know 'bout the West Bank is that it's run by a gangsta named 'Fat Friday.' 'Sides the fact that he's 'bout four hundred pounds, they say he got his name 'cause he's in the habit of makin' all his payoffs on Fridays. Wit' all those extra presidents in circulation, everyone on the West Bank expects a fat Friday fo' business – from the cocktail waitresses in every hole-in-the-wall blues bar in Algiers to the hookers workin' 'round the naval station off General Meyer Avenue. The West Bank is the smallest an' least profitable piece of the New Orleans pie, an' Fat Friday pretty much keeps his nose outta Uptown an' Downtown business.

"That brings us to The Cardinal. Things are a l'il diff'rent outside New Orleans. I guess the white boys there don't feel as much loyalty to their suburbs as we feel to our wards, so it's been easier to bring 'em all together under one organization. Several years ago, each of the surroundin' parishes had its own boss, but one-by-one, The Cardinal got control of St. Bernard, Plaquemines, an' Jefferson Parishes. If the local boss wasn't willin' to kiss The Cardinal's ass, he died, ya heard me? Simple as that. The Cardinal got his name as a kinda joke, 'cause he runs mo' parishes than a Bishop, an' 'cause all the blood he's spilled would stain his clothes red like the robes of a cardinal.

"He's been movin' into St. Tammany Parish on the North Shore, an' he has his finger deep in Orleans Parish now, too, wit' muscle in the riverboat gamblin' business an' in The Quarter. But most of the neighborhoods here are still firmly in the hands of Callio Cal, Big T, an' Fat Friday. It's gonna be hard fo' a white boss to take over the business in the projects, but everyone expects The Cardinal to make a play fo' all of New Orleans soon. One thing f'sho' – he won't give up wit'out a body count that'll make last year's murder rate look like an ice cream social. It's gonna be a long, hot summer in New Orleans."

As they neared the south end of the causeway, the New Orleans skyline loomed ahead, with the ever-dominant Superdome in the foreground. Sean stared out the window, pondering all that he had been told. In his years as a sports writer, he had ducked blows a few times as angry and frustrated athletes had vented the rage of defeat against interviewers whom they perceived to be taunting them. But this was a long way from locker room scrapes. For the first time he could remember, Sean truly feared for his life.

After a long minute of silence, Sean looked up to face Z and asked, "How does a smart college-kid who's all of twenty-four, twenty-five years old know so much about the inner workings of every criminal organization in New Orleans? There's got to be something more to this story that you're not telling me."

Z turned and looked at Cool again, who shook his head forcefully.

"Don't do it, Dawg!" Cool urged. "You've already told this reporter too much. How do we know we can trust him?"

Glancing back over his shoulder into the back seat, Cool continued. "No offense, Whodi, but you're way over yo' head. You have no idea what you're dealin' wit', an' you're jus' gonna end up gettin' us all killed. I told Z to jus' leave it alone an' mind his business. You've gotta know you can't jus' write everythin' he told you. You'll start a war in New Orleans, an' we'll be the first casualties. Like Z said, people don't play down here, an' they *will* find out where you got yo' four-one-one."

"Look," Sean countered. "I didn't ask to be here, remember? Your friend Z called me out here from California, then the four of you kidnapped me at gunpoint. I can assure you, I'm not going to write a damn thing until I sort out what's really going on – I have no particular wish to die, myself. You're right, I don't know what I'm involved in, but like it or not, I *am* involved and now I need all the information I can get."

"He's right," Z interjected, brushing off one last warning glare from Cool. "I've gotta tell him the rest. We'll all be better off if he knows where to step, an' where not to." With that, Z leaned back over the seat and, looking Sean squarely in the eyes, answered his question.

"The reason I know so much 'bout all the organizations is 'cause Big T is my uncle. I've never been involved in his operation – Momma wouldn't allow it – but when I was younger, I used to do some legit work fo' Uncle T in his hardware store. You know, cleanin' up an' unloadin' trucks, shit like that. I used to hear a lotta phone calls that I knew weren't 'bout hardware, ya heard, an' I started seein' some of the other merchandise he had comin' in on those trucks.

"When Momma got wind of what Uncle T was really 'bout, she stormed down to his office one day when I was there an' read him like I've never seen anyone read befo'. I've never seen my Momma curse like that. She cursed him fo' havin' me there wit' all the drugs an' guns, an' told him he was no longer her brother. Then she yanked me outta there by my ear, hollered at me 'til she lost her voice fo' not tellin' her what was goin' on, an' gave me the worst lickin' I've ever had. That was over eight years ago, ya heard me, an' I don't think they've spoken since. If they pass on the street, Momma'll look right through Uncle T like he's not even there, an' keep right on walkin'.

"When you've got someone in yo' family runnin' an organization like that, you make it yo' business to know everythin' that's goin' on. Callio Cal or The Cardinal wouldn't think twice 'bout choppin' my Momma's house up to send a message to Uncle T. If Big T ever gets on the losin' end of a war, I'm gonna want to know what's comin' so I can look out fo' Momma an' my l'il sister. That's why I know what I know."

(10)

Z, Cool, Roderick, and Dewayne drove Sean back to the Hotel Maison Dupuy, and he invited them in to the privacy of his room to continue their conversation. Z continued his monologue detailing the power structures and pitfalls of New Orleans' criminal organizations. He also assured Sean that his uncle, Big T, would never work with The Cardinal, and therefore, could not be involved in the conspiracy against the five athletes. Before leaving Sean alone in his hotel room to plan his next move, Z gave him a phone number, with instructions to call if he came up with any answers or needed help of any kind.

The next morning, Sean set about to locate Mack Vanderhorn and Tyrone Freeman. The key to the puzzle, he reasoned, would be in determining the common link among the athletes on the presumed hit list. With Cassius Banks in intensive care and Hat Trick Hathaway under arrest on felony charges, it would obviously be all but impossible to contact them. Besides, Sean reasoned that it was too late to help either of them, but hoped to be able to warn the remaining two. Sean soon discovered that contacting Tyrone Freeman was going to be a major problem. The football player was at his summer condo in San Juan, Puerto Rico, and his unlisted number there was a closely guarded secret.

Mack Vanderhorn, on the other hand, turned out to be the lucky break – he was at home in New Orleans. Lucky for Sean, that is, but unlucky for Mack. This was the week of the All-Star game, and in earlier years Mack Vanderhorn would have been assured of a place in the starting rotation for the National League team, but that was before his fall from grace. Mack had been arrested on heroin possession charges three seasons earlier, and had been on a rapid slide from glory ever since. As part of a plea bargain agreement, he had been forced to sit out half a season, ending his chances for a third straight twenty-win year.

After that, things got worse. His drug addiction and lavish lifestyle caught up with him financially and he was forced to file bankruptcy, selling his multimillion-dollar estate on the shores of Lake Michigan. That was the last straw for his wife, Gracie, who filed for divorce and took their two children to live with her parents in Vermont. Then, in the spring of last year, Gracie went public with charges that Mack had not sent a single dollar in child support in over a year. The voting for that year's All Star game had already been tabulated, and Mack was among the starting pitchers, but thousands of fans had booed him when he had taken the mound. Newspaper headlines around the country had dubbed him the "All Star Deadbeat Dad."

This year, Mack Vanderhorn was sitting at home in New Orleans, trying to avoid the glare of publicity that had so forcefully illuminated his past indiscretions. After a half dozen calls to some of Mack's close associates, Sean successfully tracked down his unlisted home number and tried several times to reach him. Each time, his call was answered by voice mail, with an automated female voice instructing him to leave a message. The first three times he called, he simply left his name and the hotel phone number in hopes that Mack would return his call. As the morning passed into afternoon, Sean realized that Mack was not going to be in a rush to talk to a member of the press without a very good reason, so on his fourth and fifth calls, he recorded a warning to Mack. He informed Mack that Jackhammer Hamilton's death might not have been an accident, and that Mack's name had been mentioned in connection with Jackhammer's, closing with an "urgent" plea to return his call.

Sean stayed by his phone throughout the day, hoping Mack would call. He even ordered room service for lunch to avoid leaving his room. But the call never came. Sean would have been frustrated to learn that Mack Vanderhorn had been home all day with his telephone ringer turned off. He had wanted to get through this painful day without interruption, and had nearly succeeded. His tranquility had only been disturbed once, by a satellite dish repairman who had knocked insistently on the front door until Mack had opened it and greeted him with an icy glare. Mack's first inclination had been to physically throw the repairman off the property, but he had realized that he was about to vent the rage of a lifetime on an innocent bystander. In the end, he relented and let the man go about his work, returning to his poolside chaise and bottle of Jack Daniels.

When no call came by six in the evening, Sean decided to take a walk in search of dinner and fresh air. He stopped by the front desk on his way out and instructed the lone desk clerk to give special attention to watching for his messages, impressing the importance of the request with a twenty-dollar bill folded into the young man's hand.

At six-fifteen that evening, just as Sean was being seated in the lively, art-deco dining room of the Acme Oyster House, Boudreaux Dupre was driving the last few blocks home from work in his satellite repair van. Boudreaux was grinning from ear to ear and humming along with the zydeco melodies blasting from his dashboard stereo, barely able to contain his glee. This had been a very special day.

Although he was now employed as a satellite dish technician, he had worked a number of years as a locksmith and was quite skilled at both trades. An acquaintance, with whom he frequently shot pool at his favorite watering hole, had recently introduced him to a man who had expressed great interest in Boudreaux's dual careers. The man had offered Boudreaux ten thousand dollars for a very simple thirty-minute job. Boudreaux was to enter the home of Mack Vanderhorn under the pretense of performing routine maintenance on his satellite dish, then surreptitiously take a master imprint of Mack's front door lock. After returning the imprint to the man, he would be paid his reward on the spot. The man had identified himself as a private investigator working for Gracie Vanderhorn's attorneys, and said they needed a way into the house to search for documentation of assets Mack was hiding from the legal discovery process.

Boudreaux had done exactly as he had been instructed. His heart had sunk with disappointment when Mack initially failed to answer the door, fearing that the deal might be a one-day only offer. Once Mack had let him in, however, it had been easy to slip back to the front door while the drunken baseball star lounged by his pool. Returning the imprint at a pre-arranged meeting point, he had been handed a small burgundy leather briefcase filled with five neatly arranged stacks of twenties.

Boudreaux really didn't care about the legalities. He understood that lawyers frequently skirted the letter of the law to achieve the desired results for their clients, and he had bent a few

71

laws himself. *I know one more law that's gonna be broken, today*, he thought to himself. *The IRS will never get their hands on this bonus income!* Reaching across to the seat next to him, he flipped open the latches and took another peek at the cash, whistling softly at the sheer bulk of the green currency. Clicking the latches closed again, his mind was filled with a score of possibilities that would now be open to him: a dream vacation; a down payment on a new car; a hot tub in the back yard – the modest hopes of a working man who had lived most of his life a half step behind the American dream and a half step ahead of financial ruin.

He never saw the car approaching from behind. As he slowed at a stop sign two blocks from his home, he was suddenly jolted by the impact of another car crashing into the back of his van. Instinctively, he slammed on his brakes, then sat in a moment of dazed silence after he had come to a full stop. The other driver, however, did not hesitate for a second. Wearing loose-fitting coveralls, welder's goggles, and what appeared to be a flak jacket, he bolted from his car, dashed forward, and swung open Boudreaux's door. In a neatly choreographed series of actions, the second driver cracked Boudreaux's forehead open with a short iron pipe, stretched his left hand across the unconscious man's torso to grab the briefcase, then reached under the vehicle with his right – depositing a small plastic device directly under Boudreaux's seat. After dashing back to his own vehicle, the killer just had time to throw open his trunk, hitting the deck as Boudreaux's truck exploded in a huge orange fireball.

Instantly, the assassin jumped to his feet, stripped off the blood-spattered coveralls and gear, and tossed them into his trunk before abandoning the vehicle and strolling casually up the sidewalk – wending his way through the rapidly gathering crowd of onlookers. When the first police cruiser arrived at the scene moments later, the officers' attention was drawn to the thick smoke billowing from the flaming wreckage, so they barely noticed the businessman walking along the sidewalk with a small burgundy-leather briefcase. As the sounds of multiple fire engines and ambulances approached, the businessman rounded the corner, stepped into a parked car, and drove away, disappearing into the steamy New Orleans evening.

Even if Sean had heard the sirens, he would not have known that they heralded the death of a loose end, the imminent destruction of another man's life, and the successful completion of a plan that had been set in motion weeks before. Of course, he did not hear the sirens; the accident had occurred several miles from the French Quarter, and the boisterous frivolity of Bourbon Street shielded its visitors from any sensory connection to the larger city and world beyond. Sean walked back to the Hotel Maison Dupuy, checked with the front desk for messages, then tried calling Mack Vanderhorn one last time. It was nearly nine in the evening, and there was still no answer. Exhausted, Sean fell across his bed and slept.

(11)

Sean had failed to leave a wake-up call, and didn't awake until nearly ten-thirty the next morning. The frenetic pace of his first three days in New Orleans had finally caught up with him. He dialed Mack Vanderhorn's number again, and was greeted once more by the monotonous metallic voice of the automated answering system. He felt his frustration boiling to the surface as he slammed down the receiver, and decided to forget the story for a few minutes and take a long, hot shower.

Upon emerging from the shower, Sean dressed in shorts, sneakers, and a tee-shirt before heading downstairs for breakfast – he had learned how to dress for summer in New Orleans. Seated at his favorite window-side table at Dominique's, he ordered the house special "American Breakfast:" a waffle with pecan butter, orange juice, and coffee. Sean neglected to ask for a newspaper, but in just one more example of the "lagniappe" service that he was growing to expect in New Orleans, the waitress remembered Sean's request from two days prior, and delivered a Times-Picayune along with his coffee and juice. In an off-hand manner, she commented, "It looks like they finally got that deadbeat Vanderhorn."

"What do you mean?" Sean asked, puzzled that his waitress would make an unsolicited comment about the man he had been trying to contact for the past day and a half.

"Right there, Sug" she said, unfolding the newspaper and pointing to the bottom of page one. "They got him dead to rights in his own home this time. He's through."

Sean followed her direction, and nearly spilled his coffee when he read the headline: "Vanderhorn Busted in Police Raid; Heroin Stash Confiscated."

Quickly scanning the text of the article, Sean read that the New Orleans Police Department had received a tip that Mack Vanderhorn had turned to heroin distribution as a way out of his current financial troubles, and they had raided his house last night.

74

He had been home, alone, with over two kilos of pure heroin in his possession.

"I'll be damned!" Sean muttered. Then, turning to the waitress, he canceled his breakfast order, dropped a five on the table for the coffee and juice, and rushed back to his room. Flipping through the pages of his notepad, he found the phone number Z had given him, and was about to lift the receiver to dial, when he noticed that the message indicator light was blinking. He picked up the receiver and punched the speed dial button for his room's voice mailbox.

After an automated voice announced that he had one message, logged at eleven fourteen this morning, he heard Z's voice with the simple message, "Call me at this number," followed by seven digits. Sean noted that it was a different telephone number than the one he had jotted on his notepad.

He held down the receiver for a few seconds, then dialed the new number. The voice that answered was familiar, but was not Z: "Yeah?"

"Hello," Sean responded. "May I speak to Z?"

"Who's callin'?"

"This is Sean McInness."

"Oh, hey. Wuzzup, Whodi? This is Cool. Let me get Z – hold on."

After a few seconds, Z came to the phone. "Aye yo! Ya heard the news?"

"Yeah. I just read it in the Times-Picayune. Seems like quite a coincidence that Mack gets busted the same day I try to warn him that he may be in danger. What would you say are the odds that bust is clean?"

"It's clean awright," Z agreed in a sarcastic tone. "Every fingerprint that might give up the *real* source of that heroin has been wiped an' polished, ya heard me? There's no way this ain't a set-up."

"I agree. So if this was part of Connor's plan, what does that tell you about who else might be involved?"

"There's no 'might' 'bout it – Connor most definitely has some cops doin' jobs fo' him. Since Mack's house is in the Garden

District, Uptown, an' since all the bad cops in the Sixth District there report to Callio Cal, Cal prob'ly supplied the heroin fo' the set-up. That can only mean two things, ya heard: either Connor is playin' Cal an' The Cardinal off 'gainst each other, or worse, he's found a way to bring 'em together. Either way, things jus' got 'bout twenty times mo' dangerous."

"So what do you recommend, now?" Sean asked. "I still haven't been able to reach Tyron Freeman."

"That depends," Z replied. "How bad do you want this story? Are you willin' to die fo' it?"

"Hell, no!" Sean replied incredulously. "I'm a sports reporter, for God's sake, not some front-line war correspondent!"

"Then I'd say back off, go home, an' fo'get 'bout it. If they think you've quit fo' good, maybe they'll leave you 'lone."

"Maybe? *Maybe* they'll leave me alone? Or what? Have some truck run my Miata off Highway One next week or next month? I can't spend the rest of my life looking over my shoulder."

"Then you got a problem. As fo' me, I've always believed the best defense is a good offense. Maybe you can flush 'em out somehow."

"I could try to go see Mack in jail."

"You crazy?" Now it was Z's turn to be incredulous. "You think you can jus' walk into Tulane an' Broad an' talk to an inmate 'bout how dirty cops set him up? Mack'll never talk to you – not if he's smart, ya heard? He'll know he'd be found dead in his cell the next mornin'."

"Then what?"

"I don't know, Whodi. I already told you everythin' I know. Whatever you do, watch yo' back. Outside the Nint' Ward, I wouldn't trust anyone right now."

Sean hung up the receiver and sat on his bed for some time, pondering his next move. It had been six days since Jackhammer's accident and he still had no proof to back up his suspicions. Meantime, Connor had apparently claimed three more victims in rapid succession. There had to be something he could do, but he could not think of anything.

He picked up the phone again and dialed a number in San Francisco. Like clockwork, the phone rang once, then, "Lillian Kramer."

"Lil, it's Sean. Look, this Jackhammer story has taken some unexpected twists; I haven't been able to close it out yet. I need more time, but while I'm here, I'll get a story together on the Vanderhorn arrest. None of the other Bay Area papers has a man on location here to get the local reaction, so it should be worth a buck."

"It better be worth more than a buck. Your expense account on your last out-of-town assignment ran nearly four hundred dollars per day. I can't afford to pay that just to get a couple of man-in-the-street interviews. Unless you have something solid, you're on the next plane back to Oakland."

"The truth, Lil, there *is* more. I don't have enough to go on yet, but I'm certain the Vanderhorn arrest is connected to Jackhammer's death, and perhaps even to Hat Trick Hathaway's assault on Cassius Banks."

"What?" Lillian nearly screamed into the phone. "What possible connection could there be between the DUI accident of a basketball star in California, a hockey stick assault by a jilted husband, and the drug bust of a washed-up pitcher in New Orleans? Are you out of your mind?"

Sean considered telling her the whole story of his encounter with Z and his friends, and about the conversation Z had overheard. Then he realized how crazy it would sound to tell Lillian that he believed the unsubstantiated tale of four young thugs who had kidnapped him at gunpoint.

"Lil, all I can tell you right now is that there is definitely more to this story, and there may be still more athletes involved. I think Tyrone Freeman is also in some sort of danger. You've got to let me stick with this a few more days."

Lillian sighed. She had long since resigned herself to the conviction that headaches and ulcers were just part of the cost of doing business with Sean McInness. She knew her only choices were either to fire him or go with the flow. One more time, sensing that his maddening ability to find a quagmire of complexity in the simplest story just might have some merit, she chose the latter. "But I'd better hear something more substantial from you within two days, or I swear I'll charge your expenses back to your next paycheck!"

At about the same time, J. Richard Connor was receiving a telephone call that he found similarly troubling, from Lieutenant Morris Lynnwood of the New Orleans Police Department, Sixth District.

"J. Richard Connor here."

"Connor, this is Lynnwood. We have a problem. You know we had Vanderhorn's line tapped the past two weeks, so we would know his movements. It seems that one Sean McInness, a sports reporter with the San Francisco Star-Reporter, called Vanderhorn's private line five times yesterday. The last two times, he specifically alluded to Jackhammer's death, and told Vanderhorn he needed to see him urgently. It appears that he knew Vanderhorn was next on our list. At this point, we must assume the whole operation has been compromised."

"I see," replied Connor, the even tone of his voice showing no evidence of concern. "Our reporter friend has found his way closer than I had thought. Thanks for letting me know – I'll have it taken care of immediately."

J. Richard Connor reflexively massaged his graying temples with his fingers, the pronounced wrinkles of his forehead making him appear a full decade older than his fifty-seven years. Pouring a glass of Scotch from a decanter on the corner of his huge mahogany desk, he leaned back in his oversized leather chair and contemplated the view from his twenty-third floor window. He could see the top of the Superdome a block from his high-rise office, the Arena just beyond, and in the distance he could see one of the casinos on the lake Ponchartrain shoreline. *My empire*, he mused. Then, reaching into the top left drawer of his desk, he removed a picture of Sean McInness that he had downloaded from the San Francisco Star-Reporter's web site. Turning the picture over several times in his fingers, he congratulated himself for once again staying two steps ahead of any and all who stood in his way.

After taking another sip of his Scotch, he picked up the phone again, and dialed a number from memory.

"Yo! Speak yo' piece."

"Cal, this is Connor. I've got another job for you."

(12)

Sean decided the best thing he could do would be to call all of Mack Vanderhorn's associates, just as he had previously contacted Jackhammer's, in hopes that one of them would know something he could use in his investigation. Following his standard priorities, Sean contacted Mack's personal assistant, then his agent, coach, trainer, and teammates, followed by business partners, friends, and any past associates he could locate. He immediately encountered a brick wall even more solid than the one that had confounded his inquiries following Jackhammer's death. In that case, no one he spoke to had known anything useful, while this time, Sean found that no one wanted to talk to him at all. Mack had just become too much of a pariah, and no one wanted to take the chance of being quoted in defense of a drug dealing deadbeat. Even Darius Houston, Mack's personal assistant, refused to talk to Sean.

Sean sat on the edge of his bed, peering out his window at the pool and lush courtyard below. It struck him how hollow the trappings of success are if you cannot find so much as one friend who will speak up for you. Mack Vanderhorn had been tried and convicted already in the court of public opinion, so it almost didn't matter what Sean's investigation turned up. Vanderhorn's career – and life as he had known it – was finished.

As Sean sat quietly contemplating Mack Vanderhorn's transient fortunes, the phone rang. Answering, Sean immediately heard the loud crackle of static.

"Hello?"

"Hello, is this Sean McInness?"

"Yes, it is. Who's this? You need to speak up – we have a bad connection."

"This is Darius. Darius Houston. I couldn't talk to you on my home phone, earlier. I'm not sure if it's safe. I'm at a pay phone a few blocks from my home. Can you hear me?"

"Yeah, I can hear you, but the static is pretty bad. Is there someplace we can meet?"

"I can meet you for lunch tomorrow. The Dry Dock Cafe, in Algiers Point. It's just down the hill from the ferry terminal – little mom an' pop tavern. I'll be there at twelve noon."

"What have you got for me, Darius?"

"Nothin' definite. Just suspicions. I really don't trust your phone line, either, so let's talk tomorrow."

Sean hung up the phone, but let his hand linger for a few moments on the receiver as his forehead wrinkled with concern. It had not crossed his mind before that moment that he should not feel secure using the phone in his hotel room. He contemplated how much effort would be required to obtain an illicit wiretap on a hotel telephone. Shuddering as he concluded that it probably wasn't nearly as difficult as he would like to believe, he decided not to make any more confidential calls from his room.

Sean realized there wasn't anything more he could do to prove his conspiracy theory, so he spent the rest of the afternoon assembling the Vanderhorn article he had promised Lil. His first stop was the Sixth District police headquarters at Claiborne Avenue and Melpomene. Although the station was located squarely in the heart of the inner-city corridor which included the Magnolia, Melpomene, and Calliope housing projects, its jurisdiction also included a large share of the antebellum mansions of the city's Garden District. It was this district's officers who had conducted the raid on Mack Vanderhorn's home, and it was here that Mack had been booked on felony charges.

Sean approached the duty officer at the desk, presented his press credentials and California driver's license, and asked for a copy of Mack Vanderhorn's arrest record. The officer scowled at him, muttering under his breath that "every goddam reporter" in the Crescent City had been in to bother him today, and now the out-of-staters were arriving. He picked up the phone on his desk and placed a quick call to the records room, saying, "send up another press copy of the goddam Vanderhorn file." Then, without speaking or looking up from his desk, he motioned Sean toward a pair of wooden chairs with a flick of his wrist.

Sean took a seat, and waited nearly twenty minutes, feeling somewhat surprised to find beads of perspiration forming on his forehead. He knew that even a district full of bad cops wouldn't be so brazen as to assault or abduct a reporter right in the station house, but he still felt as if he were behind enemy lines. Finally, a young clerical worker emerged from the secured doors to the records room, and following a quick nod of the head from the duty officer, handed Sean a manila portfolio. Sean remained seated as he flipped through the pages of reports inside, to the obvious displeasure of the scowling duty officer. He almost expected to find a signed confession, but was pleasantly surprised to find that Mack had pleaded "not guilty" at his arraignment earlier that day. *Good! Don't let these bastards win easily – put up a fight!*

Sean had hoped to find a discrepancy of some sort – anything that might send up a red flag that the bust had been wrong – but he found nothing. Sean had reviewed arrest records every time a Bay Area athlete had found himself on the wrong side of the law, but this was the most solidly documented case file he had ever seen. Every "i" was dotted, and every "t" was crossed. It seemed too perfect. A stiff-lipped half-smile formed on Sean's face. *These guys are good*, he thought.

Sean asked to speak to the arresting officers, but the desk sergeant tersely informed him that they were unavailable for interviews, and that all press inquiries were to be directed to the District Attorney's office. With that, Sean left the station and proceeded to track down several local luminaries in the world of sports, gathering sound bites for his article. The verdict of his informal public opinion survey was unanimous, just as it had been among Mack's own associates that morning: Mack Vanderhorn was a disgrace and deserved what was coming to him.

The next morning, Sean decided to leave early for his appointment with Darius Houston, to enjoy a little more sightseeing. He needed a break from the stress of the past few days, if only for a couple of hours. He wound his way down Bourbon Street, which was nearly deserted and strewn with liter from the previous night's revelry, and back to the Café du Monde, where he ordered café au lait and beignets for breakfast. Sitting in the shade of a brightly colored canopy, he quickly decided that this world-famous sidewalk café was even more charming in daylight than it had been on his previous nighttime visit. Decatur street, to his right, was filled with a chaotic, churning human river of tourists, street musicians, performance artists, carriages, automobiles, and tour buses, all seemingly well-versed in some unwritten rules of engagement. To his left, young dreamers and love-struck couples climbed the steps of the Mississippi river levy to find solitude strolling the Moon Walk, interrupted only by the occasional melodic bursts of the authentic steam calliope on the paddlewheel Natchez or the rumbling passage of the Riverfront Streetcar.

Finishing his breakfast, Sean elected to tour Jackson Square and the St. Louis Cathedral, which served as the geographic, artistic, and spiritual center of the French Quarter. Flanked on both sides by the Pontalba Apartments – the oldest rental units in America – Jackson Square was a simple park in design, but boasted the finest ingredients any park could claim: richly carpeted lawns, towering shade trees, broad walkways, a huge bronze statue of Andrew Jackson, and the magnificent façade of the St. Louis Cathedral as a backdrop.

The pedestrian malls on each side of the park were crowded with street vendors working almost elbow to elbow. While there were purveyors of souvenir trinkets, incense, and other merchandise, the vast majority of the vendors represented a profession uniquely suited to the oddball mystique of this city: fortune tellers. Seers of every imaginable variation hawked their skills, from tarot card and palm readers to crystal ball gazers, spiritual guides and even voodoo priests and priestesses, each claiming a special gift of clairvoyance or the legitimacy of a centuries-old family tradition.

Continuing past the soothsayers of Jackson Square to circle behind the cathedral, Sean found himself on Pirate's Alley. Although the whispered history of this short and narrow passageway included duels, double-crosses, and perilous meetings with Jean Lafitte himself, Sean found it bright and pleasant. Smaller alcoves and passageways too small to appear on any map led to a handful of tiny cafes and specialty boutiques, while itinerant artists displayed their works of oil and pastel along the wrought iron fence that lined the alley.

Sean checked his watch and saw that it was already past eleven. He continued his walk around the other side of the cathedral and cut through the French Market to a platform where he could catch the Riverfront Streetcar. Consulting the small map he had folded in his hip pocket, he saw that it was three stops to the foot of Canal Street, where he would catch the ferry to Algiers Point. The Riverfront Streetcar was a vintage electric tram with polished wooden seating, windows that could be opened widely to create an open-air sensation, and a conductor whose friendly and conversant manner seemed typical of New Orleans' transit employees. Sean enjoyed the scenic views of the river and the informative chatter of the conductor, but most of all, he enjoyed the cool breeze as the train rushed with surprising speed from one station to the next.

Stepping off the platform at Spanish Plaza, Sean found himself immersed in a sea of humanity. This was ground zero for both the city's tourist and convention industries, with the Aquarium of the Americas, the Riverwalk shopping center, and the World Trade Center all steps away. A live band was performing at Le Moyne's Landing, an upscale oyster bar with open-air seating on the plaza and more under the shade of a giant canopy. Sean stopped briefly to take in the panoramic scene and enjoy the music, then hurried up the ramp of the ferry landing when he saw a boat approaching.

The ferry was huge, slow, and simply-furnished compared to the sleek catamaran ferries Sean often rode across the San Francisco Bay. On the other hand, it was free, there were departures promptly every fifteen minutes, and the vistas of New Orleans from the center of the river were fantastic, which more than sufficed to earn a positive rating for the experience. He arrived at Algiers Point in the West Bank at ten minutes before twelve, and walked swiftly down the ramp and out onto the street to find the Dry Dock Café. Spotting the rustic wooden-framed building to his right, he continued down a short incline and stepped inside with several minutes to spare.

Almost immediately, he thought of the theme song from "Cheers." This definitely seemed like the kind of place "where everybody knows your name." The interior was built on a split-level to conform to the contour of the hill upon which the building sat. The lower level, nearest the entrance, was the bar. The walls were plastered with an odd assortment of trinkets and memorabilia, most notably hundreds of photographs of customers laughing and wearing outrageous costumes at the café's annual Halloween bash. Behind the bar, two steps led up to a small dining room.

Sean recognized the stocky build, dark chocolate complexion, and wide smile of Darius Houston at one of the tables near the back of the dining room, having met him on several of the Cubs visits to San Francisco, dating back to the years when the Giants still played at Candlestick Park. Darius waved, and Sean walked up the steps and approached the table. As Sean reached his seat, Darius rose halfway and stretched out his hand in greeting.

"Hey, Sean. Long time."

"Yeah, it's been, what, three or four years?"

"I guess that's 'bout right. The last time I saw you was for our series against the Giants at Pac Bell Park – er, I guess that's SBC Park now – in September, 2000. Bad memory. So, how do you like New Orleans?"

"As much as I've been able to see of it, it's a wonderful town. But I'm afraid I've been a bit preoccupied with work."

"That's not good," Darius asserted with a grin. "You know what they say 'bout 'all work...' N'awlins is definitely a town for the 'play' side of life."

"How did you ever find a little place like this?" Sean asked.

"I grew up right 'round the corner – the West Bank is my old 'hood. I've been with Mack in Chicago for goin' on nine years now, but I still make a point of stoppin' by the Dry Dock whenever I'm back in town."

The waitress approached the table, nodded and smiled at Darius, and asked if they were ready to order.

"Ever had a Muffuletta?" Darius asked.

"A muff-a-what-a?" Sean replied, glancing first at Darius, then at the waitress in hopes of enlightenment.

Ignoring the question, Darius turned to the Waitress. "Anna, be a sweetheart an' bring us two Muffulettas an' whatever you have cold on tap."

After Anna had left to deliver their order to the kitchen, Darius turned back to face Sean, his expression suddenly serious.

"Sean, this bust is bullshit. It's pure fiction. I can't prove it, but I'm as certain of that as I am of my own middle name. Someone set Mack up."

Sean nodded thoughtfully, then replied with equal gravity. "I've been looking at that possibility, myself. I have good reason to believe you're right, but I have no proof – just a few hunches and pieces that don't fit together. I need some hard facts. What can you give me?"

"I'm afraid all I can give you is more of the 'hunches an' pieces that don't fit,' but you've got to believe me. Mack is no dope dealer. To begin with, I can give him a character reference: Mack has had a turbulent past, an' he can be a real asshole at times..."

"What a way to start a character reference!" Sean interjected, with a half laugh.

"We both know it's true," Darius shrugged. "He can be an ill-tempered, self-absorbed, anti-social jerk on his bad days, but that's a long way from pushin' drugs to school kids. I know how Mack feels 'bout dope – especially heroin. I'm the one that got him into Narcotics Anonymous, an' I've been with him at every meetin' since. I was a user myself before I got cleaned up an' caught a break workin' for Mack. It's true what they say, that it takes one to know one. I'm painfully familiar with the lies, the deception, an' the games that go hand in hand with addiction. I would know if he was full of shit. Sean, that man knows what heroin did to his life. He knows it cost him his marriage an' his career. He had the American Dream an' a guaranteed place in the Hall of Fame; now he sits home alone, watchin' as his career fades from his former fans' memories. He despises everythin' drugs represent, an' he would never get involved in pushin' that destruction on others."

"You're not going to convince too many people that Mack's a saint," Sean responded. "What kind of man makes four million a year, and won't send his kid a winter coat?"

"I'm not sayin' he's a saint. He's an ass, okay? I can't tell you how many times he an' I have argued 'bout the child support situation. I told him he was flat wrong, an' that he was throwin' away whatever's left of his reputation an' career – not to mention his relationship with his son. I guess he felt betrayed when Gracie left him. He felt like she kicked him when he was down, when he needed her by his side more than ever. He's got his lawyers tryin' to work out some kind of trust arrangement for the kid, but he flat refuses to send money if there's any chance Gracie will benefit from it. He's an ass, but he's not a drug dealer.

"Sean, you've got to understand that I handle all of his business for him. *All* of his business. He spends most of his off-days sittin' by his pool with a bottle of Jack Daniels – he knows he's supposed to stay clean an' sober, but he thinks easin' his pain with alcohol will keep him off the heroin. I would have known if there were any visitors, any phone calls, or any financial transactions tied to a major drug sale. I would have known."

The waitress delivered their food. The Muffulettas were huge sandwiches, with mounds of salami, ham, and melted Provolone cheese stacked high on a round Italian loaf, then smothered in a chopped-olive relish. Served with spicy seasoned fries and a cold beer, it was just one more unexpected surprise from New Orleans' culinary repertoire.

Picking at his sandwich, Darius continued. "Sean, someone had Mack's house staked out before the bust, an' I don't think it was the police. Mack noticed a car with two men in it parked just down the block from him almost three weeks ago. We did a little discreet surveillance of our own, an' sent a friend they wouldn't recognize to make a close pass by their car. He said they were smokin' blunts – he could smell the marijuana from outside the car. We figured it was some private dicks workin' for Gracie. But now..." Darius shook his head as his voice trailed off.

Sean suddenly lost his appetite as he sensed a growing unease in the back of his mind. *Accusations. Rumors. Whispers. But no proof. Where was the proof?*

(13)

Sean spent the rest of the evening and most of the next morning sitting in his hotel room, pouring through his notes in search of answers. He knew something terrible was happening. Some mysterious, undefined danger had killed five people in a horrific car crash, destroyed two men's lives in a single violent incident, sealed the coffin on another man's career, and threatened yet another in a still-unknown manner. *Lil had hit the nail squarely on the head in their last conversation,* he thought to himself. *How did she put it? What possible connection could there be between the DUI accident of a basketball star in California, a hockey stick assault by a jilted husband, and the drug bust of a washed-up pitcher in New Orleans?*

He had conducted thirty-seven telephone interviews following Jackhammer's accident, in addition to the in-person contacts with Lieutenant Vasquez, Dr. Hahn, and LaTanya Harrison. Just in the past forty-eight hours, he had met with Darius Houston, visited a police precinct headquarters, and conducted another thirty-one interviews related to Mack Vanderhorn's arrest. Then there had been the lengthy encounter with Z and his friends, as well as several phone conversations with Z. He had worked harder on this story than any other in his life, and had filled four notebooks with interviews and sidebars, and yet, he had nothing. If a crime had been committed, he had nothing to connect his prime suspect – no motive, no smoking gun, no evidence, no trace. Nothing.

He had flipped through his notes so many times, the pages were ripping loose from their spiral binders. He could virtually recite every word in those notepads from memory. Glancing at his watch, he saw that it was nearly two in the afternoon, and he had not yet eaten lunch. Suddenly, it dawned on him that the most obvious starting point for his investigation had been staring him in the face since his first minutes in New Orleans. *The Superdome!* He had not visited the Superdome or the new Arena because they were not connected in any meaningful way to any of the five athletes that he was investigating – Jackhammer and Cassius Banks had played at the Arena occasionally with visiting teams and Tyrone Freeman had visited the 'dome only once with the Patriots in 1998 to play the Saints. Hat Trick and Vanderhorn had probably only visited the structures as spectators. The dome was, however, intimately connected to J. Richard Connor and his new team, the New Orleans Cajuns. If he was ever going to flush Connor out, he reasoned, there would be no better way than to start snooping around his home turf. *That cab driver from the airport earned his tip —I think I'll take that tour!*

With that, he scooped all the notepads into his briefcase, which he slid under his bed, then locked his door, rode the elevator to the hotel lobby, and stepped out into the blast furnace of a New Orleans summer afternoon. Consulting his pocket map, he saw that the quickest route to the Superdome was to follow Rampart into the heart of the central business district, four blocks past Canal Street, then turn right on Poydras. He walked one block up to Rampart, near where he had caught the Esplanade bus to City Park, and began walking toward the gleaming towers of downtown. *No, that's "uptown,"* he corrected himself, smiling at the perversity of a city that doesn't know which end is up.

As he crossed Canal Street, the barren landscape that character- ized North Rampart gave way to glittering tinted-glass, magnificent facades, and meticulously manicured parks as the street changed names to South Rampart. When he reached Perdido, one block before Poydras, he caught a glimpse of an amazing sight: the world's tallest clarinet, a trompe-l'oeil painted onto the side of a Holiday Inn. The detail of reflections curving along the contours of the instrument's metal keys, along with the artist's masterful grasp of light and shadow, gave the piece a three- dimensional appearance so striking, Sean decided to take a closer look to determine whether it was, in fact, a painting or a bas-relief sculpture. Departing from his planned route, he crossed South Rampart and continued up Perdido to approach the mural.

Some unconscious instinct honed from years of professional observation caught his attention. Something was wrong. A car was turning the corner behind him, but was moving much too slowly. Feigning the random glances of a tourist, Sean was able to catch a glimpse out of the corner of his left eye. It was a silver BMW with two men in the front seat, and it was creeping at a snail's pace only a dozen yards behind him. *How long have they been following me?* he wondered with a chill. He quickly realized that the relatively deserted parking lot behind the Holiday Inn was the worst place he could be, so he decided to get back to the crowds of Canal Street as quickly as possible. He cut diagonally across the lot, hoping to put a little more distance between himself and the car, and found himself oddly distracted by the recognition that, even upon approaching within a few feet of the clarinet he still could not be entirely certain whether the depth was real or illusion. Turning onto Elk Place, he walked briskly toward Canal Street, glancing backwards only once to verify that the BMW had turned the corner to follow him.

When he got to Canal Street, he decided that the abundance of retail storefronts would afford him an opportunity to get a better look at his pursuers, under the guise of window-shopping. In addition, if the men in the BMW made a threatening move, he could try to dash through one of the stores, although he would run the risk of being cornered if the store he entered had no back door. This section of Canal Street was occupied primarily by tourist tee-shirt and camera shops intermingled with discount jewelers, athletic shoe retailers and fast foods. Sean found that the revolving racks of postcards just inside the doorways of many of the souvenir shops provided ideal opportunities to conduct surveillance. Positioning himself to face back up Canal Street, he would peer through the rack while pretending to select a postcard.

The men behind him seemed to be interested in nothing more than observation. Stopping and starting, sometimes pulling into an available parking space, they maintained a discreet distance about half a block behind Sean. After four blocks, Sean found his opportunity to make a move. One of the intricately restored streetcars of the St. Charles line spun around the corner just behind him, clattered past along Canal Street, then slowed noticeably as it turned the corner in front of him. *It's going to stop just around the corner!*

After only an instant's hesitation, as he remembered that the BMW was currently parked in a metered space, Sean broke out running as fast as he could. With a quick glance over his shoulder as he turned the corner, he could see that the car was trying unsuccessfully to force its way out into the street in front of an airport shuttle van. Just then, he felt his cell phone bounce out of his pocket, and heard the disheartening sound of plastic and circuitry shattering on the hard pavement. He slowed and looked back, frozen briefly by the uncertainty of deciding whether to rescue his phone, but he could see that it was ruined. Turning to look ahead, he saw that the streetcar had just come to a stop, with a small group of passengers embarking, so he accelerated again and sprinted for the vehicle.

The timing worked exactly as he had hoped. He reached the streetcar platform just as the last passenger was boarding, and managed to squeeze on board before the silver BMW turned the corner. Ducking down in the first seat he could find, he kept his head below window level, and listened intently. Just as the streetcar started rolling forward, he heard the screeching of a car turning the corner behind them far too fast. The unseen vehicle applied its brakes audibly, then pulled alongside and shadowed the streetcar for several seconds. Drenched in sweat, Sean took a deep breath in relief when he heard the car's engine racing as it accelerated past the streetcar and turned the next corner, disappearing into the bustling hum of urban noise.

After a minute or so had passed, Sean tentatively raised his head, peering out the open windows for any sign of the silver BMW. It was not there. As the St. Charles streetcar, or "Charlie Car" as the locals sometimes called it, curved around Lee Circle, Sean had a clear view of St. Charles Avenue behind them. Seeing that the BMW was still nowhere in sight, Sean decided he should get off at the next stop – it would only be a matter of time before his pursuers would take a second look at the streetcar. He pulled the cord to request a stop and waited until the streetcar was fully motionless before taking one last look behind, then darted out the open rear door.

He immediately began walking down the nearest street toward the river, hoping to reach the relative safety of the tourist crowds at Spanish Plaza. He had walked three blocks before he noticed a street sign and identified the street he was on as Calliope. *Calliope. That has a familiar sound to it.* Suddenly, he remembered that Calliope, pronounced by locals to rhyme with Calico, was the name of one of the three notoriously violent Uptown housing projects Z had described to him. He felt a sudden chill as he surveyed the warehouses and vacant lots surrounding him and realized that he had no idea where the Calliope projects were located. He certainly did not want to walk smack into the middle of Callio Cal's home turf, so he decided it would be best to backtrack a half-block to the nearest cross street, and cut over a few blocks before continuing his trek toward the river.

As soon as he turned, he froze in horror, the odd tingle of adrenaline-laced blood rushing throughout his body. The silver BMW was stopped in the intersection only a few dozen yards behind him, and two large black men were emerging, one from each side of the car. Sean's mind was shouting for him to turn and run, but his legs remained motionless – the only portion of his anatomy that seemed to be functioning was his pounding heart. Then, as the two men stepped fully out from behind the open car doors, he saw something so unexpected – so horrifically incongruous – that, for a brief and dangerous moment, he simply could not comprehend it. Both men were clad in white tee-shirts bearing a large silk-screened image of his face. *They're wearing my face...* Then, as comprehension gradually crystallized in his consciousness, confusion gave way to terror. *They're wearing my face! Oh, God! Run!*

Time seemed to pass in slow motion. Just as his legs finally began to respond to his mind's urgent commands, he saw both men reaching under their tee-shirts. Acting on sheer instinct, with no time for reasoned calculations, he dashed diagonally across the street toward a row of parked cars, reaching them just as he heard the first loud pops in a rapid series of gunfire erupting behind him. It seemed as if every car window and windshield on the street was exploding, and Sean turned his head slightly to the left to shield his face from the glass and shrapnel that filled the air all around him. Keeping his head as low as he could without losing his balance, he seemed almost to be falling forward as he ran. The sounds of gunfire and shattering glass were accompanied by the odd thuds and whistles of bullets striking metal and fiberglass at random angles, as well as the rapid footsteps of the two large men behind him.

"Fuck!" Sean heard one of the men exclaim. "The mutha-fucka's gettin' away! Get the car!" Not daring to look back, Sean continued running as he heard one set of footsteps suddenly reverse direction and begin fading into the distance, while the other set seemed to be slowing and falling further behind. *Thank God I ran track in college!* Sean thought between steps, noticing that the gunfire had temporarily ceased. *And thank God those two guys are more out of shape than I am!* Suddenly, the gunfire erupted again in a rapid burst, as the assassin nearest him opened fire with a fresh clip. Then Sean heard the dreadful sound of a car engine turning over and revving, the wheels spinning furiously a block or so behind him. *Got to get off this street!*

Looking ahead, Sean saw that the next intersection was angled oddly, as Calliope Street curved and two other streets intersected it. Sensing that this would be his only opportunity to lose the rapidly approaching BMW, he made a sharp left at the intersection, and was relieved to see that there was another intersection just a half block ahead. The car behind him screeched to a stop. Sean heard the passenger door open and slam closed, then the car once again accelerated loudly, its tires screeching against the pavement for traction. Sean raced forward past a series of warehouses and was about to turn right at the next corner, when he spotted the "do not enter" signs directly in front of him, and realized he was running against the flow of a one way street.

His instant prayer was answered as a small group of cars emerged around a bend in the road, filling both lanes of traffic. Swerving onto the sidewalk, Sean continued running against the flow of the traffic, and heard the screeching of tires and blaring of horns just behind him as the oncoming traffic snarled in the path of the BMW. There were angry shouts in half a dozen voices and the sound of multiple car doors opening and slamming. From within the auditory melee, Sean could just discern the sound of two pairs of feet running behind him. *They're on foot again.*

Seeing the street signs at the next intersection, Sean turned from Tchoupitoulas onto the broad, tree-lined Diamond Street and ran directly down the center of the shady median strip, hoping the trees would provide some cover as he serpentined between them. The tranquil beauty of the avenue was sporadically interrupted by the rapid pops of gunfire and the splintering of tree limbs near him. Seeing that Diamond Street was nearing a dead-end, Sean zigged to the left past the bright murals of the Praline Connection Restaurant, ran down another long block of warehouses, then zagged right again, toward the river.

Directly ahead, he saw a huge, canopied escalator and overhead walkway leading into a large building, which he surmised was part of the Riverwalk complex. Quickly, he calculated the merits of ascending the escalator. If he could do it, he thought, he could widen his lead over his pursuers, as they would climb the steps at a slower pace dictated by their greater weight. On the other hand, if they were too close behind him at the moment of ascent, he would be a sitting duck with no cover in the narrow passageway. He decided his only chance was to sprint for the escalator and try to get to it with sufficient lead-time to reach the top in safety. Reaching deep into his soul, to a place he had rarely visited in the two decades since his college graduation, he sprinted at maximum speed toward the foot of the escalators, his consciousness fully focused on the goal before him.

When he reached the escalator, he nearly flew up the steps, taking them three and even four at a time. Just as he reached the top, the sound of gunfire erupted at the bottom, the bullets pinging off the metallic escalator steps and handrails. He dashed across the elevated walkway and dove through a pair of glass doors, finding himself in a large open food court that he instantly realized provided no protection at all. Glancing frantically around him, he saw a retail department store to the right, a series of vendor carts cluttering the long expanse of a mall to the left, and a glass-fronted balcony ahead. He bolted to the left and rushed toward the heart of the mall, hoping to find cover beyond the food court before his would-be killers reached the top of the escalator.

As he emerged past the row of Cajun, Creole and ethnic food vendors, he was greeted with the gaudy, theme-park décor of Mardi Gras Madness, an open-air store displaying a wide assortment of bright party regalia, masks, costume jewelry, and paraphernalia. Had he been strolling the mall, he likely would have wandered into Mardi Gras Madness to marvel at the decadence of a city most famous for its parties, but under the duress of his present situation, he found the brazen frivolity of the store unnerving. After only a few more steps, he passed a fudge shop where the confectioners were singing in a "call and response" style to a large crowd of onlookers. *What a strange place.* Making his way past the revelers, he saw an escalator leading to a level below and, glancing quickly behind him, saw his two pursuers emerging into the food court and turning to follow him.

Surging down the escalator, Sean emerged into a much shorter section of mall filled with neat little wooden carts displaying a variety of inexpensive handicrafts and baked goods. At the end of the artisan's strip, there was another escalator, brightly decorated with extravagant art-deco neon fixtures. He jumped headlong down the second escalator, and emerged into another long strip of mall, this one dominated by distinctly upscale clothiers, specialty shops, and gift boutiques. He continued to sprint down the length of the mall, feeling the burning pain in his lungs that signaled he was nearing the limit of his stamina. Reaching the end of the long corridor, he glanced back and saw the two thugs clamoring down the art deco escalator seventy yards or so behind him.

As he veered around a corner, he saw yet another long strip of retailers stretching out before him. *My God! How long is this Riverwalk Mall?* His pace was slowing dramatically and he felt the first stabs of muscle cramps creeping up his calves and thighs. At the same time, the surreal quality of the chase struck him again, as he brushed passed a Warner Brothers outlet store replete with larger-than-life statues of Bugs Bunny and other cartoon characters, followed a few steps later by a jeweler whose storefront was guarded by living replicas of the Buckingham Palace Grenadier Guards engaged in the intricate choreography of the "Changing of the Guard." *What a strange place to die...*

After forty or fifty yards, the retail space gave out onto a large foyer, with an information kiosk and a large, illuminated display detailing the history and folklore of the mighty Mississippi River. Beyond the foyer, he could see bright sunlight where the Riverwalk Mall exited into the crowded terraces of Spanish Plaza. Sean raced into the sunlight and dove headlong into the densest parts of the crowd. Primal instincts welling inside him wanted to keep running, but reason took control forcefully as he realized that running through the crowd would make him far easier to spot. Fighting to restrain the urges of outright panic and feeling the very real prospect of physical collapse, he walked slowly across the plaza, trying to blend in with the milling tourists. He could not look back, not wanting to risk the possibility that one of the assassins would recognize his face. As he continued walking toward the Aquarium of the Americas, he struggled to maintain his composure and silently prayed that he would not feel the cold steel of a gun pressed against the back of his head.

Traversing the riverfront side of the aquarium, he continued along the pedestrian trails of Woldenberg Park, which was bustling with tourists, lovers, panhandlers, performance artists, and ice cream vendors. He stopped for a few seconds to catch his breath, his badly out-of-shape lungs burning as if he had inhaled liquid fire, and took the opportunity, finally, to look back toward the Riverwalk. He saw no sign of his pursuers. Nonetheless, he vowed not to be overly confident in his escape as he had been back on the St. Charles streetcar. Lack of due caution had nearly killed him, he realized. He spotted a Riverfront Streetcar pulling into a station only a few steps away from him, across a grassy knoll, and decided to run for it.

He climbed aboard the streetcar and fumbled through his pocket for correct change, finally depositing five quarters under the watchful eye of the conductor. The streetcar pulled away from the station, slowly at first, then rapidly gained speed, leaving Woldenberg Park and his executioners behind. He jumped off at the very next stop, directly in front of the home berth of the steamboat Natchez, and dashed into the Jackson Brewery, a large shopping and eating mall of the converted-warehouse style. Winding inside the structure, well out of sight from any exterior doorways, he found a pay phone. After fumbling through his pockets again for the number Z had given him four days before, he dialed.

"Aye yo?"

"Is this Z?"

"Yeah, who's this?"

"This is Sean. McInness."

Sean's voice was faltering, as he struggled to find enough breath to speak audibly.

"Wuzzup, Whodi? You awright? You sound like you're havin' a heart attack or somethin'."

"They tried to kill me. Two men. My picture. On their shirts. Chased me. All the way from St. Charles. Shooting at me."

"Where y'at?"

"Inside a place. Called Jackson Brewery. You know it?"

"F'shiggity! I know where it is. They know you're there?"

95

"No. I don't think so. I think I lost them. Back at the River-walk."

"Stay there an' stay outta sight, ya heard me? We'll be right there."

With that, Sean hung up the phone, then collapsed onto the concrete floor under the phone booth.

14

When Z and Cool found him, Sean was slumped against the wall next to the pay phone, still breathing rapidly, and resisting the nearly overpowering compulsion to pass completely out of consciousness from exhaustion. When he saw them approaching, he waved weakly and initiated a futile effort to rise from the floor.

"Aye yo! You awright? What happened?" Z inquired as he and Cool rushed to help Sean to his feet, each taking hold of one of Sean's arms.

"They tried to kill me. I spotted two men following me in a silver BMW at Rampart and Perdido, you know, where that huge clarinet is painted on the side of the Holiday Inn. They tailed me around to Canal Street, then I jumped on a streetcar and rode until just past the circle. I thought I'd lost them, but they caught up with me again on Calliope, a couple blocks off of St. Charles. They got out of the car and started walking toward me, and when I saw they were wearing my picture, I ran. I ran all the way to the Riverwalk and kept running right through the mall, from one end to the other. Damn, that Riverwalk is long! I finally lost them in the crowds near the Aquarium. They shot at me! They had semi-automatics, and they must have fired five or six clips at me."

"Let's get him outta here," Cool said, turning to Z. "They'll be lookin' fo' him."

"I can't go back to my hotel. They must have followed me from there, so they know where I'm staying."

Z seemed lost in thought for a few moments, then, looking over to Cool, said, "Let's take him back by my crib."

"I just need to make a few calls," Sean continued. "I can't use my credit cards without using my real name, and I don't want them to find out where I'm staying. I'll have the paper wire me some cash, then I can get another room."

"We're parked a coupla blocks from here – it was the only place we could find this time of day. You gonna make it?" Z inquired, continuing before Sean could answer, "We don't wanna attract too much attention draggin' you down the street, ya heard me?"

"Yeah, I'll be okay. My legs feel like they're going to fall off, and I think I need a lung transplant! I haven't run like that since my college track days, and that's been a long, long time. But I can manage."

Cool and Z released their grips on Sean as they emerged from the Jackson Brewery into the bright sunlight and bustling activity on Decatur Street, but maintained their positions on either side of him. They turned right and walked briskly past Jackson Square and the Café du Monde, then turned right past a gilded statue of Joan of Arc to cut through the fruit and vegetable stands of the French Market. Behind the market was a series of three small commercial parking lots, and they quickly located Cool's car in the last one. Sean had been under such extreme duress the last time he had seen this car, that he had not thought to identify its make and model, but now he saw that it was a Nissan Sentra, dark blue, and in excellent condition for a late-eighties model.

They wasted no time getting out of the area – paying the parking attendant then turning right onto North Peters for the quickest departure from the French Quarter. Veering around a bend onto Elysian Fields Avenue, they passed through a somewhat gentrified neighborhood of restored antebellum homes and towering shade trees. Then they turned onto St. Claude and rushed eastward along what appeared to be a major commercial artery, stopping only for occasional traffic lights until they reached a line of vehicles waiting for a drawbridge to descend ahead of them. The conversation was minimal, as all three maintained a vigil for any signs that they had been followed, Z and Cool each monitoring their respective rear-view mirrors while Sean turned around in the back seat so he could watch out the rear window.

Traffic started moving across the bridge and Z turned in his seat to look at Sean. "This is the St. Claude bridge," he explained. "Barges cut 'cross the canal from the river to the lake, or turn up to the NASA factory in Michoud. The Port of New Orleans is right over there," he continued, gesturing to their left. As they crossed the bridge, Z smiled and announced, "Welcome to the CTC –

you're deep in the Nint' Ward now, ya heard? Cal's boys would be crazy to follow us here."

"F'sho'," Cool nodded in agreement before turning off of St. Claude onto a small residential street lined with modest homes and neatly kept lawns. After two more turns in rapid succession, they pulled to a stop in front a pastel yellow home with a white picket fence delineating its small front yard. Cool and Z stepped from the car, gesturing for Sean to follow, and Z took the lead, extracting keys from his pocket as they stepped onto the front porch. Then, stepping to the side after unlocking the double-bolted door, he gestured to Sean and Cool to enter the home, with a simple, "Go on in."

They passed through a brightly-lit living room with the crowded but somehow comforting appearance of a lifetime's accumulation of knickknacks and furnishings, along with a half-dozen assorted green plants. As they moved through the house, Z provided narrative to accompany their guided tour. "That's the kitchen off behind the front room. My Momma an' sister have rooms on the other side of the house, an' I have the two rooms on this side. This is my bedroom, here, an' my studio is the next room down the hall."

"Studio?" Sean inquired.

"Yeah – check it out." Z swung open the door to a small room with one wall filled nearly floor to ceiling with audio equipment – multiple CD and cassette decks, turntables, tuners, mixers, keyboards, huge speakers, and several sets of earphones. The remaining walls were padded with eggshell styrofoam, and a microphone dangled from the ceiling on a long cord in one corner.

"Cool, D, an' Rod have a group called the K-Nines. They've been doin' gigs at a few local clubs an' some private parties, ya heard? I've been deejayin' a lotta the same places, plus producin' a few events."

"How long have the four of you been in the music biz?" Sean prodded.

"We used to sing an' dance together jus' fo' fun when we were growin' up," Cool answered. "Rod an' D both got mad chill voices. Their momma had 'em in the church choir 'most befo' they could walk. I've always been into poetry, so a coupla years ago they asked me to write some raps fo' 'em. We've been together as the 'Nines ever since, an' I do backups on the keyboard."

Turning back toward Z, Sean asked, "Why aren't you in the K-Nines?"

"'Cause he's a sorry-ass, no-talent, ain't-got-no-rhythm, frog-voiced, K-Nine wanna-be!" Cool interjected, laughing, before Z could answer.

"Yeah you right," Z retorted with a sarcastic laugh. "You may think that you're the Master of Rhymes, but most of yo' lines have been felonious crimes! You can dis me now, you can dis me later, but 'least I ain't no playa-hater!"

"Day-am!" Cool exclaimed, drawing out the word into two long syllables. "Playa-hater? Why you have to go there?"

Then it was Sean's turn to interject. "Uh, I hate to interrupt this little battle of wits, but have you forgotten that I just got shot at? Is there a phone I could use to call San Francisco? I'll put it on my calling card."

"Fo' shiggity! Use the phone in the front room," Z motioned back down the hallway. "It's right by the door."

As Sean left the room to make his dreaded call to Lil back at the newspaper, Cool and Z resumed their good-natured war of words. "Did you hear that?" Cool asked rhetorically, his voice dripping with mock incredulity. "He called me a player-hater! Day-am! I can't believe my dawg would play me like dat!"

Sean was not sure how to react to the young men's levity. On the one hand, it seemed oddly inappropriate, considering the seriousness of the situation they were all now in. On the other hand, Sean had to concede that the distraction had helped to restore his sense of composure...just in time to hear Lil's fury. He took a deep breath, then dialed the familiar numbers of his calling card access code, followed by Lil's direct line.

"Lillian Kramer."

"Lil, this is Sean."

"Sean..." She let the name dangle for a few seconds, as if trying to recognize a long-forgotten acquaintance. "Do you have a story ready for the copy desk, or is that an unreasonable expectation?"

"Lil. Someone tried to kill me this afternoon."

"Oh, really? Well, I certainly have a motive, but I've got an alibi – I was at my desk doing my job! One of us has to, you know."

"Lil, I'm serious! Two men followed me in a BMW for several blocks, then got out of their car and opened fire on me. I ran halfway across New Orleans before I managed to lose them in a crowd on the river front. Lil, this wasn't some random mugging – they were both wearing tee-shirts with my picture. I was *targeted.*"

Sensing that Sean was telling the truth, Lil's voice grew suddenly serious. "Are you all right?"

"Yeah, I'm all right. I think I lost about ten pounds, but I managed to dodge all the bullets. Lil, they wouldn't be trying to kill me if I weren't on to something big with this story. I'm certain Jackhammer, Banks, Hat Trick, Vanderhorn, and Freeman are on some kind of hit list, and I believe J. Richard Connor has something to do with it. I have a credible source to back that up, but no proof to run a story with. I'm still trying to come up with a motive – I can't figure out what connection these five guys have. I've got to stay down here and try to work it out. There's just one problem."

"There's always 'just one problem' with you, Sean," Lillian lamented. "And it almost always involves spending vast sums of the newspaper's limited funds."

Ignoring her jibe, Sean continued. "Lil, I can't return to my hotel room – they obviously knew where I was staying. I need you to have my things at the Hotel Maison Dupuy shipped back to the newspaper. Then I need you to wire me a couple thousand in cash so I can buy some clothes and check into another hotel under a bogus name. Oh, and have my cell-phone deactivated – I dropped it when I was running."

"Sean, you're the most talented writer on my staff. It's a pity that your talent isn't for writing! Someone shoots at you this afternoon and you find a way to make that an excuse to go on a shopping spree this evening. Of course, you wouldn't just do the sensible thing and contact the police. Unbelievable." After a long silence Lillian let out an audible sigh, and continued. "I'm going to do this, just because some little part of me desperately wants to believe it will pay off in the end. I'll wire you two thousand, and have Amy take care of your things. But if you don't come up with a blockbuster story out of this, you'll have *me* chasing you down the street with a gun. And Sean…"

"Yes?"

"I earned a marksmanship medal in the Navy!"

15

Sean was just hanging up the receiver and turning back toward Z's studio room, when there was a sharp banging on the door, accompanied by two loud voices uttering the single sound "Z" in a deep and thunderous harmony. The fear of the day's events surged inside him and he was so startled that he knocked the phone off its stand.

Emerging into the room, Z saw Sean replacing the telephone on the table, visibly shaken, and immediately understood his guest's reaction. "Sorry," he apologized, laughter seeping through the words. "I fo'got to tell you I left a message fo' Rod an' D to pass by."

Z stepped to the door and opened it, greeting his two friends with tapping fists. Roderick and Dewayne were surprised to see Sean standing there and turned to Z, allowing their faces to express their unspoken inquiry.

"Some of Cal's boys tried to pull up on Mr. McInness a coupla hours ago," Z explained. "He says they had his picture on their shirts. Cool an' I drove down to The Quarter to get him from the Jackson Brewery, an' brought him back here so he can make some calls an' get his shit straight, ya heard me?"

Nodding their understanding, they both turned back to Sean, Dewayne speaking up to ask, simply, "You awright, Whodi?"

"Yeah, it's gonna take more than a couple of Uptown thugs to keep this reporter from getting his story to press," Sean quipped. "Hell, my boss, Lil, scares me more than Callio Cal!"

They each cracked a smile as they returned to Z's studio. Cool was seated in the room wearing a pair of earphones, nodding his head to the beat of the unheard music. When they entered the room, Cool removed the earphones and turned the output knob to "speakers" while turning the volume down. It was a pair of female rappers, singing rapid-fire rhymes with an excellent sense of timing and harmony. "Who are you listening to?" Sean inquired.

"Oh, that's the Ghetto Twins," Cool answered. "They're Z's favorite group, 'sides the K-Nines, of course! They're an 'ol' school' group from the Nint' Ward – been around since we were all in middle school."

"Gotta give 'em their props," Z chimed in. "It's hard fo' any group from the Nint' Ward to make it these days. See, Callio Cal runs the drug trade in the Uptown wards, but he's a shot-caller wit' the studios all 'cross town, ya heard me? Anyone who wants to burn a CD in New Orleans has to kiss Cal's ass. So anyone who's got a beef wit' Cal's Uptown soldiers, well, they can jus' fo'get 'bout rappin' in this town. That's the real reason I'm not in the K-Nines. My family ties to Big T would've iced any chance fo' the band to make it. So I went my own way, doin' the deejay thing here in the Nint' Ward – that's somethin' Callio Cal couldn't control."

"F'sho'," Roderick agreed, joining the conversation. "Truth is, none of us wants to work wit' Cal. He ain't shit! 'Sides havin' his finger deep in the Uptown drug trade, he has a bad rep wit' the artists he produces, know what I'm sayin'? Off top, he takes a much higher percentage than most other producers, then adds in all kinds of bullshit expenses, but they all know if they bitch 'bout it he'll send a carload of soldiers to chop up their houses. Once you sign wit' Cal, he's gotcha by both nuts. 'Sides, we're tryin' to put out a positive message an' Cal's not into producin' that, know what I'm sayin'? What would happen to his uptown business if the young brothas an' sistas on the street started turnin' away from drugs, choppers, an' the gangsta life?"

"That's one of the reasons I like the Ghetto Twins," Z interjected. "They've put out some tracks wit' a real positive message, ya heard me, like the one Cool was 'bout to play." Watching the digital counter as he fast-forwarded the tape, Z found the start of the song he wanted Sean to hear. Sean listened to the fast-rhyming female singers framed between refrains of two young men singing in a slow and melodic harmony, as Z continued to speak.

"This one's called 'Responsibility', from one of their early albums, an' it's all 'bout steppin' up as a man to take care of yo' children – payin' befo' playin'. It's the kinda positive message we wanna put out. Young brothas have had a negative image fo' too long, ya heard – and not jus' to white folks, but really to ourselves.

No one gives a fuck when they hear there's been 'nother drive-by or pull-up – it's jus' another brotha off the streets. When we're growing up immersed in so much violence none of us expects to make it to our twenty-first birthday, ya heard me? How you gonna build a future like that? That's gotta change, an' we gotta do it fo' ourselves. If 'nough of us can start puttin' out a positive message in our raps, you'll see a new generation layin' down their guns, walkin' away from the gangsta lifestyle, an' puttin' their families first."

"You're very passionate in what you believe, aren't you?" Sean noted.

"F'shiggity! I guess I got that from my Momma. She always told me that my name represents hope an' victory fo' the African people."

"What does she mean by that?" Sean asked, intrigued by the statement.

"My real name is Zimbabwe. People always think I was named fo' the country in Africa, but the truth is, I had the name first, ya heard? Momma was into the civil rights movement in the sixties an' boycottin' the governments of Rhodesia an' South Africa in the seventies. I was born in 1980, when the war in Rhodesia was comin' to an end. Momma named me Zimbabwe as a sign of faith that a new nation would be born outta that blood. She was right – Rhodesia became Zimbabwe jus' a month after I was born."

Sean marveled at the story – few people he knew had such genuine significance attached to their names. Most parents chose names to honor a living or deceased relative, to invoke a patron saint or national hero, or simply because they liked the sound the name played off the tongue.

"Your 'Momma' sounds like a very interesting woman," Sean observed. "What's your last name?"

"Williamson," Z answered.

"Glad to meet you, Zimbabwe Williamson. And that goes for the three of you as well," Sean said, gesturing toward Cool, Dewayne, and Roderick. "And while we're talking about names, please call me Sean. Nobody calls me 'Mr. McInness'."

Just then, they heard Z's younger sister walking in the front door, accompanied by a young man.

"Kenyetta! Q-B!" Z shouted. "Come back by the studio, ya heard me?"

The young couple appeared in the studio doorway a few moments later. Kenyetta was strikingly pretty, with piercing black eyes that showed a definite family resemblance to Z's. The young man Z had referred to as Q-B was tall and slender, though with a well-toned physique and visibly muscular arms.

"Kenyetta, this is Mr. McInness ...er, Sean, the reporter I told you 'bout. Sean, this is my sister, an' this is Keith, but everyone calls him Q-B."

Sean stretched out his hand, first to the slightly bemused sister. "It's a pleasure meeting you, Kenyetta, and you, Q-B. It doesn't take a sports writer to know what those initials stand for. Who's team do you play for?"

"I jus' graduated from Frederick Douglass. Our team's been havin' some rough years, but I got to play the All-Star game fo' Orleans Parish in the Superdome. We whupped St. Bernard!" Q-B answered. "I'll be goin' to Tulane on scholarship this fall."

"Tulane's a good school," Sean allowed. "But with their starting quarterback graduating this year, they definitely need some new talent. Sounds like you've got an open field ahead."

Q-B smiled broadly and Kenyetta jabbed him playfully in the ribs. Then Z interrupted their horseplay with a serious tone. "Kenyetta, Sean's here 'cause two of Callio Cal's thugs tried to kill him this mornin'. This is serious, ya heard me, so I want you to be careful an' stay on top of yo' game like I taught you. If you see any cars creepin' by the house, you know what to do."

"I'll watch out fo' her," Q-B volunteered, the seriousness of his tone matching Z's.

"You'd better! I'll be yo' worst nightmare if you let anythin' happen to my 'Special K'. An' 'nother thing, I know I've told you befo' to get her home by ten-thirty on school nights. Don't think I didn't hear her sneakin' in after midnight last night, ya heard me? Momma may be sound 'sleep 'cause she works hard all day, but I sleep light. If you keep her out past curfew again, I'm gonna ground her an' break up yo' l'il romance."

Kenyetta glared at Z with a look that was at once angry and mortified with embarrassment. Icily, she reached past Z to extend her hand to Sean. "Nice meetin' you, Mr. McInness. You be careful." With that, she took Q-B by the arm and turned to leave the studio.

After the young couple had departed, Sean turned to Z and asked what school she was attending in the middle of July.

"Kenyetta's always been the best in school – she was Valedictorian of her class, ya heard me? She's startin' at Xavier this fall – they have a kickin' pre-med program – but she wants to finish in three years, so she's takin' summer classes at UNO. She wants to go to medical school, an' wit' all those years 'head of her, she's tryin' to get a jump-start. That's why I call her my 'Special K' – she's one-of-a-kind. She gets mad when I play the big brother role, but she knows I would do anythin' fo' her. As fo' Q-B, he's awright wit' me, but I keep him in check so he doesn't ever fo'get to treat her right."

Glancing at his watch, Sean saw that it was nearly seven o'clock. "This has turned out to be an interesting afternoon – I'm glad I got the chance to get to know all of you a little better. Now I've got to get down to a Western Union office, then check into a new hotel. Cool, could I impose on you for a ride?"

"F'sho'. There's a Western Union in the Winn-Dixie on North Carollton, over by City Park, where we, uh, kidnapped you."

"Thanks for reminding me!" Sean laughed. "You know, after these thugs chased me halfway across town, I have to tell you I appreciated the fact that at least the four of you had the courtesy to give me a ride while assaulting me!"

They all laughed, bid their farewells, and one-by-one, Z, Dewayne, and Roderick offered assistance should the need arise in the future. Cool and Sean then made their exit, and nearly collided with Z's mother as she was coming in the front door. She was tall and slender, wearing a work uniform that Sean did not immediately recognize. She was quite attractive and, though Sean guessed that she must be in her mid forties, she looked considerably younger. It made Sean feel suddenly old to realize that the mother of a college student looked younger than he did. Looking quite startled upon seeing Sean emerging from her house with Cool, it was obvious that Z had not told her about their earlier encounter. Thinking quickly, Sean decided it was probably just as well for her to remain in the dark for the moment.

"Hello, Ms. Williamson," Sean said as he reached out his hand to her. "I'm Sean McInness, with the San Francisco Star-Reporter. I just had a chance to speak to Q-B about his upcoming football season at Tulane, and spoke with your son, Zimbabwe as well. Incidentally, he told me the story behind his name. I must say, you sound like quite an interesting woman. I really wish I could stay to talk, but I've got a deadline to meet." With that, Sean nudged Cool and turned to make a quick escape out the front door.

"It was nice meetin' you, Mr., uh, McInness?" Ms. Williamson stammered. "Write somethin' positive for Q-B – he's a good boy." She stood in the doorway and watched as Sean and Cool got in the car and drove away. Shaking her head as she turned and closed the door behind her, she lamented "What have these boys got themselves into this time?"

16

After stopping by Western Union to pick up his cash, Sean asked Cool for a recommendation on another hotel in the French Quarter. Cool had a cousin who had worked at the Omni Royal Orleans, and he believed the hotel could be recommended equally on the strength of its comfortable accommodations and its discreet staff. "He got me an' my honey into a room at the Royal O on prom night, an' everybody was chill even though they knew I wasn't payin' fo' the room. That place was off da heazy! They even hooked me up wit' room service an' a bottle of White Star. I dropped some mad tips there that night!" Without hesitation, Sean accepted Cool's recommendation and asked Cool to drive him there.

Immediately upon arriving at the front door, he knew the Omni Royal Orleans was going to be a bit pricier than he had planned. The doormen wore uniforms consisting of khaki shorts, light colored shirts, and safari-style pith helmets, giving them an image befitting the colonial trappings of some small island nation in the British Commonwealth. Inside, the foyer was decorated with simple elegance. A large but tasteful chandelier illuminated twin stairways, each flanked by large potted shrubbery and a modest selection of classic statuary. Just behind the foyer was a large pen and ink rendition of the St. Louis Hotel, which had occupied the site from 1838 to 1916 – before the present structure was built – and which had once served as the State Capitol.

Sean stopped at the registration desk and learned that his financial concerns were justified: The rooms started at nearly three hundred dollars per night. He seriously considered turning and walking away, but he didn't know any other hotels in the area and Cool's assurances regarding the staff's discretion carried a lot of weight under the circumstances. Besides, the location was perfect – just two blocks from Jackson Square, the Omni sat smack in the heart of the French Quarter. Sean withdrew a roll of crisp hundred dollar bills, and prepaid for three nights. *I wish Cool's cousin* could "hook me up" he thought. *Lil is going to kill me.* He requested a receipt in the name of Kramer Lillianson, the name he had told Lil he would use, and had half of his remaining cash placed in the hotel safe.

His room was stunning. A massive four-post bed dominated the space, its thick, burgundy comforter perfectly complimenting the matching floral patterns of the linens and draperies. With a window facing Chartres Street, Sean could glimpse the St. Louis Cathedral to the left, while the high-rises of the central business district were silhouetted against the twilight sky to the right. The physical and emotional drain of the day's events finally overpowered his adrenaline and he almost involuntarily accepted the invitation of the soft mattress and fluffy pillows, not even taking time to remove his clothing. He slept deeply for thirteen hours.

The next day, Sean fumbled with his PDA – he was much more comfortable with his dog-eared old Rolodex at the office – and set to work calling every name that was in any way connected to any of the five athletes or J. Richard Connor. He had already spoken to most of these people earlier in the week, but he wanted the opportunity to ask a few more in-depth questions in light of his growing certainty that all six were connected in some unknown way. It was a slow process, because Sean had decided to walk to a different location and use a pay phone for each call. By the end of the day, he had crisscrossed the French Quarter three times, and had called fewer than half the names on his list.

Across town, in a twenty-third floor office overlooking the Louisiana Superdome, another call was in progress. J. Richard Connor had a problem, and he knew one man he could count on when all other options had failed. He dialed the pager number which he had long ago committed to memory, and which was his only means of contacting The Cardinal. After inputting his own private telephone number, he replaced the receiver, and reached for his bottle of Scotch. He had just begun to pour when the phone rang. *The Cardinal is always prompt,* Connor smiled to himself. Pressing the speakerphone button, he answered, "Connor."

"This is The Cardinal. What can I do for you?"

"I have a small problem that requires your expertise," Connor began in the clipped, confident cadences of a Fortune 500

110

executive. "You recall our previous conversation about the reporter from San Francisco, who was sniffing around the Jackhammer accident a bit too enthusiastically? As you had suggested, I put in a call to Callio Cal to take care of it for me. To make a long story short, Cal fucked up. He apparently put a couple of overweight, over-the-hill triggermen on the job, and they let that middle-aged snoop outrun them. Now I've lost him – he's been too damn smart to return to his hotel, or to check into any other hotel as far as my contacts can ascertain, at least not under his real name. I know he's still in the city, because he's been making more calls today, but I can't find him. It occurs to me that he must have contacted his newspaper, probably either collect or with a calling card. I was hoping you could use some of your national connections to trace those calls for me. I'm afraid our entire operation may be in jeopardy if we can't get a fix on him quickly."

"I'll get right on it," The Cardinal replied, then hung up the phone. He believed in keeping business transactions short and to the point. As he sat in his deceptively modest Chateau Estates villa in Kenner, The Cardinal quietly pondered the full implications of what he had just been told. To begin with, he had gained valuable information about a future rival, learning that Callio Cal could be sloppy and ineffective in carrying out his business. That was very good news, indeed, for a man who was planning to launch a territorial war against Cal in just a few weeks.

He had suggested that Connor call on Cal under the guise of territorial courtesy, but had, in fact, hoped to gain any insights he could about Cal's organization and capabilities. He had also steered the contract on the reporter toward Cal in order to keep his own hands clean. This was a dangerous assignment, there was to be no mistake about that. Hits among rival organizations were relatively risk-free in many important respects. Despite protestations to the contrary, the cold and simple reality was that police forces, as a rule, would not commit significant resources to their investigations where the victim was himself a known criminal. There was an unspoken understanding that those who live by the sword die by the sword.

But Sean McInness was a noncombatant. As a presumably innocent victim, his murder would justify a full-scale police investigation. Even worse, he was a bona-fide member of the press, so the newspapers would almost certainly blow the story of his death into a banner headline, and the Police Commissioner would know that he would have reporters dogging him daily until the case was solved. This was one can of worms he would have gladly seen opened by Callio Cal.

Now the assignment had returned to him, and he decided immediately to farm it out to his "national connections," as Connor had phrased it. The Cardinal was not formally affiliated with the Mafia, and was certainly too independent to ever consider allowing any outside organization to swallow his little empire. Nevertheless, his Italian roots had proven valuable on more than one occasion, and he had developed a cordial working relationship with one of the dominant New York area "families."

The Cardinal dialed the number of his Cosa Nostra contact and quickly briefed him on the situation, finally asking that he utilize the mob's considerable resources to trace any calls made in the past twenty-four hours on Sean McInness' calling card back to their source.

"That's gonna cost your client big," the New Yorker had asserted. "You know the long-distance companies have some of the tightest security around. We'll be putting our resources at serious risk to pull those records."

"I understand," The Cardinal replied. "Let's just say our client is well-funded and has made clear that the stakes justify any reasonable expense."

"That's good. That's good. Okay, here's what I'm gonna do. I'm gonna make some calls for you. Give me a couple of hours – I can have those numbers for you by the close of business today."

"Excellent!" The Cardinal agreed. "Can you have a couple of your boys on the next plane down here? We're going to need them to do the follow-up on this. There are…political considerations that require our own organizations to keep a low profile."

"What you mean is, you need to keep your hands clean! Watsa matta, you afraid of a little bad publicity?" the New Yorker laughed. "Yeah, we can fly in a couple of our guys to handle it. I'll have them call you when they get to New Orleans International. They'll have the information you requested when they call, so you can set up your action directly with them."

"Perfect! We owe you on this one."

"Heeey! What are friends for, eh?" With that, the New Yorker terminated the connection, and The Cardinal replaced the receiver on his phone.

Now all he could do was wait patiently, as one more obstacle was swept aside in his well-planned effort to take full control of the New Orleans trade. Callio Cal was his most formidable rival, but The Cardinal felt confident that Cal's music business would prove to be his undoing, distracting him from managing his organization. Once Cal fell, Big T and Fat Friday would surely roll over and seek an alliance with him, realizing that keeping a percentage of their former business was better than losing it all. With J. Richard Connor in his pocket, he already had a lock on the casino and sports businesses. By the end of the year, he would be fully in control of New Orleans and four surrounding parishes.

Shortly after ten that evening, The Cardinal's patience was rewarded. The phone on his desk rang and, when he answered, a heavily accented voice greeted him over the background static of a pay phone.

"The choir boys have arrived at New Orleans International to sing for The Cardinal," the caller announced. "Our friends in the Archdiocese of New York send their warmest regards, along with tidings of great interest. The call that interested you was made at four forty-two yesterday afternoon, to the private office line of Lillian Kramer at the San Francisco Star-Reporter, Sports Desk, and charged to a calling card belonging to one Sean McInness. The call originated from a private residence in New Orleans, listed in the name of Regina Williamson. I've got the address – shall we pay a courtesy call?"

"I'm not interested in Ms. Williamson," The Cardinal snapped, annoyed by the mocking tone of the unseen hit-man. "It's Sean McInness who needs your services. I want you to stake out this Williamson house and watch for him – you should have received a fax of his photo from our client. Check in with me tomorrow afternoon, or when the job is finished. And don't screw up!" The Cardinal slammed down the receiver.

An hour later, a late model rental car cruised past the Williamson house, slowing slightly as it passed, then accelerating again. Z was in his studio, headphones directing a hip-hop beat directly to his eardrums; Kenyetta was studying in her room; and Ms. Williamson had already turned in for the night, since her job required setting the alarm for five-thirty in the morning. None of them had any reason to suspect the danger that had suddenly come directly to their doorstep. The car drove several blocks past the Williamson home, circled a block, then crept back down the other side of the street. Finding a suitable spot in the shadows of a deserted warehouse three-quarters of a block from the targeted home, the car came to a stop and the two men inside began their vigil. One by one, the lights in the home darkened, as the occupants each lay down for a peaceful and carefree night's slumber.

(17)

One light came on at five-thirty the next morning, followed shortly by two others as Regina Williamson prepared for work. She wasn't due at her job in the central business district until seven-thirty, but she always started her day with a solid southern-style breakfast, a long cup of coffee, and the morning newspaper. After completing her morning ritual, Ms. Williamson emerged from her front door at precisely six-fifty-five, dressed in the crisp uniform of a hotel concierge. Stepping into her late-model Ford Tempo, she started her engine and pulled away from the curb, beginning her twenty-minute commute to the uptown Sheraton.

Just a few car-lengths behind her, a second vehicle started its engine and crept slowly onto the street. The hit-men from New York had watched the home all night, taking turns grabbing half-hour catnaps. They knew nothing of Regina Williamson or the other occupants of the household, and had decided to follow each one as they emerged from the home, gathering as much information as they could and hoping one would lead them to Sean McInness. As they pursued Ms. Williamson at a discreet distance along St. Claude Avenue, the passenger scratched detailed notes onto a small pad of paper, recording the make, model, and license number of the car, along with a few descriptive comments on Ms. Williamson and her attire. When Ms. Williamson pulled into the employee parking entrance at the Sheraton, the hit-men waited just long enough to confirm that she was reporting for work there, then returned to their chosen parking spot across from the Williamson home to continue their surveillance.

At nine o'clock, Kenyetta Williamson emerged from the home, toting a large book bag, and walked four blocks to the bus stop on St. Claude. The hit-men followed, maintaining a distance of one to two blocks behind her. They positioned their car at an intersection two blocks down St. Claude where they would have a clear view of the bus stop, and waited until Kenyetta boarded an inbound line. Following a bus was a particularly difficult task, because of the need to adjust to the frequent stops and starts. But the hit-men were skilled in their profession and followed an established routine – turning right at the first intersection every time the bus stopped, pausing long enough to see whether their quarry had stepped off, then continuing half a block, turning around, and emerging back onto the main thoroughfare.

Kenyetta Williamson changed buses once, at Elysian Fields, and continued her ride northward, toward the lakeshore. Finally, she stepped off the bus where the line ended in the heart of the University of New Orleans campus and walked across the grassy lawns to her classroom building. The New Yorkers watched from a safe distance as she entered the facility, the passenger jotting notes on his pad as the driver conducted a methodical tour of the area. After completing their informal cartography of the campus and its surroundings, they returned once again to their stakeout of the Williamson home. After several hours with no visible activity, they concluded that any additional occupants of the home must have slipped out while they were following the others. They decided to take a break to grab lunch and a shower before returning for an afternoon stakeout.

Meanwhile, Sean had decided it was time to turn the tables on J. Richard Connor, tightening the screws on him more forcefully. For the moment, he forgot the five athletes at the center of his investigation and decided to gather all the information he could about Connor and his business activities. Spending half his day pouring through microfiche records at the New Orleans Public Library, which sat at the appropriately academic intersection of Loyola and Tulane Avenues, and the remainder walking to pay phones to call Connor's various offices and business contacts, Sean dove headlong into Connor's world. The man had a carefully constructed veil of secrecy obscuring his private transactions, but Sean was able to learn a great deal about him nonetheless.

J. Richard Connor had been born into a wealthy family, his father having made a small fortune in the local seafood industry and a larger one in real estate. Connor had continued the family endeavors in those two areas, but had also diversified significantly, with his real estate holdings now predominantly focused in the booming hospitality industry, and had his finger in the casino business and construction as well. However, Sean learned, his real passion – his obsession – was professional sports. He had made several attempts over the years to acquire ownership of the New Orleans Saints and the Zephyrs, New Orleans' Triple-A minor league baseball franchise, but had never been able to obtain a controlling interest in either team.

For nearly two decades, Connor had been one of the city's most prominent voices for obtaining additional professional teams. At first supporting a bid for an expansion baseball team, Connor had eventually decided that luring a basketball team to New Orleans was more commercially promising.

So, for fourteen years, Connor had led the charge to lure an NBA team to New Orleans. Then it had all fallen apart. The consortium Connor had assembled to finance a team collapsed in the wake of the riverboat gambling scandals, and before he could regroup, another syndicate had seized the opportunity to lure the Charlotte Hornets to the newly-built New Orleans Arena. Connor's dream had come true without him.

Undaunted, Connor returned to his first love – baseball. He knew that the first step was to gain the support of New Orleans' people and political leaders, hoping that the city's wild enthusiasm for its football and basketball teams would extend to baseball as well. Conner had mounted a massive public relations campaign to remind the people of New Orleans that baseball had always been a part of their history. The Crescent City's first minor league team, the New Orleans Pelicans, dated to the nineteenth century, and had been the proving grounds for the likes of Shoeless Joe Jackson, while the Black Pelicans had a proud history with the Negro Leagues and had once been home to the great Satchel Paige.

Conner then turned his attention to acquiring a team. He had put together a bid for the Montreal Expos as they sought to avoid extinction by relocating to a more profitable market. Connor argued passionately that the Montreal Expos *belonged* in New Orleans. After all, the French-speaking Cajuns of southern Louisiana had originated in the Acadia region of Canada, not far from Montreal, before their exile by the British following the French and Indian War. Connor proposed renaming the team "The Cajuns" and soon the city was awash with "Welcome Home Cajuns!" billboards and bumper stickers, and their counterparts in French: "Bienvenue Acadiens!"

Connor and the city were devastated when Washington, D.C. won the bid for the Expos and promptly moved the team to the nation's capital with the moniker "Washington Nationals." A few days later, Connor had held a press conference in which he promised to keep the dream of a "Cajuns" baseball team alive. Within a few months, he finally achieved his lifelong ambition: using his considerable influence to leverage friendships with both local and state political officials, Connor was able to broker a sweet offering that included tax incentives, revenue guarantees, an immediate home in the Superdome, and the promise of a brand new ball park within five years. Major League Baseball was impressed with his offering and with the outpouring of enthusiasm from the people of New Orleans, and agreed to an expansion team. The deal would benefit Connor in several ways, over and above his ownership stake in the team. Most directly, his cronies in city hall promised him that a large piece of the construction contracting for the new stadium would be assured for Connor Enterprises. In addition, stock in his hospitality holdings would soar as the new team brought additional visitors into the heart of the city.

Finally, his friends in the casino business would owe him a very large debt of gratitude for bringing to the city the sort of high profile high-rollers that only a professional sports team can command, helping to boost revenues for the deeply troubled Harrah's casino. After the unceremonious departure of most of the riverboat casinos that had flooded the city briefly a few years earlier before moving upriver, Harrah's had represented the gaming industry's last best hope in New Orleans. However, the giant casino had itself spiraled into one of the costliest and most embarrassing boondoggles in the annals of myopic city planning – its convulsions had included two bankruptcies, a tax-relief bail-out approved by the state, a class-action lawsuit by laid-off employees, and an epic power struggle with the Board of Directors of it's affiliated holding company. An influx of new gambling revenues would be welcome relief.

No sooner had Connor achieved his life-long dream of owning a professional sports team, however, than the disappointments and headaches set in. During the second week of the season, the City of New Orleans had been rocked as first one, then two of its new stars were jailed on serious charges. One was arrested in a vice squad sting operation in New York for soliciting underage prostitutes in his white stretch limousine. The other was charged with assault in the brutal beating of his girlfriend. The national press exploded in a feeding frenzy, and even the hometown Times-Picayune couldn't resist the headline "Cage the Cajuns!"

The fledgling team never recovered from the disorientation of the morale-shattering scandals, and fell quickly to the basement in the standings. They finished the season with a staggering record of one hundred ten losses versus fifty-two wins and, by August, the tide of local public opinion had turned solidly against them. Truckloads of Cajuns tee-shirts, caps and other merchandising gear were being returned from retailers unsold; local officials were openly reneging on their support for the tax breaks that had been afforded the team; and the Times-Picayne ran an editorial forcefully asserting that the Cajuns had become the laughing stock of the nation and were not worthy of sharing the Superdome with the ever-popular New Orleans Saints.

Connor had lost millions overnight and stood to lose much more if he could not stem the tide. Sean concluded that Connor must be both angry and desperate, but despite the wealth of information he had learned, he could still find nothing that would tie Connor to the five athletes on the hit list. "What is the connection?" he muttered aloud to himself, as he emerged from the library. It was mid-afternoon, and Sean realized that the library was only a block from the Holiday Inn where he had seen the huge clarinet mural. Confident that he had not been followed, he decided to take another look at the painting, without the duress of his previous visit, and continue on a leisurely stroll through the Central Business District. He needed a chance to clear his head and ponder all that he had learned.

Only a few blocks away, J. Richard Connor was also pondering the questions raised by Sean's research. He dialed The Cardinal's pager, then slammed down the receiver after punching in his return number. Impatiently, he circled from behind his desk and paced over to the picture window overlooking the Superdome and Arena. No sooner had he reached the window, than the phone rang. Dashing back to his desk, he picked up the phone. "Connor here!" he nearly shouted, the agitation in his voice evident.

"This is The Cardinal. What can I do for you?"

"You can take care of that goddam reporter! That's what you can do! There's no doubt he's on to something – he spent this entire morning calling all of my business offices trying to scratch for anything he can find. That goddam snoop even had the audacity to call my personal secretary and ask to have a copy of Connor Enterprises' quarterly report mailed to his newspaper! We need to take him out, NOW! You must understand how much is at stake here. Surely you realize how much you stand to gain if our plan succeeds and how much you'll lose if we fail. I don't give a damn what you do – blow up the fucking house where he's staying. Just get rid of him! Are we clear on that?"

"Crystal clear. We haven't located him yet, but I believe I know a way we can get to him. Don't worry, I'll take care of it."

"Don't worry?" Connor snapped. "Hell with that! This reporter already escaped one hit – he'd damn well better not escape again. You and I can have a long and prosperous partnership ahead or we can be finished today. The question is, can you deliver?"

"I'll deliver, you can count on that," The Cardinal replied, his voice carrying an undertone of contained anger. He didn't like being questioned, challenged, or threatened, and Connor had just done all three. He hung up the receiver and checked his watch. Five minutes to three – his New York contractors should be calling in just a few minutes, he thought.

The rage that Connor's call had provoked quickly faded as he thought of his own contribution to the day's efforts, a smirk of self-satisfaction coming to his face. The name and address provided by his Mafia contacts had struck a chord of familiarity somewhere deep in his recollection. It had only required a couple of phone calls for him to confirm that Regina Williamson was Big T's estranged sister. It had then been equally easy for him to assemble an impressive dossier on all three members of the Williamson household – Regina, Zimbabwe, and Kenyetta. Based upon what he had been able to learn about the three of them, he had guessed that Zimbabwe was most likely the one in contact with Sean McInness – his interest in sports, his devil-may-care personality, and his previous employment working for Big T all pointed to his involvement. *So, the first shots in the great New Orleans turf war will not be fired against Callio Cal, after all,* he mused. *The shocking triple-slaying of the Williamson family should crack Big T's hold on the Ninth Ward. After all, who will trust him or have confidence in his strength if he can't even protect his own family? This is a perfect chance to kill two birds with one stone.*

At precisely three o'clock, The Cardinal's phone rang. It was one of the New York hit-men calling to report on the progress of their surveillance. He quickly described how they had tracked the mother and sister to their respective destinations, but had not yet seen the reporter.

"There's been a change of plans," The Cardinal cut off the New Yorker. "Our client is getting impatient and wants us to move more quickly. There's a third occupant of the home – a young man named Zimbabwe, and I believe he's the one who can lead you to McInness. I want you to grab the sister and the mother, then use them as bait to get the information you need from the young man. Once you've got the reporter, kill them all."

At three-forty-five, Kenyetta Williamson stepped off the bus on St. Claude and found Q-B waiting for her there, as he always was, to walk her home. He was making a half-hearted effort to conceal something behind his back, until she was within reach. Removing his hand from behind his back with an exaggerated flourish, he presented her with a single red rose completed with a spray of white baby's breath and a large silk bow. "Happy Anniversary!" he announced.

"Anniversary?" Kenyetta asked, her confusion tinged with concern that she had forgotten an important date.

"Yeah, K, this is our anniversary – we've been goin' together fo' one year, five months, two weeks, an' four days!"

After a moment of confused silence, Kenyetta burst out laughing. "What kind of an anniversary is that? Q-B, you're crazy!"

"Crazy 'bout you," Q-B replied, as they turned to walk away from the bus stop. "I think we oughta jus' make every day our anniversary, 'cause every day I'm wit' you is a special day."

"Listen to you! You're jus' runnin' yo' game – my brother warned me 'bout boys like you!"

"Oh yeah? An' what did yo' brother tell you 'bout me?"

"He said a boy like you will say anythin' to get what he wants!"

"There it is! What I want is you – you an' me, forever – an' I would say anythin' or do anythin' to make that happen."

"You jus' need to stop!" Kenyetta smiled, not wanting him to stop at all. She loved the way Q-B treated her, like she was the most beautiful, desirable, and wonderful woman on Earth. She touched the rose to the tip of her nose, catching its subtle scent.

"Let me get yo' book bag fo' you," Q-B offered, lifting it from her back and pulling one of the straps around her arm before she could answer.

"You don't have to be doin' all that," Kenyetta protested. "I can carry my own weight – I'm a *strong* black woman!"

"Yeah you right, but you're still *my* woman, an' you don't need to be carryin' anythin' but yo' rose."

Suddenly, a car slammed on its brakes just a few feet from them, and before the young couple had time to react, two men jumped from the car. One of the men grabbed Kenyetta from behind, locking her arms behind her back, as the other landed a solid blow to Q-B's jaw, knocking him to the ground. Without a second's hesitation, Q-B jumped to his feet, brushed past his attacker, and lunged for the man struggling with Kenyetta.

"What the fuck? Who the hell you think you are layin' a hand on my woman? This is the Nint' Ward, muthafuckas, an' you jus' stepped to the wrong brotha! Get off my woman befo' I fuck you up!"

Before either of the New Yorkers could react, Q-B hammered the kidnapper's face with a rapid series of blows as Kenyetta kicked repeatedly at one of his knees, causing him to loosen his grip on her and sending him reeling backward. Q-B maintained the offensive, continuing to pummel the man as he fell to the ground.

"Run, K!" Q-B shouted as he continued to batter her attacker. She turned to run, but ran squarely into the waiting arms of the second kidnapper. He knocked her to the ground with a powerful backhand, then lunged on top of her, pinning one of her arms behind her with one hand, and yanking her head backward forcefully by her hair with the other.

Seeing that Kenyetta had not escaped, Q-B turned away from his first target, rose to his feet, and took a step toward Kenyetta and the second attacker. The first attacker, lying on his back on the sidewalk, took the opportunity to pull a gun from his shoulder holster, took aim, and squeezed the trigger. The single shot crashed through the back of Q-B's shoulder, and he crumpled to the ground. Rising to his feet, the gunman approached, wiping blood from his nose and peering angrily through his swollen eyes. He viciously kicked Q-B in the ribs and abdomen several times as the other attacker dragged Kenyetta kicking and screaming into the car, struggling to hold a chloroform-soaked rag over her mouth and nose. "I oughta pop your punk ass right now, boy, but I need you to deliver a message. You tell your bitch's brother to sit by his phone and do what he's told if he wants to see his sister alive again."

With that, the New Yorker kicked Q-B hard one more time, spat on his back, and turned to get into the car, waving his gun menacingly at several witnesses who had gathered at a safe distance across the street. Turning to his accomplice, he growled, "Get us to the Sheraton – let's get the mom so we can finish this!"

The bystanders rushed to the fallen young man's aid as the car sped away, the first one to reach him shouting back to the others, "It's Q-B! He's bleedin' bad, ya heard me? Get an ambulance!"

18

With over a dozen witnesses to the brazen daylight assault, word spread like wildfire through the neighborhood. Z was at Cool's home a few blocks away when Trey, his fourteen-year-old neighbor, burst through Cool's front door.

"Q-B's been shot!" the breathless teenager announced. "An' they got yo' sister!"

Jumping to his feet, Z rushed toward the youth and grabbed him by the shoulders, as Cool sat motionless, frozen with shock. "What do you mean they got my sister?" Z demanded.

"Two white guys in a Chrysler Le Baron snatched her walkin' home from the bus stop, 'bout a block off St. Claude. Q-B tried to stop 'em, but they shot him. I saw everythin'."

"When?" Z pressed, his face contorted into a fearsome mix of rage and desperation.

"'Bout half an hour ago. Q-B an' Kenyetta put up a hell of a fight – they woulda got away if one of the white dudes hadn't pulled a gun. I stayed wit' Q-B 'til the ambulance took him, then I started lookin' fo' you."

"Where'd they take Q-B?"

"To Charity. He lost a lotta blood – I've never seen so much blood! I don't know if he's gonna make it."

"Let's go!" Z commanded, turning toward Cool. Cool jumped to his feet and they all ran out of the house to Cool's car. Trey started to jump in the back seat, but Z ordered him to stay behind. "You did good comin' here to find me, but Cool an' I gotta handle it from here."

Cool drove wildly to the hospital, reaching the emergency entrance in just a little over ten minutes despite the early rush hour traffic. Z stepped from the car, and turned around to lean back in the open window. "I'm gonna check on Q-B to see if he can tell us anythin' mo' 'bout the gangstas that got Kenyetta. Go by the

Sheraton an' tell my Momma what happened, ya heard me? Tell her it's not safe at our house, then take her by my Auntie Cecee's – you know where she stays. I'll call you there."

Z turned and ran into the hospital, quickly learning that Q-B was in emergency surgery, and that there was nothing he could do but wait. Cool drove to the Sheraton, double-parked in front of the entrance, and ran inside to the concierge desk. It was five minutes to five, and Ms. Williamson was just packing her things to go home for the evening. Looking up to see Cool, she smiled a greeting to him, then her smile faded as she read the expression on his face.

"What is it, Cool? What's wrong? Oh, Lawd, is it Zimbabwe?"

"No, Ma'am," Cool stammered. "Zimbabwe's awright. It's Kenyetta. She's been kidnapped. An' Q-B's been shot."

Ms. Williamson sat down reflexively -- her jaw dropped open and her body quivering visibly. "Oh my Lawd! Who would kidnap Kenyetta? Why? When did this happen?"

"Trey told us it was two white guys – I don't think they hurt her. Z says it's not safe at yo' house, so he wants you to pass by his Auntie Ceecee's. He'll call you there soon as he knows anythin'. Come on, let me help you to the car."

"Ceecee. That's fine. Ceecee, yes. Oh, Lawd! They've taken my baby!" Ms. Williamson exclaimed breathlessly as Cool helped her to her feet, her voice quavering as the distant expression in her eyes betrayed deep shock. The evening concierge had been standing nearby and overheard the entire exchange. He assured Ms. Williamson that he would notify their supervisor and keep her in his prayers, as Cool escorted her out the door. Cool helped her into the passenger seat, then ran around to get in the driver's side door, rushing away just in time to avoid being ticketed by a rapidly-approaching traffic officer.

Behind the Sheraton, just across the street from the employee parking entrance, two men sat in a Chrysler Le Baron, one of them still nursing a bloody nose. They were expecting Ms. Williamson's beige Ford Tempo to emerge shortly after five, but it never did. At six-thirty, they abandoned their vigil and returned to an empty warehouse in the down-river suburb of Chalmette where they removed Kenyetta's unconscious body from the trunk of the car and bound her for the night.

Z was nearly out of his mind with anxiety, desperately wanting any information that could help him to bring his sister back safely. He paced anxiously in the waiting room as the minutes stretched to hours, stopping only once to call his auntie's home and verify that Cool and his mother had arrived safely. Finally, just past eight, a nurse approached him in the waiting area.

"Mr. Williamson. Your friend Keith is out of recovery and two police officers have just finished interviewing him. You can see him now, but only for a couple of minutes. He's suffered a major trauma, and will need lots of rest for the next few days."

Z followed her directions, nearly running down the hallway to the room where Q-B had been taken. Q-B turned his head away as soon as he saw Z entering the room and when Z reached the bedside, he could see tears beginning to stream down the younger man's face. Instantly understanding, Z reached out and placed his hand on Q-B's head. "It's cool, Dawg. It's cool."

Turning to face Z, Q-B began to speak, choking on every second or third word. "I tried to handle my business. I tried to step up like a man an' protect her. I'm sorry I let 'em take her. If anythin' happens to her...I don't know what I'll do."

Turning away again, he coughed and grimaced, obviously in extreme pain.

"You did all you could do, ya heard me?" Z assured him. "Trey saw everythin', an' he said you fought yo' heart out. He said you woulda kicked both their asses if they hadn't shot you. I jus' need to know anythin' you can remember 'bout 'em, anythin' that might help me find Kenyetta."

"Off top, they weren't from 'round here," Q-B replied, gritting his teeth and pursing his lips as he tried to think. "I know that fo' true. I think they were from New York – they had that movie gangsta accent, like the Sopranos or somethin'. An' they knew you, or knew 'bout you. They knew Kenyetta had a brother, an' they told me to give you a message to stay by yo' phone an' do whatever they say if you wanna see her again."

Z nodded his head as he considered the information, realizing immediately that the men were probably working for Connor or

The Cardinal. Shifting his gaze back to the injured young man, he responded, "Then I guess that's what I'd better do. How 'bout you, what did the doctors say?"

"Good thing they got me in the right shoulder – I guess they didn't know I'm a left-handed quarterback. The doctors told me I'll prob'ly have to sit out my freshman year, but I should be throwin' touchdowns fo' Tulane next year."

"Good – Tulane needs a playa with heart like you! I guess I'd best get back by the house an' wait fo' that call. You get some rest, ya heard?"

Z turned to leave the room, but as he reached the door, he turned back with an afterthought. "I know I come down hard on you some times – I've gotta look out fo' my Special K – but you're cool wit' me. When we get her back, I'm gonna tell her she'd better hang onto you. I wouldn't wanna see her wit' anyone else."

The younger man smiled weakly and lifted his uninjured arm to wave as Z bolted out the door and hurried down the hall. Z found a taxi in front of the hospital, and pulled a twenty-dollar bill from his pocket as he slid into the back seat, announcing that the driver could keep the change if he got him home in less than fifteen minutes. Twelve minutes later, Z stepped from the cab at his front door, where a large group of friends and neighbors had gathered to maintain a quiet vigil on the Williamson's front stoop. Roderick and Dewayne lived some distance away, in East New Orleans, and had apparently not yet heard the news. Z took a moment to answer his friends' questions, telling them Q-B was going to recover, but that Kenyetta's whereabouts were unknown. He then excused himself to enter the house, after asking a few of the larger young men to stay nearby in case he needed back-up on short notice.

At nine o'clock, the phone rang, and when he answered, Z immediately noticed the heavy Brooklyn accent of the caller.

"Listen-up, homeboy. We've got your sister, and man, is she a pretty young thing! It would be a real shame if somethin' happened to that pretty little face of hers."

"I swear," Z countered, barely able to contain his rage. "If Kenyetta has even one bruise when I get her back, I'll cut you up so bad they'll never find yo' fuckin' body!"

"Ohhhh! I'm scared!" the New Yorker mocked. "That's some big talk. Where I come from, if you're gonna talk big like that, you'd better be ready to back it up, or you'll find your balls cut off and stuffed into that big-talkin' mouth. Now shut-up and listen! We don't give a shit about you or your pretty little sister. We want Sean McInness. You give up where we can find him and you'll get your sister back."

Z briefly considered denying any knowledge of the reporter, then thought better of it. *I'd better not fuck wit' these guys – not wit' Kenyetta's life on the line.* "Okay. You got a deal – I'll give you Sean McInness, ya heard me, but there's no deal unless I know my sister's okay an' have a way to get her to safety. That means bringin' her to a very public place, like Bourbon Street. I'll bring Sean McInness an' we can swap."

There was silence for several seconds, as the New Yorker contemplated the deal. Finally, he responded. "Yeah, okay. We'll bring your sister and you bring McInness. There's a place I know from my last visit to your city, called Razzoo – I remember they had a flaming fountain in their courtyard. That's where we'll meet. Have the reporter there at noon tomorrow."

"Awright, I'll be there. If you've got my sister an' she looks okay, I'll turn him over to you, then you do what you need to do. All I care 'bout is my sister."

"You cover your bases pretty good, kid," the New Yorker agreed. "Just remember – you try anything funny and you'll get to watch your sister's brains blown out the side of her head. No cops. No guns. No double-crosses. Got it?"

"I got it."

"See you tomorrow, kid. Sweet dreams!" With that, the phone went dead.

Z immediately dialed his Auntie Ceecee's number. After assuring his mother that Kenyetta was okay and would be freed tomorrow, he asked to speak to Cool.

"Cool, I need you to get Rod an' D together, an' meet me at yo' crib fo' ten o'clock. We need to put together a plan. We may have to ice some people."

"Damn, Z! We ain't never been caught up in no drama like that befo'. Are you sho' you don't wanna let the NOPD or FBI handle it?"

"Cool, they've got Kenyetta – they've got my Special K! *I've* gotta handle this, *my* way, ya heard me, an' I need to know if my dawgs are gonna back me up."

"We don't even have any straps," Cool protested, " 'cept fo' Rod's piece of shit that we used to hustle Sean – I don't even think it works."

"Don't worry 'bout that, I have all that covered. I jus' need to know if you're in or out."

After a brief silence, Cool answered. "I've got yo' back. You know I always have yo' back. I'll call Rod an' D."

"Thanks, Dawg." Z hung up the phone, then rifled his wallet for the scrap of paper with Sean's phone number at the Omni Royal Orleans. Luckily, Sean was in his room and answered on the second ring.

"Hello?"

"Aye yo, this is Z. Somethin's come up. I need to pass by there tomorrow mornin'. Can you meet me down in yo' lobby fo' eleven-thirty?"

"Sure," Sean replied, sensing the urgency in Z's voice. "What's this about?"

"I can't tell you any mo' right now. I'll give you the four-one-one when I see you. Jus' be there – it's important, ya heard me?"

"Okay, I'll be downstairs at eleven-thirty sharp."

"Cool." Z hung up the phone. After a long hesitation, he picked up the receiver one more time, and dialed a number he knew from memory, although he had not called it in over eight years.

"Wuzzup?"

"Uncle T. This is Z, yo' nephew. I need to ask you fo' a big favor. Can you get me five clean nines tonight?"

19

By eleven-thirty the next morning, Z's plan was already fully in motion. Cool, Roderick, and Dewayne had taken up their assigned positions, ready to attempt their rescue with precision timing. The plan was relatively simple, relying on the age old weapon of surprise and the presumption that the New Yorkers would be less familiar with the turf, as well as a little help from the crowds of revelers who would certainly be filling Bourbon Street by midday on a sunny weekend. Z had decided that he could not tell Sean about the planned meeting with the New York hit-men. With his sister's life at stake, he could not take a chance that Sean would refuse to go along.

When Z walked into the Omni Royal Orleans hotel at precisely eleven-thirty, Sean was seated on a marble bench just inside the front door, reading the morning paper. Looking up, he greeted Z with a smile, folding the paper into his lap. "So, Z, what's this about?"

"My l'il sister, Kenyetta, is in trouble an' needs our help. I need you to go wit' me to a place called Razzoo, right 'round the corner on Bourbon Street. I don't have time to explain, but there are jus' three things you need to know. First, when we get there, I'm gonna leave you to chill in a jewelry store next door an' you gotta stay outta sight. When Cool comes to get you, I need you to walk straight into Razzoo an' come to my table. Kenyetta an' a coupla white guys'll be there wit' me. Second, once you get to the table, don't ask any questions, ya heard me, don't say *anythin'* wit'out thinkin', an' don't look surprised, no matter what you see or hear. Finally, remember what I told you befo' 'bout New Orleans: when I say 'run', don't hesitate an' don't look back – jus' follow my lead."

"What the hell is going on?" Sean felt the emptiness in his stomach that had become all too familiar in recent days.

"I can't tell you any mo'. We've gotta go now." With that, Z reached out and took Sean by the arm, leading him through the double doors into the bright sunlight. Bourbon Street was just a block away, with Razzoo and the adjacent jewelry boutique straddling the block parallel to the Omni Royal Orleans, so they reached their destination in less than two minutes – not enough time for Sean to digest what he had been told. Approaching the boutique cautiously and observing the crowds for any sign of the hit-men, Z deposited Sean in the jewelry store before returning alone to the patio club. "Remember, stay outta sight – away from the door. Cool will know where to find you when it's time."

Z walked into the restaurant and gave the hostess his name – he had had the foresight to reserve a table for five, lest a lack of lunch-time table space spoil his only hope of seeing Kenyetta alive again. Seated near the flaming fountain, as the hit-man had instructed, he made brief eye contact with Cool, who was sitting at a small table on the far side of the patio, trying to remain incognito, dressed like a tourist and sipping a daiquiri. Z checked his watch, and looked around the patio nervously as he waited for the last ten minutes before noon to pass.

At just past twelve, the two New Yorkers entered the patio – one of them marked with two black eyes and a bandaged nose – accompanied by a very frightened and dazed Kenyetta. When she saw Z, she started to cry out to him, but one of the hit-men quickly covered her mouth, and Z could see the bulge in the man's jacket where his gun was pressed against her side. While one hit-man paused with Kenyetta at a safe distance, the bandaged one walked briskly toward Z, maintaining a forced smile as he commanded, "Give your old Uncle Guido a big hug!"

Z did not understand at first, but did as he was told, standing up and holding out his arms in a mock greeting. The hit-man took him in a seemingly friendly bear hug, then in a single swift motion, ran his hands down to Z's buttocks, smoothly around the sides of his hips to his front belt buckle, then brushed past his crotch down to his inner thighs. Satisfied that Z was unarmed, he gestured to his partner with a quick motion of the head, and the other hit-man joined them, along with Kenyetta. As the hit-men took their seats, Cool slipped unseen from his table, and rushed next door to get Sean.

"So, where's our mutual friend?" one of the hit-men asked.

"He should be here in a minute. I've already sent a signal."

"Good boy! I sure hope he shows up quickly, because I have a bet with my partner here. He says you're a fuck up, and we're gonna have to waste you and your kid sister right here in this pretty little patio, but I say you're a bright boy and you're gonna deliver like you promised. Loser has to buy the other a Hurricane at Pat O'Brien's, and I know he's getting really thirsty, so you'd better come through in a hurry."

Just then, Sean walked through the entryway into the patio area, hesitating for a moment when he saw the two men with Z and Kenyetta. Surveying the scene quickly, he could not miss the look of fear on Kenyetta's face, nor the emotionless expression on Z's. It was obvious this was not a friendly encounter, and he desperately wished Z had provided him with a better explanation. He had no idea what he was supposed to do from this moment on. He took one tentative step forward, then took a deep breath and tried to seem casual as he continued to walk toward the table. One of the unfamiliar men, whose face was badly damaged from a recent altercation, stood and walked toward him, arms outstretched in an almost jovial pose. "Sean McInness! Give your Uncle Guido a big hug!"

Sean glanced toward Z, who nodded his approval. Taking the signal, Sean stretched out his arms to greet the approaching stranger. As the man worked his hands down to Sean's waistline, it occurred to Sean that he was being patted down. A shudder ran down his spine as he realized that the situation he had walked into was even worse than he had guessed. The hit-man grabbed him by the arm forcefully and pushed him toward the group's table, all the while smiling broadly and carrying on a meaningless banter for the benefit of any nearby prying ears.

Once they were all seated at the table, the hit-man continued his conversation with Z. "Well, well, well. It looks like I just won myself a delicious Hurricane! I knew you were a smart kid. In fact, as smart as you are, I'm sure you realize we need to finish our transaction in a more private location. Shall we go?"

The hit-men both stood, one pulling Kenyetta up with him, the other pulling his jacket to the side so both Z and Sean could see his weapon. Sean looked to Z, desperately hoping for a cue or a way out, but Z simply stood and gestured for Sean to do the same. The five of them walked out onto Bourbon Street, where the hit-men herded them into a manageable configuration, with gunmen flanking Sean and Kenyetta on each side, and Z walking in the middle, between the others. As they emerged into the teeming crowd, the hit-men pressed their guns snugly against their intended targets, and reminded Z that if he tried anything they would shoot both hostages.

A few dozen yards ahead of them, Sean caught a glimpse of two familiar faces. Two young black men, who appeared to be boisterously drunk, were staggering aimlessly toward them. As they drew closer and emerged from the mass of tourists and partyers, Sean realized that it was Roderick and Dewayne. Seeming completely oblivious to their surroundings, they were laughing loudly, gesturing frenetically, and drinking greedily from their huge, forty-ounce daiquiri cups. The hit-men tried to steer their hostages around the impending collision with the two loud drunks, but there was not enough room to maneuver.

Roderick bumped into the hit-man nearest Kenyetta, spilling most of his bright red daiquiri onto the man's front. With an embarrassed laugh, he began apologizing loudly while making a vain effort to wipe the frozen, sticky concoction off the man's shirt. The irritated hit-man tried at first to brush off what he presumed was an obnoxious drunk, then began shoving him forcefully aside with his free arm. For a few seconds, they almost appeared to be playing "patty-cake" as they tussled with each other's arms. Without warning, Dewayne spun around and threw his drink into the second hit-man's face – glass and all – then lunged at him in a body-tackle motion, while Roderick simultaneously grabbed the first hit-man's trigger hand and yanked the gun up away from Kenyetta's side. Z reached out to grab Kenyetta's hand and shouted "Run!"

Sean bolted just a half step behind Z and, understanding that Kenyetta was even more mystified than he was, he grabbed her other arm and tried to match his stride to Z's, as they both pulled Kenyetta through the crowd. Following Z's lead, they turned into the same jewelry store where Sean had waited before the meeting. As they sprinted through the upscale establishment, Sean saw that Z was intentionally knocking over jewelry cases as they passed, sending shattered glass and precious stones flying across the floor and setting off ear-splitting alarms. They crashed through a pair of doors at the back of the store and found themselves passing through the lobby of the Inn on Bourbon Street, one of the toniest addresses in the French Quarter. After only a half-dozen steps, they flung open another set of double doors and emerged into a swimming pool patio, replete with Greek statuary and lush shrubbery in neat brick planters.

Sean could see that they had reached a dead end, with an eight-foot brick wall at the back of the patio area, but Z continued to run full speed toward the wall with Kenyetta, and Sean followed. As they reached the wall, Z shouted, "Now, Cool! Now!" Then he turned to Sean and yelled, "Help me get her over the wall!" As Z reached down to grab one of his sister's legs, Sean mimicked the action and grabbed the other. Together they thrust her upward until her waist was even with the top of the wall. "Jump, K!" Z commanded, just as two bulging backpacks flew over the wall and bounced with soft thuds on the concrete a few feet from them. Kenyetta tumbled over the wall as Z and Sean gave a final push, and they heard Cool's voice from behind the wall, shouting, "I've got her!"

"Get her outta here, NOW!" Z shouted back, as they heard car doors slamming and wheels spinning. Then he turned and lunged for one of the backpacks near the pool, kicking the other pack toward Sean as he shouted a series of quick orders, "There's a nine-millimeter stuffed in a pillow inside. Get the gun out an' get the safety off!"

No sooner had Z spoken, than the two New Yorkers burst through the double doors behind them, guns drawn. Roderick and Dewayne had wrestled with the hit-men and pinned them to the ground just long enough to buy the escapees a few desperately-needed seconds, then had bolted in the opposite direction – disappearing into the Bourbon Street crowds as the New Yorkers got to their feet and gave chase after their quarry.

The New Yorkers immediately opened fire, and Sean dove for his pack and rolled behind one of the brick planters, scrambling to retrieve the carefully padded weapon. Z had made it to the planter on the opposite side of the pool, and they both returned fire at the hit-men as panicked hotel guests screamed and dove headlong into the pool for cover. The gun battle lasted only a few seconds, but nearly a hundred rounds were unloaded from the four weapons. The air throughout the patio was thick with the smell of gunpowder, and scores of fresh pock-marks scarred the brick walls and planters, as well as several statues. Sensing the danger of being cornered in this dead end when the police arrived, the hit-men suddenly ceased fire and retreated through the hotel lobby, disappearing onto the street beyond.

"We gotta get outta here!" Z shouted to Sean. "Let me help you up onto the wall, then you can pull me up. Throw yo' gun over the wall, NOW!" Sean quickly stuffed his gun into the nearest backpack, then tossed it over the wall, as Z knelt so that Sean could step up on his knee. Grabbing the top row of bricks, Sean pulled himself up while Z boosted from below, then he straddled the wall and tried to balance himself so he could assist Z. Z tossed his gun over the wall in the second backpack, then jumped, grabbing for the top row of bricks as Sean reached for the back of Z's shirt and pulled as hard as he could – ripping the fabric. After slipping back twice, Z took a few steps backward, then with a running start he leaped for the wall, finally pulling himself up unassisted. As the sound of police sirens approached, Sean and Z dropped over the backside of the wall, just as Roderick and Dewayne pulled into the alley in Dewayne's battered old Monte Carlo. With no need for further instructions, both of them scooped up their backpacks from the pavement and lunged into the back seat of the car, the door slamming shut by its own inertia as the car accelerated out of the alley.

They emerged onto Toulouse, which ran one way back toward the river and across Bourbon Street. As they crossed Bourbon Street, they saw the first in a series of police cruisers pulling to a stop in front of the jewelry store, the officers jumping from their vehicles with pistols drawn and shotguns at the ready. They continued to the next corner and turned right, following the dictates of the French Quarter's ubiquitous one-way streets. Dewayne could have turned right again at the next street to head north out of The Quarter, but wishing to avoid the congestion of police vehicles, he continued two more blocks, before turning right on Bienville. As he turned, he glanced in his rear-view mirror. "Uh, oh!"

The others all turned to look behind them, and saw the two New Yorkers in their Chrysler Le Baron following almost directly on their bumper. "Oh, shit!" exclaimed Roderick, as Sean and Z exchanged glances with equal parts disbelief and exasperation.

"Get 'cross the canal!" Z shouted. "We can lose 'em in the Nint' Ward."

Dewayne punched the accelerator as they crossed Bourbon Street again, dodging pedestrians, parked cars, and mule carriages along the narrow cobblestone street. Seeing that they had been spotted, the hit-men accelerated to keep pace and the passenger leaned out his window and opened fire, shattering Dewayne's rear window. "Oh, shit!" Roderick repeated.

Sean and Z exchanged glances again, then, without a word spoken, they both pulled their weapons from the backpacks, leaned out their windows and returned fire at the pursuing car. As several bullets found their marks, piercing the Le Baron's windshield, the hit-men's car fell back to a slightly safer distance, then the passenger leaned out his window again and unloaded another clip at the rear of Dewayne's car.

Dewayne narrowly missed colliding broadside with a city bus as the car lurched out onto North Rampart, the tires squealing as Dewayne forced the car to turn onto the broader, four-lane road. As soon as he had regained control, he jammed the pedal to the floor, accelerating like a rocket up the boulevard. Looking back, they saw the Le Baron turn the corner a few seconds behind them, bumping the side of an oncoming car and sending the innocent victim spinning into the "neutral ground." The Le Baron accelerated behind them, and the chase was on in earnest. Reaching speeds in excess of eighty miles per hour, Sean and the young men all squinted and said silent prayers as they ran three red lights in a row, watching cars swerve, slide, and honk all around them, but miraculously avoiding a collision.

The road curved noticeably after crossing Esplanade, and became McShane, then a few blocks later changed names again, to St. Claude. It would be a straight shot from there on into the CTC. Cross The Canal. The Nint' Ward. Safe haven. Only one thing stood between them and certain escape from their pursuers: the drawbridge. They had just crossed Poland Street, the last turn-off before the bridge, when the lights ahead of them began flashing, signaling the raising of the drawbridge over the canal. Dewayne was the first to see it and he stole the words from his brother's mouth, exclaiming, "Oh, shit!"

Having seen cars jump drawbridges in a dozen action movies, Dewayne would not have hesitated going for it, but the bridge over the Inner Harbor Navigation Canal rises only on the western side, providing no ramp for an eastbound car to jump. It only took a few seconds before Dewayne – and everyone else in the car – realized they would never make it. "We've gotta ditch the car!" Dewayne shouted as he slammed on the brakes.

Z turned to Sean, and asked, "Do you know how to swim?"

"You've got to be kidding!" Sean responded, his mind both unable and unwilling to fathom the next stage of their getaway.

Before the car had even come to a complete stop, Roderick and Dewayne were rolling out their respective doors, and Z had flung his door open. Grabbing Sean's arm, Z yanked him from the vehicle before there was time to protest. "Come on!"

They ran forward along the elevated roadway, past a row of cars that had stopped ahead of them. Behind, the Le Baron screeched to a stop and the hit-men jumped out, opening fire as they chased the foursome. Sean and the three youths came to a concrete stairway leading down to the ground level twenty feet below, and all four flew down the steps, ducking around behind before the hit-men got close enough for a clear shot. Running directly toward the canal, Sean could see the slow-moving hulk of a barge passing under the raised bridge. "We'll be awright if there's only one barge," Z shouted between strides. "If there's 'nother one behind that one, you'd better be a fast swimmer!"

They reached the water's edge just as the hit-men reached the bottom of the stairs, opening fire on them across clear terrain. Z had been the only one among the four of them who had thought to reload his gun with a fresh clip when evacuating the car. He turned back toward their pursuers, fell prostrate on the ground, and opened fire, briefly pinning the hit-men behind the stairwell some fifty yards away. "Go! Go! Go!" he shouted to the others. Sean, Dewayne, and Roderick dove simultaneously into the canal, looking just a bit like a sad audition for a synchronized swimming team.

Z glanced over his shoulder, noting with relief that there was only one barge, leaving a zone of safe swimming in its wake. He remained on shore for a few more seconds, emptying his clip at the hit-men as the sounds of police sirens became audible from somewhere in the distance. Finally, he pushed himself up from the ground, spun around, took three long steps, and dove into the canal, shoving his gun tightly into his waistband just as he splashed through the surface of the water. Swimming frantically to catch up with the others, he could hear gun shots behind him and saw several small splashes directly in front of his face, but he remembered his own rule: never look back.

By the time he reached the far shore, the hit-men had expended all of their ammunition, and Sean, Roderick, and Dewayne were waiting to pull him from the water. Soaked with the foul-smelling water of the canal, the four stood for a brief moment facing their pursuers across the channel, with first Roderick and then all four of them flipping a finger in defiance. Then they turned and disappeared into the back alleys of the Ninth Ward.

20

Taking a circuitous path through back yards and side streets, they reached the safety of Cool's home in about ten minutes, still soaking wet. Cool was not home, as he had taken Kenyetta directly to her aunt's home, but Cool's mother needed no explanation upon seeing the four dripping wet bodies standing at her door. She ushered them in with an exasperated sigh, handed each a towel, and pointed the way to her home's two bathrooms. Then she began scavenging Cool's room for shorts and shirts that might passably fit the four men, all of whom were considerably taller than Cool. Sean and Z deferred to Dewayne and Roderick for first shift in the showers, and Z went immediately to the phone in the front room to call his aunt's house. After speaking with his mother, Kenyetta, and Cool, Z felt reassured that they were all safe for the moment.

They both sat quietly on plastic patio chairs for several minutes awaiting their turn in the showers and pondering the violent turn of events that had befallen them. Z broke the silence first, realizing that Sean was still unaware of the full scope of the day's events.

"I guess you'd like to know what this was 'bout, huh?"

"Well, it's not every day that I get shot at *and* swim across the Mississippi River!" Sean cracked. "Those were obviously two more of Connor's creeps looking for me, but how did your sister get caught up in all of this?"

"They snatched her from the bus stop a coupla blocks from my house, an' told me they'd kill her if I didn't turn you over to 'em, ya heard me? Q-B got shot tryin' to stop 'em. You remember meetin' Q-B the other night over by my crib?"

"Damn! Is Q-B...okay?"

"Yeah, he's awright," Z nodded. "I talked to him fo' a minute last night tryin' to find out anythin' he could tell me 'bout the kidnappers. He took a bullet in the shoulder an' had some cracked ribs an' a bruised liver. He'll be awright, but he's gonna miss his first season at Tulane."

"Well, I'm glad he's going to be okay. As something of an expert in the field, I can tell him that missing a freshman season is not a major calamity – just an unplanned redshirt season. Tell him I'll be watching for him to take Tulane to a bowl game next year."

After another awkward pause, Z broke the silence again.

"I hope you understand why I couldn't tell you what was really goin' down off top this mornin'."

"I understand," Sean nodded. "If I had to choose between my sister and a near stranger, I would have done the same thing. Hell, I'm amazed you didn't just cross me like they wanted you to."

Z shook his head. "I've seen how the game is played too many times, ya heard? I knew they never meant to let me or Kenyetta walk away. I played it out the only way I could."

"You know you can't go back to your house until this is all over," Sean observed. "In fact, I think it would be wise to get you and your family the hell out of New Orleans for a while – they'll definitely come looking for you again. I'm going to make some calls when I get back to my hotel room, but I think I can promise you that my newspaper will pick up the tab to fly you, Kenyetta, and your mom out to California. You can disappear out there for a while. I'll call Lori and Vicki, two friends of mine, to see if you can stay with them for a few days. I think that would be the perfect place to hide you. Lori and Vikki are two of my best and most trusted friends, they have a large Victorian house in a quiet neighborhood, and they have no connection at all to the newspaper, so Connor will have no way to trace you to them. Just one thing I guess you should know, they're lesbians."

"Lesbians? Momma's gonna trip hard on that – she's all up into her church, ya heard me – but it's chill wit' me." After a moment to ponder the offer, Z chuckled softly. "I gotta agree wit' you – stayin' in a big house in San Francisco wit' two lesbians is prob'ly the last place Connor or anyone else would think to look fo' us."

"Well, talk to your mom, make sure she understands how much danger you're all in if you stay here. I'll call Lori and Vikki, and my boss Lil, and see what I can work out."

Just as Sean was finishing his conversation with Z, Dewayne emerged from his shower, followed a few seconds later by Roderick. "Yo' turn," Dewayne announced. Sean and Z looked at the two brothers, both wearing very tight fitting shorts and tee-shirts which fell a good two inches short of reaching their waistbands. Sean and Z looked at each other then back at the two brothers, and both burst out laughing. "Just go ahead and shoot me if I have to look that stupid," Sean quipped.

"What 'bout you?" Z asked, turning back to Sean. "What'll you do after you send us off to Frisco?"

"I'm going to Puerto Rico to find Tyrone Freeman. It's clear now that he's in grave danger, and equally clear that he's our last hope for solving this riddle. If I can only talk to him face-to-face, maybe he'll have some idea of the connection he has to the others on Connor's list."

"Won't Connor be expectin' you there?"

"Probably so, but I'll stay in a small bed & breakfast under a bogus name, so I shouldn't attract any attention. I'll just have to be careful."

With that, Sean and Z decided to take their turn in the showers, emerging dressed in equally misfitted clothing. Cool's mother drove Dewayne and Roderick home, then transported Z to his Aunt Ceecee's, where he was reunited with his sister and mother. After thanking Cool for his part in the rescue mission, Z pulled his mother aside for a long conversation, spelling out for her in detail the events of the preceding days. She had been reluctant to take time off from her job, and had been disturbed by the prospect of sharing a home in a distant city with two strangers. As Z had anticipated, she was also put off by the knowledge that the women were lesbians. In the end, though, she agreed that evacuating the family from New Orleans was the only way to assure their safety.

Sean called a cab to return to the Omni Royal Orleans, where his first priority was to change into his own clothes, and his second was to make a series of telephone calls to arrange the necessary logistics for himself and the Williamsons. First among them was the dreaded call to Lil. He could hardly contain himself as he imagined the expression on her face when he informed her that he needed to spend several thousand dollars more of the paper's money and still had no story to print. After a few side comments about hiring her own hit-men to eliminate her most expensive and least productive reporter, she agreed to pick up the charges on the Williamson family's airfare, as well as his own excursion to San Juan. After securing the finances, he called Lori and Vikki, who agreed to host the Williamsons for an indefinite stay until the danger passed.

With each of the women on a separate extension, they held a three-way conversation with Sean. After he explained the situation, Vikki was the first to respond. "We'd be delighted to have your friends stay with us for as long as they need," she asserted. "It would be so nice to have some new faces around. It gets a little boring here – you know Lori isn't much of a conversationalist."

Not one to let a jab pass without retaliation, Lori shot right back. "Oh, and I do hope they can share a few Creole cooking secrets with us. You know, fried rice is Vikki's specialty, but unfortunately, it's her *only* specialty. A little change in our diet might do us both good."

Now, now!" Sean interceded mirthfully, knowing how his two friends enjoyed sharing their sarcastic sense of humor together. "I didn't call to set off a major domestic conflagration! You two behave and make nice. I really do appreciate your helping out on such short notice."

"It will really be no trouble," Vikki replied, resisting the temptation to fire back another zinger at Lori. "We have the whole upstairs closed off. Just give us a few hours to sweep and tidy up a bit, and it should be perfectly suitable as guest quarters."

"When will your friends be arriving?" Lori asked.

"I'll have to call you back with their flight information as soon as I get all that settled, but you won't need to meet them at the airport. My Miata is still in long-term parking there, so I'll just give them my keys and directions to get to your house."

"Good! We'll look forward to meeting them!"

After speaking to Lori and Vikki, Sean called the airlines and booked reservations for all four of them. He then called a friend whose husband managed a travel agency, asking for a recommendation on lodgings in San Juan – taking care to explain the need for discretion to protect his anonymity. Sean's friend called back a short time later with her husband's recommendation: The El Canario Inn. Sean called the number she had provided and made a reservation for three nights under the name Dean N. Califano. He congratulated himself on the pseudonym because it would be easy to remember – when listed last name first in a hotel registry, it bore a mnemonic resemblance to "California Dreamin'."

At seven o'clock, the phone rang in Sean's room, and he knew by previous arrangement that it would be Z.

"Aye yo, this is Z. You got everythin' set up?"

"Everything's set. I've got all three of you booked on Delta, departing at nine-twenty tomorrow morning, and my friends have agreed to let you stay in the upstairs rooms of their home. It's near Alamo Park in a really beautiful part of The City. You'll need to bring jackets and warm clothes – the temperatures in San Francisco are going to be a shock to you. Their names are Lori Roth and Vikki Kwan, and they have a two year old daughter named Ashley. Just so you'll recognize them, Lori has long frizzy blonde hair, and Vikki has long straight black hair. Other than their hair color and obviously different ancestries, they could almost be twins. They're both early thirties, both medium height and slender, and both would rather eat ground glass than wear heels or anything with a designer label. The house cost them a small fortune, but in every other respect they live simply."

"How do we get to their house from the airport?" Z inquired.

"That's the *really* cool part," Sean answered, with a smile. "Do you drive a stick?"

"F'shiggity!" Z answered, excited anticipation showing in his voice. "Why?"

"Because when I meet you in the morning to give you your tickets, I'm also going to give you the keys to my Miata and my parking receipt. You and your mom can use my car for whatever you need, but if you wreck it, you'd better just drive off a cliff – that would be a less painful death than the one I would have in mind for you."

"I've never had a wreck or ticket in my life!" Z boasted. "You don't have to worry 'bout yo' car."

Sean realized that those words, when spoken by anyone under the age of twenty-five, were a near-certain kiss of death for the vehicle involved; but he also realized there were much more pressing matters for him to worry about. "How's Kenyetta, and how's your mother taking all of this?"

"They're both shook up, but I think they'll be awright once we get outta this town. K's already talkin' 'bout everythin' she wants to do when she gets to Cali, ya heard me? It's gonna be a big vacation fo' her, like spring break or somethin'. I think Momma's gonna want to jus' sit up in the house an' chill – she says she feels like this day aged her ten years."

"Well, I guess we're all set then. I'll meet the three of you for breakfast at the airport about seven tomorrow morning. Your flight leaves about an hour before mine."

Sean hung up the receiver, finished packing his bags, then fell across the bed for a last night's sleep in New Orleans.

The next morning, everything worked perfectly according to plan. Z, Kenyetta, and Ms. Williamson were waiting in the airport coffee shop when he arrived at three minutes past seven, and they enjoyed a pleasant conversation along with their overpriced breakfast. Sean turned over the tickets, car keys, and parking receipt, along with Lori and Vikki's address and the phone numbers of half a dozen friends in San Francisco and Oakland they could call if they needed anything, then walked with them to their gate. They boarded on time and he watched as their plane disappeared into the western sky, before turning to walk the short distance to his own gate.

His flight also boarded on time, and he was pleased to find that the two seats next to him were vacant, allowing him the rare comfort of ample leg and elbow-room throughout the six-hour flight. Soon, they were in the air. He watched the Big Easy disappear below as they crossed the bogs and marshes of Plaquemines Parish on the way to the open, blue waters of the Gulf of Mexico. When the flight attendant passed by to offer beverages, it suddenly occurred to him that there was something he hadn't done in several days.

"I'd like a gin and tonic, please. Actually, make that a double, and could you drop a couple of olives in it?"

21

When Sean landed at Luis Muñoz Marin International Airport in San Juan, it was late afternoon and the tropical sun was beating down with an intensity surpassing even the blast furnace he had left behind in New Orleans. The heat was literally breath-taking, and Sean found himself drenched in sweat almost as soon as he stepped out the front of the building to hail a taxi. "Bueno' dia', Señor," the driver greeted him, with the uniquely Puerto Rican intonation that dropped the final "s" from each of the first two words. "Where you going?"

Sean knew some Spanish, but in California he had learned the inflections characteristic of Mexico. The Spanish spoken in Puerto Rico sounded significantly different, so he immediately decided not to attempt to communicate in that language. "Please take me to the El Canario Inn, on Ashford Drive in Condado."

The driver nodded and pulled away from the curb, rapidly accelerating into the crowded lanes of traffic exiting the airport. As soon as they turned onto the main road, Sean could see the glistening high-rise hotels of the Isla Verde district, San Juan's most glamorous and exclusive beach resort area. Dominated by glittering casinos, four-star hotels, and secluded condominiums, Isla Verde was not for the budget tourist. They crossed a narrow neck of land, where Sean caught his first glimpse of the azure waters of the Atlantic to the right, and the equally blue Laguna Los Corozos to the left. After a short distance, the road veered away from the water's edge and they passed through the middle-class residential neighborhoods of Santurce. As they turned right on Avenida Jose de Diego, Sean noted directional signs indicating that they were approaching Condado. After just a few blocks and a couple of quick turns, the taxi pulled into the driveway of the El Canario Inn.

A handsome young man, perhaps twenty-five years of age, with naturally wavy black hair, chiseled features, and a bronze complexion stepped out from an entry foyer and reached to open

Sean's door. "Bueno' dia', Señor. Welcome to the El Canario Inn! Let me get your bags."

"Thank you, but I just brought one carry-on," Sean replied. "I can manage."

The young man nodded graciously and waved to the taxi driver as he backed out of the driveway to hunt for a new fare. As Sean entered the arched foyer, the young man stepped behind a small podium and hit a few keys on the computer console, then looked up to ask Sean's name. Somewhat surprised by the young man's instant transformation from doorman to reservationist, Sean stumbled on his words, nearly forgetting to use his pseudonym. "Sean, er, Dean N. Califano."

Glancing at him with a flicker of light-hearted suspicion in his eye, the young man responded. "Yes, Señor Califano, we've been expecting you. I have a note from your reservation that you may have some special needs."

"That's right. My business here is very sensitive – I'm a sports agent on a recruiting mission. It's absolutely vital to the success of my mission that both my identity and my client's remain strictly confidential. I may receive calls from any one of these people," Sean directed, handing the young man a small slip of paper with the names of Tyrone Freeman, Lori and Vikki, Zimbabwe and Ms. Williamson, and Lillian Kramer written on it, folded neatly with a crisp new hundred-dollar bill. "All other callers should be denied any information regarding my whereabouts. Similarly, I'm expecting no visitors while on the island, with the possible exception of Tyrone Freeman."

The young man, already smiling from the generosity of Sean's gratuity, burst into a broad grin. "Tyrone Freeman! I know him! That is, I know of him. He plays for the New England Patriots! You know he lives on the beach, not more than two blocks from here? They say his penthouse is the most expensive apartment in all of Puerto Rico. I have seen it only from the outside – his windows must be as tall as this building."

Sean was oddly embarrassed by the young man's gushing admiration for the star football player, as if his guise as a talent scout somehow placed him in the same spotlight. He was also a bit concerned that the young man's enthusiasm could lead to a poorly timed outburst that would blow his cover. Trying to regain the sense of urgent secrecy, Sean continued in a hushed voice. "You would recognize Tyrone Freeman out of uniform?"

"Si, of course! I would recognize him easily from across the avenida."

"Good, then there should be no mistake. No one else is to visit my room or know anything about my business here."

"Of course, Señor Califano," the young man answered, in an equally serious tone, crumpling the note and bill into the front pocket of his shorts. "No one."

The young man accepted Sean's cash payment for his first night in advance, completed the registration, then showed him to his room. Sean was a bit taken-aback by the small size of the room, but it was neatly decorated with sturdy wicker and rattan furnishings flanking a queen-size bed. Blue-gray tile floors accented the pastel salmon walls. A rapidly spinning ceiling fan supplemented the room's air conditioner, maintaining a very comfortable temperature. From his window, he had a charming view of the inn's secluded terrace, with umbrella-covered tables and inviting patio chairs set in the shade of towering palms and lush ferns. After the young man had provided a verbal tour of the facilities, explained checkout procedures, and handed Sean his keys, Sean thought to ask him his name.

"Hector," the hotel employee replied, his posture straightening visibly in a prideful pose. "Hector Muñoz, at your service!"

"Thank you, Hector. Do you work every day?"

"I work some days and some nights, while attending the Universidad de Puerto Rico. Any time I am here, it will be my pleasure to assist you."

I'll be counting on you," Sean asserted.

Hector smiled and, with a quick nod of his head, backed out of Sean's room, pulling the door securely behind him. Sean exhaled deeply, surveyed his room, and checked his watch. It was nearly six o'clock. Sean knew the first thing he wanted to do was to jump in the shower – six hours of travel from subtropical New Orleans to tropical San Juan had taken its toll, and he needed the refreshment that only a long, hot shower could provide. After he emerged from the shower, Sean decided to spend the evening acquainting himself with the city. He realized that time was running against him – he urgently needed to reach Tyrone Freeman before Connor did. On the other hand, Sean reasoned, it would be wise to gain some familiarity with his surroundings before exposing himself to another potentially dangerous situation. In addition, he realized that he really had not thought through how he was going to approach the linebacker. He needed to come up with a cover story to tell the personal assistant, bodyguards, housekeepers, and others who would be screening Tyrone's calls and visitors. He needed time to develop a strategy.

Donning sandals, shorts, and a loose fitting Hawaiian shirt, Sean stepped from the El Canario Inn and began walking west along Ashford Avenue. It struck him that the street name seemed oddly out of place. Most of the other streets he passed had names like Avenida Caribe and Calle Condado which matched the Latin language, culture, and ambiance of the island. Ashford Avenue seemed to be a rather jarring reminder of the colonial status under which the Commonwealth of Puerto Rico had existed for the better part of five centuries.

After two blocks, Sean came to the Marriott Hotel and Casino. He had opted against staying in one of the major hotel chains for fear that his identity and whereabouts would be more easily tracked in their worldwide reservation systems, but he decided to step inside to have a look around. The lobby was spacious and elegant, as he would have expected from a Marriott, with large floral-patterned oil paintings behind the reservations desk, the enticing casino entrance on the far side, and a comfortable lounge and piano bar occupying the space between. As he walked toward the back of the lobby, he caught a glimpse of the hotel's outdoor pool one level below him. It was stunning. Actually two separate pools, the larger one shaped in an angular, multisided configuration, with an expanse of pale blue water broken by a series of striking pink and white granite obelisks rising from the surface. Dozens of majestic palms circled the pool, their tops swaying gracefully in the sea breeze and, behind them, Sean could see the white sand beach and the deep blue waters of the Atlantic. *I wish I was here for rest and relaxation,* Sean thought with a touch of disappointment, as he turned to leave the Marriott behind.

Before leaving the El Canario, Sean had asked Hector to recommend a good restaurant nearby where he could sample authentic local cuisine in a casual atmosphere. Hector had suggested the Café del Angel, which was across the street just a short distance past the Marriott. Sean stepped into the café, and was immediately greeted by a pleasant older gentleman Sean guessed to be the proprietor. The man treated Sean as if he were the establishment's only customer, or an honored family friend. He patiently explained every item on the menu, and Sean ultimately deferred to the man's recommendation – trying Mofongo, the house specialty. It was a casserole of mashed green plantains, stuffed and baked with garlic and shrimp, then topped with Mohinto Sauce, a simple brew of wine, oil, vinegar, and garlic. The thought of garlic and banana in the same dish was both intriguing and off-putting, but Sean was very pleased with the results – it was one of the most outstanding meals he had had in quite some time. When Sean had finished with his meal, the proprietor advised him that homemade "tres leches cake" was available, speaking in the hushed yet excited tones of one who is revealing a carefully guarded secret. Sean capitulated and agreed to stay for dessert.

After dinner, Sean continued westward along Ashford Avenue as it traversed a narrow neck of land that separated the Laguna del Condado from the Atlantic Ocean, passing a series of high-rise hotel casinos and low-rise condominiums. Finally, he reached land's end, where a short bridge spanned the symbolic gulf between the glamour and excitement of Condado and the historic charms of Old San Juan. Sean turned back and decided to walk along the beach as he returned to his room.

The one-mile walk back to the El Canario Inn was both slower and more strenuous in the sand, but Sean was rewarded with a cool ocean breeze and fantastic views of one of the world's finest beach resort areas. It was approaching sundown, but the beaches were still alive with vacationers and locals alike, some swimming or wind-surfing in the warm ocean waters, others running and playing in the sand, and still more reclining on towels and beach chairs, soaking up the last rays of the Caribbean sun. As he neared his destination, he passed a pair of lodgings that he quickly surmised were popular among the island's gay visitors. A large number of scantily clad and gym-toned young men were congregated on the beach, while others sipped tropical concoctions and watched the scenery from the balconies of patio bars above.

The atmosphere of relaxed, friendly frivolity reminded him vaguely of Bourbon Street. *Bourbon Street. That was only a few days ago,* he recalled wistfully, *but it seems a million miles away now.*

Continuing a few hundred yards past the back of the El Canario, Sean came to the end of the beach, as a rocky outcropping abruptly interrupted the narrow strip of soft sand. While the surf rolled gently onto the sandy shoreline elsewhere along the beach, the waves here crashed against the jagged stones, which appeared to be of volcanic origin, sending a spray of salty mist into the warm evening air. After about fifty yards, sandy beach reappeared and continued unabated into the distance, and just a few yards past the point where the beach resumed stood the Olympic Tower condominiums, home of Tyrone Freeman. Sean had asked his friend's husband, the travel agent who had booked Sean at the El Canario Inn, to find a suitable establishment for him near the Olympic Tower. He smiled as he realized just how well the travel agent had fulfilled his request.

The Olympic Tower was a magnificent structure, rising eleven floors from sea level, its ivory and beige tones complimented by the natural hues of the surrounding beach. A dense grove of dark green palms abutted the front of the building, and long burgundy awnings draped the private balconies on every floor. Tyrone Freeman's penthouse suite occupied the front portion of both the tenth and eleventh floors, with huge plate glass windows spanning both levels. It was certainly an address worthy of one of the highest-paid athletes in America.

Somehow, Sean thought, he would have to bypass the building's ironclad security to reach Tyrone Freeman without revealing his identity to anyone else. He still had no idea how he was going to accomplish that task. He turned, and was greeted with the spectacular view of sunset over the Atlantic – the luxury high-rises of Condado and the feathery leaves of nearby palms silhouetted against a brilliant sky glowing in a dozen shades of pink and gold. It had been a long day of travel and there was much to be done tomorrow, so Sean decided to turn in for the night.

22

The next morning, Sean was awakened by the ringing telephone as Hector provided Sean's requested wake-up call. Sean hurried to shower and dress, then found his way to the continental breakfast in the patio area. As was typical of lodgings throughout Puerto Rico, breakfast consisted of an assortment of fresh tropical fruits, coffee, juice, and locally baked pastries – attended by small lizards that scurried to within inches of Sean's patio table in search of scraps. By ten o'clock, Sean was standing in front of the Olympic Tower condominiums, rehearsing the script he had finally devised.

It was too risky to identify himself as a reporter, whether or not he used his real name – anyone working for Connor would be looking for a reporter to make contact with Freeman. Besides, he was certain Tyrone would not wish to be bothered by a reporter here at his off-season island paradise. It was also impossible to claim, as he had told Hector, that he was a talent scout for a competing team. Tyrone and his personal assistant would both be savvy enough to know the names of every team's scouts. Sean had decided his best chance was to play the role of marketing representative for a new line of sportswear, in search of a major athlete's endorsement. With no business card, brochure, or samples, it was going to be difficult, but he only needed to get his foot in the door. Once in the private company of Tyrone Freeman, he would reveal his identity and outline the danger they both faced.

After taking a deep breath, Sean approached the front door of the building. He could see a security guard seated at a console just inside the lobby and, after making eye contact, the guard buzzed the door open and motioned for him to enter. Sean approached the desk, reached out his hand in greeting, took a deep breath, and launched into his script.

"Ola! I'm Dean Califano, with Millennium Fitness Products! You may have seen our new ad campaign on TV, with our slogan:

'Fitness isn't a fad – it's your future!' Actually, as I think of it, we're planning a Spanish-language version for release later this month. In any case, I'm here to see Tyrone Freeman."

The guard cocked his head, bewildered by the fast-talking sales pitch, but could not be dissuaded so easily from his security protocols.

"Si. Is Señor Freeman expecting you?"

"Well, not exactly," Sean continued, having expected the question. "My secretary has been trying to reach him for several days now, but has missed his return calls twice. It's hard to get good help these days, you know. I was in Miami for a sportswear marketing convention, and decided to fly on down to meet with Mr. Freeman today. It's rather urgent, you see. We had another spokesman scripted for our campaign, but he pulled out at the last minute. We've got to get these ads on the air by the end of the month to reach our back-to-school target market, so you see, I really must speak with Mr. Freeman right away. We have a very attractive offer for him – I'm certain he'll be pleased to hear what we have to say."

"I'll call up to Señor Freeman's assistant. He has to approve your meeting before I can admit you. Do you have a card?"

"Well, that's a funny thing," Sean chuckled, sensing that his plan was beginning to unravel. "I'm afraid I left my briefcase in the back seat of a cab in Miami on the way to the airport – business cards, promotional literature, even my day planner. It will take me weeks to recreate all the information in that planner – damned things are supposed to help us stay organized, but God help you if you ever depend on one! I've put in a call to the cab company to make a claim, but you know what the odds are on that. That briefcase was calf leather with twenty-four karat gold trim – cost me over four hundred dollars. If the next passenger didn't take it with him, the cabbie probably snatched it up to sell at a local flea market. The days when you could expect your lost wallets and purses to be returned by honest strangers are long gone, I'll tell you! My secretary is sending me a supply of cards and materials by overnight express, along with a copy of our standard endorsement contract – boilerplate stuff, mostly. Assuming Mr. Freeman likes our deal, we can crunch the numbers and be up and running to sign him later this afternoon."

The security guard stared at Sean silently for several moments, apparently trying to decide whether to believe his story. Then, while still watching Sean, he picked up the phone and dialed four digits. Although the guard spoke in a muffled voice, Sean could hear the content of the conversation:

"Hello, Señor Carpenter, there's a comerciante from Millennium Fitness Products here to see Señor Freeman...No, he doesn't have an appointment, but says he must see Señor Freeman about an endorsement. Fast-talking hombre, but I think he's just nervous...No, he doesn't have a card – says they were lost in a cab...Si...Si...What's that number? ...Si. I'll let him know, Señor Carpenter."

Turning back to Sean, the security guard handed him a slip of paper with a phone number. Sean recognized the area code as Boston.

"Señor Carpenter sends his regrets that Señor Freeman will be unable to meet with you. Señor Freeman has given strict orders that he not be disturbed during his last week before training camp. Señor Carpenter recommends that you call Señor Freeman's agent, who handles all endorsement contracts. He will be authorized to negotiate with you."

"But," Sean stammered. "You don't understand. There's no time – I've got to see Mr. Freeman today. There's too much at stake to waste time cutting through the red tape."

"I'm sorry," The security guard replied firmly. "No one sees Señor Freeman without Señor Carpenter's authorization. Bueno' Dia', Señor Califano."

The guard gestured politely toward the door, and Sean realized that the ruse had failed. Stepping outside into the warm morning air, Sean felt a sudden surge of anxiety. Five people were dead, one athlete had been beaten nearly to death and another charged with the crime, an innocent man was in jail, another young man was lying in a hospital in New Orleans, and an entire family had been evacuated from their home after the kidnapping of a young girl. On top of all that, he had been shot at for the first time in his life. Twice! If he didn't reach Tyrone Freeman before Connor, he feared there would be much more tragedy to come, but he had no idea how to get past Freeman's impenetrable wall of security. He spent much of the day wandering the beach, so thoroughly lost in thought that he barely realized he was still wearing his business suit, stopping only occasionally for liquid refreshments as the blistering tropical sun drained him. When he returned to the El Canario that afternoon, the disappointment must have been evident on his face because Hector quickly inquired about Sean's progress.

"Eh, Señor Califano, you don't look happy. Did he turn you down?"

"No, not exactly. I'm embarrassed to admit it, but I'm having a bit of difficulty getting around his gatekeepers. It seems he's too busy with his pre-season vacation to be bothered with a multimillion-dollar deal. Must be nice."

Hector smiled and nodded his agreement. Then, with a sudden look of inspiration, he spoke again.

"Señor Califano. I may be able to help. I think I know one place where you can find Tyrone Freeman alone. He's a big time gambler, you know. He plays a lot in the high-roller room at the Condado Plaza. You might be able to catch him there."

Sean pondered the suggestion for a moment, then a big smile came across his face. "It just might work!" he observed, more to himself than to Hector. "I'll be damned, it just might work. Thank you Hector – if this works, you can be sure there will be another good tip in it for you."

"Hector Muñoz, at your service!" the young man shrugged with a smile.

Sean glanced at his watch. It was almost four-thirty. He knew that Puerto Rico was actually four time zones ahead of California, but since the island doesn't observe Daylight Savings Time, it would be one-thirty in San Francisco. *Lil should be back from lunch by now.* He raced to a nearby pay phone, removed the calling card from his wallet, and dialed the San Francisco Star-Reporter.

"Lillian Kramer."

"Lil, this is Sean..."

Before he had a chance to finish his sentence, she interrupted with a terse inquiry: "How much?"

"Uh, well," Sean stammered, caught off-guard by her abruptness.

"I know you're calling for more expense money. God forbid you should ever call with a completed story! I don't even want to know what it's for this time, just tell me how much so I can have it wired."

"Ten thousand dollars," Sean answered.

There was a long silence, then Lil spoke again. "I was wrong. I *do* want to know why."

"So I can go gambling. Actually, it's not what it sounds like..."

Lillian interrupted him again. "It's never what it sounds like with you, Sean McInness. Just do me a favor, okay? Come up with something a little more eloquent than 'so I can go gambling' on your expense voucher. You know how picky that silly Board of Directors can be about things like that. That wouldn't be too great a stretch for your writing talents, would it? And remember, unless I get a damned good story out of this, I'll be docking your pay for the rest of the century!"

Sean had seen a Citibank branch near the El Canario, so he instructed Lillian to have the funds wired there. He knew that it would take until the next morning to complete a transaction of that size, so he decided to use the time to put together a plan. He would not be able to speak to Tyrone at length in the casino – they would need someplace quiet, private, and safe to meet afterward. He asked Hector for an appropriate restaurant recommendation, and Hector immediately suggested La Mallorquina, "The oldest restaurant in the Caribbean. Shall I call a taxi for you?" Sean agreed, and rushed up to his room to change into more comfortable clothing. By the time he returned to the foyer, a taxi was waiting to take Sean to Old San Juan.

La Mallorquina was located on Calle San Justo in historic Old San Juan, about midway between the Plaza de Armas and El Castillo de San Cristobal. The former served as the heart of the Old San Juan business district, while the latter was a true architectural marvel. San Cristobal, built by the Spanish over three centuries ago, consisted of an elaborate array of ramparts and battlements rising nearly one hundred fifty feet above the beaches below, with stone walls some twenty feet thick. The structure, and its larger cousin El Morro, dominated the landscape of Old San Juan, and both were visible above the skyline as Sean's taxi approached the restaurant.

La Mallorquina itself boasted a lovely but unpretentious façade of pink stucco accented with ornately carved white wood door frames and a row of potted plants lining the balcony railing above, the dense green foliage and bright red blooms perfectly accenting the building's color. Inside, the ceilings were high and a series of broad arches contributed to a feeling of openness, as if dining outdoors on a patio. The décor was elegant and immaculate: white tablecloths creased and folded to a crisp point at each corner, and matching white cloth seat covers lining the backs of every chair. Sean found the Maitre d' and first inquired if he would be there for the dinner shift the next day as well.

"Si, Señor. There is only me."

Good," Sean continued, pressing a hundred-dollar note into the man's hand. "I need to reserve your most private table for two, from six o'clock until you close tomorrow night. The name is Califano."

"Of course, Señor Califano! Shall I have something from our wine cellar reserved for you?"

"Yes, please. Would you select a red wine for me in the moderate price range?"

"Certainly. I'll personally see that your table is ready for you."

"Gracia'," Sean thanked the man, feeling increasingly confident of his ability to pronounce a few simple words and phrases in the Puerto Rican style.

After leaving the restaurant, Sean strolled the narrow streets of Old San Juan, taking in the sights and enjoying the ambiance. Although this was American soil, and every Puerto Rican a United States citizen, Old San Juan had an old-world charm utterly unlike any city in the fifty states. The narrow streets, paved with shiny gray bricks fashioned from iron ore, were lined with rows of stucco homes and shops, each one painted in a different pastel shade. The traffic flow had the feel of modulated chaos more typical of the back streets of Madrid, Lisbon, Paris, or Rome, with many intersections completely lacking any traffic lights or signage. There was a distinctive rhythm of life here as pedestrians, passenger cars and tour buses competed for the single-lane passageways and narrow walkways that traversed Old San Juan's steep hills.

After meandering among the varied shops along Old San Juan's two major commercial thoroughfares, Calle San Francisco and Calle Forteleza, Sean found a high-end men's clothier and stepped in to find appropriate attire for his planned excursion to the high-roller gaming room. He was startled to see a price tag very nearly approaching four-digits for an Armani suit, but decided it was a necessity. *Lil is going to kill me, but I can't afford to let anything screw up this chance.* He pointed out the suit he wanted and asked if he could have it tailored by early the next afternoon, adding that he would need a suitable pair of Italian shoes as well. The salesman seemed put off by the directness of Sean's requests, as if disappointed that there would be no opportunity to show various designers and interject his own personal recommendations. Nevertheless, he nodded politely and, without speaking a word, produced a cloth tape measure to carefully record Sean's size requirements. After the measurements had been taken, Sean produced a credit card, asking that it be used only to guarantee the purchase, as he would be returning the next day to pay with cash.

After a quick snack at one of the countless bistros in Old San Juan, Sean caught a cab back to Condado and retired for the night in his room at the El Canario. The next morning, he walked across the street to the Citibank at precisely nine o'clock to inquire about his wire transfer. The funds had arrived, but the tellers were necessarily cautious about turning over such a large sum to a non-resident of the island, and the branch manager was summoned to participate in the transaction. Luckily, Sean had an account with Citibank in Oakland and he produced his Citibank ATM card, along with his passport, his California driver's license, and his newspaper's corporate credit card. Even with such an array of legitimate identification, the branch manager still felt it necessary to obtain additional verification. After making Sean wait until after noon when he could call the bank in California, the executive finally directed one of his tellers to proceed. The teller counted out one hundred hundred-dollar bills.

Restraining his impatience as he thanked the teller and man-ager, Sean folded the thick stack of currency into his front pocket and felt a sudden uneasiness as he wondered how many people had seen him pocket the large sum of cash. The prospect of being robbed of his ten thousand dollars had not occurred to him until that moment. Glancing around the bank nervously, he saw that no one seemed to be interested in him or his cash, so he left quickly and walked briskly the two blocks back to the El Canario. By the time he reached his room, the combined effects of his newest anxiety and the burning rays of the sun had produced a torrent of sweat from head to toe.

He took a long shower, as much for its calming effects as to wash away the residue of his nerve-wracking foray into high finance, then called Hector at the front desk to request another cab. Stashing all but fifteen hundred dollars into his pile of soiled laundry, he hurried downstairs to find his cab waiting already. An hour later he returned, dressed to the nines in his perfectly tailored suit. Retrieving his hidden bankroll, he added it to the change left over from his shopping expedition and counted eighty-seven hundred dollars, not including the small bills that he knew were in his wallet. He checked his watch and saw that it was approaching three o'clock. He let out a long sigh, shoved the money roll deeply into his pocket, cracked his knuckles, and announced to his empty room, "It's time to play!"

23

Sean entered the main casino floor of the Condado Plaza Hotel and was greeted with a multimedia assault on his senses. Shimmering chandeliers and gleaming gold and silver fixtures, a chorus of bells, alarms and whooping sirens signaling slot-machine winners, and the raucous hum of human voices – shouting, laughing, gasping, and whispering, all contributed to a sense of excited anticipation; of possibility. One felt that fortunes were being won here – lives were being forever transformed from their prior bleakness and monotony to the glamour and bliss of instant riches. It was an image that had been carefully devised, promoted, and fine-tuned by the gaming industry, which had found its own instant riches in the booming popularity of its establishments.

Even Sean, a veteran reporter with a well-developed dose of cynicism, found himself taken in by the carefully orchestrated appeal to his senses and emotions, bursting into a wide-eyed smile as he took in the view. He had seen the inside of a casino before. It was only a short drive from Oakland to Reno or Lake Tahoe, and a short hop by air to Las Vegas, but gambling had never caught his fancy. Consequently, it had been several years since his last visit to a casino, and tonight the experience seemed new again.

He strolled the aisles and corridors of the casino at a leisurely pace, taking in the surroundings and glancing occasionally into the corner room where high rollers played. Tyrone Freeman was not there. As he toured the facility, he quickly recognized with both amusement and journalistic interest that there was a remarkable difference in the attitudes of those playing the various games.

Those most deeply affected by the dream of fantastic riches and, not coincidentally, those who could least afford to lose their money, were mostly seated at the slot machines. Inserting coins and working the levers in a nonstop rhythm, sometimes for hours, they resembled factory workers in some chrome-gilded, automated assembly line – earnestly believing that with the drop of just one more quarter, or perhaps another, a million-dollar jackpot was sure to appear. Second to the slots, roulette held the greatest promise for quick payoffs. The players here frequently let their bets ride on one or a handful of favorite numbers, ascribing cosmic significance when "their number" hit, with payoffs ranging into the hundreds for a five-dollar bet. The group that seemed to have the most boisterous fun gathered tightly around the craps table. As something of a group sport, every player at the table had money at stake while they cheered the "roller" – an honor they each took in turn. Quite the opposite of this proletarian game was baccarat. Baccarat was a game more commonly associated with the Old World casinos of Monte Carlo and was quite unfamiliar to most American players, resulting in a noticeably cliquish ambiance.

The only game for a truly professional gambler, however, was blackjack, for two related and equally important reasons. First, it is a steady game, rarely characterized by extreme swings, whether favorable or unfavorable. While it is true that one can win vast sums in mere minutes at the other games, one is even more likely to lose just as quickly. Playing blackjack, a gambler can sit down with a modest stake, and feel relatively certain that he will still be in the game an hour later. That is crucial for the professional gambler, because playing is where he wants to be. The other attraction that is unique to blackjack is the perception – or perhaps illusion – that there is just a touch of skill involved. There is certainly skill in understanding the nature of the game and recognizing the true odds in any particular scenario – statistics that are sometimes counterintuitive at first glance. But there is an even more esteemed skill known as "card-counting," in which an experienced player keeps track of every card that has been played and extrapolates a census of the cards still remaining in the dealer's deck. If this skill is truly mastered, it is widely believed that a professional gambler can actually shift the odds and beat the house. Of course, the continued prosperity of casinos around the world belies the significance of such skills.

On his third circuit around the casino, Sean spotted Tyrone Freeman swaggering through the main entrance, as two of the pit bosses, as casino supervisors are called, rushed to greet him. Hector had been quite accurate with his information – Tyrone was obviously a beloved regular patron. After a few moments of friendly banter and laughter, the pit bosses subtly began to maneuver the football star toward the back room parlor. Sean maintained a discreet distance, smiling as he recognized the skillful human relations techniques at work. *These guys are shrewd manipulators – they make him feel like the most important man in the world. I wonder how many "most important" customers they have?*

Tyrone entered the high-roller room in the back corner of the casino, which included one blackjack table, one roulette table, and two baccarat tables. He chose the blackjack table, and the dealer greeted him like an old friend, as did the lone player who had been at the table for some time. Sean was not close enough to overhear conversation, but he saw Tyrone lean forward to ask something of the dealer. The dealer gestured with a quick hand signal, and a pit boss was at his side moments later. The pit boss handed Tyrone a pen and a slip of paper, waited as Tyrone scribbled a few marks on it, then retrieved the document from him. Leaving the table as swiftly as he had appeared, the pit-boss was gone for no more than two minutes before returning and handing a smaller slip of paper to the dealer. The dealer initialed the document, slipped it into his cash slot, then pushed a large stack of hundred-dollar chips toward Tyrone. *He plays on markers*, Sean realized, aware of the system all casinos employ to give temporary credit to their valued customers – valued, of course, not for their celebrity status but for their impressive losses.

Sean watched Tyrone play for the better part of an hour, while going through the motions of moving about the casino and occasionally playing a game or two, so he would not attract attention. He was hoping the second player would leave, allowing him a better opportunity to speak to Tyrone with some privacy, but the second man stayed, apparently unable to gain a decisive victory and unwilling to admit defeat.

Finally, Sean decided he could not risk waiting any longer, so he entered the fray. Gliding smoothly through the unguarded entrance to the high-roller area, he knew that if he acted as if he belonged there, he would be welcome. The football player had spread out his chips on a large portion of the table and held his elbows out in an extended posture that effectively claimed the space of the stools nearest him on both sides. The other player was seated in the furthest right position at the semicircular table -- a position selected to assure that he would always receive the first card dealt. Sean pulled up a stool two spaces to Tyrone's left and produced his roll of cash. Counting out forty of the bills, he placed the currency on the table in front of him, pushing it slightly toward the dealer. The dealer picked up the bills, counted them in a mechanical, almost ritualistic manner, then announced aloud "change forty black," denoting the color of hundred-dollar chips as he pushed the stack toward Sean. "Good luck!"

With that, the dealing resumed. Contrary to the previously noted stability of the game, Sean lost his first four hands in a row, two of them due to amateurish mistakes in his strategy. The other players glared at him pointedly, as if his poor performance was somehow shifting the karma of the table against all of them. Even without the disdainful looks of the star linebacker and the unknown gambler, Sean had quite sufficient reason to feel beads of sweat breaking out on his forehead: at five-hundred dollars per hand, he had already lost almost a quarter of his cash in just the first few minutes.

The next time around, Sean was dealt a pair of eights, while the dealer's visible card was a five. Sean knew enough of the game to recognize a classic scenario to "split" his hand. Splitting required that he double his bet, which he had no stomach to do, but he feared that another amateur blunder might provoke the others to quit and leave the table, costing him his chance to speak with Tyrone. Sean pushed five more chips onto the table and asked the dealer for a split. The dealer separated his two eights and dealt another card onto each. To his consternation, the dealer dealt a three onto the first eight, and another eight onto the second. Sean pushed his last two stacks of five chips each onto the table, and asked to have the first hand doubled and the second hand split. The dealer complied, dropping a card face down onto the eight-three combination, then separating the new pair of eights and dealing a new card onto each. The first was another three, while the other was an ace. The conventions of blackjack required that he double each of these new combinations as well, so he pulled ten more bills from his pocket and dropped them on the table. After converting the cash into chips, the dealer proceeded. *Three thousand dollars!* Sean realized how much he had just bet on this one hand. If he lost, he would be in real danger of losing his entire stash.

The premise upon which the splits and doubles had been made related to the frequency of cards in the deck with values of ten, or close to ten. In the circumstances which had presented themselves, such high-value cards would be quite beneficial to each of Sean's hands, while a ten in either the dealer's hold card or his draw would almost certainly spell doom for the house. The dealer turned over his hold card. It was a six. *Oh, shit! If he draws a ten now, he's got twenty-one!* Sean felt the clamminess of his palms, and could barely stand to watch the dealer draw the next card. It was another five. *Thank God! Now he's got sixteen. He's got to draw, and he'll almost certainly bust!* The dealer drew again – a four. The dealer had twenty. *Oh my God! Have I just lost three thousand dollars?*

Sean watched as the dealer first turned over the hidden card of the unknown player. The man had eighteen, and the dealer swept away his bet. Next, the dealer turned Tyrone Freeman's hold card, revealing a sum of twenty. "Push," the dealer announced, rapping the top of Tyrone's chips with his knuckles, but leaving them in place. Finally, he came to Sean's triple hand, revealing each one in turn. Eight-three-queen. Eight-ace-ace. Eight-three-ten. Sean had pushed on one hand and won the other two, with double bets on each. The dealer pushed a stack of twenty black chips toward him, announcing "twenty black out."

Tyrone Freeman leaned over, slapped Sean jovially on the back with his huge open palm, and grinned at him. "Nice hit, man! Way to go!" The other player also smiled and flashed a thumbs-up sign to him silently. He had joined the fraternity. He had been accepted as a bona fide member of the high-roller elite. He had won. As play continued over the next forty-five minutes, the tide ebbed and flowed several times, with the unknown player taking on the unwelcome role of biggest loser. Finally, he cashed in his remaining chips, dropped a hundred-dollar tip on the table for the dealer, shook Tyrone's hand heartily, and wished Sean good luck as he left. After two more hands, Sean sensed that his moment had arrived, so he leaned over as near the linebacker as he could, cupping a hand over his mouth to prevent the dealer from hearing him. "Tyrone. I'm Sean McInness with the San Francisco Star-Reporter. Your life is in danger. Please meet me at La Mallorquina in an hour."

Sean detected a brief tensing of the star player's muscles as the unwelcome message registered but, outwardly, he showed no hint of recognition – continuing to play several more hands as if nothing had happened. Sean decided there was nothing more to do but hope the athlete would respond to his plea. Asking to be cashed out, Sean was stunned when the dealer totaled his chips. "One hundred eighteen black going out," the dealer announced. Sean had won nearly seven thousand dollars, bringing his cash total to fifteen thousand and change! After dropping three black chips on the table for the dealer, he hesitated briefly, hoping Tyrone Freeman would give some sort of signal of his intentions, but the football star kept his eyes focused on the dealer, refusing to acknowledge Sean's presence in any way. Sean turned and left, catching a last glimpse of Tyrone playing another hand as he walked toward the casino exit.

Sean arrived at La Mallorquina a few minutes before seven, after making a quick stop at the El Canario to stash the bulk of his winnings, and found the Maitre d' he had spoken to the previous day. The man greeted him enthusiastically, exclaiming that the best table in the house was waiting for him. Sean was escorted to a meticulously set table in the rear of the restaurant, a bottle of La Rioja Alta Gran Reserva centered next to a hand-painted candleholder. Sean thanked the Maitre d' and asked if he was familiar with Tyrone Freeman.

"Si! Si! Of course. Señor Freeman lives on the island for several summers now. He has been to La Mallorquina many times!"

"Good, I'm expecting him to meet me here. Please be sure that he finds his way to my table if, or when, he arrives."

"Of course, Señor Califano!"

Sean waited until nearly nine, politely turning away several visits by the waiter. He was preparing to settle his tab and leave when the Maitre d' appeared, escorting Tyrone Freeman, whose large frame seemed even more impressive when standing next to the restaurant's petite tables and chairs. After seating the new arrival, the Maitre d' handed each of them a menu, and asked if he could bring them a drink. Tyrone answered before Sean had a chance, with a smooth graciousness that seemed almost comical juxtaposed against his imposing physical presence.

"No thank you – the wine will be fine. I'm certain it's an excellent vintage."

The Maitre d' smiled, nodding his head approvingly, then signaled the waiter with another quick nod. The server walked crisply to the table, decanted the wine into two glasses, then replaced the bottle on the table, leaving as briskly as he had arrived. Turning to face Sean for the first time, the cordial smile and gracious demeanor instantly disappeared from Tyrone Freeman's face. "What the fuck was that all about at the casino? What do you mean my life is in danger? If this is some bullshit game to get an interview, I'm in a mood to fuck someone up, ya dig? I dropped twenty G's after you left."

Sean took a deep breath, hesitated for a moment, then began his story. Starting with the suspicions he had first felt following Jackhammer's crash and his bedside visit with LaTanya, Sean recounted everything that had happened since. It was a tale of shootings, police frame-ups, crimes of passion, kidnappings, and seamlessly choreographed escapes, buttressed with a healthy dose of rumor and innuendo. As he narrated the chronology of events for his skeptical audience, he realized how incredible it must sound. He finished with an earnest plea for the athlete to take every precaution to assure his own safety, along with a request for any information the star might provide which would explain the link between the five targeted victims on Connor's list.

"There ain't no damn connection," Tyrone replied bluntly. "I've never met Jackhammer or Banks or Hathaway or Vander-horn – or Connor for that matter, ya dig? I really can't see what any of this has to do with me.

"I appreciate your concern for my safety," he continued with a sarcastic edge, "If that's really what this is about, but I think it's all bullshit. If you'll excuse me, I have another meeting I need to get to." With that, the big man rose from his chair and turned to walk away – ignoring Sean's stammered entreaties and providing no acknowledgment as Sean called out to him with the pseudonym under which he was registered at the El Canario.

"Look me up if you change your mind," Sean implored, realizing the futility of the request.

That was it. The meeting was finished. The mission had failed.

Sean remained at La Mallorquina for another hour and a half. He finished the bottle of wine with his meal, then ordered his trademark gin and tonic. Then another. He was at a complete loss, and couldn't think of any way to get ahead of the story and get out of harm's way. All he could do was rehash the evening's conversation in his head again and again, wondering if there was anything he could have said or done differently to persuade the Patriot's star of the veracity and seriousness of his warning. *Coulda, shoulda, woulda* he thought, as the liquor began to exacerbate his frustration. Finally, dropping two hundred dollars on the table to cover a tab of just over half that amount, he staggered into the night air. After walking the mostly quiet streets of Old San Juan for nearly an hour, he caught a cab back to his room.

Meanwhile, at eleven o'clock, Tyrone Freeman was preparing for his second covert meeting of the evening. Although Tyrone's fortune was in the tens of millions, he rarely had large sums of cash in his possession. Most of his wealth was tied up in real estate holdings, business investments, mutual funds, and his automobile collection, and most of his financial transactions were conducted by his business manager. Tyrone had found that the fickle tides of luck at the blackjack table sometimes left him needing more cash than the meager "allowance" his manager provided for him. Thus, as a convenience, he made a regular habit of dealing with a local loan shark – sometimes borrowing ten, twenty, or even fifty thousand dollars, to be repaid from future winnings or from his next cash disbursement, whichever came first.

Tonight, he was to meet his regular "financier," Miguel, to repay a prior debt of fifty thousand, but he was a little short of the full amount following the afternoon's losses. *No problem,* he consoled himself. *Miguel knows I'm good for it.* In addition, he reasoned, his bodyguard, Leo, always sets up these meetings and always accompanies him for security. Donning his favorite leather jacket, which was a bit out of season for a tropical summer evening, he saw that it was time, and signaled to Leo to accompany him down the elevator and out into the Puerto Rican night.

The regular meeting place was just a short walk from his penthouse apartment at the end of Paseo Don Juan, a short frontage road that ran parallel to the water's edge. There was a low concrete wall along the ocean side of the road, where the earth dropped precipitously down a rocky twenty-foot embankment to the crashing surf below. At this time of night, the roadway and the surrounding beaches were deserted and all but a few lights in the nearby buildings were dark. Tyrone and Leo strolled up the slight incline of Paseo Don Juan together, but as they neared the regular rendezvous point, Leo fumbled with a cigarette lighter that had apparently spent its fuel.

"Damn cheap-ass Bic!" Leo cursed, his Philadelphia accent enhanced by the irritation in his voice. "I just bought the damn thing this week. Lemme run back to the garage an' use the limo's lighter. I'll be right back. You'll be aiight – it's only Miguel. He's cool."

Tyrone nodded his agreement, and Leo took off in a half trot back toward the Olympic Tower complex at the far end of the road. Tyrone leaned against the concrete railing, looking out at the nighttime ocean, the waves sparkling in the light of a nearly full moon. The rhythmic crashing of the surf against the rocks below was punctuated at random intervals by the melodic love-calls of the coqui – tiny tree frogs beloved by this island's people as harbingers of good luck. It was a beautiful night, and Tyrone regretted that he would have to leave his island paradise behind next week to rejoin his teammates in training camp. Suddenly, an unfamiliar voice called his name from behind. Tyrone turned, and seeing a stranger standing across the street, began to speak. "Where's Miguel?"

Without speaking another word, the stranger pulled a forty-five from his waist, aimed directly at Tyrone's chest, and squeezed the trigger four times. The multiple impacts knocked the football star off his feet, sending him reeling backward over the stone barricade. The hit-man stepped swiftly across the street, peering over the edge of the barrier with his gun poised to fire if Tyrone still showed any sign of life. There was no sign of life at all. There was nothing but the crashing surf quickly washing the traces of blood from the nearby rocks.

24

Sean arrived back at the El Canario Inn shortly after eleven-thirty. He was frustrated by the seeming impossibility of his mission to stop Connor's hit list, angry with Tyrone Freeman for his flippant dismissal of Sean's allegations, and drunk. Although Sean was a regular drinker, he rarely crossed the threshold of insobriety as he had tonight. *Bullshit.* Sean pondered the words of the star linebacker, replaying them again and again in his mind. *Five people are dead, a half-dozen others have had their lives torn apart, I've been hunted by professional killers, and I flew a thousand miles to warn him – and all he can say is 'bullshit?' Hell with him!*

Sean felt rage boiling just beneath the surface of his consciousness, and decided spontaneously that it was time to end this mission and go home. Without a minute's hesitation, he picked up the phone by his bed and called his regular airline to book a flight back to San Francisco. Cost was no object, he told the reservationist – he just wanted to get back home as quickly as possible. After only a few moments, the airline representative confirmed Sean on a nine-fifteen departure from Luis Muñoz Marin International Airport, stopping once in Atlanta, and arriving in San Francisco early in the afternoon. Sean pressed his finger to the receiver, then released it and dialed zero for the front desk.

"Buono' noche', El Canario," answered Hector.

"Hector, this is Dean Califano in room two-twelve," Sean announced, smugly self-satisfied that he had remembered to use his alias despite his inebriated condition. "I see you're on one of your night shifts. I'd like a wake-up call for five-thirty and a taxi waiting to take me to the airport at six-thirty. I'll be checking out."

"Checking out so soon?" Hector questioned. "You've only been here three days. I hope you were successful in your meeting with Tyrone Freeman."

"Well, actually, no," Sean replied. "I'm afraid Mr. Freeman has decided to stay right where he is. Thank you for all of your assistance, though. You were a big help."

After hanging up the phone, Sean busily set about packing his things, stuffing crumpled clothes into his suitcase without bothering to fold them. He wanted to be ready to leave on time in the morning. Satisfied that he was fully packed, except for the clothes and toiletries he would need in the morning, Sean pulled down the covers on his bed, switched off the overhead light and bedside lamp, and glanced at the clock-radio as he turned in for the night. It was twelve-thirty. *Not bad. I got my reservations and packed in exactly one hour.*

Sean fell almost immediately into a deep, alcohol-enhanced sleep and had been unconscious for little more than an hour when he was suddenly awakened by a loud banging on his door. As his mind grudgingly came fully awake, he realized there was a voice accompanying the persistent knocking.

"Señor Califano! Wake-up! Señor Califano, it's me, Hector. Wake up, please!"

Stumbling out of bed, Sean found his way to the door, pausing to respond before unlatching it. "What is it, Hector? It's almost two in the morning! What do you want?"

"Señor Califano, you have a visitor. I think you need to speak with him urgently."

A visitor? Too drunk and sleepy to remember his own security precautions regarding unwelcome guests, Sean unlatched the door without asking the visitor's identity. He squinted as the bright light from the hallway temporarily blinded him, then saw Hector standing in front of him, a peculiar nervous smile on his face. Behind Hector stood the imposing presence of Tyrone Freeman, his clothing tattered and covered with sand and mud. Blood was streaming from deep abrasions on his head and left arm. Sean stood silently, at a complete loss to understand why Tyrone was there or what would account for his brutalized appearance. Finally, all he could think to say was "What happened?"

"I think we should come inside, Señor Califano," Hector said, not waiting for a reply as he reached back and put his hand on the big man's shoulder, gesturing for him to step into Sean's room.

Sean nodded his assent as he stepped out of the way, and Hector followed Tyrone into the room, looking down the corridor to be sure they had not been seen before closing and latching the door behind them.

"What happened?" Sean repeated, more lucidly this time.

"You were right," Tyrone answered. "They tried to kill me tonight."

"What do you mean?" Sean asked, incredulous. "Who tried to kill you? Tell me exactly what happened."

"I don't know who it was – I've never seen the face before, ya dig? But someone shot me four times in the chest just a couple of hours ago, and I know I was set up by my bodyguard."

"Wait a minute, wait a minute!" Sean interrupted, shaking his head and unconsciously forming a "time-out" signal with his hands. "Back up. What do you mean someone shot you in the chest four times? You look bad, but not that bad!"

"Oh, right," Tyrone nodded his understanding of Sean's confusion, as he unzipped his leather jacket and revealed a thick kevlar vest underneath. "I was wearing my vest. It saved my life, ya dig, but it damn sure doesn't stop the pain – I think I have a couple of cracked ribs."

Sean found himself sliding even further into non-comprehension. "I don't understand. Why were you wearing a bulletproof vest? Why don't you start from the beginning and tell me everything that happened."

"Okay, okay," Tyrone agreed, signaling a concerned glance with his eyes toward Hector.

"Oh, he's all right," Sean answered the unspoken question. "I think it may be the right time for him to get up to speed on the real purpose of my meeting with you."

Now it was Hector's turn to give Sean a questioning glance. Turning to Hector, Sean gave him a brief synopsis of the truth. "I'm not really a talent scout. I'm a sports reporter from San Francisco, and I've uncovered some kind of conspiracy behind the death of Jackhammer Hamilton, the altercation between Cassius Banks and Hat Trick Hathaway, and the arrest of Mack

Vanderhorn. I came to San Juan to warn Tyrone that he appeared to be next on the hit list."

"What hit list?" Hector asked, his jaw dropped wide in disbelief.

"It's a long story, and we don't have time right now," Sean replied. Then, turning to Tyrone, he prompted the football player to continue. "Please, tell us what happened tonight, just since I saw you at La Mallorquina."

"Okay. I told you I thought your conspiracy story was bullshit, but that was just a front. Truth is, I've had suspicions for some time, ya dig? You know, the press plays me as some dumb jock who was just lucky enough to be big and fast. I guess I play into that image when it suits me, but I'd like to think I'm a serious player in the business world as well. I have six people on my payroll—an agent, a trainer, a bodyguard who drives my limo, an accountant, a housekeeper, and my personal assistant – but I don't just turn my life over to them. I keep track of every decision made and every dime spent.

"Over the past six or eight weeks, I've suspected something was up with my bodyguard, Leo. He's been spending a lot of money all of a sudden – a lot more than I pay him, ya dig? There's been a brand new Lexus, a Rolex, and lots of top rack clothes. Then, I noticed some unusual calls on the cell-phone bill – several calls to one number in New Orleans. I checked it out and found out it was Connor Enterprises. I figured Connor was paying Leo for some kind of information, or perhaps acting as an intermediary to persuade me to accept an offer from the Saints. When you told me Connor had me on a list with Jackhammer, Banks, Hat Trick and Vanderhorn, I knew some serious shit was going down, ya dig? That's when I decided to wear my vest.

"I was supposed to meet up with Miguel, my financier, at eleven o'clock. Leo was with me, but excused himself at the last minute. Then, someone I don't know called my name and shot me as soon as I turned around. Damn forty-five knocked me right off my feet, ya dig, and I fell over a concrete wall, then rolled about twenty feet down the rocks – I guess one thing I've learned in the NFL is how to duck, cover, and roll. Luckily, there was a little indentation in the rocks right at the water line, and I rolled up underneath where the shooter couldn't see me from above.

"Then I heard Leo running back up the street. I thought he was coming to back me up, and I hoped he would get his piece out before the shooter turned and fired on him, but when he reached the scene, he just asked, 'Is it done?' Then he stood there and talked with the shooter like they were old friends. The shooter told Leo he had got me clean in the chest, and that he thought my body had washed out in the undertow immediately. Then Leo told him they were to meet at the statue of Louis Armstrong in New Orleans at ten o'clock this Saturday night to get the rest of their payoff. God damn punk-ass schemer! I'll break his back if I ever see him again! I must have passed out after that, from this bump on my head. When I came to, I crept along the beach until I was out of sight from my building, then came here to find you – lucky I remembered that fake-ass name you said you were using."

Sean listened in awe to Tyrone's amazing story, trying to think what they should do next. Hector, also in stunned silence, looked back and forth from Sean to Tyrone, his jaw still hanging open. After finishing his tale, Tyrone glanced down at his arm as if noticing his wounds for the first time, and asked Sean, "I really need to use your shower. You got any bandages?"

"Yeah, uh, no," Sean rambled, trying to answer the football player's immediate request without losing his train of thought on the larger issues. "Please, feel free to use the shower – there are plenty of towels. Hector, do you have any medical supplies?"

"Si, we have a first aid kit in the office," Hector replied.

"Good. Please get some bandages and aspirin for Mr. Freeman. And do you happen to personally know any shopkeepers in San Juan who would have some clothes in Mr. Freeman's size?"

"Si, Señor Califano, but the shops are all closed at this time of night."

"Of course, but if you can contact someone personally, tell them I will pay a thousand dollars cash to have two sets of clothes delivered here within the hour – one casual – shorts and sneakers, the other a bit dressier – slacks and shoes. Do you think you can do that?"

"Si, I think so."

"Tyrone," Sean half-shouted, so the football player in the next room could hear him. "Tell Hector all your sizes."

"Yeah, okay," Tyrone responded, as Hector scrambled to jot the answers down on a notepad by the telephone. "Thirty-six waist, thirty-eight inseam, eighteen and a half neck, and forty-eight chest. Size twelve shoes – a size larger for sneakers so I can double up on the socks."

"You got all that?" Sean asked, continuing when Hector nodded affirmatively. "If a thousand isn't enough, I can go up to two. You negotiate a reasonable deal, but just get the clothes here within an hour. Can you do it?"

"Si!"

"Make the calls first, then bring us back the bandages," Sean instructed. "And, Hector, thanks for all your help."

"De nada. No problem, Señor, I'll get right on it."

With that, Hector flew out the door. After a few minutes, Tyrone emerged from the bathroom, one towel draped around his waist, and another wrapped tightly around his left arm. He was pressing a third towel against the cuts on his forehead, and four dark bruises were clearly visible on the milk-chocolate colored skin of his chest. "What's next in the playbook?" he asked Sean as he took a seat in one of the wicker chairs.

"We've got to get you off this island, and we have to make sure no one else knows you're still alive. If they know you survived, they'll come for you again – I've already learned that lesson once. We have to get back to New Orleans in time for that meeting Saturday night – it's our one chance to catch these guys red-handed. We can't fly out without revealing your identity, not to mention the possibility that they may be watching for me at the airport. Do you know anyone with a boat – someone you know you can trust?"

"Yeah, I do," Tyrone answered. "I can call my home-boy Marcus. He's the architect who hooked up my penthouse when I first bought the place in ninety-seven. He did a damn-good job on it, too, ya dig? We've done some deep sea fishing and snorkeling the past few summers. I'm pretty sure he invites me out on his boat because he gets off on seeing me in my Speedos, if you know what I mean, but that's cool. He knows where I stand, and all we do on the boat is chill, so it's all good. You'd be surprised how many of the players, trainers, and crews in the NFL are gay, ya dig, so it doesn't bother me."

"Okay, call your friend Marcus, and tell him you need to get off this island as soon as possible. If I remember my geography, the Virgin Islands are just east of Puerto Rico and the Dominican Republic just to the west. I guess the Virgin Islands would be a better bet – at least they're American territory. Tell you friend we need to get to the Virgin Islands as fast as his boat will take us."

(25)

Tyrone called his boating friend, Marcus, from the phone in Sean's room and, after apologizing for the late hour of the call, explained the situation as concisely as he could. After telling his story, he listened intently, occasionally interjecting an "okay" or "right." Then he thanked Marcus and hung up the phone, turning to speak to Sean.

"He'll do it. But he says we can't come down to the marina by his crib at Laguna del Condado – the place is crawling with Coast Guard, DEA, and the local press after some big drug bust earlier this evening, ya dig? He says the only way to get me off the island unseen is to meet at a small dock he knows in La Perla."

"Where's La Perla?" Sean asked.

"La Perla – The Pearl. It's the barrio on the north shore of Old San Juan," Tyrone explained. "There's a wall the Spanish built running all the way around Old San Juan. La Perla sits on a narrow strip of beach outside the wall, completely cut off from the rest of the city, except for one entrance through a narrow stone gate. They call it the prettiest slum in the world, but it's also got a reputation as one of the most dangerous places on Earth. The local police long ago gave up on controlling the area – coming through that gate is a set-up, ya dig? It's pretty much a no-man's land of gangs, drugs, violence, and lawlessness – kinda like those 'Escape From New York and LA' movies."

"And we have to go through this hell on earth to get on your friend's boat?" Sean asked, feeling the now-familiar queasiness gripping his stomach again.

"Yeah, but we'll synchronize our timing so we get in and get out quickly."

Hector had dropped off the bandages while Tyrone was on the phone, but had not yet returned with his new clothing. Tyrone returned to the bathroom to begin wrapping his wounds and Sean suddenly realized that, with the time-zone differential, it was not yet midnight in California. He decided to call Z to update him on the situation. Dialing the area code and number directly so it would be charged to the room of one Dean N. Califano, Sean listened as the phone rang four times. On the fifth ring, a sleepy voice answered.

"Hello?"

"Hello, Vikki? This is Sean. Sorry to wake you."

"That's okay. Are you all right?" Vikki asked, the sincerity of her concern undisguised by her drowsiness.

"Yeah, I'm fine. Is everything okay out there in The City?"

"Everything's fine here. Your friends have been no trouble at all. I guess you're calling to talk to them?"

"Yeah, could you put Z on the line?"

"Sure, hold on a minute."

After a brief silence, Z picked up the phone. "Aye yo! Wuzzup?"

"How's everything out there?" Sean asked, choosing to bypass Z's inquiry for the moment. "Any sign of trouble?"

"Nah. As far as I can tell, no one knows where we are."

"Good. And is everything working out okay with Lori and Vikki?"

"F'shiggity! That Vikki can really cook, ya heard me? You know she's got her own caterin' business? An' last night they took us out fo' sushi when we told 'em none of us had tried it befo'. I gotta admit I always thought sushi sounded nasty, but that hot green sauce was kickin'!"

"Oh, you mean the wasabi?"

"Yeah, I guess that's what it's called. We went by this place where the sushi floats right past you in l'il boats, so you jus' grab what you want. By the time we finished, I had 'bout twenty of those l'il plates piled up in front of me!"

"And," Sean paused, "What about your mom. Is she handling everything okay?"

"Oh, yeah, 'bout that. The first night we were here, Momma jus' stayed in her room – said she wanted to catch up on her readin', an' she tried to press me an' Kenyetta to do the same. But by mornin' I guess she'd thought things through, ya heard, that Lori an' Vikki were cool wit' lettin' us come an' stay wit' 'em. She really warmed up an' started askin' a lotta questions 'bout their life. When they told her none of their parents had ever come to visit the baby, that seemed to really bother her. Since then, she's been playin' wit' l'il Ashley 'most non-stop, ya heard me? Kenyetta ribbed her befo' she went to bed tonight an' told her she'd best be careful not to get too attached, 'cause we're only stayin' a few days. Then Momma said 'that l'il girl is gonna be so mixed up wit' two mommas, she jus' might as well have a black gramma, too!'"

"Good," Sean answered, both amused and relieved by Z's recounting of their California exile. "It sounds like everything is going well. What about my car – you haven't wrecked it yet have you?"

"Oh, yeah, I was gonna ask you 'bout that. Does it always make that metallic screechin' sound when you shift gears?"

"What screeching sound?" Sean demanded, his voice shrill with alarm.

"Psyche!" Z retorted. "Ha! Ha! Yo' car's fine, Whodi. Chill!"

"Veeery funny!" Sean laughed. "Okay, it's time to get serious, so listen. A lot has happened out here – they tried to kill Tyrone Freeman tonight, but he escaped. He's with me now, and we're getting off the island in about an hour. I'll be on a boat to the Virgin Islands, and from there I'm going to try to charter a plane back to the Gulf Coast. I don't have a map with me, now, so off the top of your head, do you know the nearest major airport outside New Orleans?"

"I guess that'd be Mobile."

"Okay. I'm going to leave a message for my boss, Lillian Kramer, on her voice mail. I'll ask her to book you on the first plane she can to Mobile. I don't think it would be safe to fly back into New Orleans – they might be watching the airport for us. When you get to Mobile, stash your luggage in an airport locker, then find your way to the main public library. Find a good book and settle in. I don't know exactly how I'm going to get there or how long it'll take me, but I'll find you there as soon as I can. I'll ask my boss to front you some cash, so you'll have money to eat."

"What's our next move?" Z inquired.

"Something big's going down in Armstrong Park on Saturday night and we need to be there. I'll fill you in when I see you in Mobile. We'll need to get in touch with Cool, Roderick, and Dewayne before we get to New Orleans, but don't call them yet. I want to keep this under wraps as long as possible – at least until I get Tyrone out of harm's way."

Hector returned at that moment, announcing his presence with a soft knock on the door before letting himself in. Sean ended his call to Z, then turned to see what Hector had been able to come up with. There were two pairs of shoes – one pair of size thirteen Nikes and a pair of Italian designer shoes a size smaller, along with an armful of clothing. Hector and his merchant friend had also provided boxers, socks, a belt, a tie, and even a leather duffel bag – all items Sean had neglected to order. Nodding approvingly at the selection as Tyrone reentered the room to view his new wardrobe, Sean asked Hector what the total tab would be.

"My friend is very reasonable, Señor Califano. The regular price on these items would come to just under eleven hundred dollars. He only asks two hundred more for the late-night service, as a personal favor to me."

"That's reasonable," Sean agreed. "I'm going to leave you an even two thousand to cover the clothes, my last two nights here, and any incidental charges. Whatever's left over is yours to keep. You've been worth your weight in gold to us tonight. I must ask you for two more favors. First, we need a cab to La Perla right away. Second, I need you to use your very best judgment about what you've seen tonight. If anything should happen to either of us, I want you to contact the authorities as quickly as possible and tell them everything you know. But if anyone else comes snooping around, you must forget that Tyrone Freeman was ever here."

"I understand perfectly, Señor, and you have my word. Just one small problem – you will never find a cab to take you into La Perla."

"Can the cab drop us just outside the area?"

"That is also a very bad idea, Señor," Hector advised. "You don't want those chulo thugs in La Perla to see you stepping out of a cab before you walk through the gates. Very bad idea. You should have the cab drop you a few blocks over the hill, perhaps at Calle Tanca and San Sebastian."

"Then that's what we'll do. Tyrone, let's get that boat rolling."

Tyrone called his friend Marcus, who reiterated the precise location of the dock where they were to meet and agreed upon a rendezvous time of three forty-five. Hector excused himself to call a cab from his office phone, Sean scooped his remaining personal items into his luggage, and Tyrone dressed in the shorts and sneakers, folding the remaining items neatly into the duffel. By the time they got down to the front entrance, their cab was waiting in the drive. Hector met them at the door, signaling to the cab to wait while he pulled Sean aside for a short private conversation.

"Señor Califano," Hector began, as he pressed a snub-nosed thirty-eight caliber revolver into Sean's hand. "Or whatever your real name is, take this. You need it more than I do – no one is going to rob El Canario tonight."

"This must be worth several hundred," Sean objected. "Here, let me pay you for it."

"No, no, you have been most generous already," Hector insisted as he reached out to grab Sean's hand, preventing him from removing the money roll from his pocket. "If I can help Tyrone Freeman escape whatever trouble he is in, that will be reward enough. Just ask him to send an autographed football for my nephew, José."

Sean was sincerely touched by the extraordinarily generous and trusting gesture from a near stranger. After thanking Hector again for all of his help over the past two days, Sean stepped into the cab where Tyrone was already scrunched in a rather uncomfortable looking position in the back seat. With a wave, they were off, thirty minutes ahead of their planned embarkation from the dock in La Perla.

The cab dropped them at the corner Hector had suggested and they walked up a steep incline toward the crest of the hill, their footsteps echoing eerily on the deserted street. As they came over the hill, they could survey all of La Perla in one panoramic view.

At the foot of the hill, one block to their right, was the entryway, a narrow graffiti-lined drive barely wide enough for a single car to pass, terminating under an ancient stone archway which opened onto a small plaza. To the left, past several blocks of two and three-level tenements whose pastel colors glowed eerily in the moonlight, they could see the dock that was their ultimate destination. La Perla was menacingly dark, with no lights visible anywhere along the narrow strip of land. It seemed at first glance to be utterly devoid of human habitation. Upon closer inspection, however, they could see a small crowd loitering against the walls in the plaza, some concealed in the shadows, while others revealed their presence with the glowing embers of cigarettes and joints.

Sean and Tyrone exchanged a glance, then both checked their watches. It was three thirty-five, and their boat was due in ten minutes. They nodded their silent agreement that it was time to go and began walking swiftly down the hill toward the entry corridor. As they passed under the gate and into the forbidden plaza, the voices began almost immediately – calling out greetings and taunts from a half dozen hidden recesses in the aged and crumbling structures that surrounded them.

"Oye, 'mano, que pasa?"

"Hey! What you buyin'? I got the best, man!"

"Oye, Norte Americano, ven aca un momento."

"What you got in the suitcases, homies? Let me take a look!"

"Foquin touristas! You got credit cards?"

"Give up those Nikes o te rompo el coco!"

"Hey, I'm talkin' to you!"

Sean and Tyrone walked swiftly through the plaza and continued along the main road that ran parallel to the beach. Aware that several of their shadowy taunters were following not far behind, Sean felt the salty sting of sweat dripping into his eyes. He gripped the strap of his bag tightly with his left hand, securing it over his shoulder, while using his right hand to first press his money roll as deeply into his pocket as he could, then to finger the butt of the revolver which was snugly residing in his waist band. *I've got over thirteen thousand dollars cash on me and we're about to get jumped in the heart of the barrio. Oh, shit!*

As they approached the dock, Sean glanced at his watch again. Three-forty-three. *Where's the damn boat?* Sean and Tyrone stepped out onto the dock and exchanged a knowing look, as they were both well aware that they had walked directly into an indefensible dead end. Continuing out to the very end of the dock, trying to place as much distance as they could between themselves and their pursuers, they both set their bags down and turned to face the inevitable.

Tyrone spoke for the first time since leaving the cab. "I know a little boricua slang. Let me do the talking."

"Sure," Sean replied. "But if it comes down to it, I've got a thirty-eight. Where the hell is your friend?"

Before Tyrone could answer, the crowd of young thugs emerged from the shadows, approaching the end of the dock. One, who appeared to be the defacto leader, stepped forward and began to speak, the switchblade in his right hand catching the reflected light of the moon and sparkling as he twirled it deftly in his palm.

"Que pasa? What you touristas doin' in La Perla? You lost? This is *my* barrio, *my* ciudad! Nobody walks through my plaza without payin' the toll!"

Just as the leader took a first, tentative step onto the far end of the dock, Sean thought he heard the high-pitched buzz of a boat engine. Taking his eyes off the provocateur briefly, he glanced over his right shoulder and saw the red, white, and green lights of a large boat heading directly toward them. The young men on the shore spotted the boat at about the same moment and scattered instantly into the darkness, apparently fearing that the boat belonged to the Coast Guard, DEA, or some other law enforcement agency.

Sean and Tyrone both understood the reason for their attackers' retreat and equally understood that the hoodlums would regroup and renew their assault as soon as they realized the approaching boat was a private vessel. As Marcus' yacht came clearly into view, Tyrone began signaling for him to approach at full speed until the last possible moment, his frantic and exaggerated hand gestures taking on an almost choreographed rhythm. For a moment, Sean feared that the yacht was going to ram the dock, but when it was just a few dozen yards away, Tyrone's friend Marcus skillfully turned his rudder and threw his left engine into full reverse. A roiling white wake surged past them as the back of the boat swung around and slammed into the dock, the impact sending a creaking shudder along the length of the wooden structure and nearly knocking Sean and Tyrone off their feet. Without hesitation, they each threw their bags onto the boat then took a running jump on board, as Tyrone shouted, "Go! Jam it, man, jam it!"

The engine revved to a deafening level and, after a short pause as it gained enough thrust to overcome seven tons of inertia, the boat finally began to accelerate into the open sea. When they were a few hundred yards from shore, Marcus finally slowed the acceleration to a more sustainable pace. They could hear fading shouts from the dock behind them, just audible over the reduced engine noise. "Man, are we glad to see you, Marcus!" the football star asserted. "I've tackled some rough characters in the NFL, but they usually don't come after me with knives!"

Marcus was a pleasant looking man in his early thirties who stood an inch or so taller than Sean, with very dark skin and short cropped black hair. He turned to look over his shoulder at the two evacuees sitting against the railings in the back of his boat, and announced the bad news. "Yeah, well, you boys better hang on – it's going to be a rough ride. They just upgraded tropical storm Bella to hurricane and she's slamming Guadalupe and Dominica right now. We'll be lucky to get into San Thomas ahead of her. I hope you both know how to swim."

Sean could think of only one response. "You've got to be kidding!"

(26)

Tyrone collapsed almost immediately from the exhaustion of his ordeal, so Sean was left on his own to plan the next phase of their escape. He quickly realized that, if reaching the Virgin Islands by sea was going to be a problem, getting off the islands by air would be an even bigger one. If they didn't get off before the approaching storm, they could be stranded for days in Bella's aftermath. Sean walked to the cockpit, reaching out one hand to greet Marcus while steadying himself against a railing with the other.

"Hello!" he announced, speaking loudly to compensate for the engine noise and the rhythmic crashing of surf against the hull. "I'm Sean. I know Tyrone filled you in on our predicament. You're a real life-saver – coming out in the middle of the night to rescue us like this."

"Don't mention it," Marcus answered, keeping both hands on his wheel but turning his head to look at Sean. "Tyrone and I go back several years. He's easily my most valuable client and he let a couple of trade journals do photo spreads of the work I did in his condo – did wonders for my career. We've become real friends these past few summers, so I wouldn't hesitate to drop everything if he needs help. He's really a good person, you know. The public sees the tough linebacker and the press sees the gambling, but those of us who know him personally know how much of his money he gives to worthwhile causes, and how much of his time he gives, as well. If I can help him out of a jam, it's a privilege."

"Well, you helped us both out, and we really appreciate it. Listen, we've got to get off San Thomas ahead of the storm – we desperately need to get back to the mainland, and we can't take regular airlines. Do you happen to know any private pilots on the island?"

"As a matter of fact, I do. Bob Green. He's done some aerial survey work for a couple of development projects I've been involved with. Good man. He's sort of a jack of all trades; he'll take any flying assignment as long as the money's good."

"How much do you think he'd charge to put us down somewhere in the vicinity of Mobile, Alabama?"

"I really don't know," Marcus answered, scratching his temple reflexively. "His work for me was billed on an hourly basis. But if you're talking about flying in under radar and evading U.S. Customs, I'm sure that'll cost you plenty."

"Do you have any way to contact him?"

"I think I have an old number in my card file below deck. I can take a look and try to call him on my cell phone before we get too far from shore. You ever drive a boat before?"

"No," Sean answered, surprised by the question.

"Here, take the helm," Marcus commanded, releasing his grip on the wheel and gesturing for Sean to take over. "There's really only one rule out here on the open sea: don't hit anything!" With that, the boat's captain stepped forward and opened a small door leading down into the cabin, disappearing behind the door as it swung closed. Sean glanced over the controls and quickly spotted a compass, indicating that they were traveling almost due east. The throttle was set at three-quarters full and the speedometer showed that they were cruising at a little over twenty knots. As he continued to survey the craft's cockpit, he was impressed with the variety and technological sophistication of the instrumentation. There was a Global Positioning Satellite transmitter/receiver into which Marcus had programmed their "way point," or destination; there was a radar, a depth indicator, and both VHF and Ham radios; there was a gas fume detector and a fully automatic halon fire extinguishing system; and finally there were a variety of status gauges, controls, and warning lights for the twin diesel engines. It was all very interesting, but he reminded himself that he really only needed to know one thing. *Don't hit anything.*

Focusing his attention on the view ahead, he found the experience exhilarating. The sky was partly cloudy, as the leading edge of the massive Caribbean storm was just beginning to reach them. The moon shone brilliantly over his right shoulder, only occasionally obscured by a passing cloud, and cast a bright glade across the rippling waters. The boat rocked in a steady rhythm as it bounded over the crests of waves approaching at a forty-five degree angle. Each time the bow crashed into the water it sent a fresh cloud of sea spray into the windowless cockpit, stinging Sean's face like an aftershave and leaving a salty taste on his lips. He had been at the helm for ten or fifteen minutes and was just beginning to feel comfortable with the role, when Marcus emerged from the cabin.

"You're in luck, or at least partly so," the ship's owner announced. "I got through to Bob, and he's available to take you to the mainland, but he say's we're going to be cutting it pretty close. The forecasters are predicting gale force winds on the island an hour or two after sunrise, which would close all the airports. We need to put this boat of mine to the test and see what she can do."

With that, he took over the helm from Sean, checked and adjusted several of the indicator dials, then pushed the throttle forward to seven-eighths. The engine roared at a noticeably higher pitch, and Sean had to grab a nearby railing as the boat accelerated rapidly up to thirty knots. Realizing that Marcus needed to concentrate on captaining his vessel, Sean returned to the stern, where Tyrone had fallen sound asleep with his head and shoulders propped against the starboard railing. Sitting down across from the football player, Sean began planning the next phase of their mission, back in New Orleans, but the rocking of the boat soon lulled him to sleep as well.

He awoke with a start as a large volume of water splashed his face. The waves were nearly twice as high as they had been when he left the boat's cockpit, some of the crests reaching twelve to fifteen feet. The sky was completely overcast, the wind whistled dramatically overhead, and it was beginning to rain lightly. Sean crawled across the boat to shake Tyrone awake and shouted that they should go forward to the cockpit. Tyrone nodded and they both crept forward cautiously on their hands and knees, dragging their baggage and slipping precariously on the wet surface as the boat rocked wildly in the waves. When they reached the cockpit, they could see that Marcus was struggling with the wheel, only occasionally releasing his grip with one hand to make a quick adjustment to one of the engine controls or trim tabs. Sean noticed that Marcus had unrolled a clear vinyl windshield and pushed the throttle all the way to full.

"We're about an hour from San Thomas," Marcus shouted, most of his voice lost to the wind and engine noise. "It's getting pretty rough out here. I think you two better go below."

"Is there anything I can do to help?" Tyrone shouted back.

"No. This boat's really a one-man show and I know her like the back of my hand. If she's going to make it, she'll do it for me. You'll find life vests in the locker by the door – I suggest you put them on and take a look around to familiarize yourself with the inflatable and the rest of the survival gear you find down there. I have the radio set to the universal hailing channel, in case we need to put out a distress call."

"Is it really that bad?" Sean asked, already knowing the answer.

"This is going to be about the worst weather I've ever navigated. I think we'll get through it okay, but we'd be wise to be prepared for anything."

Sean and Tyrone followed their captain's instructions, going below deck and taking a few minutes to look in all the cabinets and pinpoint the locations of flashlights, waterproof rations, ponchos, and other potentially crucial items. After they had conducted their inventory of the boat's emergency equipment, they both donned life vests and took seats facing each other. As Sean surveyed the cabin's interior, he was amazed by the luxurious accommodations that had been packed into such a small space. The bed and furnishings consisted of gleaming brass frames girdling plush upholstery; there was an entertainment center boasting a color television, VCR, DVD player, stereo, and laptop computer; and there was even a complete vanity with a swivel chair and a mirror encircled with tiny globe light bulbs.

The boat rocked violently, and they both found it necessary to grip their seats firmly to avoid being tossed to the floor. Piloting the boat had been a pleasure a few hours earlier, but Sean could only guess how much strength it must take to hold the wheel steady against such powerful swells. *We're going to owe this Marcus character big time if he gets us to San Thomas in one piece.* After half an hour of violent rocking, with no horizon to steady his gaze, Sean found himself suddenly regretting the evening's excessive indulgences in alcohol. Rising from his seat, he stumbled forward to the boat's tiny lavatory, reaching the

186

plumbing facilities just moments before losing much of the aforementioned liquid refreshments. He never returned to his seat, remaining instead crouched in the lavatory, frequently revisiting that singular error in judgment.

Suddenly the ordeal was over. The rocking almost completely ceased and the boat slowed to a crawl as the engine was throttled down. The door swung open and Marcus shouted down to them. "We're in San Thomas harbor. I've already called in to the Harbor Master to let him know we're coming in, and they've got a slip ready for us. Come on up and you can help me secure her."

"You all right, man?" Tyrone asked as Sean staggered from the lavatory. The intonation of Tyrone's inquiry was serious, but there was just a hint of mirth on his face.

"Yeah, I'm fine. I'll just never drink again, that's all."

Tyrone burst out laughing, as he reached out a hand to steady Sean's ascent up the narrow stairs. "Let me help you up."

Above deck, the view was ominous. The waters were relatively still in the protected portion of the harbor, but just two or three hundred yards behind them Sean could see huge crests of twenty feet or more battering the shoreline. It was not currently raining, but dark clouds boiled menacingly overhead, ready to dump their heavy cargoes of water at any moment. It was approaching eight o'clock in the morning, but still quite dark. The boat pulled gently into it's mooring, and Tyrone jumped onto the dock while barking instructions to Sean. "Throw me that rope! The one there, in front! Yeah, then the one in back."

In just a few seconds, the boat was securely tethered and Marcus emerged from the cockpit. "Hell of a ride!"

"Hell of a good job getting us through that mess," Tyrone responded, with Sean nodding in agreement.

Letting the praise pass, Marcus continued. "You two need to get out of here right away – I think you'll be able to get off the pier unseen if you hurry. They'll be closing the airport any minute. Here," he said, pulling Bob Green's business card from his pocket and handing it to Sean. "Grab a cab at the end of the pier and tell the driver to take you to hangar three at the airport. Bob will be expecting you and should have a flight plan filed for immediate take-off."

"You sure you don't need some help securing the boat?" Tyrone asked.

"No, I've got it. I just need to cinch the tethers on the cleats and pull down the tarps. Go! And good luck."

Sean tossed all the baggage onto the dock, then jumped off the boat. He and Tyrone picked up the totes and dashed toward the end of the pier. Luckily, they found a cab immediately and promised the driver a generous tip for a quick trip to the airport. The streets were all but deserted, as nearly all the island's residents were indoors preparing for the storm, so it took only a few minutes to reach hangar three. Paying the driver, Sean and Tyrone jumped out of the cab, grabbed their luggage from the trunk, and ran to the closed door of the hangar. Sean knocked rapidly.

"Come on in!" a voice shouted from inside. Sean opened the door, and they both stepped inside to find a man sitting behind an antique desk, the surface of which was strewn several inches thick with piles of loose papers. It seemed inconceivable that the man could actually find anything on that desk. The man was in his mid fifties but quite lean and muscular, with a very short haircut that gave a pronounced graininess to his salt and pepper hair color. He looked exactly as one would envision a retired marine drill sergeant.

"You're late. They've announced the airport will be closing at eight-thirty, so we need to get airborne. Now, as I understand it, you two want me to put you down in Mobile or thereabouts, and don't want your ID's checked at Customs. Is that about the size of it?"

"Yes," Sean answered, recognizing the need for brevity.

"Okay, now we're talking about six hours of flight time, plus my return trip. Then there's the risk factor for an unauthorized landing on the mainland, plus the dangerous conditions for takeoff here. I think fifteen thousand should cover it."

Sean did a quick mental calculation, remembering that he had just over thirteen thousand dollars on him. He knew that he would need some of that cash for the remainder of his trip, so he hoped to negotiate the price down to eleven. "Do you give a cash discount?"

A big grin came across Bob Green's face. "Cash discount?" he chuckled. "Cash is the *only* kind of business I do for a deal like this."

Thinking quickly for a way to close the deal, Sean realized he didn't need Bob Greene to get them all the way to Mobile. They only needed to reach the mainland. "How about Miami?" Sean asked. "How much to get us to Miami?"

"Hmmm," the man pondered, appearing to be making some mental calculations of his own. "That cuts the flight time just about in half, and it's a more desirable place for me to put down for a night or two while Bella blows over. On the flip side, a Miami landing increases the risk factor a notch or two – damn DEA watches South Florida like a hawk! I'd say twelve grand. It'll take me a couple of minutes to file a new flight plan, so we need to do it now."

"I've got to hold some cash to get from Miami on to Mobile," Sean bargained. "I can go to eleven."

"Done! Now, I don't ask any questions, but I do insist on searching your luggage. I've got two teenage daughters, so I won't transport drugs. Are either of you packing?"

It took Sean a few seconds to recognize the lingo, then he admitted that he was carrying a thirty-eight revolver.

"I'll keep that locked up until we get to Florida," the pilot demanded. "I don't want some trigger-happy asshole starting a firefight if we get intercepted, and I damn sure don't plan to get hijacked."

Sean surrendered the weapon and Tyrone unzipped their bags. The pilot conducted a quick but professional search, checking for false bottoms and hidden compartments. When he was satisfied that the cargo was innocuous, he returned to his desk, made some quick notes on a chart, then picked up his phone and called in the new flight plan. Replacing the receiver, he rose from his desk and motioned toward the luggage. "Get your gear, we're rolling now."

They rushed out of the hangar, pausing briefly as the pilot padlocked his door. In just the few minutes they had been inside, it had started to rain and the wind had increased markedly. Following the pilot, they ran about fifty yards to a green and white Piper Comanche 250 that was parked at the end of a long row of general aviation aircraft. A number of workers were busily tethering all the aircraft to steel rings imbedded in the tarmac, but they had not yet reached Bob Green's plane. Climbing up on the wing proved moderately challenging, as the steel was wet and slippery. Sean slipped on his first attempt, hitting his elbow hard on the wing's tailing edge, but luckily injuring neither himself nor the aircraft's fragile fuselage. Tyrone gave him an assist on his second try, then handed up the luggage before climbing aboard himself.

The single-engine plane was a four-seater, which was quite cramped when one of the passengers was a linebacker who stood six foot three and weighed in at two hundred thirty pounds. Sean immediately recognized the fortuitousness of his decision to fly only as far as Miami – this was going to be an uncomfortable ride. While they buckled their safety straps, Bob Green ran a quick checklist of his numerous gauges and controls, then radioed the tower for clearance. Sean heard the radio crackling with the reply as the tower announced that they were clear for immediate takeoff on runway one, followed by a warning that the airport would be closing in five minutes.

"It's now or never, boys!" the pilot announced. "Get ready for a wild ride!"

He revved the engine, taxied out to the end of the runway, and stopped momentarily as he made a final check of his engines and navigational readings. Then Sean felt himself sinking deeply into his seat as the plane accelerated rapidly. The Piper swerved precariously as the gusting winds shifted unpredictably. The pilot pulled back on the stick and the nose of the plane came up with a shudder. Airborne, they rocked and swayed violently in the near gale-force winds, with no tire traction to help keep them on a straight course. Within seconds, they were inside the dark clouds and the visibility instantly dropped to zero as the windshield was pelted with heavy rain and pea-sized hailstones. The pilot was turning knobs and flipping switches with his right hand almost too quickly for Sean to follow the actions, and gripping the wheel in his left so tightly that the tendons could be seen tensing the full length of his forearm.

A sudden downdraft caught the plane, and Sean felt himself rising out of his seat as the plane dropped beneath him. He felt nauseous, but was grateful that he had lost the full contents of his stomach back on board the boat.

After what seemed like an eternity of turbulent rocking and swinging inside the dense black cloud layer, the plane popped out above the storm, the brightness of the sun temporarily blinding Sean. The air above the clouds was relatively calm and the plane leveled out into a smooth glide.

"This is your captain speaking!" the pilot announced, turning to look at Sean and Tyrone with a broad smile on his face. "We have reached our cruising altitude and expect to land in the Miami area at approximately twelve noon, local time. Refreshments will not be served on this flight and, in case of emergency, reach beneath your seats, bend your head forward, and kiss your asses goodbye!"

Once the Piper had reached its cruising altitude and left the storm behind, it wasn't long before the monotonous droning of the engine and the gentle swaying of the aircraft lulled Sean into a deep sleep. Tyrone also slept, slouching forward with only his safety belt restraining him from sliding out of his seat. It had been a very long and stressful night, and both of them welcomed the opportunity to rest for a few hours. As they approached the mainland, the pilot skillfully dropped his craft to within a few dozen feet of the ocean's surface, the white crests of the waves rushing beneath them like static lines on an old television set. Years of entrepreneurial piloting had provided Bob Green with comprehensive knowledge of every Coast Guard radar station, DEA facility, and private airstrip along the South Florida coast and he charted a zigzag course around every known obstacle. They crossed land just south of Miami, then curved northward across the suburban portions of Dade County, flying just above treetop level. He put the craft down at a tiny landing strip just outside Hialeah and taxied toward a small hangar at one end.

"This is where you boys get off," he announced, as his two passengers rubbed the sleep from their eyes. "I need to get you off-loaded in a hurry and get airborne again. I filed a flight plan into Fort Lauderdale, with an airspeed that would put me there in half an hour. I've got to retrace my steps to about fifty miles out, then let radar track me back in for my legitimate landing."

Sean and Tyrone gathered their gear and the pilot opened his cockpit lock box, withdrawing Sean's revolver. Taking great care to wipe his own fingerprints from the weapon, he held it out to Sean, dangling it from one outstretched finger. "Here you go," he offered. "Whatever you two are running from, I wish you luck."

Sean and Tyrone slid down the wing and jumped to the ground below. Then, without further delay, the pilot closed the door to the cockpit, turned the aircraft in a tight semi-circle, flashed a thumbs-up sign at them, and roared back down the runway. The two fugitives watched the craft become airborne, reaching an altitude of no more than fifty or sixty feet as it disappeared from view behind a tall stand of coconut palms.

The airstrip was completely abandoned, and they decided it would be wise to leave the area as quickly as possible. Climbing through a large tear in the rusty chain link and barbed wire fence that surrounded the facility, they stepped onto a single lane dirt road and walked about a quarter mile before reaching a highway. The Miami Canal paralleled the road on the far side, carrying both fresh water and commerce between Miami and Lake Okeechobee, fifty miles to the northwest. Sean and Tyrone began walking toward the distant high-rises of Miami, which shimmered like a mirage in the scorching heat of the Florida summer. They crossed under the Florida Turnpike and continued walking for three more miles, during which time each of them lost several pounds of fluid volume as their bodies' cooling systems worked overtime.

When they finally reached a small strip mall in Hialeah Gardens they both dropped their bags and rushed to the self-serve soft-drink dispenser inside a convenience store. Filling the largest sized cups, they guzzled the contents then filled the cups a second time before stepping up to the cashier to pay for the life-saving drinks. Sean asked to borrow a telephone directory, then stepped outside to a payphone attached to the outer wall of the store. He called three rental car agencies before finding one nearby with a full-sized vehicle available. Sean read the address of the store off the front window and the reservationist agreed to send a courtesy car to pick them up. They sat down on their luggage, taking advantage of the store's awning to provide shade, and waited.

The rental agency's driver found them within a few minutes, and after a short drive to the rental office, they completed their transaction and drove off the lot in a black Ford Explorer. It was one of the few vehicles available with enough room for Tyrone to ride or drive comfortably. After a quick stop at a drive-through fast food, they headed North on the Florida Turnpike. It would be a grueling seven hundred miles from Miami to Mobile, so Sean and Tyrone took turns behind the wheel with the cruise control set at seventy-five. The afternoon slowly faded into evening, then to night. Sean was in the driver's seat when they finally crossed the causeway over Mobile Bay and entered the heart of the city. It was almost one o'clock in the morning, and Sean knew the library would be long-closed, but he asked directions and drove past the building just in case Z was waiting out front. He wasn't.

In the rushed planning the night before, Sean had failed to account for the possibility that he would not reach the rendezvous point before closing time, and now he wondered where Z would have gone, alone in a strange city. He found a twenty-four hour service station where he purchased a local city map, and sat quietly pondering the location of the library in relation to the business district. *Which way would Z have gone?* Suddenly, it dawned on him that Z would have called Lori and Vikki – after all, his mother and sister were still staying with them. Sean handed the map to Tyrone and dashed to the pay phone at the edge of the service station's lot, then dialed the codes for a long-distance collect calling service.

Vikki answered before the first ring had finished, and quickly accepted the charges. "Sean?"

"Yeah, this is Sean. Hi, Vikki."

"Hey, everyone, it's Sean!" he could hear her announcing to the rest of the household before she returned to continue speaking to him. "Where have you been? Are you okay? We've all been so worried about you! The last thing we knew, you were on a boat heading for the Virgin Islands. When we heard how hard Bella was hitting the islands this morning, we were very concerned. They're calling it the worst storm in that area since Georges. Then, when you didn't show up in Mobile to meet Zimbabwe, well, let's just say none of us expected to sleep tonight."

"I'm sorry," Sean responded. "I should've called earlier. It's been a really hectic day – we just barely got off San Thomas before they closed the airport, and I've driven all the way from Miami this afternoon. Me and Tyrone Freeman, that is."

"Well it's a relief to hear that you got out before the storm hit," Vikki sighed. "They're saying quite a few people have died, and the pictures on TV look awful."

Changing the subject, Sean got to the point of his call. "So, I gather Zimbabwe has been in touch. Do you know where he is?"

"Yes, he's at the Holiday Inn downtown. Hold on a minute, I have his number here somewhere by the phone." Sean could hear papers rustling as Vikki searched for the scrap of paper with the message from Z, then she returned to the phone and read off both a telephone number and a room. "He said he reserved a second room for you and Mr. Freeman."

"Thanks a lot, Vikki. I guess we'll go find Zimbabwe and get checked in for the night. I'll be in touch – I promise!"

Sean held down the receiver for two seconds after ending his long-distance call to California then dialed the Holiday Inn, asking to have the call put through to Z's room. Z was there, and wanted to repeat all the same questions Sean had just answered for Vikki. "I'll be there in ten minutes," Sean objected. "I'll fill you in on everything as soon as we get there."

Z was waiting for them in the lobby when they arrived, his face beaming as he greeted them. Temporarily star-struck, Z ignored Sean and turned first to Tyrone, extending an opened-palmed handclasp as he spoke. "Dawg, my heart's gotta be wit' the Saints, but I admire yo' game, ya heard me? As many interceptions an' fumbles as you've run back fo' TD's, you've prob'ly scored mo' than most of the receivers or runnin' backs in the NFL!"

Tyrone reached out to shake the young man's hand, glancing toward Sean for an introduction. Sean took the cue and interceded with the necessary information: "My enthusiastic young friend here is Zimbabwe Williamson, known to his friends and loyal listeners as Deejay Z."

"'Sup, Z?" Tyrone nodded, holding up a fist and pausing briefly as Z made his own fist and met the star's in midair. "I have nothin' but respect for your Saints – they'll have a tough offense again this year."

Finally, the initial high of meeting a sports superstar beginning to subside, Z turned to speak to Sean. "Where've you been? I think I read half the books in that damn stuffy-ass library today!"

"Sorry we kept you waiting," Sean retorted, sarcasm dripping from each word. "We had a minor detour around a hurricane and drove half way across North America today, but I'm sure that was nothing compared to enduring a boring day at the library! Come on – let's get this stuff up to our rooms. We have a lot of work ahead of us. We need to get to New Orleans and put a plan together by sundown Saturday."

The three travelers slept late, then enjoyed a large meal at a nearby pancake house before calling Z's friends. They finished loading up the Explorer and checked out around mid-afternoon, then set off on the two and a half hour drive back to New Orleans. I-10 hugged the Gulf of Mexico west of Mobile, skirting the Mississippi coastal cities of Biloxi and Gulfport before turning southward just past the Louisiana border and crossing the mouth of Lake Ponchartrain. From there it continued into East New Orleans and Z's home turf in the Nint' Ward.

They reached Cool's front door a few minutes before six. Roderick and Dewayne were already there, and the three young men greeted Tyrone with a reception line worthy of a rock star or the President, then greeted Sean and their old friend Z. After the greetings, the six of them sat down to begin seriously planning strategy. Luckily, they still had the five guns they had obtained earlier from Z's uncle, Big T. With the thirty-eight Hector had given Sean in Puerto Rico, they had just enough weaponry for each of them.

Sean and Tyrone filled in the details of their encounter in Puerto Rico and their escape to the mainland, while the four New Orleans youths listened attentively. Sean explained his hope that they could capture the hit-man, Tyrone's bodyguard, and whoever came to pay them. It seemed to be a safe bet that they could capture their quarry without firing a shot, since they would out-number their opponents six-to-three and would have the element of surprise in their favor. Then they would turn the miscreants over to the police, after calling in enough media coverage to ensure that there was no cover-up. That would be enough to crack open the case, Sean argued, as the three captives would likely trade testimony against Connor in exchange for immunity or reduced sentences.

With the certainty that Sean's plan was their best hope to bring an end to the violence which had threatened all of their lives, they set about busily preparing their ambush. First, they decided to thoroughly familiarize themselves with Armstrong Park both in the dark of night and by the light of the following day, so they convoyed to the park in Cool's Sentra and Sean's rented Explorer. Parking their vehicles on opposite ends of the park and walking into the grounds in pairs, they strolled among the park's trees and lagoons, taking their time to survey the landscape.

It was a perfect setting for an ambush: a half dozen small bridges arched across the fingers of the lagoon. Some were wood-frame structures, while others were built of concrete and stone – each aligned in a different direction since the placement of the bridges was dictated by the random curvatures of the water. A huge and brightly lit art-deco archway spanned the entrance to a short drive at the front of the park, which terminated in a circle around the statue of Louis Armstrong. The broad glass and steel façade of the New Orleans Center for the Performing Arts effectively blocked the back of the park. A dozen steps spanned the full breadth of the building and a series of simple fountains and pools accented the front. There would be an abundance of hidden and protected enclaves from which to observe the blood-money transaction at the statue the next night.

After each of them had seen all they wanted to see of the park's layout, they returned to Cool's house, allocating duties for the next day to complete their preparations. Z and Cool would call upon Big T to secure an abundant supply of ammunition for all of their guns. Roderick and Dewayne would borrow Sean's Explorer to visit a nearby hardware store, procuring ropes and bungee cords to have on hand for securing any uncooperative hostages, and obtaining copies of the Explorer's ignition key. Cool already had a duplicate key for his car, and they had decided it would be wise to have a second set of keys for each vehicle to facilitate any necessary chase or escape. Sean would place a few calls to his coworkers back in San Francisco to obtain names and direct lines for a half-dozen of New Orleans' most respected print and television journalists. He would then be able to call them to the scene from a nearby pay-phone before the police had a chance to take the criminals into custody. Tyrone's most important assignment was simply to stay out of sight, so he nursed his wounds and secured an Ace bandage for his ribs, preparing to go onto the "playing field" with the others despite his injuries. By late Saturday afternoon all of their preparations were complete. They made one last trip to Armstrong Park to walk through their plan and select the best locations for each to lay in wait for their prey. Now, they just had to wait until dark to set their trap for Connor's conspirators.

(28)

At nine o'clock Saturday night, just as twilight's last vestiges faded into the starry darkness of a moon-less night, the six men entered Armstrong Park. They were all dressed in dark clothing, with loose-fitting shirts concealing the bulges of weaponry and spare ammunition. Just as they had done on both of their scouting visits, they left their vehicles on opposite ends of the park and entered the grounds in three pairs, walking casually and indirectly to their assigned positions. They had decided that Tyrone and Z would take a position on a bridge near the center of the park from which they could direct the operation. Tyrone was the only one who would recognize his errant bodyguard and the man who had shot him, while Z was the de facto leader among his Ninth Ward friends, so the success of the operation was in their hands. Sean and Cool found cover on an arched bridge about forty yards to the left, commanding a clear view of the statue of Louis Armstrong, while Roderick and Dewayne loitered and strolled the meadow on the opposite side, planning to duck behind trees or light posts at the critical moment.

Time crept at an agonizingly slow pace, as the competing emotions of anticipation, impatience, and fear fed a steady stream of adrenaline into Sean's veins. At about a quarter to ten, a shadowy figure slowly approached the statue, stopping in the circle drive a few feet away to light a cigarette and gaze thoughtfully at the great jazz musician. A few minutes later, a second man emerged from the shadows of the trees that lined the front of the park. He, too, approached cautiously, walking in a wide circle around the statue before finally joining up with the first man. Sean could see the first man checking his watch as they spoke in voices too low to be heard across the distance that separated them from his location. He and Cool nodded to each other before turning to look for the signal from Z which would indicate that Tyrone had confirmed the visitor's identities. Peering through the darkness, Sean could just discern a single thumb raised above the railing of the central bridge. *This is it – it's show time!*

Sean checked his own watch and saw that it was five minutes before ten. The bagman should be arriving any moment with the payoff for the hit-man and bodyguard. Sean removed the thirty-eight from his waistband and looked over his shoulder to see that Cool had already drawn his nine-millimeter. They waited and watched. Suddenly, a commotion erupted from the back end of the park. Sean turned to look in the direction of the noise and saw a crowd emerging from the Center for the Performing Arts, where a rare summertime theatrical production had just ended. Scores of patrons were pouring out into the warm night air, walking mostly in coupled pairs, and uniformly attired in black tuxedos and satiny evening dresses. The hum of soft laughter and buoyant conversations spilled across the park, as many of the theater-goers congealed into small groups and lingered among the steps and fountains, hoping to extend the magic of their evening if only by a few minutes.

At that precise moment a dark sedan turned under the gateway arch, headlights dimmed, and rolled slowly toward the pair waiting at the statue. Perhaps it was the unnerving distraction of the crowds that had suddenly interrupted their quiet rendezvous; perhaps it was the dimmed headlights and oddly disconcerting pace of the approaching vehicle; or perhaps Leo, the bodyguard, recognized one of the car's occupants – something caused him to turn and run just as the car came to a stop in front of them. The passenger-side window started to retract, and Sean saw a steel barrel emerge from inside the vehicle. At the same instant, the driver jumped from his door, swirled around, and leaned over the top of the car with a second weapon. The evening stillness was ruptured by the distinctive high-speed chattering of two AK-47's as the waiting hit-man, who had not followed Leo's cue, spun wildly through the air, collapsing into a crumpled heap on the grass. Pandemonium exploded across the park as the crowds in front of the theater screamed and scrambled for cover, many of them diving into the lagoon or ducking behind the fountains. The few strollers in the nearby meadow either ran or threw themselves to the ground.

"Oh, shit! They got choppers!" Cool exclaimed, ducking securely behind the concrete side of their bridge. Leo had found his way to a small stone monument, returning fire at his assailants, as Sean felt compelled by his journalistic curiosity to peer over the railing at the full-scale urban warfare unfolding before his eyes. *Damn, they're cleaning up loose ends! That bodyguard is our only link back to Connor!* Either Tyrone or Z must have realized the same brutal truth, because someone from the other bridge opened fire at that moment, shattering the windshield of the attackers' car. The driver turned to spray Tyrone and Z's position with a long burst as the passenger rolled out of the car and dashed for cover behind the Armstrong statue, continuing to pin down the beleaguered bodyguard with his weapon.

Suddenly, gunfire erupted from sixty or seventy yards behind the assassin's car as Dewayne and Roderick joined the battle, opening fire from behind two trees. The driver turned and razed their positions with a steady stream of automatic fire. Sean could see medium-sized tree limbs crashing to the ground as the chain-saw effect of the impacting shells severed them from their trunks. "We've gotta cover 'em!" Cool shouted, as he raised his weapon over the edge of the railing and began squeezing the trigger rapidly, firing a dozen rounds in quick succession. Sean raised his weapon, took aim, and quickly squeezed off three shots at the driver, one shot ricocheting off the car's roof as the other two missed their mark entirely.

The bodyguard and the second assassin continued to duel from behind their respective statuary, undeterred by the multifaceted battle raging all around them. The professional assassin clearly intended to fulfill his objective. Seeing that the bodyguard was out-gunned and would surely soon be out of ammunition, Sean signaled to Cool that they should turn their attention to the assassin behind the statue, leaving their four friends to deal with the driver. Sean and Cool opened fire simultaneously, unleashing nearly twenty rounds at the statue in a matter of seconds. Sean could hear the assassin curse loudly, as shrapnel chipped from the marble injured the man's face. Turning his full fury against them, the assassin blasted their bridge in a long, sweeping arc, shouting a steady stream of obscenities as he did. Sean and Cool ducked just in time and crouched low, with their backs to the wall, as whistling projectiles and concrete dust filled the air over their heads. Then, much to their relief, they heard the sound of gunfire coming from the direction of the bodyguard's position as he resumed his one-on-one duel with his would-be killer.

Meanwhile, Tyrone, Z, Roderick, and Dewayne were failing in their effort to pin the driver in a cross-fire, as the two brothers were on the defensive in their exposed positions. There was no room to maneuver from behind their trees, so both of them were relegated to spending most of the time leaning tightly against the trunks, only rarely reaching around to take a wild shot. Sensing their predicament, the driver reached inside his car, emerging with something that looked like a can of hair spray. Twisting and pulling on the end of it, he reeled back and threw it as far as he could toward the trees. It rolled to within a few feet of Dewayne's feet, emitted a loud pop, and began spewing thick white smoke. Sean recognized the device from riots he had witnessed during his early years as a journalist. *Tear gas!*

Sean instantly realized the mortal danger this new element posed for Roderick and Dewayne. Within moments, they would begin to cough and buckle involuntarily, exposing themselves from behind the safety of their tree trunks. It would be easy picking for the driver. "We've got to keep that driver pinned down while they run for it!" Sean urged Cool. "I'll shoot while you load, then you cover while I load." Sean spun around, rested his arms on the bridge railing, and fired six shots in a steady progression. Just as he dropped back behind the wall, Cool opened fire, also discharging his allotted ammunition at a measured pace. Sean frantically raced to dump his empty shell casings and reload, snapping his cylinder closed just as Cool fired his last shot.

Dewayne began to cough as the first wisps of the noxious smoke curled behind his tree. "Run, D!" Roderick shouted. "I'll cover you!" Dewayne stumbled out into the open meadow, disoriented as the fumes stung his eyes. Seeing the desperate plight of his younger brother, Roderick stepped from behind his tree, fully exposing himself to the assassin's line of fire as he leveled his nine-millimeter sideways, took careful aim, and began shooting in a rhythm that matched his stride. He walked directly toward the driver, popping new clips into the semi-automatic pistol as quickly as he could unload them. "Take this, mutha-fucka!" he was shouting. "Take these hot boys!"

201

Z stood up from behind his protective wall, holding a pistol in each hand, and opened fire on the driver as he shouted for Roderick to back off and take cover. Tyrone, who had tossed his weapon to Z, dashed out from the end of their bridge and nearly tackled Dewayne, scooping him up by the waist and spinning around in a tight circle back toward the concrete abutment. "Run, Rod!" Z implored. "Get the fuck outta there!" Rage had fully gripped Roderick, however, and he continued a steady advance toward the assassin's car, firing and cursing at the driver with a steely singularity of purpose...until he ran out of clips. Realizing the fatal indefensibility of his position – standing in the open, unarmed, less than twenty yards from the driver and his assault weapon – he threw his gun at the car in a defiant gesture, yelling a simple "Fuck you!" in a thunderous voice that reverberated across the park.

The next few seconds happened so quickly, every action and nuanced motion seemed to float in time like a still photograph. The driver stood from behind the door of the car where he had taken cover during Roderick's onslaught, and began to lower his assault rifle to take a clean shot at the easy target. Sean and Cool stood and began firing in unison; Tyrone dropped Dewayne behind the concrete, scooped the gun from his hands, and twisted sideways to begin firing immediately; and Z continued to rain fire from both hands while shouting futile pleas for Roderick to turn and run. With all of their weapons unloading simultaneously, they would never know who fired the critical shots, but clouds of red exploded from the driver's shoulder blade and forearm as two bullets found their target.

The assault rifle flew from his hand as he lurched forward onto the ground, grimacing in pain. He groped for the gun with his uninjured arm, swung it up into the car like a bat-boy tossing a bat, then pulled himself into the car while shouting to his accomplice to get in. The second gunman backed slowly toward the vehicle, continuing to fire at the bodyguard's position, then turned to spray the two bridges one last time before ducking into the car. As he fired in a semicircular pattern across the park, the stream of tumbling shells strafed the front of the Performing Arts Center, shattering the huge glass panels that covered the entire front of the building. The impacts of scores of projectiles sent a glittering torrent of fragmented glass to the ground, the collective tinkling of the shards sounding like the roar of a metallic waterfall. The car accelerated, burned rubber as it spun around the circle drive, and disappeared through the gate onto Rampart Street.

It was over. For a brief moment, an eerie silence fell across the park, then bedlam resumed with the sounds of crying, shouting, and screaming among the stunned crowd of bystanders. The wail of distant police sirens could be heard approaching from three directions.

Before any of the others could react, Tyrone bolted across his bridge, emerged onto the lawn, and passed Sean and Cool with astonishing speed. "I'm gonna break that muthafuckin' Leo's back!" he cursed as he dashed past them. The bodyguard froze with fear, as if he had seen a ghost, then dropped his gun and turned to run. Sean took off in pursuit, shouting back over his shoulder for the others to get to the cars. The four local men scattered, with Z dashing for Sean's rented Explorer, and the others running for Cool's car – Roderick detouring briefly to retrieve his discarded weapon, then sprinting to catch up with the others.

Leo had begun with a sixty-yard lead, but starting from a cold standstill, he never stood a chance against one of the greatest defensive backs in NFL history. Tyrone took a flying dive and swept his bodyguard's feet up off the ground just as they reached the sidewalk lining the front of the park. Rolling on the concrete with no apparent awareness of his injured arm or ribs, Tyrone reached back and grabbed Leo's ankle to prevent him from getting to his feet, then pulled himself up over the smaller man and began to pummel him. Sean dove into the middle of the altercation, physically thrusting himself between the enraged football star and the object of his fury. "No!" Sean shouted. "Tyrone, stop! We need him alive – and conscious! He's our only lead! Let's just get out of here!"

Tyrone knocked Sean to the ground with a backhanded sweeping gesture and grabbed Leo's collar, jerking his head up from the pavement violently. Pulling the dazed bodyguard to within inches of his own face, he glared into the other man's eyes. "I'm not through with you yet, muthafucka!" he growled before slamming Leo's torso back down onto the pavement. "Try to set me up and think you're gonna get paid for it? I'll finish with you later!"

With that, Tyrone stood, reaching down to yank Leo up by his collar with one hand and reaching out the other hand to help Sean back to his feet. "Sorry, man," he said, rage punctuating his voice. "I just lost my temper with this lying, two-faced bastard, ya dig? I didn't mean you any harm."

The Explorer screeched to a stop just a few feet in front of them, and Z gestured for them to pile in quickly. Sean jumped in the front passenger seat, while Tyrone pushed Leo ahead of him into the back. The other three pulled up on the opposite side of the street in Cool's car as the approaching sirens sounded no more than one block away. Leaning out his window, Cool urgently asked, "Where?"

"The swamp!" Z shouted in reply.

29

Z and Cool showed remarkable restraint for the circumstances, both of them resisting the nearly overwhelming, instinctive desire to speed from the scene. Driving casually at a speed safely below the legal limit, both vehicles escaped the attention of the onrushing parade of police cruisers, and Tyrone maintained a seemingly chummy arm around Leo's neck. The threat was understood, and Leo sat quietly as the Explorer circled around behind Armstrong Park, turned right onto Claiborne where it ran directly underneath the elevated portion of I-10, and continued across the canal into the safety of the Ninth Ward. After following a meandering path through several quiet residential blocks, the Explorer crossed another small bridge and entered the vast industrial wasteland of the Port of New Orleans. During daylight hours, the narrow lanes weaving among the loading docks would be congested with tractor-trailers hauling wares to and from the countless barges of the Intracoastal Waterway and Mississippi River; but at this late hour, the facility was nearly deserted.

Turning right, Z continued on a zigzag course, skirting the edges of the Port's domain, finally spotting Cool's car parked on the shoulder ahead, and easing the Explorer to a stop just behind it. They had found their way to a particularly dark and desolate corner of the city. A concrete dike paralleled the roadway on one side, separating dry land from the marshy bogs of the bayou, while the cranes and massive junk piles of Southern Scrap stood silhouetted against the New Orleans skyline on the other. Cool and the two brothers were standing a few yards from their car and, as the occupants of the Explorer stepped from their vehicle, they could hear Cool and Roderick arguing.

"You mus' be outta yo' mutha fuckin' mind!" Cool was yelling. "What the hell was that Rambo bullshit you pulled back there? You think you can jus' walk up to a chopper an' stick yo' finger in the barrel?"

"I had to do somethin'!" Roderick protested, extreme levels of adrenaline magnifying both the volume and pitch of his voice. "Dewayne was in trouble – you saw how he was startin' to choke on that tear gas shit. I wasn't gonna jus' hide behind a tree an' watch my l'il brother get cut in two by some asshole wit' a chopper."

"All I know is, I hope I *never* get caught up in no drama wit' you again – you're one crazy mutha fuckin' fool!"

"Hey, bras," Z interrupted. "We can settle this later. Right now, we've got a job to finish."

"I call dibs on poppin' that muthafucka!" Roderick growled, turning his attention to glare icily at the hapless Leo while fingering the nine-millimeter tucked in his waistband. "He damn-near got us all killed, know what I'm sayin'?"

"I think Tyrone gets the honors on this one," Sean responded, finding it useful to play into his angry accomplice's blood lust. There had been no opportunity to coordinate a new strategy after the violent turn of events at Armstrong Park, so it was unclear who among them was serious in their threats against the bodyguard and who might be bluffing. For now, Sean felt it entirely appropriate to allow Leo to fear imminent death and at the same time to try to take subtle control of the situation in order to avoid a premature execution.

Turning to Leo, Sean continued, "But first, I think Leo has a few things he might like to share with us. How about it, Leo? Do you want to make this easy or difficult?"

Cowardice can be a powerful motivator, and Leo fairly sputtered over his words as he tried to appease his captors. "Man, I'll tell you whatever you wanna know! Just don't kill me! You gotta promise if I tell you what I know, you won't kill me."

"Fuck you!" Tyrone exploded. "The only promise I'll make you is that if you don't start talking NOW, you *will* bleed and suffer all night long before you die!" Drawing his nine-millimeter, Tyrone pressed the barrel of the gun into the inside of Leo's left elbow, positioned to blow a hole all the way through the joint. "We'll start with the elbows, then the knees, and maybe blow your shit off for good measure, ya dig? Then we'll drop you over this wall into the bayou and see how long it takes the 'gators to get to you!"

"Aiight! Aiight!" Leo begged, tears beginning to flow from his eyes. "I'm sorry, man! I never shoulda set you up, but when he offered me a hundred G's for doin' nothin', I couldn't turn him down."

"Who?" Tyrone demanded. "Who offered you a hundred G's?"

"J. Richard Connor. When you an' I were here for Mardi Gras, he looked me up an' asked me to come up to his office. I didn't know what he wanted at first. I figured he was gonna try to broker a deal to sign you for the Saints or somethin', but he told me he wanted me to set you up. I wouldn't have to pull the trigger; hell, I wouldn't even have to be there. I just had to give him a time an' place an' make sure you were unprotected for a minute or two. He pulled fifty thousand presidents outta his desk drawer an' handed the cash to me right there, then promised there'd be another fifty when the job was done. He also said if the job worked out right he'd hook me up with a spot in his organization an' pay me twice what you're payin' me. I told him about your meetings with Miguel, by the beach. Then he gave me his private number an' told me to be in touch to set up a day an' time. That's it, man, that's how it went down!"

"So it was just about money?" Tyrone snarled, dumbfounded at the tale of deceit by his trusted assistant.

"Man, it's *always* about money! Hell, you should know that – you're livin' large with all the coins you make. Do you know how frustrating it is for me livin' in your shadow all the time? I spend all my time in *your* condo, in *your* limo, in *your* chartered jets, watchin' over you an' *your* women. I've gotta have *mine*! Can you understand that? I couldn't have all the things I wanted off of what you were payin' me!"

"You greedy, ungrateful punk!" Tyrone sneered, pushing Leo to the ground. "I took you off the streets when you had nothing! Nothing! All you had was a bad-ass attitude and a record for some petty shit! Who would've given you a job? *I* gave you a job because you were a friend of my cousin. I took you into a world you never would've touched, ya dig – a world you and that triflin' crowd you ran with could only see in movies. You got to travel all over the world, you got into parties you never would've known existed, and got to meet big-name stars like it wasn't a thing. You fucking greedy little prick, that wasn't good enough for you?"

Tyrone let the question hang in the night air – the tension palpable as the others watched the superstar confront his betrayer. Finally, Tyrone spit on the ground at Leo's feet, then turned his back on the bodyguard, arms folded across his chest. "That punk isn't worth my spit," he announced to the others. "Do whatever you want with him."

"I called dibs!" Roderick repeated, pulling the weapon from his waistband with a flourish. "I get to pop his sorry ass. Anybody else got business wit' him first?"

"Yeah," Sean answered. "I've got a couple more questions."

Turning to Leo, Sean continued. "If you want to live, you need to give us more. We need proof. We need something we can hang Connor with. You say he paid you in cash – do you still have some of the money, perhaps with Connor's fingerprints?"

"No, man, that money's all gone. I never had money like that before, an' there was so much I wanted, so much I'd waited all my life for. I was supposed to get another fifty G's tonight."

"Okay, so what about the hit-man. There's a body lying back there in the park. Do you have any way to connect him to Connor?"

"No, man, I never saw him before that night in San Juan. I don't even know his name. Connor found the guy through some of his other connections – all I was ever supposed to do was look the other way."

"Damn it, man, work with me!" Sean implored, exasperated with the dead ends. "You haven't told us anything new. We already knew it was Connor – Tyrone is the fifth athlete Connor has tried to take out of the game. We just don't have enough to prove it, and an unsupported accusation by a third-rate loser like you won't be enough to bring down a man who can afford to hire half the lawyers in Louisiana. I've got a couple of pissed-off young men here who are getting very impatient for their chance to blow your brains across the bayou. Give me something I can use and maybe you'll live through the night."

His voice trembling with emotion, Leo begged for his life. "Please, please don't kill me! I swear I'd tell you if I knew more! I swear it! I don't know what I can tell you to give up Connor."

Leo paused in deep concentration, his faced twisted in an exaggerated scowl as if trying to physically squeeze a life-saving memory or tidbit of information from his mind. Suddenly, he looked up. The scowl turned to a blank and questioning expression, then to the child-like excitement of an unexpected discovery, as he spoke again. "Wait a minute! There was something! When I was in his office talkin' about the hit on Tyrone, Connor was takin' notes. He was writin' notes to himself in a little black notebook. Then he stashed the book in the false bottom of his cigar case. The son of a bitch has written notes about the whole set-up! I don't know how you'll get your hands on that book, but I'm bettin' my life he's got notes about the others you say he's tried to kill!"

Sean and Z exchanged a glance, both of them apparently trying to calculate the value of this new piece of information. Z shifted his gaze and with a subtle tilt of his head signaled Roderick and the other members of the K-Nines to put their firearms away, as Sean resumed the questioning.

"The book was in the bottom of a cigar case? Where, on his desk, or in a drawer?"

"It's sittin' right out on top of his desk – looks like it was custom made from the same mahogany his desk is made of."

"Did you actually see what he wrote in it?"

"No. I couldn't see from where I was standin', but I think I remember seein' him make some notes when I told him where to plan the hit. I think he might have also written something down about how much he was gonna pay me. I don't know. I'm bein' straight-up with you, man!"

"Okay, okay," Sean inquired. "Now, think very, very hard. Was the cigar case locked? Think back and remember – did you ever see Connor use a key to open or close the secret compartment?"

Leo closed his eyes and thought silently for several seconds, then opened his eyes wide. "No. I'm sure I never saw him use a key. That cocky son of a bitch is keepin' a murder diary right out in the open on his desk. I guess he don't think anyone'll be snoopin' around in his office."

Sean cast a questioning glance toward Z, unsure if the answers Leo had given could be put to any practical use. Z gave him a tentative nod, the pensive expression on the younger man's face showing that he, as well, was trying to devise a plan to make the most of Leo's information. Sean turned his attention back to Leo and spoke again.

"Give me the names and addresses of your three closest relatives – your next of kin."

"What?" Leo asked, confused by the sudden shift in Sean's questioning.

"Give me the names and addresses of three relatives or people you stay in touch with frequently." Sean pulled a notepad from his pocket as he repeated the demand.

With a tone of utter bafflement in his voice, Leo complied with Sean's inquiry, rattling off names, addresses, and even phone numbers, for his mother and sister in New Jersey, as well as a brother in the Marine Corps who was stationed at Cherry Point, North Carolina. "I don't know the zip code there, but it's right down the road from Camp Lejeune."

After closing his notepad, Sean looked squarely into Leo's eyes. "I know you'll stay as far from Connor as you can, since he tried to have you killed tonight. We're not ready to take this to the police yet – we have reason to believe Connor has some bad cops in his pocket as well – so you just need to disappear for a while. When the time comes, you'll have to turn yourself in and make your best deal with the prosecutors, trading your testimony against Connor for any charges that come from your involvement in the hit on Tyrone. Make no mistake – if you don't come in voluntarily, we *will* find you! I'm a journalist with all the investigative resources of a major newspaper at my fingertips and Tyrone has enough money to hire six busloads of private eyes. With the information you just gave me as a starting point, we'll find you. Now, get out of here, but I expect you to call for me at the San Francisco Star-Reporter in forty-eight hours. If there's no message for you, keep checking back every two days until I get word to you on our next move."

Sean gave a nod to Tyrone, who understood the signal and pulled the gun from his waistband, brandishing it in a threatening gesture. "Get the fuck out of here, punk!" he shouted. "Get the fuck and do exactly what you've been told, ya dig? If I have to come looking for you, I'll hurt you worse than you've ever imagined!"

As Leo stood and turned to run, Tyrone reached out and kicked him in the buttocks, sending him reeling to the ground again. Scrambling back to his feet, Leo took off running into the scrub brush lining the bayou, disappearing into the darkness as Roderick and Dewayne shouted taunts after him.

"Watch out fo' 'gators an' wild pigs!"

"Yeah! An' snakes!"

Sean turned to Z and asked, "How are we going to get that book out of Connor's office?"

"I think my Uncle T might be able to help. I told you he handles his business diff'rent than some of the others, ya heard me? Callio Cal has dirty cops workin' for him, usin' their muscle to back him up, but Uncle T has a friend or two in City Hall who could be useful right 'bout now."

30

Sean and Tyrone returned to the Days Inn on Canal Street where they had checked into adjacent rooms upon their arrival in New Orleans the previous night. They hoped that Tyrone's identity would remain undiscovered in the discount hotel where no one would be expecting to see a multimillionaire superstar. Z crashed on the couch at Cool's home for a second night, while Rod and D returned to their own home. The next morning, while waiting for Z to obtain the anticipated assistance from his Uncle T, Sean rose early to have a peaceful breakfast at the adjoining Louie Louie's restaurant. Although it was not yet eight o'clock on a Sunday morning when Sean left his room, he could hear rhythmic pounding coming from next door, as Tyrone jogged in place and performed various calisthenics. *Oh great! He's not only attracting the attention of half the guests in this hotel, but he's going to get us tossed out of here!*

After ordering a breakfast of biscuits and gravy, with grits and bacon on the side, Sean picked up the Times-Picayune to read the accounts of the prior night's gun battle in Armstrong Park. The debacle had landed on page one. Sean immediately saw the irony that he had been more successful grabbing headlines when he *made* the news than when he wrote about it, and chuckled softly to himself. *Lil would have a stroke!* According to the New Orleans paper, police had found one body – tentatively identified as a free-lance hit-man, known to have dealt variously with the Mafia, at least one Colombian clan, and local criminal organizations in half a dozen cities. They had also found significant blood stains indicating a second casualty, but so far there had been no reports of a "John Doe" corpse or of a suspect visiting any of the local emergency rooms. The New Orleans Center for the Performing Arts had canceled a Sunday evening performance pending emergency repairs and clean-up. In fact, the entire park had become a giant crime lab as forensic teams from the New Orleans Police Department methodically scoured the scene for every stray slug and empty shell casing.

As Sean read the detailed eyewitness descriptions, with seemingly every witness recalling a significantly different chain of events, his eyes strayed across the page. He nearly spilled his coffee when he happened upon a second front-page article, with the headline: "Patriot's Star Missing – Presumed Dead," centered over a portrait photograph of Tyrone.

Although they had been taking precautions to keep Tyrone's identity and whereabouts secret, it had been done with the sole purpose of deceiving J. Richard Connor. With so much happening in such a short time, Sean had not contemplated the full magnitude of the media frenzy that a disappearance like this would generate, especially right at the start of the pre-season hype. Sean quickly scanned the second piece, to learn what he could about the status of that investigation.

According to the article, a number of Tyrone's associates had contacted San Juan authorities when the star failed to keep several previously-scheduled appointments and didn't return urgent voicemail messages for over twenty-four hours. Upon receiving reports of Tyrone's disappearance, San Juan police had quickly made a connection to gunshots that had been reported by several residents in the star's neighborhood the night before. A full-scale investigation had been launched, including a thorough review of Tyrone's gambling habits and contacts, and authorities had discovered the slain body of Miguel Lopez, one of Tyrone's gambling associates. In addition, Tyrone's photo had been faxed to every hospital and law enforcement agency in the Caribbean. The New England Patriots had refused to issue a formal statement beyond a simple expression of concern for Tyrone's health and safety. Private sources, however, were reporting that the team's management was in a state of unbridled panic as they braced for the prospect of starting the season without their most valuable defensive player. The most tantalizing fact in the article, however, was that San Juan police had interviewed several witnesses who claimed to have recognized the football star walking on the beach in wet and tattered clothing at least an hour after the reported gunshots.

Just as Sean was finishing the article, Tyrone found him in the restaurant and pulled up a chair. "You're dead," Sean announced in a deadpan voice, handing the newspaper across the table for the football player to see. "Well, almost anyway."

"Damn!" Tyrone cursed with mock sincerity. "Then I'm rich! I have a ten million dollar life insurance policy, ya dig, but collecting on it will be a bitch!"

"Seriously," Sean continued, "You're on the front pages today, so we'll need to work even harder at maintaining your low profile. I don't know a tactful way to put this, but I think doing jumping jacks in your room is a bad idea."

"I'm due in training camp tomorrow," the football player shrugged. "I've got to stick with my regimen."

"Yeah, well, I think staying alive has to be your number one fitness goal right now. Go ahead, read the rest of the article. You did manage to get the jump on all of your fellow players in the *real* competition – the race to become the media's darling."

Tyrone nodded his head and smiled wryly as he read the article. "I guess I know how Mark Twain felt about premature obituaries!"

"Yeah," Sean agreed. "I'd say this worldwide manhunt is both good news and bad news. The bad news is that time is running against us – we desperately need to flush Connor out before my colleagues in the press flush you out. The good news is that bringing you back from the dead just might give us some leverage at a key moment in our little break-in scheme."

Tyrone nodded his head thoughtfully for a few moments, then agreed. "I think I know exactly what you have in mind. It just might work."

They finished their breakfasts quickly and returned to the safe haven of their rooms, where Sean called Cool's house to check on Z's progress. Z had just returned and came on the phone excitedly. "Aye yo! Uncle T says he can get us what we need tomorrow mornin', ya heard? I'm supposed to pass by his office to pick the stuff up for ten o'clock."

"Excellent. Let's hope they're convincing enough to get us past Connor's secretary. Tyrone and I think we've come up with a plan to get Connor out of the way for a few minutes. You and I need to go shopping this afternoon for appropriate attire, and we need to spend some time rehearsing our roles."

The rest of the day was consumed with preparations for Monday's planned incursion into the heart of enemy territory. When Monday arrived, Cool drove Z to Big T's office, where two official City of New Orleans Fire Prevention / Code Enforcement credentials were waiting, along with a sheaf of official forms and documents. After taking a moment to thank Big T, Z returned to the car, and they drove to the Days Inn to meet with Sean and Tyrone. They all synchronized watches, then three of them departed in Cool's car, destined for Connor's office on Poydras Avenue, leaving Tyrone behind to fulfill his assigned function. The threesome circled the block in front of Connor's office several times before finally locating a parking spot with a favorable view of the building. It was a striking structure – towering twenty-three floors above the Louisiana Superdome, the building featured a multifaceted, angular design so that nearly every worker had a corner office.

Then they waited.

At eleven-forty, Tyrone left his room in the Days Inn, took the stairs to the first floor, and stepped out into the hot New Orleans sun. He jogged twice around the block, hoping to induce a noticeable breathlessness, then stopped at a pay phone to dial the private telephone number Leo had provided them. The phone rang once, then Connor answered.

"Connor here."

"J. R. Connor!" Tyrone repeated, his breathlessness serving to bolster his feigned excitement. "This is Tyrone Freeman. I'm in New Orleans! Someone tried to kill me in Puerto Rico, ya dig, but I got away. I've been on the run and didn't know who I could trust – it must be someone with the Patriots organization who set me up. I've been hiding out here in New Orleans since the morning after the shooting and finally decided to call you for help. I'll be at The Quarter Scene Restaurant in fifteen minutes, one of the tables at the rear, on the upper deck, with my back to the room. I'll be on the down low, ya dig, wearing wrap-around shades and a wide brim hat. Be there." Without giving Connor a chance to respond or ask any questions, Tyrone hung up the receiver. His mission completed, Tyrone returned to his room in the Days Inn to wait and hope that the amateur sleuths on his team would score.

J. Richard Connor replaced the receiver on his desk and sat in silence for several seconds. A dozen questions raced through his mind, chief among them being how the star athlete had survived being shot at nearly point-blank range and why he had chosen New Orleans as his refuge. At the same time, although the hit in Puerto Rico had failed, Connor realized he might have a small window of opportunity right in his own back yard. If Tyrone Freeman had been successful in his efforts to remain incognito, it might be possible to lure him from the restaurant and finish the job without a trace. *A very lucky break*, he thought. He quickly picked up his telephone and placed two short calls – the first to his secretary, asking her to have his car ready in five minutes; the second to The Cardinal's pager. As always, the Cardinal was prompt in his response.

"What can I do for you today, Connor?"

"I've got a rather urgent problem, along with a ready-made solution. It seems our contractor in San Juan wasn't as thorough as we thought – I just got a call from Tyrone Freeman, and he's right here in New Orleans. I'm supposed to meet him at The QSR in just a few minutes. He says no one else knows he's in town, so I think we should settle this matter immediately. Can you have someone there by twelve-thirty to meet Mr. Freeman as he leaves the restaurant?"

"I'll have someone there," The Cardinal asserted, his voice betraying both irritation that the original hit had gone awry, as well as confidence that he could handle any situation on his own turf.

Connor dashed from his office, told his secretary he'd be back in an hour, and rode the elevator to the parking garage beneath the building. As he emerged from the underground facility in his black stretch limo, Sean, Z, and Cool were watching.

31

"There goes the limo, right on schedule," Cool observed. "It mus' be him."

"Let's go!" Sean decreed as he opened his door and stepped from the car. Z jumped out of the front passenger seat, and they both walked swiftly toward the main entrance. They were dressed in matching uniforms consisting of black slacks and dress shoes, white button-down shirts, red ties, and fire marshal badges pinned to their lapels. Each had a plastic pocket-protector and a selection of pens and pencils in their front pocket, and Sean was carrying a clipboard filled with official forms and papers, while Z had a small briefcase in his hand.

Inside the lobby, they passed by a small photocopy shop which they had noted on a reconnaissance drive-by the previous evening, then paused briefly at the security console to confirm Connor's suite number on the building directory. Speaking to each other, but in tones just loud enough to be overheard by the security guard, they conferred and agreed that they would start their building inspection on the top floor and work their way down. Sean rehashed their plans aloud as they rode the elevator to the twenty-third floor, anxious to avoid any missteps with his young partner.

"I got it, I got it, ya heard me? Dayam!" Z objected, just as they reached the top floor. "You jus' keep the secretary busy an' I'll do the rest."

The elevator opened onto a small but airy foyer, the limited dimensions more than offset by the openness of a large skylight. Three suites occupied the twenty-third floor, and the two ersatz inspectors quickly identified the entrance to Connor Enterprises. They stepped into a lushly furnished lobby, and Connor's secretary immediately greeted them. Dressed crisply in a conservative business jacket and knee-length skirt, the woman appeared to be in her mid-fifties, and her voice projected the twin requirements of authority and cordiality which characterized a true professional in her field. Surveying the suite, Sean saw that there were five offices. The largest, obviously Connor's, was positioned directly behind the secretary's desk, with two others flanking each side. Occupants were visible through the two open doors on the right, while the offices on the left had their doors closed. Three small alcoves lined the wall opposite the secretary's desk, housing a photocopier, a kitchenette, and a supply closet. *This is not going to be easy*, Sean realized.

Reaching forward to extend a hand in greeting, Sean introduced himself, "Matt Wilson, with the New Orleans Fire and Safety Codes Division. This is my assistant, Jett Johnson. We're just doing a quick walk-though of the building today – shouldn't take long."

Sean tipped his head slightly to Z, signaling him to get going, as he pulled a pen from his pocket and began studying the papers on his clipboard. Z started toward the office furthest to the left, which had a closed door, and knocked authoritatively on the wood panel. The secretary began to rise from her seat, gesturing toward Z as she spoke in urgent tones. "Excuse me! Excuse me, young man! You can't just walk into our offices without an appointment!"

"Actually, Ma'am," Sean replied while gesturing for Z to proceed. "City ordinance specifically authorizes the Fire Prevention and Code Enforcement Division to conduct unannounced inspections. I'm sure you run a tight ship here at Connor Enterprises, but you would be shocked to learn how many businesses operate day-to-day with egregious violations, then try to clean everything up for a day or two when they know we're coming. I'm sure you understand."

The secretary stammered, trying to squeeze a word in edgewise, but Sean forged ahead with his monologue. "Now, the sooner we get started the sooner we can be out of your way. I'm guessing you're responsible for all of your office's supplies and maintenance contracts, so I will likely have a few questions for you. Would you accompany me, please, ma'am?"

Without waiting for her reply, Sean turned and walked directly into the kitchenette, kneeling down to inspect the electrical outlets, and running his fingers along a half dozen cords leading to various appliances. "I can tell you right now that you're exceeding the wattage on this circuit," Sean said, shaking his head and clicking his tongue.

"Look at this, ma'am," he commanded as he pointed to an outlet underneath a small coffee table. The woman kneeled carefully, drawing her skirt up slightly so it would not drag the floor, and looked to where Sean was pointing. "You've got an automatic coffee maker, a microwave, a three-quarter size refrigerator, a lamp, and a hot & cold water dispenser all plugged into the same outlet, using a surge protector as an outlet multiplier. Absolutely a violation – you can only have two appliances on this circuit. You'll need to have two more outlets installed, with appropriate circuit work and fusing. For now, three of these appliances have got to go. I'm guessing the refrigerator and the coffee maker would be your priorities?"

Before the secretary could answer, Sean unplugged the surge protector from the wall outlet, then plugged the refrigerator and coffee maker cords directly into the wall, darkening the room as the lamp clicked off, and leaving the microwave and water dispenser unconnected. The secretary objected loudly, reaching out her hand as if to rescue the discarded appliance plugs. "The sales rep at the office supply assured me that this surge protector could handle these appliances!"

"It's a big problem," Sean nodded his head in agreement. "I'm guessing half the surge protectors sold are used improperly. You have to understand the real problem is in your internal wiring. There's nothing you can do short of shelling out the cash for a certified electrician. If you wish, I can take a formal report on your office supplier – knowingly selling electrical equipment for unauthorized use is also a code violation."

The secretary shook her head no, rising to her feet and stroking the front of the microwave as one might bid farewell to a deceased pet. As Sean continued to hold her attention, Z slipped into Connor's office, spotted the cigar box, and quickly found the false bottom. *There it is!* He held his breath as he lifted a small black leather notepad from inside the red felt-lined compartment under the authentic Cuban cigars. Stashing it inside his briefcase, he crept past Sean and his unwilling audience, reaching the outer foyer without detection. As he waited impatiently for the elevator to take him downstairs he clicked open the briefcase to take a quick look, confirming the presence of a roll of quarters that had been obtained from a supermarket the day before. They had decided it would be best to make a copy and replace the original, so that Connor would not know that they had found their proof – buying them valuable time while they planned their next move.

The elevator arrived and, after several stops on other floors, Z emerged into the building's first floor lobby. Walking briskly toward the copy center, he made some quick calculations in his head: the notebook appeared to contain about forty or fifty pages, but was small enough to copy two pages at a time. That meant twenty or thirty copies he would need to make within ten minutes. *I've gotta do at least three copies a minute.* As he stepped into the copy center, his jaw dropped and he froze as he tried to comprehend the terrible sight before him. The front panels of the store's only self-serve copier had been removed and a technician was laying prone on the floor, intent on his work as he reached a screwdriver deep inside the copier's mechanisms. Nuts, bolts, and small components were strewn all about the technician, and the copier's main drum sat on the floor near his feet. A handwritten sign was taped to the top of the machine, needlessly pointing out that the copier was out of order.

With thin streams of sweat starting to run down his temples, Z turned his attention to the full-service counter, where two people stood in line ahead of him. The person at the head of the line was comparing color samples produced on two different grades of paper, and was alternately holding each one up to the light, turning the samples over and over in her hands. "I just don't know," she was repeating, "I just don't know." The sales representative was making his best pitch for the more expensive paper, but the customer seemed hopelessly frustrated by the need to choose between lower price or higher quality. "I don't know," she continued, "I just don't know."

Z considered bullying past the indecisive customer and appealing for emergency service, but he could not immediately think of a way to explain the "emergency" without calling dangerous attention to his mission. He fidgeted nervously, checking his watch frequently as two, three, then four of his precious minutes were consumed by the first customer in line. Finally, she made a decision, bowing to the salesman's pressure to choose the better paper, and he issued her a receipt. The next customer stepped forward, flopped a briefcase onto the counter, opened it, and pulled out a large handful of originals. There must have been three to four hundred pages, paper-clipped and rubber-banded in several dozen smaller sets and subsets, with yellow sticky notes attached to the front of each batch. Z rolled his eyes and felt his heart skip a beat as the customer began to meticulously explain the instructions for each set to the man behind the counter.

Twenty blocks away, J. Richard Connor had reached The Quarter Scene Restaurant at just past noon and found the restaurant crowded with lunch-time guests. Every table was occupied, including the ones on the upper deck that Tyrone had specified, but there was no sign of the Patriots' player. After waiting fifteen minutes for Tyrone to show up, Connor used the voice-activation on his cell phone to dial his secretary's number in order to ask if there had been any additional contact from the football star. When there was no answer at his secretary's desk, Connor was enraged. "Goddamit!" he shouted as he slammed the phone closed against his open palm. "She knows not to leave her desk until her twelve-thirty lunch hour. Goddam wild goose chase! I don't know what kind of stunt that bastard Freeman is pulling, dragging me out here like this, then standing me up! Get me back to the office, NOW!" Connor stepped into the back seat of the limo, slamming the door behind him before the driver had a chance to close it for him. Without delay, the driver walked around to the front of the car, stepped inside, and gunned the engine.

Sean checked his watch discreetly, noting that nearly twenty minutes had elapsed since they entered the office, and began to feel a sense of desperation as he groped for details to elongate his inspection tour. They had finished with the kitchenette, then spent several minutes in the copy room as Sean had opened up the front of the photocopier and pretended to inspect its inner wiring before moving on to the supply closet. The phone on the secretary's desk had rung several times, but Sean had managed to pin her down with questions and observations throughout the entire inspection tour. Once in the supply closet, Sean shifted gears from the "fire" component of his counterfeit jurisdiction to the "safety" aspects, inquiring about first aid kits, sharp objects, toxic inks, and any other credible concern he could dream up.

Twenty-three floors below, Z finally reached the head of the line, pulling the small notebook from his briefcase. "I need every page of this copied as quickly as possible!" he urged the counter man.

The sales assistant looked over his shoulder to the large commercial machine behind him which was spitting out finished copies at a rate of nearly two per second, then checked his watch. "I've got a job on the machine now that won't be done for another two hours or so," the sales representative responded. "If you want to leave your book, I could have it finished for you by three."

No! No!" Z nearly shouted, leaning over the counter in an intimidating posture. "I've gotta have this NOW, ya heard me? I'll pay extra for the rush – jus' DO IT!"

"I'm sorry, sir," the attendant answered coolly. "But I can't shut down the machine for you – that job has a rush order on it as well."

Groping for a solution, Z asked the man if there was another self-serve machine nearby. "The nearest copy center I know of is on St. Charles, near Lafayette Square. That's about five blocks from here."

"This is *all* fucked up!" Z cursed, as he turned and hurried from the copy center. He paused for a moment in the lobby, checking his watch and contemplating what his next move should be. It was twelve-twenty. They were rapidly approaching the red-zone of their allowable time. With no options remaining, Z darted to the elevator and made his way upstairs. As he quietly entered the lobby of Connor Enterprises, he could hear Sean continuing his verbal assault on the exasperated secretary.

"Okay," Sean was saying. "Now for your log books. I'd like to see your smoke detector logs."

"*What* smoke-detector logs?" the secretary nearly shrieked, incredulously. "What do you mean?"

"Your logbooks – when the smoke detectors were purchased, when the batteries were changed, you know. You don't expect the City of New Orleans to just take your word that you've been keeping those batteries fresh, do you?"

Z tiptoed past, slipped into one of the other unoccupied offices, then emerged loudly a few seconds later. "All done!" he announced as he approached the supply closet, glancing at his watch pointedly and conveying a warning glance to Sean. Uncertain how to interpret Z's visible uneasiness, Sean shot back a questioning glance of his own. Z shrugged his shoulders uncomfortably and tilted his head slightly toward the door. Turning back to face the secretary, Sean began to wrap up his lengthy interview with her, while pretending to complete some of the paperwork on his clipboard.

"Well, that should just about be it for today, if you can just sign here."

The secretary's anger finally boiled to the surface. "Now just a minute! Before I sign anything, I have a few questions of my own!"

Outside the building, Cool's nervous anxiety turned to outright panic when he saw Connor's limo pull into the driveway and disappear underneath the building. "Oh, shit! Get outta there!" he exclaimed aloud, fully realizing the futility of the unheard warning. The driver pulled the limo to within a few feet of the elevator, letting J. Richard Connor out of the car before driving on to his reserved parking space a few feet ahead. Connor stepped onto the elevator and pressed the button for "twenty-three," cursing and muttering audibly as the elevator doors closed.

"I'm really fed up with all the red tape we have to put up with running a business office," the secretary raged. "This whole inspection has just been the most obnoxious, intrusive, and ridiculous exercise in bureaucratic double-speak that I've ever witnessed. I want your badge numbers and the name of your supervisor so I can write a formal letter of complaint."

Thinking quickly, Sean pulled an answer from the top of his head. "I apologize for the inconvenience, ma'am. I don't make the rules and neither does my supervisor. I recommend that you raise your complaint with your City Council member. Only they have the power to cut the red tape. If you file a complaint with our department, there will be a formal grievance procedure with hearings, depositions and such – it'll take a lot more of your time."

The ascending elevator stopped at the first floor lobby where a small crowd of workers returning from lunch surged inside,

223

shoving J. Richard Connor to the back. When the jolly and conversant workers pushed buttons to stop on six different floors, Connor felt his face flush as his blood pressure boiled to a crescendo. The elevator ascended to the third floor, then to six, then eight. At the fifteenth floor, one worker emerged, but another stepped on, pulling a janitorial cart behind him, and pushed the button for "sixteen." Connor's fury could barely be contained.

"We really must go, ma'am," Sean announced to the secretary, "We have twenty-two more floors to inspect this afternoon. Again, my apologies for the inconvenience." With that, Sean and Z made a hasty departure, stepping into the sun-lit foyer and pressing the down elevator button. There were two elevators side-by side and Sean looked up at the status displays above them. One was on sixteen, the other on fourteen, with both currently ascending toward them. Following Sean's gaze, Z also looked up at the displays. They both watched impatiently as the two elevators seemed to be playing leap-frog on the way up – one stopping as the other moved, then vice-versa.

Finally, the status light above the left elevator flashed a red "down" arrow, while the elevator on the right was still two floors below. The doors opened, and out stepped a pair of executives, each carrying a take-out bag from Popeye's Fried Chicken. Sean and Z stepped into the elevator, Z pressed "one," and the door closed behind them just as the light for the right elevator flashed on. Connor exploded from the other elevator, stormed into the lobby of his suite, and began yelling at his secretary – not allowing her an opportunity to explain the source of her distraction – before stomping into his office and slamming the door behind him.

32

As soon as they were safely aboard the descending elevator, Z apprised Sean of the change in plans occasioned by the defective photocopier and uncooperative counterman. Sean's curiosity to view the contents of the black notebook was temporarily outweighed by the sense of urgency to put some distance behind them, knowing that Connor could open his cigar box at any moment and discover the missing journal. They stepped off the elevator, walked briskly past the security guard at the lobby console, and broke into a trot as they reached the sidewalk, rushing to jump into Cool's car. Cool saw them coming and had his engine started, waiting only until both of his passengers had lunged into the vehicle before throwing it into gear and pulling rapidly from the curb. "Get us outta here!" Z urged, "an' make sho' no one's tailin' us."

As they cruised down Rampart toward the Ninth Ward, Sean finally had an opportunity to look at their prize. Opening Z's briefcase, he took out the black notebook, thumbing quickly through the pages as he scanned the contents. As the pages turned, Sean began to linger a bit longer on each page, trying to absorb the full magnitude of what he was seeing. The names of Jackhammer Hamilton, Cassius Banks, Hat Trick Hathaway, Mack Vanderhorn, and Tyrone Freeman had been scrawled in the first few pages, along with an odd assortment of shorthand notations. There were dates, times, addresses, names, nicknames, and dollar amounts scribbled in a seemingly random order on the pages accompanying each name, along with a brief thumbnail sketch of each of the athlete's greatest public relations snafus or character flaws. Under the name "Jackhammer" were the simple notations, "Cocaine," "Promiscuity," and "DUI." Cassius Banks' name was followed by his nicknames – "The Philly Philanderer" and "The Washington Womanizer" – as well as the name "Giselle Hathaway," and Hat Trick Hathaway was noted on the following page for "Violent Temper" and "Assaulting Official." Mack Vanderhorn's name was followed by "Heroin" and "Deadbeat Dad," while the single word

"Gambling" accompanied Tyrone Freeman's entry. Each page was marked with a giant red "X" as if to negate the contents.

But as Sean turned the pages, he saw that there was much, much more. Jackhammer and the others were but the first in a long list of celebrity athletes, each annotated with a brief description of legal or image problems they had experienced, as well as the same sort of random notes that accompanied the first three.

The names on Connor's list seemed to jump from yesterday's sports page headlines. Perennial pariahs Mike Tyson and Darryl Strawberry were listed alongside all-but-forgotten charges such the Baltimore Ravens' 2001 Superbowl MVP, Ray Lewis, tagged with "Murder Cover-up," as well as relative newcomers such as NBA superstar Kobe Bryant with his sensational "Rape Trial." The annotated "charges" against each ranged from the trivial to the truly horrific: Anthony Mason, Milwaukee Bucks, noted for "Fights" and Darren Perry of the New Orleans Saints, listed for "DUI Hit-and-Runs" while Bill Romanowski of the Oakland Raiders was tagged for "Assaulting Teammate" and Latrell Sprewell listed for "Choking Coach" during his time with the Golden State Warriors. Vancouver Canucks forward Todd Bertuzzi and former Boston Bruins star Marty McSorley were each charged with "Hockey Assault," Darrell Russell of the Oakland Raiders listed for "Rape Allegation," former NBA star turned commentator Jayson Williams for "Manslaughter," and the Baltimore Ravens' Jamal Lewis for "Cocaine Trafficking."

Then there were the group listings. A number of players made the list for "Peeping" in on the Philadelphia Eagles cheerleaders' dressing room, while three members of the Detroit Lions football team and one Miami Dolphin player were charged with "Group Rape Incident." Patrick Ewing, Andruw Jones and others implicated in the Gold Club scandal merited the simple notation, "Strippers." And in the grand-daddy of all sports scandals, a litany of the most prominent names in baseball were linked to the "BALCO Steroid Scandal," including Barry Bonds, Mark MacGwire, Sammy Sosa, and Jason Giambi.

It seemed to make no difference if the purported offenses were proven or merely rumored, recent or old news, adjudicated or not. The only distinction that Sean could find among the various names in the journal was that some had been marked with the large red "X." Letting out a low whistle, Sean exclaimed, "Holy Shit!"

"What's in it?" Z inquired, reaching over the seat to take the notebook from Sean's hand. Sean stared out the front of the car and repeated his expletive as Z began flipping through the pages of the small black book.

"Check this out, Cool!" Z exclaimed. "He's got Kobe, Tyson, Sprewell, an' 'bout forty other players in this book."

Unsure whether Z was fully grasping the contents, Sean directed his attention to the red "X's" over the first five names. "Those are the *finished* jobs – this is some kind of "Who's Who" of everyone in professional sports with any kind of bad reputation, and that crazy son of a bitch is planning to get rid of all of them!"

"Day-yam!" Cool exclaimed, swerving as he leaned toward Z to try to catch a glimpse of the book, as Z stared at the book, trying to grasp the spectacular dimensions of the truth they had uncovered. Reaching the end of the target list, there were a number of blank pages, but Z flipped all the way to the back and, on the last page before the inside cover, he spotted the name of Sean McInness.

"Look!" he pointed to Sean, passing the book back over to him. "He's got *yo'* name in the book, ya heard me, wit' some website called 'www.sfstarreporter.com', an' he's got my phone number! There's some other number, there, right under my digits."

"That's my calling card!" Sean realized aloud. "That's how they connected me to you! I used that calling card to call my office from your house the day Callio Cal's thugs chased me through the Riverwalk."

"An' look, there!" Z said as he reached over and pointed to the top corner of the page. "There's the name 'Cal,' scratched out, wit' the name 'Cardinal' next to it. I guess he changed his plan after Cal fucked up that first hit on you."

"We've got to stop this bastard before he gets a chance to kill anyone else," Sean announced, gravity replacing the excitement of a moment before. "We've got to bring him down *today*."

When they reached Cool's house, Tyrone, Roderick, and Dewayne were waiting, relieved to see that the other three had returned safely, and anxious to hear about the daring daylight burglary. Sean and Z recounted the events at Connor Enterprises, rushing through the details quickly in anticipation of reaching the punch line. Opening the book, Sean held it out for all three of them to see as he flipped through the pages and revealed the names of one superstar athlete after another.

After they had all contemplated the hit list in awestruck silence for several minutes, Sean spoke again, urgency and determination marking his tone. "We have to move *now* to stop this guy. He knows Tyrone is alive, and we can only assume he will soon discover that his book is missing. It won't take him long to get a description from his secretary and realize it was us. Considering the magnitude of what's in this book, he'll stop at nothing to hunt us all down. I would guess by sundown tonight there will be an all-points-bulletin to every hoodlum, hit-man, and dirty cop in this city to find us. At the same time, I've looked over these pages carefully and I'm just not sure there's enough here to prove anything or convict Connor of any crime. All he needs to walk away is a reasonable doubt, and I can almost hear some slick lawyer coaching him to say he wrote these notes *after* the first four incidents – claiming that he was, in fact, trying to help solve the crimes. We need more. We've got to set him up, somehow, and get him on tape."

"How do you plan to do that?" Tyrone asked.

"I don't know," Sean answered, his voice trailing off as he considered the dilemma. Thinking aloud, Sean continued. "Getting Connor to meet with me would be easy – he'll certainly want his book back. But he would unquestionably bring muscle with him and they would be smart enough to search me and the surroundings for weapons or wires. I just don't know how to catch him on tape."

There was silence, as all six of them pondered the problem, then Roderick spoke up. "How 'bout a pie?"

Every one in the room turned to stare at Roderick with expressions of dismay. Then Cool retorted, "A pie? What the hell you mean 'a pie,' Dawg? Don't you think of anythin' but food?"

"No! No! No!" Roderick insisted. "Peep this out! Stick a mike in a pie. You know, like 'fo'-an-twenty blackbirds' an' all that shit. The joint where D an' I work makes some big-ass crawfish pies –

it'd be easy to scoop out the crawfish an' plant a microcassette inside – then set it on the table in front of Connor."

Sean was flabbergasted by the preposterousness of the suggestion, but wanted to hear more of Roderick's idea. "How do we get Connor to order a crawfish pie, and then how do we keep him from eating it?"

"Awright," Roderick answered, defensively. "So we don't set it in front of Connor – we set it in front of *you*, wit' the mike pointed 'cross the table to pick up Connor's voice."

Again, the group fell silent, as they all mulled over the merits of Roderick's idea. Sean began to rattle off a litany of questions, prodding to discover and resolve any weak spots in the proposal. Roderick fielded each inquiry, his voice becoming more excited as he realized that he just might have dreamed up a winning idea.

"What if the microcassette gets damp, or too hot?"

"After we scrape out the crawfish, the crust won't hold 'nough heat to do any harm, an' we can wrap the microcassette in wax paper to keep it dry."

"How would I turn the microcassette on and off?"

"You won't. We'll turn it on in the kitchen jus' befo' we bring it to you, then come get yo' plate befo' you run outta tape."

"Will the cassette record through the crust?"

"We can poke some holes in the crust wit' a fork."

"Are you and Dewayne scheduled to work tonight?"

"Dewayne's on the schedule as a waiter tonight. I have tonight off, but I'm sho' the other line cook, Corey, would trade a shift wit' me if I kick him a few bucks."

Sean pondered the scheme silently, flipping again through the pages of the black notebook. He noticed that at least two of the remaining victims had dates in late July penned next to their names – only a few days away. *Time is running out.* Sean looked up from the book and saw that everyone else in the room was watching him, waiting to hear his decision.

"Let's do it!" he proclaimed. "Let's set this madman up tonight!"

(33)

They decided to make preparations first, before contacting Connor, in order to allow their nemesis as little time as possible to plan a counter-strategy. Roderick called the restaurant, speaking first with his fellow line cook, Corey, then with his boss. He replaced the receiver and announced to the others that he had succeeded in swapping shifts. He had also determined that his boss would be leaving him in charge of the restaurant for the evening – a stroke of luck that would allow the others access to the restaurant's kitchen at the critical moments. He and his brother then donned their uniforms, and left early for work, hoping to gain a head start on their regular prep and set-up duties so they could buy some valuable time. Cool drove Sean to a nearby electronics outlet where Sean purchased the microcassette recorder, tapes, and batteries they would need, while Z and Tyrone drove with the brothers to the restaurant – located off of St. Charles Avenue in the lower Garden District. Their assignment was to survey the vicinity in detail and determine the best sites for reconnaissance and get-away vehicles.

Finally, the stage was set and Sean called Connor from a pay phone a few blocks from Cool's house. The phone rang twice, then Connor answered with a shortness that telegraphed his irritability. "Connor here!"

"Well, well," Sean mocked. "*The* J. Richard Connor. This is Sean McInness. I understand you've been trying very, very hard to contact me."

Sean let the allegation dangle in the tense silence for a few moments before continuing.

"As it happens, I have something of yours which I think you might value even more highly than the pleasure of meeting me. Speaking as a professional journalist, I'd say the notebook you kept in your cigar box would make a record-breaking bestseller."

"I really can't imagine what you're talking about," Connor asserted, his voice carefully modulated in an attempt to restrain his rage. "I know of no one named Sean McInness."

"Well, that may be," Sean continued. "But you are apparently quite familiar with Jackhammer Hamilton, Cassius Banks, Hat Trick Hathaway, Mack Vanderhorn, Tyrone Freeman, and numerous other sports icons, with a keen interest in their personal hang-ups and the precise circumstances of their untimely accidents. Rather a strange hobby, if I say so myself."

"What do you want, Mr...McInness?" Connor pretended he could not remember the reporter's name, clearly concerned that the call might be tapped.

"I want to meet for dinner, tonight at six o'clock. If you eat all your vegetables, I just might give you your little book back." Without waiting for Connor to reply, Sean quickly rattled off the restaurant's address, then hung up the receiver. Walking back to Cool's car, he checked his watch and saw that it was five fifteen. "I think he took the bait," Sean told Cool as he slid into the front passenger seat of the car. "Let's get to the restaurant."

When they arrived, they spotted Z and Tyrone in the Explorer, parked about a half block from the front entrance. The sport vehicle had been precisely positioned so that it also had a clear view down the alley that led to the side delivery door into the kitchen. Z's task for the evening would be to remain out of sight in the Explorer, maintaining a careful vigil and honking a prescribed signal if he saw evidence of any unexpected trouble. Cool let Sean out before backing his car into the alley, and Sean motioned to Z and Tyrone to meet them at the back kitchen door.

Entering through the front, Sean saw that it was a very small restaurant, with no more than ten tables arranged in a long narrow space, and another five tucked around a corner behind the bar. Sean found Dewayne making change at the cash register behind the bar and pulled him aside for a brief conversation, passing a small package to him discreetly as he spoke. After nodding his agreement, Dewayne led Sean into the kitchen. Sean gestured toward the service entrance as Roderick looked up to greet them, and the older brother opened the door to admit Z, Tyrone, and Cool. Roderick had been working on his culinary masterpiece between regular orders. With the pride of a master chef, he presented his work to the others.

"When I got here, I realized our crawfish pies are too small fo' yo' microcassette recorder. The pies are made up by the mornin' prep crew, then refrigerated for quick bakin' durin' lunch an' dinner. It's an appetizer, so it's gotta be outta the kitchen eight to ten minutes from when it's ordered, know what I'm sayin'? Anyway, I saw it was too small, so I split open two of 'em an' sealed the crusts to make one bigger one. I went 'head an' baked it wit' the fillin' inside, to keep the crust from gettin' too dry an' brittle. 'Soon as it cools, I'll cut it open, scoop out the crawfish, an' put the microcassette inside. When Connor's peeps get here, jus' tell 'em you've already ordered somethin', know what I'm sayin'? I'll start the tape rollin', close the top crust, an' have Dewayne bring it out to you. The sound quality is gonna be a problem, recordin' through the crust, so you'll have to run it on the faster tape speed. That cuts the recordin' time in half, so Dewayne will have to take the plate back from you after twenty-five minutes – befo' the tape clicks off. Whatever you want on tape, you'll have to make sure he says it within twenty-five minutes, know what I'm sayin'?"

Sean nodded approvingly as he looked at the oversized turnover crust. Then they quickly reviewed their assignments before taking up their respective positions. While Sean took a seat at an isolated table near the back of the restaurant, Roderick and Dewayne continued to perform their regular duties and Z resumed his surveillance mission from the parked Explorer. Cool occupied the driver's seat of their get-away car in the alley near the kitchen entrance, poised to rush the occupants of the restaurant to safety should their plan go awry. Tyrone loitered inside the kitchen. His job would be to take the finished tape from Dewayne and sprint to a secure location with the crucial evidence. They were ready.

Roderick had waited until the last possible moment to begin his dissection of the pie, allowing the contents to cool thoroughly. He had just finished scraping the crawfish from the crust and was carefully dabbing the inside with a paper towel, when Connor made his entrance – flanked by the same two New York thugs who had kidnapped Kenyetta. The one who had taken the brunt of Q-B's wrath was still visibly bandaged and bruised. Dewayne caught sight of them from across the room and turned his head quickly before they could recognize him. Hurrying into the kitchen, he burst through the swinging doors and lunged toward his brother. "It's them!" he whispered. "It's the same two gangstas we jumped on Bourbon Street! They'll recognize me in a heartbeat – I can't serve the table!"

"Oh, shit!" Roderick exclaimed, almost loud enough to be heard in the dining room. Reflexively reaching up to cover his mouth, he lowered his voice as he temporarily halted work on his pie creation. "Why didn't we think of that? Oh, shit! We've gotta do somethin'! Damn! We shoulda known he'd be usin' the same posse as befo'."

"Cool!" Dewayne shot back, as Tyrone approached to try to join in on the brothers' panicked conversation. "I'm gonna get Cool an' switch places with him!" With that, Dewayne turned and darted out the kitchen door.

"What's going on?" Tyrone asked.

"The muscle Connor brought with him tonight are the same ones we tangled wit' last week on Bourbon Street. If they spot Dewayne they'll smell a set-up, know what I'm sayin'? Cool is the only one they haven't seen face-to-face."

"Oh, man!" Tyrone exclaimed. "Sean's out there on a limb, ya dig – we've got to pull this game together in a hurry!"

In the dining room, Connor quickly lost his patience when no one showed up to escort them to the table. Signaling his hired hands to follow him, he marched through the restaurant, brushing past several other guests as he searched out the object of his quest. When he spotted Sean around the corner behind the bar, he motioned to the New Yorkers, who stepped in front of him and walked briskly to Sean's table.

"Give your Uncle Guido a big hug," commanded the bandaged man who had performed the searches at their previous encounter. Sean stood and permitted the pat down, while the other thug searched the booth thoroughly, looking under the table and running his hand deeply into the crevices in the upholstery. Satisfied that the area was devoid of recording devices, bugs, or weapons, the two New Yorkers nodded to Connor, and he quickly joined them.

Meanwhile, Dewayne was outside, breathlessly explaining the situation to Cool.

"I can't do that!" Cool protested. "I've never been a waiter – I don't know what to do."

"It's our only chance!" Dewayne insisted, as he stripped to his underwear right in the middle of the alley. "You gotta put on my uniform an' get in there, NOW! Jus' fake it, Dawg! You got game – jus' talk yo' way through it!"

Cool, reluctantly realizing that there was no other way, stepped from the car and began stripping his clothes, trading them for Dewayne's discarded items. With Cool standing nearly seven inches shorter than Dewayne, the uniform could only be described as ill-fitting. Cool wore the pants with the waistband riding as high as possible so the legs wouldn't drag the floor, using the apron to conceal the embarrassingly nerdy look.

"Oh, shit! I 'most fo'got one mo' thing..." Dewayne announced just as Cool was opening the kitchen door. Dewayne directed Cool's attention to the object in his apron pocket, and recounted Sean's brief conversation with him.

"I can't do that!" Cool cried again. "I ain't got no skills doin' no shit like that!"

"You've gotta try, Dawg. He said it was important, so you jus' gotta try, know what I'm sayin'? Now, go on – get in there!" With that, Dewayne pushed Cool through the kitchen door. As Cool crossed the kitchen toward the dining room, Tyrone stared at the poorly fitting uniform, then covered his eyes, simultaneously lowering and shaking his head while letting out a long sigh through clenched teeth. When Cool emerged into the dining room, Sean quickly caught his eye, signaling an unmistakable plea to hurry with the next phase of the plan.

Sean was finding it increasingly difficult to hold Connor at bay, trying to keep the murderous mastermind distracted with small talk and tangents, hoping to postpone the key portions of their meeting until the microcassette pie arrived.

"Do you have the book?" Connor demanded.

"You'll get your book in due time. I'm actually quite anxious to discuss the, ah, what shall I say? The literary merits of it. But before we get down to serious business, I have just a few preliminary questions for you."

Sean stopped to take a long, slow sip of his gin and tonic, paused to twirl the olives on their toothpick, then looked back up at Connor with a mock-quizzical expression on his face. "I'm sorry, what was I saying? Oh, yeah, a few preliminary questions. Oh, I almost forgot to mention – I ordered an appetizer before you got here. You don't mind if I nibble a bit as we talk do you? Anyway, like I was saying, I have a couple of preliminary questions for you…"

Dewayne was just putting the finishing touches on his masterpiece. He had loosely wrapped the microcassette in a sheet of wax paper, carefully trimming the edges to fit flush inside the empty pastry shell. Then he started the recorder, dipped his finger in a saucer of oil, and lightly moistened the cut edges of the pastry, before replacing the top and gently pinching the crust together along the seams. Finally, he selected a serving fork with large tines and pierced the front of the turnover several times, producing a tic-tac-toe square of small holes for the microphone. Just as he removed the fork from the third insertion, the top of the pastry shell began to collapse inward, creases and cracks forming where it had buckled. It was just too weak to hold its shape without support from the filling.

"Oh, shit!" Roderick scrambled to save his creation. Thinking quickly, he grabbed a pastry spatula and hurriedly reopened the cut around the edges, then lifted the top off gently, turning it upside down on his cutting board so he could press it back into shape. Tyrone exhaled deeply, pursed his lips, and shook his head as he watched the calamity unfolding. Roderick was visibly shaking as he tried desperately to think of a way to salvage the situation.

"What are you going to do?" Tyrone asked.

"I don't know!" Roderick answered.

34

"The Fuckin' crust is too weak!" Roderick cursed. "It can't hold its own weight. I've gotta think of somethin', know what I'm sayin'?" He began to rustle through his kitchen equipment randomly, in a panic-stricken search for something that could provide the necessary structural support inside the turnover. Brushing aside dozens of utensils, measuring and mixing tools, he was reaching a state of utter desperation, when he spotted a quart-sized carton of whipping cream on a counter behind Tyrone.

Cool popped into the kitchen at that moment, announcing that Sean needed the recorder immediately. Roderick nearly shouted for him to stall another minute or two, and Cool went back out to make another quick sweep through the restaurant, smiling, nodding, and pouring water at every table, then hurrying away before any of the customers could ask him for something more substantial.

Roderick dumped the contents of the dairy carton, sliced off the top with a large kitchen knife, then hurriedly rinsed out the inside. Eyeballing the dimensions of the recorder and the inside of the pastry shell, Roderick trimmed an additional two inches off the open end, then sliced the carton vertically. Inserting one half into the other, he created a sturdy cardboard structure with one open end, something like a tiny garage. Placing the cardboard device carefully over the top of the recorder, he again took a mental measurement of the fit, and realized the cardboard was still too low and flat to hold up the rounded top of the pie crust.

Tyrone had been watching with fascination, his sense of dread gradually turning to admiration as he observed the creative improvisation of the younger man. Understanding the final technical obstacle, Tyrone glanced around the kitchen, and spotted an oval-shaped scrub sponge on a counter. "Here!" he whispered as he tossed the sponge to Roderick.

"Perfect!" Roderick agreed with a smile. He rewound the tape, started the recorder, and placed the carton over it with the sponge on top, finally flipping the crown of the crust in place. There was no time left for perfection, so he quickly crimped the crust in a half-dozen spots around the edges, just finishing it when Cool popped in the door.

"Take this, NOW!" Roderick commanded, as he scooped a generous handful of fries onto the plate, surrounding the pie, both to conceal the roughly joined edges and to give Sean something he could legitimately nibble on to avoid suspicion. Handing the dish to Cool, he pointed out the fork holes and reminded the novice waiter to set the plate down with the holes facing Connor.

Connor was losing his patience rapidly. His face was turning visibly crimson as Sean continued to regale and bamboozle his captive audience with pointless small talk and irrelevant details. He reached his limit just as Cool set the turnover on the table.

"I'll be damned if I'm going to sit here while you have a leisurely dinner! Where's my goddam book!"

"Okay, okay," Sean conceded. "I guess it's time to get down to serious business. I'll give you your damn book, but first, my insatiable journalistic curiosity has a few questions for you. I know what you've been up to. I've known almost from the beginning that you were behind the death of Jackhammer Hamilton, I'm certain you set up Mack Vanderhorn, and I believe you had a hand in instigating Hat Trick Hathaway's assault on Cassius Banks. I knew you were going to make a move against Tyrone Freeman even before you did it, and now I've seen your list of targets, complete with dates and details. I'd say that pretty well covers the journalistic 'who, what, when, and where.' Now all I really want to know is the "why' and the 'how.' Why would you be going after players who have nothing to do with your flagship New Orleans Cajuns or any of the other teams you have interests in? And how have you been able to pull off such a wide-ranging conspiracy? As soon as you've satisfied my curiosity, I'll let you take your marbles and go home."

"Why?" Connor replied. "*Why?* Because they're destroying America's professional sports, that's why. Not long ago, being a rough-edged superstar was trendy, fashionable, but the fad played out its time and wore out its welcome. The public has gotten sick and tired of crybaby heroes, spoiled-brat millionaires, and common criminals parading across their television screens as role models for their children. It's hard enough for the public to come to terms with pouting punks who make millions going on strike or demanding trades and concessions, when they themselves can no longer afford the price of a lousy ticket to take their kids to a game. When you throw in the drugs, the arrests, the lawlessness, and the visible contempt for the fans and even for the game itself, the public just can't accept it anymore."

"So you've taken it upon yourself to be judge, jury, and executioner?" Sean asked, incredulously.

"Not at all – that's the beauty of it, don't you see? Every player I take down is going to fall from his own weakness, or at least appear to. It was only a matter of time before Jackhammer had an accident resulting from his multiple intoxications. How many wives could Cassius Banks screw before a jealous husband hunted him down, and how many times could Hat Trick Hathaway lose control of his temper before someone pressed charges against him? Mack Vanderhorn would have succumbed to his heroin addiction sooner or later, and Tyrone Freeman was gambling with his life every time he carried thousands of dollars to a midnight meeting with a loan shark. All I've done is speed up the timetable. It will be the same with all the others – they'll each be crushed by their own petty vices."

Sean continued to prod, amazed at the straight-faced depravity of the megalomaniac's twisted thinking. "You think it's your mission in life to save America from its bad sports?"

"I do have a passion for my business," Connor responded. "And my business is professional sports, but I'm a rational man. I'm not doing what I'm doing just to feel good. The bottom line is that America's loss of faith in its sports heroes is translating into major financial losses across the board. All across the country attendance is plummeting at professional sporting events, and the ratings for television viewership have dropped dramatically. The losses are easily reaching into the hundreds of millions. I've personally lost over twenty million dollars in just one year with the disastrous first season for my Cajuns. That's a good enough motive for murder. There's your 'why' for you."

"It seems to me you might want to look a little closer to home for your scapegoat," Sean retorted in disgust. "After nearly twenty years as a sports reporter, I've had plenty of opportunity to watch owners in every major sport sweet-talk elected officials into spending hundreds of millions of taxpayer dollars for their stadiums and arenas, only to threaten those same officials and taxpayers with abandonment the very next year in order to extort even more money and concessions. That kind of brazen greed and political blackmail by the owners probably has a lot to do with your declining attendance and revenues. In any event, I guess I still don't understand why you're hitting players that aren't even on your teams. Hell, half of them aren't even in sports that you have a stake in. Why not just use your power as owner or share holder to clean up your own team?"

"How?" Connor asked rhetorically. "How do you clean up a team when the worst offenders have multi-year, multimillion dollar contracts in their pocket? You can't fire them without being liable for the value of those contracts. That's a lot of money on the line. Besides, I'm convinced it's a problem that can't be solved halfway. It has to be all or nothing. See, this country, this generation has developed a serious character flaw – no one can see the big picture anymore, or take responsibility for how they fit into the big picture. Look at Congress – ninety percent of the public says Congress is corrupt, that they should all be run out on a rail, and yet ninety percent of the incumbents keep winning reelection. In effect, the people are saying 'get rid of all the other cheats, but let us keep our cheat, because he cheats for us!' It works the same way in sports. Locally, a 'bad boy' may be popular with certain elements and generate a core of enthusiasm. It's hard for an individual team owner to walk away from that short-term cash cow. In the long term, though, the sport itself is being weakened. The only way it can end is for someone to step in and do spring cleaning across the board."

"And that someone is you?" Sean sneered. "You and who else? I guess that brings us to the 'how' question."

"Oh, I've had no problem finding allies. I'm not the only one who sees what's happening. Sports gambling has been declining right along with attendance, so there are some powerful interests, nationally, who have wanted to see exactly the sort of solution I had in mind. Locally, I've been able to team-up with two of the city's biggest operators, each for his own reason. One, who runs the uptown wards around the Superdome and Arena, stands to profit handsomely if the sports complex can bring more people and money into the heart of town. The other, who has major ambitions to expand his control across the city, saw this endeavor as an opportunity to acquire the indebtedness and loyalty of businessmen like myself, whom he would expect to support him in his future endeavors."

Just then, Cool returned to the table, glancing furtively towards his watch as he caught Sean's eye. "May I take this for you?" he asked, reaching to grab the plate in front of Sean without waiting for a reply. Turning quickly away, Cool hurried back to the kitchen, very nearly closing his eyes as he prayed that Connor or his thugs would not notice his lack of experience as a waiter – or his nervousness.

"Looks like dinner's over," Connor observed. "I would like my book NOW!"

Sean took another long sip from his drink, staring thoughtfully into the glass for a moment, before raising his head and looking directly into Connor's eyes. "It's not here," he announced matter-of-factly.

Connor exploded. "What the fuck do you mean it's not here? You double-crossing son of a bitch. Where the hell is my book?"

Cool returned to the table at that moment, almost sheepishly interrupting Connor's tirade. "Um, J. Richard Connor? There's a call for you."

A puzzled look came over Connor's face, as he first looked up at Cool, then back at Sean. Thinking quickly, he was certain he had not informed anyone where he would be, and sensed that something was very wrong. "Watch him!" Connor commanded, gesturing for his New York thugs to hold Sean at the table while he went to answer the unexpected telephone call.

"On the house phone, there," Cool pointed to a phone on a small console by the front door. Picking up the phone, Connor answered tentatively.

"Connor here."

There was a brief silence, followed by a few seconds more of static and unrecognizable metallic clattering, then by a high-pitched whirring sound. Finally, there was a voice. "...line is that America's loss of faith in its sports heroes is translating into major financial losses across the board. All across the country attendance is plummeting at professional sporting events, and the ratings for television viewership have dropped dramatically. The losses are easily reaching into the hundreds of millions. I've personally lost over twenty million dollars in just one year with the disastrous first season for my Cajuns. That's a good enough motive for murder. There's your 'why' for you."

Recognizing his own voice on tape, Connor flew into a rage. Slamming the phone down on the receiver, he ran back toward the table, motioning for his thugs to get up. "That mother fucker taped us! Get him out to my car NOW!"

Without hesitation, the two New Yorkers grabbed Sean by his shoulders and yanked him from the table. Pushing him along as they hurried toward the exit, they left a trail of spilled wine and water glasses, tipped tables, and startled dinner guests in their wake. Cool had just picked up some empty dishes from one of the other tables and was carrying them on a tray toward the kitchen, directly in the path of the onrushing foursome. Slamming into him, the rapidly exiting entourage sent Cool reeling, his tray of dishes crashing to the ground noisily as he stumbled and fell into their paths. Sean fell over Cool's slumping body and one of the thugs tripped as well, slapping Cool aside as he rose back to his feet. "Get the fuck outta the way!"

Grabbing Sean by his collar, the two New Yorkers dragged him towards the exit, and they all disappeared out the front door. Scrambling to his feet, Cool ran into the kitchen, shouting to Roderick as he continued full speed out the side door. "Get to the car! They've got Sean!"

Z saw Connor, Sean, and the New Yorkers as they emerged from the front door and realized immediately that something was going terribly wrong. Turning his ignition, he followed as Connor's black limo pulled from the curb and raced away from the restaurant. Within seconds, Cool's car emerged from the alley, turning to follow behind Z. Both vehicles kept pace with the limo, maintaining a discreet distance as they watched for an opportunity to rescue Sean.

Inside the limo, Connor sat alone in one seat as Sean sat facing him, the New Yorkers flanking him and tightly controlling his arms. Connor reached into a briefcase beside him and produced a chrome-plated derringer, aiming it casually at Sean's chest. "Nobody double-crosses me!" he shouted. "Nobody! I'm going to enjoy killing you myself, you nosey prick! Who the hell do you think you are?"

At that moment, Sean felt something utterly unexpected. He felt calm. In spite of all the perilous situations which had confronted him in the preceding days, or perhaps because of them, he felt a complete certainty in what needed to be said, what needed to be done. Speaking in a low and emotionless voice, Sean looked directly into Connor's face.

"You know, of course, that you can't kill me. I've left instructions with my friends, and if any harm comes to me, that tape and your book will be in the hands of the Orleans Parish District Attorney before you can get this limo back to your reserved parking space."

"You're going to use that tape, anyway!" Connor countered. "You're a reporter. If you don't send it to the DA, you'll use it in a story for your newspaper. Otherwise, what would be the point? You're going to use the tape, anyway, so I might as well enjoy the pleasure of killing you before you get the chance."

"No," Sean commanded. "That's not how it's going to happen. I anticipated your reaction, and I know that if I ever use that tape, you'll come for me to take your revenge. That tape is my insurance – it's the consideration for the contract you're going to make with me."

"What contract?" Connor asked, his rage barely tempered by curiosity.

"You and I are going to make an agreement, right now. I will pledge never to use that tape. No one will ever hear the confession I just recorded in the restaurant – not the police, not the public. There will be no newspaper story about your conspiracy to kill or ruin a score of sports icons. But, in return, I have three conditions you will have to meet."

"What conditions?" Connor asked, his voice betraying an increasing level of uncertainty, but the gun still aimed steadily at Sean.

"First, your grand scheme ends tonight. There will be no more killings, no more set-ups – no one else will be a target for you or any of your allies. It's over.

"Second, although I am pledged to silence on the larger conspiracy and the deaths of Jackhammer Hamilton and his friends, I do want a story out of this deal. I've been chased and shot at half way across North America. I've spent over twenty thousand dollars of my newspaper's money and I've put my job on the line. I can never write the real story, so what you can give me instead is a story about official corruption. I want the names of every police officer who helped with the Vanderhorn set-up and any other dirty cops you know of from your affiliation with Callio Cal. Names, ranks, situations, dollar amounts – I want everything you can tell me to bring them all down.

"Finally, I want you to write a check for one hundred thousand dollars to my young friend Deejay Z. He and his friends have dreamed and worked for years to get a break in the music business, but with your connections to Callio Cal, and his control of the New Orleans music scene, they have no place to go. They've sacrificed their futures to save the lives of strangers, so you're going to make it right for them. That's the deal."

Throughout Sean's soliloquy, Connor had stared silently at him, the flash of anger in his eyes occasionally giving way to the distant stare of one who is deep in thought. He appeared to be calculating his response as they passed the bright lights and gaiety of the French Quarter on the way toward Chalmette, where Sean knew it could all end in some desolate warehouse. Connor glared at him icily and Sean returned the stare, determined that, come what may, he would not give Connor the satisfaction of seeing him flinch. Finally, Connor retracted his derringer, reached into his briefcase, pulled out a checkbook, and asked simply, "How do you spell the goddam kid's name?"

35

The limousine turned from its Easterly path, meandering aimlessly through the Faubourg Marigny district which flanked the Eastern edge of the French Quarter. Connor had instructed his driver to change course and kill some time while he provided Sean with the requisite details to document his knowledge of police corruption in the city. The driver had opted to remain in this quiet and increasingly gentrified neighborhood where traffic would not be a problem. When the limo finally returned to the French Quarter and pulled to a stop in front of Lafitte's Blacksmith Shop, the two pursuing vehicles decided to make their move. Z steered the Explorer past the limo, stopping at an angle in front of it to prevent its forward motion, while Cool's car screeched to a stop only a few inches behind the limo's rear bumper. All four youths jumped from their vehicles and pointed their nine-millimeters at Connor's car, with Z leaning over the hood of the Explorer and the others using their open doors as cover. After a few tense moments, the limo's left side door opened slowly and Sean stepped out.

"It's over!" he announced, gesturing to them to lower their weapons. At first, none of them budged, fearing that Sean might have been coerced to make them drop their guard. They maintained their firing postures as Sean turned and closed the limo door behind him, then walked confidently toward the passenger side of the Explorer.

"It's over," he repeated. "Let's get out of here." Then, just as he reached the Explorer, Sean paused for a moment, turned, and walked back toward the limo. Without saying a word, he opened the door again, leaned inside, and threw his best punch directly into the bandaged nose of the New York thug he had known only as "Uncle Guido." "That's for Q-B!" he announced, as he slammed the limo's door a second time, trotted back to the Explorer, and jumped in. "Now, let's go!"

Z stepped into the driver's side, still holding the weapon in his right hand, and carefully maneuvered the Explorer back into the traffic lane, moving forward slowly as he watched the limo and his friends in the rear-view mirror. The limo pulled away from the curb and began to drive forward slowly, matching Z's pace, as the three remaining youths piled into Cool's car and brought up the rear. When they crossed Ursulines Street, the limo broke ranks, turning left slowly, then speeding away into the night. Only after a safe distance had been achieved did Sean's Ninth Ward friends finally believe that the crisis had passed, and the two drivers convoyed back to Cool's home for debriefing.

Tyrone was sitting on the stoop when the two vehicles pulled to a stop in the driveway. Jumping up to greet them, Tyrone extended his hand in a high-five gesture to each one as they entered the house. "Where have y'all been?" he asked, with an edge of consternation in his voice. "After I took the tape to the pay phone, you all emptied out of that restaurant so fast all I saw was your tail lights disappearing down the block! What happened?"

"I guess you're *all* wondering what happened," Sean responded, and proceeded to regale his anxious audience with the details of his conversation with Connor. He told them how he had stared Connor down in the back of the limo, and about his three demands. He told them everything he had been able to write down for his exposé on police corruption. As the grand finale, he produced the check Connor had written, handing it over to Z. "It's real," he asserted, "But if I were you, I'd get to a bank and cash it first thing in the morning before he gets a chance to reconsider."

Under the circumstances, one might have expected a tumultuous celebration, but they were all too physically exhausted and emotionally spent to fully appreciate or savor the moment. Instead, they each reacted with the sort of ambivalent disbelief that might come in the very first moments after learning that your lottery numbers had won. Understanding the understated reaction, Sean suggested that they turn in for the night and meet in the morning to discuss what would happen next. Sean and Tyrone drove back to the Days Inn, where Sean bid Tyrone good night, went to his own room, and had the best night's sleep he had had in three weeks.

The next morning, Tyrone greeted Sean in the Louie Louie's restaurant with his leather duffel bag over his shoulder, and announced that he was taking a cab to the airport immediately to catch a late morning flight to Boston. "I've already missed the first two days of training camp," he explained. "Under the terms of my contract, I'm losing fifty G's a day, ya dig? I'll look you up next time the Patriots play at Candlestick, er, 3Com, uh, make that Monster Park." With that, he was gone.

After finishing his leisurely breakfast, Sean called Cool to see if the others had arrived, then was on his way to the Ninth Ward fifteen minutes later. When Sean walked into Cool's house he could see that the celebration had begun in earnest – the magnitude of their victory had begun to sink in. Z was counting and recounting the briefcase filled with cash that he had obtained from Connor's bank only a few minutes earlier, while Roderick and Dewayne were sitting on the floor with a half dozen music-industry catalogs strewn between them.

"Peep this out!" Dewayne urged, pointing to an entry in one of the catalogs with one hand while punching the keypad of a calculator with the other. "We can get five thousand albums pressed by this company for jus' 'bout a buck a disk, an' they can do all the printin' an' packagin', too. At these prices, we could burn fifty thousand copies, then wholesale 'em for five bucks a pop, know what I'm sayin'? This catalog is off da hook!"

"Don't fo'get 'bout studio time," Cool cautioned. "At fifty to a hundred dollars an hour, that shit's no joke!"

"What do you think we should put on the cover?" Roderick asked.

"How 'bout the fo' of us," Dewayne speculated, "The K-Nines, posin' like playa's, each of us holdin' a fine young honey close wit' one arm an' a Rottweiler wit' the other."

"I hate to interrupt rehearsal for your debut album," Sean laughed, "but I need to change the subject for a moment. Z, have you been in touch with your mom and sister?"

"F'shiggity," Z answered, setting the briefcase full of cash down on the table in front of him. "I called 'em early this mornin'. They got reservations on a flight gettin' here for five this afternoon."

"Good. I'll be staying in town a couple more days to tie up some lose ends and work out a deal with the District Attorney. With the gold mine of information I have for him, he should guarantee me an exclusive when the indictments come down."

"You know, it jus' don't seem right," Roderick said, stroking his chin and looking thoughtfully at the small fortune sitting in front of them. "I mean, don't get me wrong, the money's cool, an' it's 'bout damn time somebody finished cleanin' up the NOPD fo' real – but I jus' can't see makin' a deal to let Connor walk away, know what I'm sayin'? The dirty muthafucka killed a half dozen people, destroyed Cassius Banks, put Hat Trick Hathaway and Mack Vanderhorn through hell, got Q-B an' Tyrone Freeman shot, an' had Special K kidnapped."

Dewayne, Cool, and Z nodded their agreement, all of them disturbed by the prospect of seeing Connor deal his way out of a long prison term. "It kinda makes this seem like blood money," Cool observed.

"Well," Sean responded. "I'm bound by my professional code of ethics to keep the deal I made. A journalist never reveals his sources, and never reneges on a deal made to obtain information. I can't use the tape from the restaurant."

Sean let the dilemma linger in the air for a few moments, surveying the stony expressions of Z and the K-Nines as they weighed the merits of his argument. "However," he continued, "I made no deal for the second tape."

The foursome dropped their jaws in unison, Z being the first to ask the obvious question. "What second tape?"

"On the way out of the restaurant, when I stumbled over Cool, he slipped a second microcassette recorder into the front of my slacks and it was running the entire time in Connor's limo." Nodding his head toward Cool, he continued. "I'd set that plan up with Dewayne when I got to the restaurant, knowing that he had experience as a pickpocket. When I saw that Cool had taken over as waiter, I really thought I was screwed. I can't tell you what a relief it was feeling that microcassette sliding into my waistband. I don't know how you did that so well without practice, Cool, but I got every word in the limo on tape, clear as day.

"My guess is, Connor agreed to my terms only because he didn't really believe I would be able to make my story stick. With nothing but unsupported allegations – his word against mine, the blue wall of silence would close ranks and protect the corrupt officers he named. Now I have more than my word – I have *his* word as well, on tape. I plan to turn *that* tape over to the Orleans

Parish District Attorney this afternoon. Along with all the officers who go down, Connor is sure to face indictment on charges of bribery and conspiracy. The best lawyers in Louisiana won't be able to erase Connor's voice from that tape."

"Awright!" was the unanimous response, as all the young men in the room slapped high-fives with each other and with Sean. Roderick best summarized the thoughts they all shared: "That crazy muthafucka is goin' to jail! Do not pass go, do not collect 'nother muthafuckin' sports franchise!"

As the celebrating ebbed, everyone's attention shifted back to planning for the K-Nines' break-through album. Everyone but Z, that is. Despite the fact that the other group members had invited him to participate in the group, as keyboardist and business manager, his thoughts seemed elsewhere. Finally, he excused himself.

"Where you goin', Z?" Cool asked.

"I've got some business to handle," Z answered. "I'll pass back this way fo' 'bout fo' o'clock to go to the airport."

Z pulled a backpack from Cool's front closet, stepped into the hot New Orleans afternoon, and began walking purposefully through the neighborhood, finally reaching his destination a few blocks away. He stood in front of the house for several minutes, pondering memories from the distant past, and wondering what the future held. Finally, he stepped up to the door, and knocked.

"Who's there?" a loud voice asked through an intercom beside the door, as a small video camera overhead slowly panned down to photograph Z's face.

"It's me, Uncle T, it's Z."

The door swung open, and Big T greeted Z with a friendly handshake, motioning him to come in. Closing the door behind them, Big T offered Z a cold beer, then pointed to a pair of chairs in the front room. Taking the cue, Z had a seat, holding the backpack firmly in his lap.

"So," Big T asked. "What brings my nephew by today? Need my help again?"

"No, no," Z answered. "I think everythin' is settled. Well, 'most everythin', anyway. Here, I brought these back fo' you." Z opened the backpack, and carefully laid five nine-millimeter handguns on the table between them. "I don't think we'll be needin' these anymo'."

"You sho' 'bout that?" Big T responded, concern clouding his face. "You never know when you're gonna need some firepower."

"Nah, I'm sho' I don't want 'em 'round anymo'. We needed 'em fo' a reason, ya heard me, an' the reason is finished."

Big T didn't respond, but just pondered his nephew, seated across the living room from him. Z also sat quietly, his eyes downcast.

"Somethin' else?" Big T asked, breaking the silence.

Z looked up, cleared his throat, and looked the big man dead in the eyes. "I've been 'round 'nough to know everythin' comes wit' a price. You came through fo' us twice, first wit' the nine's, an' then wit' the City ID's. I've come to ask what you want from me to settle our tab."

Big T nodded his head silently and stroked his chin, a sly grin gradually creeping over his face.

"What's yo' major, Business?" he asked rhetorically. "I could most definitely use someone like you. Muscle is easy to come by on these streets – there are plenty of hardheads walkin' 'round out there wit' no jobs an' no skills, nothin' but cocky attitudes an' expensive tastes. As long as I can keep some dead presidents in their pockets an' some gold on their teeth, they'll be loyal soldiers. But someone like you, who knows his way 'round a ledger sheet an' the IRS code – *you* could do mo' fo' my business than a hundred of those soldiers."

Z stared at his uncle blankly, as he heard the words he had most feared. His momma had worked so hard – *he* had worked so hard to make his way through the urban quicksand that had drowned so many of his friends and classmates over the years. In an instant, in a few days of urgent necessity, he had found himself ensnared by obligation to the very world he had worked so hard to rise above. He knew he owed his Uncle, and, in the Nint' Ward, a man pays his debts. The silence was deafening as the two of them locked eyes across the room.

"Nephew," Big T broke the silence. "You know the business I'm in. You know how much I do fo' the neighborhood, but you also know the price that sometimes has to be paid. You know I've got blood on my hands. I know you don't agree wit' how I handle my business, but know this – we *are* family. You're my sister's son. Yo' momma an' I parted ways a long time ago, but I'll always love her an' I'll always respect her fo' workin' so hard to raise you an' Kenyetta by herself. It would kill her if I dragged you into this business, so I won't do that.

"Word travels fast on these streets, Cap – you know that as well as I do. Rumor has it you an' yo' reporter friend have had Callio Cal an' The Cardinal on the defensive these past coupla weeks an' jus' may have landed a knockout blow on one or both of 'em. That's mo' than 'nough satisfaction fo' me. So go on, get outta here! Finish yo' degree in school an' remember what yo' Uncle T taught you many years ago, when you were young: never look back!"

Big T rose from his chair and gestured toward the door. It took Z several seconds to catch up with the surprising turn of events and Big T had to repeat his command. "Go on! Get outta here!"

Z stood, reaching out to shake his uncle's hand. Then, thinking better of it, he embraced the huge man, thanking him before turning to leave. It was nearly four, and he rushed back to Cool's house to catch a ride with Cool and Sean to the airport. When Q-B had heard that Kenyetta was returning to town, he insisted that the trio pick him up as well, despite his doctor's pleas to remain at rest for another day or two.

The four men arrived at the terminal just a few minutes before the scheduled arrival of the women's flight. They all four did a nearly-simultaneous double-take, and then broke out laughing as they passed one of the airport cocktail lounges and caught a glimpse of a special news bulletin on the television, as Tyrone Freeman arrived at Logan International Airport in Boston. With his dark brown Ray-Bans, he looked cooler than anyone had a right to as he pushed his way past a horde of reporters who had been tipped off to his imminent arrival by a scoop in the early afternoon edition of the San Francisco Star-Reporter. As the reporters asked an endless series of questions about his mysterious disappearance and sudden reemergence, Tyrone's eloquent, if redundant, response was a stone-faced: "No comment. No comment. No comment."

The events of recent days had left all four of them with a sparse reserve of patience, so they were relieved that the plane landed four minutes ahead of schedule. When Kenyetta spotted Q-B from the far end of the jetway, she dashed up the corridor, nearly stumbling over several people's luggage and creating a mobile maelstrom as other passengers ducked out of her way. Reaching the end of the jetway, she dived toward Q-B and he caught her securely in his good arm, spinning in a pirouette worthy of a world-class figure skater.

Ms. Williamson emerged from the jetway a few moments later, shaking her head and clucking her tongue as she watched the two young lovers locked in an impermeable embrace. Temporarily turning her attention from the others, she spoke first to Z. "It's so good to see you, son. I can't begin to tell you how proud I am of you for everythin' you've done these last few weeks. You're truly the man of the family."

Turning next to Cool, Ms. Williamson continued. "Cool, I'm so glad Z had you an' Roderick an' Dewayne to back him up through all this. My son knows how to pick good friends."

Finally, turning to Sean, Ms. Williamson extended her hand warmly. "I'm sorry we haven't had a chance to become better acquainted, Mr. McInness, but I can't thank you enough for all you've done. There's an extra plate at my table anytime you want some ham hocks, red beans an' rice, or jambalaya – an' the same goes for your friends Lori an' Vikki."

Turning back to see Kenyetta and Q-B still locked in their passionate embrace, Ms. Williamson threw up her hands in exasperation. "That girl wouldn't talk 'bout nothin' else the whole time we've been away. It's been nothin' but 'Q-B this' an' 'Q-B that.' You don't know what a long ride is until you've been stuck on an airplane for seven hours with a teenager in love! Lawd have mercy, get me home!"

Epilogue

After a few days of quiet meetings with the Orleans Parish District Attorney, Sean also went home. Lillian Kramer nearly popped a cork when she saw the full tab for his expensive mission compiled on her desk, but in the end she grudgingly admitted that he had landed a good story. He spent several more days burning the midnight oil at his office to put the finishing touches on that story, maintaining contact with the Orleans Parish DA's office several times a day to keep abreast of any late-breaking developments. Finally, the DA had his case ready to read indictments against a sizable group of New Orleans police officers, amidst rumors that an indictment of J. Richard Connor would soon follow. He tipped Sean a few hours in advance to give him a jump on the story. When Sean's syndicated article hit the wires, the New York Times quickly picked it up, and Sean decided it was time for a final celebration.

He called Lori and Vikki late Saturday night, advising them that his article would be in the Sunday morning Times, and invited them over for a Big Apple brunch. When they arrived at his apartment the next morning, carrying with them a gift box of Bombay Sapphire gin and a bottle of jumbo Spanish olives wrapped in red ribbon, Sean had already spent hours preparing the spread. Three lounge chairs were positioned alongside the pool, shaded by colorful umbrellas, with a small wrought iron table next to each one. On each table, Sean had meticulously set out fresh toasted bagels, cream cheese, lox, sliced tomatoes and Bermuda onions, Greek olives, baby kosher dills, chocolate-dipped strawberries, and melon balls on toothpicks, along with chilled champagne flutes ready to serve ice cold Mimosas. Finally, on each table lay a neatly folded copy of the Sunday New York Times with Sean's front-page article prominently displayed.

The headline shouted "17 Officers Indicted in New Orleans' Corruption Crackdown," with a subhead reading "Commissioner Supports Prosecutions – Reaffirms Zero-Tolerance Policy." The article was credited to "Sean McInness, Sports Writer and Syndicated Columnist for the San Francisco Star-Reporter." Further down the page, a side bar announced that Hat Trick Hathaway and Mack Vanderhorn had both been released from jail the preceding day, with all charges dropped. Still another front-page article noted that Tyrone Freeman's former bodyguard had surrendered to police in Philadelphia and was awaiting extradition to Puerto Rico on charges that he had participated in a conspiracy to murder the football superstar. Lori and Vikki were ebullient in their praise for Sean's journalistic prowess, as Sean was equally vocal in his appreciation for the hospitality they had shown the Williamson family in their darkest hour of need.

After their brunch-time gaiety came to a close, Sean made a solitary pilgrimage to the burial site of LaTanya Harrison. Her troubled soul and tragic end had somehow touched him deeply during their one brief encounter – deeply enough to set in motion all that had happened since.

Fifteen hundred miles away, aboard a flat-bottom pontoon boat lost deep within the bayous of Plaquemines Parish, thirty miles or so southeast of New Orleans, J. Richard Connor was meeting face-to-face with The Cardinal. Connor had invited The Cardinal to this private rendezvous to regroup and plan a new strategy in the wake of their recent setbacks. The arrests of so many of New Orleans finest was really a blessing in disguise, they mused, as most of them had been working under Callio Cal's auspices. With so much of Cal's muscle reigned in, his organization was in a shambles and the rumor on the street was that Cal himself was cowering in a heavily-armed house in Uptown New Orleans, fearful that he would be the target of a drive-by while his forces were in disarray. The prospects for The Cardinal's takeover of all the city's wards had never been stronger.

The real problem for Connor and The Cardinal had been the temporary halt in their plan to rebuild professional sports as a profitable enterprise – profitable particularly for the big-time developers and gambling interests who represented the core of both Connor's and The Cardinal's alliances. They had decided to wait six months before resuming their methodical elimination of players whose personal lives had become an embarrassment, after first removing Sean McInness and his New Orleans friends from the playing field. Who would notice, they reasoned, when four more young black men were gunned down on the mean streets of New Orleans, while a sporting accident seemed almost poetically appropriate for Sean McInness. Toasting each other's continued success, they relaxed in the Sunday afternoon heat, confident that nothing could stop them from fulfilling their missions. Their destinies.

Without warning, the boat exploded in a huge orange fireball, sending shrapnel, wood splinters, flaming fuel, and ash over a hundred-yard radius. It would be nearly two hours before the thick black smoke of the wreckage would attract a Coast Guard helicopter to the scene. It would be two days before the identities of the victims would be confirmed, and two months before the investigation would be relegated to the purgatory of unsolved cases, after extensive interviews with Big T, Callio Cal, and a half-dozen of the indicted cops failed to turn up sufficient evidence to charge a suspect. But it would only be two minutes before the scent of blood would ripple across the bayou, attracting the hungry attention of a dozen or more alligators, eager to consume the last remaining fragments of human flesh.

In Southern Louisiana, "The Boot," as it was know in the Nint' Ward, justice may not always function in the manner prescribed by polite society and the rule of law, but it is always swift, certain, and final. For a time – a short time, perhaps – only the good sports would remain in the game at the final bell.

Ya heard me?